Calling the Kettle Black

A Hal Westwood Restoration Mystery

WINTER 1665

by Jemima Norton

TUDOR GATE PRESS

LARGE PRINT EDITION

ISBN 0-97409494-3

LARGE PRINT EDITION

You will find the other books in this series at: www.halwestwood.com

For ordering information visit:

www.tudorgatepress

This book is dedicated to:

Isobel

Calling the Kettle Black

Hal Westwood	26	*Justice of the Peace*
Jane Carver	23	*Hal's sister*
Ambrose Carver	27	*Jane's husband*
Ned Westwood	19	*Hal's brother*
Cecily Westwood	16	*Ned's wife, sister to Guy*
Mary Armstrong	27	*Hal's elder sister; Guy's wife*
Guy Armstrong	28	*brother-in law to Hal*
Sophia Redcroft	19	*Hal & Justin's Ward*
Bess Danvers	20	*Hal's sister*
Justin Danvers	22	*Lawyer Hal's brother-in-law*
Harry Westwood	4	*Hal & Libby's son*
Baby Frances	6 m.	*Hal & Libby's son*
Doctor Phillipe Douay	35	*physician of Chawcester*
Cordelia Sandys	18	*Hal's ward*
Margery Kingscott	60	*Hal's aunt*
Katherine Westwood	40	*Hal's aunt*
Hetta Shearsby	16	*Hal's sister*
Will Shearsby	17	*Hetta's husband*

Thomas	56	*manservant*
Isaac Hughes	36	*Sheriff*
Sargent Parry	45	*Sheriff's man-at-arms*
Helen Sitwell	24	*widow of Master Sitwell*
Walter Prescott	38	*servant of Sitwells'*
Jennet Sawsby	39	*cook of Sitwells'*
Hannah Smith	20	*servant of Sitwells'*
John Goode	38	*groom of the Sitwells'*
Betty	16	*Bess's nursemaid*
Alys	30	*Westwood's nursemaid*
Adam Blackwell	25	*innkeeper of Chawster*
Jack Hollingshead	24	*kin of Cordelia*
Kit Swithland	25	*highwayman*
Francis Findlesham	25	*Royalist gentleman*
Nancy Gollen	24	*linen draper's assistant*
Jem Cookson	61	*innkeeper of Adam & Eve*

Glossary

OED- Oxford English Dictionary
BD Brewer's Dictionary of Phrase & Fable

ague	an acute fever, *OED 1611*
apoplexy	disabled by a stroke, *OED ME*
bully-boy	a person who makes himself a terror to the weak or defenceless *OED 1609*
byword	a person or thing which has become proverbial as an object of contempt or scorn, *OED 1535*
calumny	a slanderous report, *OED 1611*
Castle in Spain	castle in the air, *OED 1695*
Castlemaine	the Dutchess of Castlemaine, Barbara Villiers, mistress of Charles II
Chawcester Mop	a hiring fair, at which maids carried mops or brooms, *OED 17thc*
chit	a very young child, or contemptuously, a girl or young woman *OED 1624*

churlish	brutal, surly, ungracious, *OED ME*
cordwainer	a shoemaker, *OED ME*
Dogberry	a slow-thinking constable in Shakespeare's *Much Ado About Nothing* *OED 16thc*
dotard	one who is feeble-minded through old age, *OED ME*
doublet	a close-fitting body garment with, or without, sleeves worn by men from the 14th-18th centuries, *OED ME*
doxy	a woman of ill-repute, *OED 1530*
drab	whore, *OED 1602*
ewers	a pitcher with a wide spout used to bring water for washing the hands *OED ME*
footpad	a highwayman who robs on foot *OED 1630*
Fustian	inflated, or inappropriately lofty language, *OED 1590*
Geneva	gin
groat	a coin worth fourpence, the groat went out of circulation in 1662, *OED ME*

Glossary

hazard a game of dice, in which the chances are complicated by a number of arbitrary rules

OED ME

helpmeet a suitable helper, usually of wife and husband, *OED 17thc*

hoyden a rude or ill-bred girl, *OED 1593*

hurdle a portable rectangular frame woven with hazel or willow, used chiefly to form fences, etc.

OED OE

infirmarian in medieval monasteries, the person who had charge of the infirmary, *OED ME*

jade a term of reprobation for women

OED 1560

kennel the surface drain of the street, the gutter, *OED 1582*

kickshaws something dainty or elegant, but insubstantial, *OED 1601*

kirtle	a woman's gown, a skirt or outer petticoat, *OED OE*
laudanum	a costly medicament in which opium was main ingredient *OED 1602*
libertine	a man who is not restrained by moral law, one who leads a licentious life, *OED 1593*
linen draper's	a retail dealer in linens, garments, etc. *OED 1609*
pattern card	an example or model deserving imitation, a model of excellence *OED ME*
patch	a small piece of black silk worn on the face, either to hide a fault or to show off the complexion, *OED 1592*
peached	to accuse or inform on a person *OED 1596*
peccadillo	a small fault or sin, *OED 1591*
physic	medicine, a cathartic or purge
physicking	*OED ME*

Glossary

OED- *Oxford English Dictionary*

BD *Brewer's Dictionary of Phrase & Fable*

pillion to ride behind another on a horse

               OED 1503

poor budget poor purse   *OED 1432*

posset dish a dish to hold a posset (a drink com-
posed of hot milk, curdled with ale
or wine and spices), formally used for
treatment of colds   *OED UO*

press   a large cupboard

quinsies inflammation of the throat, *OED ME*

rubicund ruddy

sack   a type of sherry or canary wine

               OED 1590

surety   a person who undertakes some specific
responsibility on behalf of another
who remains primarily liable; one who
makes himself liable for the default or
miscarriage of another, or for the per-
formance of some act on his part (e.g.:
appearance in court for trial) *OED ME*

"Taken the shilling" volunteered for military service

termagent a savage, boisterous, overbearing or quarrelsome woman
OED 1659

tinker's cuss intensification of not caring from the reputed addiction of tinkers to profanity, *OED 1592*

traduced defamed, *OED 1586*

trumpery something of less value than it seems, hence something of no value, *OED 1456*

trunk hose full bag-like breeches covering the hips and upper thighs, sometimes stuffed with wool or the like, worn in the 16th and early 17th century, by 1643 considered old-fashioned and out of date

turnkey one who is charged with the keys of a prison, usually a subordinate, *OED 1654*

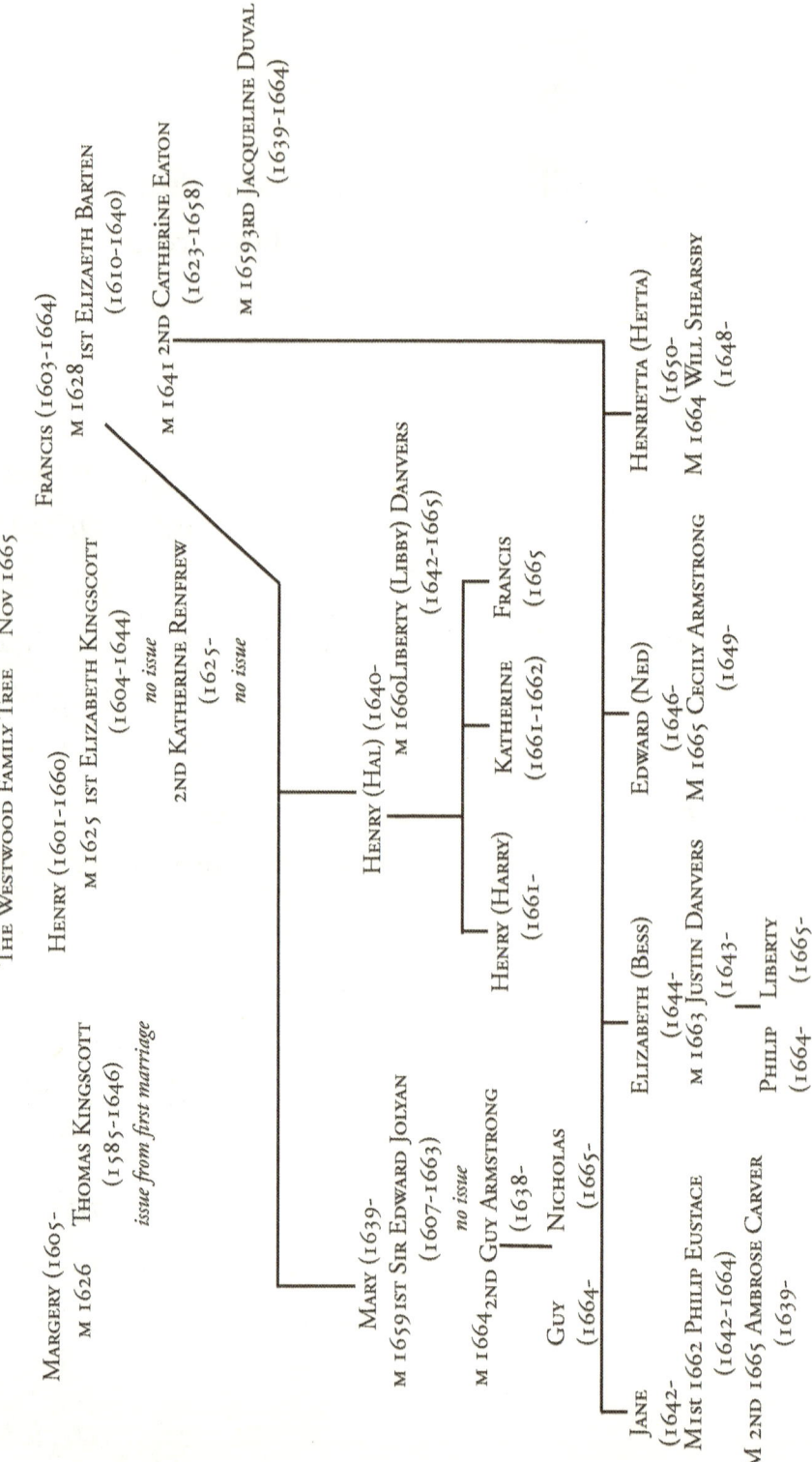

THE WESTWOOD FAMILY TREE   Nov 1665

MARGERY (1605-
M 1626   THOMAS KINGSCOTT
(1585-1646)
issue from first marriage

FRANCIS (1603-1664)

HENRY (1601-1660)
M 1625 1ST ELIZABETH KINGSCOTT
(1604-1644)
2ND KATHERINE RENFREW
(1625-
no issue

M 1628 1ST ELIZABETH BARTEN
(1610-1640)
M 1641 2ND CATHERINE EATON
(1623-1658)
M 1659 3RD JACQUELINE DUVAL
(1639-1664)
no issue

MARY (1639-
M 1659 1ST SIR EDWARD JOLYAN
(1607-1663)
no issue
M 1664 2ND GUY ARMSTRONG
(1638-
GUY   NICHOLAS
(1664-   (1665-

HENRY (HAL) (1640-
M 1660 LIBERTY (LIBBY) DANVERS
(1642-1665)
HENRY (HARRY)   KATHERINE   FRANCIS
(1661-   (1661-1662) (1665

EDWARD (NED)
(1646-
M 1665 CECILY ARMSTRONG
(1649-

HENRIETTA (HETTA)
(1650-
M 1664 WILL SHEARSBY
(1648-

ELIZABETH (BESS)
(1644-
M 1663 JUSTIN DANVERS
(1643-
PHILIP   LIBERTY
(1664-   (1665-

JANE
(1642-
M 1ST 1662 PHILIP EUSTACE
(1642-1664)
M 2ND 1665 AMBROSE CARVER
(1639-

THE HAL WESTWOOD RESTORATION MYSTERY SERIES

BOOK 1

A Flutter in the Dovecote

Summer 1660

BOOK 2

A Storm in the Wassail Bowl

Christmas 1663

BOOK 3

A Trip to Jericho

Summer 1664

BOOK 4

Dancing With Fire

Summer 1665

Refresh your memory by reading the last chapter of the previous book in this series beginning on page 432

BOOK 6

Repenting at Leisure

July 1666

Enjoy the first chapter in the next book

in the Hal Westwood series

which starts at the back of this book on page 440

Chapter One

Hal rode slowly up the avenue to the house. The frost had coated everything overnight with a powdering of white. Every blade of grass, every branch, every twig stood out in stark clarity from the blackness of its background. It was well past noon, but still the country was gripped by the thrall of cold and ice. Hal felt it had entered his soul, numbing his heart, so that it physically hurt him.

Never had Westwood looked so forbidding as on this November afternoon when already the light was fading. His horse, weary and despondent, taking its cue from its master, faltered as the great bulk of the house robbed the sky of the last brightness. It loomed over them like an ill-omened bird of prey.

The door was closed and the windows shuttered, but as he came to a halt outside, the door opened and a servant, garbed in new black clothes, scuttled forth.

"Welcome home, Sir Henry," he said. "Though 'tis an ill welcome we give you."

"Thank you, Thomas," Hal dismounted heavily, his voice sounding odd and cracked from disuse.

"Mistress Jane be inside, sir," he said, leading the horse away.

Hal straightened up as if shouldering an intolerable burden, and having quickly scanned the façade of his home with dull eyes, he pushed open the door into the hallway.

A fire smouldered in the hearth flanked by two upright chairs. On one of these sat his sister. Her strawberry-blonde hair covered with a cap, she rose to her feet. Her face was pale, and her grey eyes were shaded by grief, yet filled with sympathy. She smiled a sweet smile.

"Hal," Jane said softly. "How glad I am that you are come."

"Even if I am too late?" he added, his voice harsh.

She pressed his arm with her slender fingers. "I have no doubt you came as soon as you were able, you obviously got the note I sent to the inn at Dover," she replied calmly.

He sighed heavily. "It was waiting for me. When was the funeral?"

"Tuesday," she said, her voice almost a whisper. "We waited as long as we could, but with no word from you, no knowledge of where you were even—"

"You don't have to reproach me," he interrupted. "You cannot do so more than I do myself."

"I do not reproach you, Hal," she replied with calm dignity. "I know you well enough to know you have an active conscience. You need reproaches from none."

"Tell that to Justin, and to Mary," he replied bitterly.

"Justin is bound to take the death of his sister hard," said Jane reasonably. "Mary, too, was very fond of Libby."

"And you were not?" he asked sharply.

"I, like you, loved her dearly," she replied, "but to reproach you for something not your fault won't bring her back."

He turned and hugged her close in mute thanks for her confidence. She felt how tense he held himself, how he seemed to tremble with sheer fatigue and grief.

"How long have you been travelling?" she asked.

"Over a week, near enough," he replied. "The Loire was in flood. I had to travel miles to get a crossing. I thought I'd never get here."

"Well, you are here now," she said in a soothing manner. "Come into the parlour and I'll mull you some wine."

She led the way into the small parlour where a fire burned brightly, shining on the polished panelling. He took a chair by the blaze as she went to get the wine, extending his icy limbs to the flames. As the heat of it began to melt his hands and feet, so did the great lump of ice that was his heart. Tears slid slowly down his cheeks and dropped unheeded into his cravat. Jane, entering with a jug of fragrant spiced wine and a savoury stew, made no mention of it and gave no sign, merely putting the dish of food to keep warm, and giving a mug of wine into his unresisting hand. He drank deeply several times and was heartened by it so that he was able to control his grief enough for her to give him the bowl of stew.

"Eat this, Hal," she said kindly. "Then, I think you should sleep."

"Sleep?" he replied hollowly. "There's been no sleep for me."

"So I guessed, looking at you," she replied compassionately, "but you are home now, safe, you'll sleep."

He took a few mouthfuls of the stew. "Where is everybody?" he said, suddenly puzzled at the quiet of the house.

"Mary took the children to Elmley Park," she replied, for the first time her gaze faltering. "Libby insisted on it before she—when—well she said she—before it happened. Bess and her babies are with Justin in Adamsholme. Ned and Cecily have gone to Rushington Manor —and Ambrose is with them," she added uneasily.

The combination of the warmth, the strong wine laced with herbs and the food were having their inevitable effect, Hal's head was nodding as he struggled with consciousness. "Hetta? Hetta and Will?" he asked desperately.

"They are well," agreed Jane, removing the empty mug from his slackened grip. "Come, Hal, come to bed. You are exhausted."

Lead-footed he followed her up the shallow staircase off the hall to the gallery above. Everywhere was dim, warm and above all comforting in its familiarity. He opened the door to the left at the head of the stairs and almost staggered to the high bed hung about with curtains. He fell across it, and the last thing he remembered was his boots being removed and a cover being smoothed over him with gentle compassionate hands.

When he awoke, it was full daylight and he just

caught the sound of a softly–shutting door. He sat up abruptly, realising that he'd slept long and scrambled from the bed. The fire had been re-made and was burning brightly. Two pewter ewers stood, one filled with hot water, the other with cold, beside a basin with his razors laid out ready for him.

Unseen hands had also unpacked his clothes and washed and pressed his linen. He drank deeply of the cold water, and then poured the remainder over his head before shaving himself.

Some time later, feeling comfortable and more like his usual self than he had since he left France, he opened the door and stepped out into the corridor. To his right, the stairs led down to the hall where he could hear voices, opposite was the chamber which had been Libby's.

He crossed to it and opened the door. All stood silent, no fire in the hearth, but the bed made up fresh and her things yet still there. He stood before the toilet table, fingering the milky pearls, which had been her favourite ornament and her reflections seemed to look back at him from the fine Venetian mirror, quizzical, a little dismayed, but infinitely comforting. He felt tears prickle the back of his eyes, but controlled them, going to the closet. Here, all her gowns were hung along with her thick fur cloak. He lifted a sleeve and held it to his mouth, inhaling the smell, and then turned abruptly, closing the door and walking swiftly from the room.

The sound of voices came from below and he easily recognised those of Ned, his brother, and Ambrose Carver, Jane's husband. Quickly, he descended the staircase.

Chapter Two

"Hal!" Ned started forward as soon as Hal came into sight, and as he got to the foot of the stairs, embraced him fiercely. "Hal, I am so damned sorry," Ned said quietly. Hal stared blankly at the room over the top of Ned's vibrant red curls. Emotions Hal thought he had under control contorted his handsome face and he couldn't trust himself to speak as he returned Ned's hug with heartfelt gratitude.

Ambrose Carver, his fair skin pale, his normal cheerful smile sombre, met his eyes saying simply, "Everyone is unable to believe it, Hal. You must be so sad, I am very sorry, but you won't want to speak of it just now."

Hal gripped his offered hand and nodded, saying quietly, "Thank you, thank you."

"Are you hungry Hal?" asked Jane, coming in with ale.

"Very," he replied. "What time is it?"

"Close on noon," she replied, smiling faintly at his look of dismay.

"Noon," he replied. "Good God, I'd not meant to sleep so long."

"You must have needed it," she replied. "Did you sleep at all on your journey?"

"I snatched a few hours in a filthy inn at Cléry just short of Orleans before I was able to cross the Loire," he replied frowning, in an effort of concentration. "And a whole night in Calais waiting for the storm to subside."

"And the remainder of the time you were travelling?" asked Ned. "No wonder you look as you do."

"I couldn't sleep anyway," he replied, taking a seat at the table and accepting the mug of ale. "I was desperate to get home."

An uneasy silence fell as Jane hurried away to call for food.

"It all happened so quickly in the end," said Ned. "Justin had been agitating— for oh, more than a month now—about finding you. But we knew you'd be coming soon for Christmas and my wedding. And Libby always said to wait on your letter, that you'd write when you were ready," he sighed. "I suppose, living here with her every day I didn't notice as I should—I mean I knew she was ill—well she never recovered from Francis' birth did she? But then Mary came to stay, and she sent for Justin—for Libby and he had quarrelled—"

"Oh, dear God, that was my fault," groaned Hal.

"Well, I suppose, in essence they quarrelled over you," agreed Ned diffidently. "But Libby was very angry with Justin, it was she who said she never wanted to see him again."

Hal gave another groan of dismay and shaded his eyes. "And my poor Bess, caught between?" he asked.

"No, Bess continued to visit. I think it was Justin's way of keeping a source of news, but then Bess gave birth to a baby boy early, at the beginning of November, and she wasn't due until next week, and so she was taken up with that. Then, as I say, Mary arrived and sent for Justin, who sent his clerk to find you, but it was too late, she just seemed to fade away."

"She knew she was dying, Hal," said Jane, coming to sit along side him, laying her hand over his clenched fist. "She dictated a long letter to you one day, and I took it all down. Justin has it."

"I should have returned," he muttered. "I knew I should have returned at the end of September, once I finished assisting Phillipe, but there was another mystery, and—and I didn't want to come."

"That's in the past now," said Ned bluntly. "You can't change the past, so its no good getting upset over it." He hesitated. "When Libby was dying she said certain things, Hal, and it seemed only right to do them, especially as I wanted it." He took a deep breath. "She said Cecily and I should be married at once, and we were— last Sunday after church in Libby's chamber—at the same time as Jane and Ambrose. Guy and Mary agreed to it," he added defensively as Hal looked amazed.

"It was quite private, Hal," said Jane hastily, "so no disrespect was shown to my father's memory."

"That's why we are at Rushington. It's our home,"explained Ned.

Hal opened and shut his mouth a few times, as if he still couldn't believe it, a hurt look coming into his eyes. "I would that you had waited for me to come," he said at last.

"I would that you had come sooner. We all did, especially Libby," returned Ned brutally. "What was so important Hal, that she had to die alone, weeping for you?"

"Ned!" protested Jane, as the servants entered bearing food. Hal got quickly to his feet to hide his face from them.

"Nothing," he replied over his shoulder. "Nothing was that important, Ned, it was all my folly."

"Ned, I said you weren't to start on reproaches!" cried Jane, going to Hal and putting a tender hand on his arm. "Come, Hal, please eat, you have lost weight and look on the verge of illness yourself. You must rest and eat to get your strength back."

"Well, I beg pardon," said Ned awkwardly, as Thomas quickly ushered the maids away. "But it seems a damned shame to me. Libby was a good and faithful wife to you, Hal, she was devoted to all our interests, and yet you abandoned her in her hour of need to go off on a madcap adventure, that cannot have been necessary."

"Ned, you flew at Justin's throat on Tuesday when he said that," observed Ambrose with a faint smile. "If it hadn't been for Guy's intervention, there would have been an unseemly brawl at Libby's funeral and Justin would have had a black eye to follow her coffin. You challenged us all to speak one word against your brother in the most ferocious manner, and yet you now berate him yourself."

"I have the right," he replied coldly, as Hal and Jane

came to the table. "I am a Westwood. Justin does not have the right."

Jane smiled faintly and ruffled his ruddy locks affectionally. "He defends Hal from criticism with his life, woe betide any who speaks against his brother, but he reserves the right to speak his own mind."

"Well may he do so," agreed Hal. "He knows I'd show no mercy if he does wrong, I deserve everything any of you care to say to me, family or no, for I have been grossly at fault and made such a mess of things. Although, Ned, I take issue with you attacking Justin. Recollect, Libby is—was his sister," his voice trembled as he recollected himself over the simple mistake. "His only sister, poor fellow."

"He has taken everything hard," said Ambrose reflectively. "I noticed a change in him as soon as I joined him in July. He's grown harder somehow, less tolerant of human folly then he used to be. It was his tolerance of the human condition which so impressed one."

"Bess insists he is deeply hurt at your quarrel, Hal," said Jane as they all sat down and began to eat. "He never speaks of it—or you—but what Ambrose says in essence is so. In his disappointment he grew angry and hard and now he is, well, almost unapproachable."

"I know poor Sophie goes in fear of him," said Ambrose, helping himself to more ale. "I think that's why Libby insisted she went back to Elmley Park with Mary and the children. Up until her death, she'd been able to protect Sophie from Justin, but she knew he blamed her for everything."

"That is hardly just," said Hal his voice strained.

"That's what one notices most," remarked Ambrose. "He was the one with the sense of fair play and justice. He'd have the truth come what may, but in this matter, he won't listen to reason. Sophie was to blame for stealing your love from Libby, and thus sending you into exile, therefore, she's to blame for Libby's death."

"She never stole my love from Libby," said Hal, his tone echoing his dislike for his affairs being the subject of discussion. "I love Libby, I'll always love Libby."

"Of course you do, Hal, none doubts it," soothed Jane, seeing his agitation.

"I admit to a few weeks of mad infatuation with a pretty face, a few weeks of folly, but Libby knew, she trusted me," Hal added with difficulty.

"I have to say, she always defended both you and Sophie against Justin," agreed Ned.

"If Justin hadn't intervened, I could have handled it

all in my own way, with none the wiser," added Hal, bitterness still sounding in his voice. "No man likes to see his folly trumpeted abroad, as Justin was so determined it would be. He did none of us any good, and all of us much harm. I am branded a libertine, or a fool, Sophie a drab, and Libby a neglected wife."

"And were you not?" asked Ned bluntly.

"I was certainly a fool," Hal agreed.

"And Libby a neglected wife."

"Recriminations and reproaches are of little use to any of us," said Jane firmly. "Ned, if you can't say something pleasant, hold your tongue."

Ned glanced to her, a spark in his eyes. "Have you any idea how like Aunt Margery you sound?" he asked.

Jane looked appalled. "Ned, you can be odious!" she replied.

"That was another thing we had to endure on your behalf," added Ned. "Aunt Margery, convinced the scandal was past remedy, arrived to give Libby her support."

"And to make Sophie's life misery," said Jane quietly, "forbearance never being one of her strongest virtues."

"She terrifies me," said Ambrose. "She made me give her chapter and verse on my life before I met Jane, and then told me I wasn't fit to lick any Westwood's boots."

Hal smiled faintly in all his pain. "She does have an inflated idea of the importance of the family. In what way did she make Sophie's life misery?" There, it was out, an ordinary question about a girl who happened to be his ward.

"Oh, Aunt Margery had no hesitation in laying all the blame at Sophie's door," said Ned. "Sophie not being a Westwood, and Libby being her favourite, and the mother of the heir to the head of the family," he chuckled reluctantly. "I don't believe I've ever seen anyone square up to Aunt Margery before."

"You mean Sophie wasn't meek?" Hal asked quickly.

"Gave her as good as she sent," grinned Ambrose. "Said it was none of her affair, and when she wanted advice, she'd go to someone she trusted to give it."

"What did Aunt Margery say?" asked Hal in horror.

"Oh, that she was an impudent jade and hoyden, that if she'd had the schooling of her, Sophie'd have learnt to mind her tongue—you know, that sort of thing," said Ned.

"Then, luckily, Libby intervened before they could become daggers drawn," said Jane. "She really was the next best thing to a saint, Hal, in the way she insisted

Sophie was treated with respect and friendliness by everyone."

Hal's pallor, if anything, increased. "That had to be insisted on, did it?"

Ned coloured, for Hal was looking at him. "None of us felt in charity with her, Hal," he replied, and there was just the hint of truculence in his tone. "After all, you'd left us and Libby had been slighted, it was a difficult situation."

"No, it was an impossible situation," said Ambrose. "Excuse me, but I am an outsider. I see only too well, and you could hardly have expected different from settling your mistress in your wife's home, Hal."

"For once and all, she was not and never will be my mistress!" Hal cried enraged. "She is a young and foolish wench, who happens to be my ward, who'd suddenly become infatuated with me!"

"That's not what she said, Hal," snapped Ned bluntly. "She made it plain you had the closest of relationships. 'She slept the night in your arms,' she said, within my hearing to Cecily, and there were signs that she was, perhaps still is, with child."

Hal looked appalled, his mouth dropping open. "Then she lies," he thundered, making a recover, "and I shall call her to account for it!" Then, he recollected the night at the farmhouse, and his certainty faded before them all. "Sophie is quite childlike in some ways," he added lamely. "She might well say things, which had been misconstrued."

"A baby can be misconstrued?" asked Ambrose in amused horror.

"There is no child," said Hal quietly. "Unless of course—" For a few moments, he looked appalled and distraught. "Unless that swine Durward did ravish her, saving your pardon, Jane, and she dared to tell none! But I give you my word of honour," he looked deliberately at all three in turn. "As far as I am concerned, she was a maid."

"Well, that's a situation which will bear clarification," said Ambrose thoughtfully, recollecting, as he was sure the others did, the occasions Sophie came to the table looking pale and pinched, refusing food with a nauseous shudder, but getting plumper.

"It was from that date, in retrospect, Hal, that Libby began to fail," said Ned. "I blame myself, I should have seen it."

"No," said Hal. "It wasn't your responsibility. I should have been here to oversee everything. Justin was right, I was frightened, so I ran. Now, I am paid out for it! Where is Aunt Margery, and Aunt Kate for that matter?"

"They have gone to visit one of Aunt Margery's numerous acquaintances," replied Ned. "They were both quite overcome by the funeral, Libby was a favourite of both. So they decided to visit the Singleton-Highers, who live over beyond Chipping Barbury. I escorted them there on Thursday, they having accompanied Cecily and I to Rushington Manor."

"And I went along with them," said Ambrose. "As I went on my way to Adamsholme, and Ned came across to invite Jane to stay with them for a while."

"It is as well I came today, then, or I'd have found the house deserted but for ghosts," said Hal bleakly.

"You can't expect to abandon your family for close on five months, Hal, and not have us go on with our lives," said Ned with his usual stark frankness. "We didn't know when you were returning—if ever. For all we knew, you could have been dead."

"I knew you'd return, Hal," said Jane softly. "You've never deserted your duty yet, however difficult it must have been at times. Ned is lucky, fortune has always shone on him, he's never been put to the test. Those of us that have, and have been found wanting, will show more mercy."

Hal smiled faintly at her. "I thank heaven for your sweet sympathy, Jane, 'tis balm to my soul, which I don't doubt will be further scourged as soon as Mary arrives."

"Mary loved Libby," said Ned bluntly. "We all did. There isn't one of us she hasn't helped or stood by since she joined the family. It grieved us to see her cast aside for this chit of a girl! How could you do it, Hal? How could you treat her so cruelly?"

Hal shaded his face from their eyes, and said unsteadily, as Jane cried out in anger: "No, Jane, he—he is right—and I have no answer! I didn't want to fall in love with Sophie. I know Libby was a perfect wife, unfailing in her duty. I tried my very best not to let it happen, but to no avail."

"Ned," said Jane sharply. "You are younger and more fortunate in that father never felt the need to use you to gain an advantage. Mary and I were sold off to our first husbands to gain father either influence, or hard cash. Hal's marriage was a similar arrangement."

"But that I consented," said Hal quickly.

"As did we all, what choice did we have?" replied Jane roundly. "But Hal saw to it—indeed his marriage ensured—that you, Bess and Hetta could marry where you wanted. One must endure the penance of a loveless marriage to fully appreciate the joy of a second attachment based on true affection and respect."

"I was luckier than you and Mary," said Hal swiftly. "I held Libby in great affection and esteem, but I—I love Sophie to distraction."

Ned shrugged. "It seems a damned shame, that's all," he said simply. "I can see what Jane, aye, and Mary too, means. Philip Eustace was an unnatural monster, and we are well rid of the maniac. Sir Edward, too, was an unpleasant man, and treated Mary badly, but Libby never did anything wrong to anybody. She was next best thing to a saint, if ever a woman was."

"You are right, Ned," he agreed. "Totally and utterly correct, she never said or did a bad thing. I was the most blessed of men to have her for a wife, although it's not always the most comfortable thing in the world to be married to a saint."

Ambrose leaned across to clutch his shoulder in sympathy. "Let it go now, Ned, your brother is weary still. He doesn't need this catechism over his dinner. Leave him in peace."

"Oh, I've said what I wanted," Ned replied. "I'll add only this: I hope you don't think on wedding that hussy, Hal, for neither I nor Cecily could countenance it. Obviously, we have no jurisdiction over your actions, but for myself, I never want to set eyes on the scheming jade again—and if that means I can't visit Westwood in future, so be it. Naturally, you'll always be welcome at Rushington Manor whilst you are a widower."

"Why you insufferable young prig!" cried Ambrose. "By heaven, I thought poor Hal would have much to bear from his aunts, but I expected his own brother to stand with him!"

"I don't see that this is any concern of yours," replied Ned arrogantly.

"No, I dare say you don't, laddie," he replied incensed. "What you need, young man, is a few hard knocks to make you a little more humble—"

"Pray, don't quarrel over me," said Hal swiftly. "I am well-used to—please, a meal ended in peace would suit me at this point."

"Indeed," said Jane, fixing her husband with a look, and kicking her younger brother's shin hard enough to make him wince. "Pray, let us talk of other matters. Ned, have you settled your disputed boundary with your neighbour?" Then, as he grunted a reply, she added desperately: "You did not fall foul of our local celebrity then, Hal, on your journey home? We have our own highwayman these days, Black Jack, they call him. 'Tis rumoured he's a gentleman down on his luck taken to the road. He haunts that woodland near Tadham on the way to Rushington."

"Gentleman, my foot!" snapped Ned. "The fellow's a rogue, who has made everyone's life difficult this autumn! I don't know how many coaches he's stopped on their way to Chawcester."

"A successful rogue then," remarked Hal, glad of the change to topic.

"He's had the devil's own luck," agreed Ambrose. "Sam Wilding was in to see Justin last month, puffing and fuming! He'd been relieved of his purse last market day after he'd sold his sheep. All his profits gone for the autumn, he said."

"He certainly appears to have local knowledge," remarked Jane.

"Easily enough come by," said Hal. "Anyone could ask which day is market day in Adamsholme, and if you are going to rob a farmer, better to do so at harvest time than in the spring."

"Sheriff Hughes was saying when I met up with him at the Sessions last week that there are no new faces or strangers in the district," said Ambrose.

"That fool," muttered Ned disagreeably.

"Do you think him a fool?" said Ambrose. "I thought him rather shrewd."

"So he is," said Hal. "But not of the ilk to appeal to Ned, here."

"No, well little does, it seems, these days," Ned replied. "Now I must return home to Cecily, before sister Jane breaks both my ankles." He got to his feet. "No, don't get up, finish your meal. I wish you joy of sister Mary, Hal, and hope to see you at Rushington soon. Both Cecily and I would be greatly honoured."

With a stiff bow, he took himself off, escorted by his sister.

⚜

Chapter Three

Hal was walking in the garden the next morning. He had been tempted there by a hint of sunshine dappling the yew walk and, in spite of the nip in the air which made his nose run a little, he felt glad to have left behind the gloom of the house. Ambrose and Ned had gone on their way before supper, leaving Hal with much food for thought. He and Jane had taken a solitary meal together, after which they'd gone early to bed. Even though he still felt exhausted, he'd not slept well, being troubled by the things he'd heard. Daylight found him up and dressed and pacing the house.

The familiarity, and yet the oddness of it, was telling on his nerves. Never, not since he'd first come here five years ago, had there been so few people living in it. Indeed, often it seemed to him it was overfull to bursting, but now its quiet corridors and empty chambers seemed to echo the disaster that was his life.

Melancholy settled like a great thick blanket of despair on his shoulders and took him silent and introspective to breakfast, longing for the sound of childish voices, raised in dispute, or laughter, listening for the sound of a step on the stair. Jane had recommended a walk, seeing his unease, but had declined to join him, having tasks to do.

The sound of a shout disturbed his misery, and he turned back toward the house to see Harry running to him, his arms outstretched. He ran to meet him, catching him up in his arms and covering his face and head in kisses.

"You came, you came!" cried the little boy, half-throttling him in a hug. "Mama said you'd come before Christmas! Oh, how I missed you, father," he said, his dark eyes shining with joy. "Will Mama come back now, too? For she said, once you came, everything would be well again."

Hal dropped to his haunches so that his face was on a level with his son's, seeing with a start of amazement how he'd grown and finally left babyhood behind. Dark curling lashes screened eyes as dark as his own, and his chubby cheeks were flushed damask pink in the chill air. Hal clasped Harry to his chest, closed his eyes, and felt the tight band of iron which enclosed his heart, ease a little, then as he opened them, he became aware of another standing before him.

Instinct told him it was Sophie. Suddenly, he was as aware of her as if she'd kissed him. Keeping his eyes on Harrys' face, he continued to talk to him whilst covertly noting the tinyness of Sophie's velvet-shod feet and the beauty of the embroidery, which edged the hem of her gown.

He steeled himself to look up, and experienced another shock. She was, if anything, even more lovely! Her face was thinner, as she'd finally shed the plumpness of girlhood. It was also pale, her lovely eyes etched, it seemed, against the whiteness of her skin. But all this served only to delineate each feature, making them even more breathtakingly beautiful.

"Good morning," he heard himself say with calm politeness.

"You—you are returned," she said, her voice breathless, as if she'd been holding it for some minutes.

"As you see," he replied gravely.

"I—I am sorry about—about your wife, Libby," she stammered.

"Yes," he said, getting to his feet, Harry still in his arms. "So am I."

"Shall I take him?" she asked doubtfully, not sure what to say or do.

"He seems quite happy," he replied, as the little boy took a firm hold of his coat edge and smiled at him sweetly. "Is he in your charge?"

"No, he has a nursemaid, but—well, I've been helping a little. Whilst we were at Mary's—Mistress Armstrong's house," she hesitated, and then added in a rush, "they've been very distressed."

"With good cause," he agreed as they turned their steps back to the house.

"Indeed," she said, feeling rather lost, for he seemed infinitely remote with his black coat and pale face. She glanced sidelong at him, trying to decide whether he looked older, or merely tired. He had streaks of grey in his long black hair. He was certainly more handsome than her memory had told her. He seemed different somehow, more polished perhaps, and the fear grew in her that he'd conquered his love for her. He'd given no sign, not even so much as a flicker of an eyelid, that he held her in any special esteem. He'd made no attempt to touch her, or even initiate a conversation. Tears filled her eyes as the door opened and Guy called out, "Hal, there you are! Mary was fretting." He smiled at Sophie in a disapproving manner. "You didn't say, Sophie, that you were to take Harry into the garden."

"Jane suggested that I take him to meet his father," she replied quietly.

"Ah, yes of course," he said. "Well, Mary wants him with her now."

"I'll take him to her," said Hal. "It would seem Mistress Redcroft has been somewhat imposed upon."

"There was no imposition," she cried, blinking back tears. "I was pleased to be of use, to help where I can."

"We are greatly indebted to you," he replied with a bow. "Come Harry, lead the way to your Aunt Mary."

He turned away, leaving her at the foot of the stairs, to find Mary in the small parlour, deep in conversation with Jane.

"Hal!" Mary turned, her lovely face concerned, her black curls shining. She looked every inch the cosseted wife of a wealthy man. Jane came to take the little boy, and embraced him. "Hal, what happened? Where have you been? Couldn't you have come sooner? Don't you realise Libby was desperate to see you again?"

"Nothing happened, I have been in France, and had

I realised Libby was so ill, I most certainly would have come sooner!" he replied coldly, disengaging himself.

"But had you told us where you were, we could have sent word!" she cried quickly. "Surely you could have written, if only the once."

"I could have, but I didn't, which I regret deeply," he replied curtly.

"But, Hal, you were gone close on five months!" she expostulated. "With no word of how you were."

"I was in Gascoiny, as indeed, you all knew, for at least four of those five months, a letter sent to the town of Auch would most certainly have found me."

"Yes, well that was Justin's fault," she sighed. "I thought we should have written, indeed, I was in two minds whether to send Guy, but then I was close to my time. You have a nephew! Two nephews, for Bess has lately been delivered of a boy, too."

"Henry Liberty," said Guy, raising his mobile brows to indicate his feelings, his pointed beard wagging to emphasize the point.

"Henry Liberty?" echoed Hal in amazement.

"Bess insists on Henry, Justin on Liberty, only, since Libby's death, he's called the poor child Liberty and forbidden Bess to call him Hal, or Henry, or Harry," said

Mary, shaking her head.

"What did you call your son?" asked Hal, taking a seat and lifting his own child onto his knee.

"Nicholas, for my father," said Guy proudly.

"And he is healthy?" asked Hal, stroking Harry's curls.

"Oh yes, Hal," said Mary, her annoyance with her brother fading in the light of a much more important subject. "He's a fine strong boy, the midwife said she'd never seen a stronger baby! He was born so quickly, compared with baby Guy, who took best part of a day and a night to be born. He was here in under seven hours."

"My congratulations," he said. "Not only on a fine son, but on a safe delivery, and what appears to be a healthy recovery."

"Aye, well it wasn't without its complications," said Guy. "For a few days, I was sweating that she might take child-bed fever, but then she made a recovery. It's left you weary, lass, but you're much better now, are you not?"

"Indeed," she agreed. "That was back in October, I am more than well enough now."

"Two sons in not as many years, Guy, you are indeed to be congratulated," said Hal. "I hope your sister does her duty by Ned as well as mine does by you."

"Oh, you know about Ned and Cecily do you?" he replied. "Yes, well I gave my consent, to my mind, Libby showed great sense and courage. It's not as if the year wasn't nearly over for your father, and there was no sense in making them wait a further twelve months, indeed, I think it would have finished Ned off."

"Do you not approve, Hal?" asked Mary. "I wasn't sure, and I know you were most anxious Cecily shouldn't be hurried, but she was as eager as Ned, I assure you."

"I have no right to approve or disapprove," he replied. "Having abandoned you all, I can hardly raise objections if you choose to go your own way—or so, at least, Ned informed me."

"This marriage has been the making of him," said Mary. "You should have heard him give Justin a piece of his mind last week at Libby's funeral…" she broke off, realising that for her brother, it was all too new and unreal.

"Yes, I understood from Jane there was some sort of fracas," he said distantly.

"Well, Justin is pretty unbearable," said Guy candidly. "You know, I've never greatly cared for him, but since you bolted, Hal, he's been impossible!" he glanced to

Mary's horrified face and frowned. "What have I said amiss now?"

"Mary presumably thinks I'll be offended by your terminology," said Hal.

Guy shrugged. "I can gild it if you want, but the truth is the truth."

"However unpalatable," agreed Hal.

"What happened in France, Hal?" asked Mary. "Why were you gone so long?"

"It took me some weeks to prove Phillipe Douay innocent of a ten-year old charge of murder laid against him," he replied. "And then if you'll remember, I went also to find our father's grave."

"And did you?" asked Mary.

"Yes," he replied. "Easily, but not one for Jacqueline, or her child, and that is what detained me, finding them."

"Finding them? You mean they are still alive, they didn't perish of the plague with our father, as reported?" cried Mary.

"No, she abandoned father almost as soon as the plague was diagnosed," said Hal evenly. "Apparently, he begged her to leave to seek safety, and Madame, the inn-keeper's wife who nursed him, said she'd never seen such haste to be gone. The inn-keeper's wife had no fear of the plague, having survived a bout ten years ago. She said if Jacqueline had remained, Father may well have pulled through, for he was strong, but he'd lost the will to live. But from what she said, I guessed he'd lost the will to live earlier than that when it became clear that Jacqueline's baby would be born at Christmastide."

"Why?" asked Guy. "Surely a man of his age would be pleased and proud to have sired a child at any time of the year."

"Probably," agreed Hal. "But that he hadn't, it seemed he was abroad for the King in the previous March."

"Oh, dear God," said Mary. "Poor father, that must have hit him hard."

"Yes," said Hal bleakly. "Very hard, it seems, for he told the woman he had no doubt the child would re-semble his eldest son."

"Oh Hal! He cannot have been sure!" she cried.

"No, he cannot have been, for he did not live to see the child. I have, however."

"You've seen him? And Jacqueline?"

"No, Jacqueline died giving birth to him on the day after Christmas last year. I've seen her grave in the nun-nery at Saint-Sauvy."

"Jacqueline buried in a nunnery?" said Guy. "It doesn't bear thinking on."

"You've seen the child, you say, Hal. Is he—does he—"

"Look like me? Oh, yes," he replied bitterly. "So like his poor Mamma, the nuns said, the same dark eyes and hair. Put him beside young Harry here—or your lad Guy—and he'd pass for a brother."

"I am so sorry, Hal," Mary said simply. "What have you done with him, left him there?"

"With the nuns? No," he replied firmly. "I've left Phillipe to deal with outstanding matters and told him to bring the child to England. Phillipe intended to return anyway, his father being dead now, and I'd thought to have the child looked after somewhere close at hand. After all, if I couldn't acknowledge him as a son, he is, to all intents, our brother. But it doesn't matter now. Libby can't be hurt by me anymore, so he'll join me here and be brought up with my other children."

"What is he called?" asked Guy, as Mary looked shocked.

"Ettienne. He was born on St Stephen's Day, so he was called for the saint, as is the custom in France," he replied.

"Stephen? Good heavens, what will Aunt Margery say?" asked Mary.

"I pray God her eyesight fails her, and she is convinced of a likeness to Jacqueline," he sighed.

"We must promote it," said Mary. "We must all keep saying how like his mother he is. People always accept what they are told, if you are firm enough."

"I trust you are right, Mary, 'tis not an explanation I'd care to give Aunt Margery."

"No, no indeed," exclaimed Guy. "She's taken it all very much to heart, Hal," he added. "I don't know how many lectures we've all endured. You seem to have finally eclipsed even my behaviour, and as for Justin!" he made an expressive face.

"I thought Aunt Margery had decided to remain with her stepson," said Hal plaintively. "Didn't Libby tell me last summer that she felt it her duty to live with the Kingscotts since they'd been so beset by troubles?"

"Yes, and no," grinned Guy, "but Tom Kingscott's a downy one, Hal. No doubt he told her it was her duty to return here to assist you!"

"The rumour is, Tom Kingscott is thinking of remarriage," said Mary in disapproving tones. "And at his age, too!"

"Is Tom Kingscott so very old?" asked Hal. "Surely he is not more than five and forty?"

"Aye, and with his son Tom dead, and the heir no more than a babe in arms, I suppose it is only right he should think of remarriage, most widowers do," said Guy.

"But not before they've mourned their wife," snapped Mary. "Promise me, Hal, you'll not put us all to the blush by wedding that girl incontinently!"

Hal glared at his outspoken sister. "Remind me, Mary, how long you'd been a widow when you wed Guy? And how far gone were you with his child?" he replied coldly.

"Mary, hold your tongue," said Guy red-faced. "Look, Hal, it's not for us to criticise—"

"I am glad you realise it," he interrupted. "No, pray, say no more, Mary. Be assured, I'll mourn my wife the full term, indeed, I have no thought of remarriage at this time." He glanced from one to the other, his expression bland. "Are you making a protracted visit at this time?"

"No, Hal," said Guy hastily. "This is but a fleeting visit."

⚜

Chapter Four

Sophie hesitated outside the door to the small parlour, which she knew was called the Jericho parlour by the family, on account of the hangings which lined the walls of the room. It had not been used in her weeks at the house, now it became plain this was Hal's chamber. She wished she'd known previously, she could have gone there when she'd missed him so desperately. She smoothed the folds of the gown she'd hastily changed into, pulling out the lace which edged the neck and sleeves, patting at her unruly curls. There'd not been time to redress it, for it was plain she'd been sent for sometime ago. She only hoped he'd not notice how windswept she was by her ride out. She felt rather nervous, for they'd barely spoken in the last few days beyond the necessary for living in the same house, so that she was both bewildered and a little resentful. She thought she deserved more than to be summoned like a servant. Resolutely, she knocked on the panels of the oak door, and entered as bidden to do so.

"Sophie! At last! I sent for you an hour ago," Hal glanced up from where he was sitting at a gate-leg table, his eyes cold. Ever since Justin's clerk had finally found him and broken the news of how desperately ill Libby was, he'd been dreading this moment, this first meeting with Sophie alone. He'd put it off from hour to hour, as long as he dared, but had finally fallen back on his initial resolve, made during his interminable journey home. Once his first grief had burnt out, he'd been able to think rationally again and he had come up with the best method of dealing with what had become an awkward affair.

In an ideal world, he'd soon realised, he would never have seen her again, but his world was far from ideal, and with Justin, his co-guardian, so uncooperative and even less inclined than he to act, the task fell to him. He must deal with the matter in a manner as befitted his position and status in the world. Personal feelings need not come into it. The girl was, for better or worse, his ward, and as such he owed her a duty. He'd play the role society demanded of him and no more. None could expect any more, he was but a burned-out husk of a man, devoid of all feeling, save that of grief and despair.

"Where have you been that it takes an hour to answer my summons?"

"Out riding," she replied blankly.

"Out riding?" he repeated in surprise. Plainly, this was not the answer he expected, for he had turned his attention back to one of the many documents which littered the entire surface of the table, and he paused, the quill still in his hand. "Yet none seemed to know where you were," he said. "You must surely have told someone of your intention, or failing that, sought permission of my sister."

"No," she replied baldly and hesitated, not wanting to explain that, in the breakdown of communication at the time of his wife's death, none seemed to have cared where she went, or what she did, so that she'd become used to doing as she pleased.

He held her eyes, keeping his own cold. Treat her as you would a witness come to court, he reminded himself. She is nothing to you, but a burden laid unfairly on your shoulders, which has already cost you dear. You are required only to give justice. "Let me understand this," he said. "You have taken a beast from my stable and ridden out, unattended, with reference to none?"

"It is my own horse," she protested. "I haven't stolen one of yours!"

"You sought permission from none and told none," he repeated coldly.

"The groom knew," she replied, adding pettishly: "None care!"

There was a silence as he digested the implications of this. Then, he turned his attention back to his document, signed his name, and laid aside his pen with an air of weariness, which made her heart go out to him.

"Listen to me, Sophie, and understand," he said quietly. "For I shall not repeat myself, and I allow no convenient interpretations of my instructions. In future, you will not leave this house without informing, and seeking the permission of, one in authority over you. These being, namely, myself, Mr Danvers, and my Aunts Westwood and Kingscott. If, by some remote chance, all these people should be from home, you will seek permission from one of my sisters. If they are not by, then, here you must and shall remain. Have you understood these instructions?"

"Yes," she replied, bewildered by his manner.

"I am pleased to hear you say so. Now, tell me how it is that you were out riding and not at your studies."

"Studies?" she repeated blankly, taken aback by the question. "I didn't know I was supposed to be studying!"

"How, then, did you propose to spend this year of mourning which, if I remember correctly, you insisted as being necessary for your well-being?" he enquired coldly.

She stared back at him helplessly, noting the inflexible line of his jaw and his eyes as cold and hard as pebbles. She was totally at a loss as to how to reply, for she could hardly tell him the truth, that it had been her intention to spend it at his side, and that when he had disappeared off to France, she'd been too unhappy to care how she spent it.

She couldn't explain how, in the wreck that her life had become within days of his departure, she'd lain no plans. She couldn't tell him how it had taken all her time just to live out the day ahead, for this wasn't the same kind man who'd held her in his arms at the death of her guardian, the one who'd ridden cross-country in the dark to rescue her from Giles Durward's odious attentions. This was a cold-hearted stranger, who seemed to have little kindness or compassion for anyone.

"I—I don't know," she said at last, rather lamely. "I hadn't thought of it."

"You don't know," he repeated with an ironical inflexion she immediately hated. "You hadn't thought then of formulating any plans in the interim months since the death of Master Benton? I'd have thought five months would have been ample time for thinking."

"Yes, it is," she agreed, tears filling her eyes at the injustice of his words. "And had I known what was expected of me, no doubt I would have done so! As it is none told me, and so—and so I've just been living!"

"Just been living," he repeated, his brow raised and his cold handsome face set in satirical lines.

Anger came suddenly to her rescue. "Yes, living!" she cried, determined he'd not continue in this mode of speaking to her any longer. "Helping where I could with your home and your children! The home and children you abandoned when you went to France."

Surprise chased away his patronising air. "My home and family were adequately cared for," he snapped at once.

"Adequately cared for!" she returned, contempt in her voice. "Are children so recently bereft of their mother, abandoned by their father, to be adequately cared for by servants?"

"I left my children in the care of my wife," he cried, angered by the truth of this. "And when she died, my sisters I know, would have had every care for them!"

"Your sisters, which one?" she demanded. "Mary, who brought to bed with child so they went in fear of her life—or Bess who is so lately delivered of her baby?"

"My sister Jane—" he began swiftly.

"Who has no experience of children at all, of course," she interrupted. "Much less a child broken-hearted at the loss of both parents! No, sir, don't think to lecture me on what I've been doing since the summer, for I've been doing your duty!"

He folded his lips firmly over a retort and looked away from her lovely, impassioned face whilst he took control of his temper. He had forgotten how very provocative she could be, not only in her beauty, but in her temperament, too. He waited, counting in his head until his desire to hold her in his arms was subdued, and his anger under some control. "This is not a matter I see any necessity of discussing with you," he said in a dismissive tone. "Neither is it one you should have made your business. I shall ensure that a program of study is made up for you. You shall be expected to adhere to it, or I shall engage a tutor to make sure you do. In the meantime, I am given to understand you need to consult a physician, as your health has given some cause for concern."

"My health?" Amazement at this turn took away her indignation for his previous words. "There is nothing amiss with me."

"Indeed?" he replied swiftly. "Yet, I have had diverse reports of your health. And whilst some of it can, I am sure, be attributed to grief, others speak of odder symptoms. An inability to stomach food at certain times of the day allied with an increase, at least in outward appearances, of weight?" he looked up to meet her horror-struck eyes and noted her reddened cheeks. "A condition not incompatible with the early stages of pregnancy." There was a brief pause, then he asked harshly: "Are you with child, Sophie?"

She swallowed, unable to look away from his hard, unflinching stare. "No," she whispered.

"No," he repeated and the word fell between then like a stone dropping. "Yet, I do believe you wantonly allowed various members of my family to think you were."

"I never said so!" she cried, tears filling her eyes

"I'm sure you didn't," he agreed coldly. "You wanted them to believe it, however!"

"None ever asked me!" she cried desperately, tears trickling down her cheeks.

Some of his anger died at the sight of this, and in fear that he failed her totally, he asked quietly: "Could you have been, Sophie? I know you told me he didn't, but did that swine Durward in fact ravish you and leave you pregnant with his child, which you subsequently lost?"

"No!" she wept. "No, I told you, Hal, you got to the farmhouse in time to save me!"

"Then why?" he demanded.

"I—I don't know, Hal," she replied, still weeping. "Everything was so dreadful once you'd gone! Everyone was so horrible! They all hate me so. They hold me to blame for your going, and none had a pleasant word to say to me, not even Cecily, for Ned was so angry! I was so miserable, I missed you so much, it was a physical ache here." She held her slender hand to her breast and got control of her tears. "They expected me to—to carry on as if nothing had occurred, when my world was in ruins. None of them could forgive me for my sin of loving you and creating such a scandal, yet they expected me to sit at table and eat with them! I could not, the food used to stay in my throat and threaten to choke me. Then, they began to look side-long at me and to—to whisper behind their hands about me!" Tears overcame her for a few seconds, then she looked up, sniffing defiantly: "I—I decided to, to give them something to talk about. So, so I tied a cushion under my petticoats."

One glance to his outraged face told her the worst, and her tears came hot again, as she bit her lip, adding in a horrified whisper: "I— I beg you will believe me, Hal, I never thought they'd think you were to blame. I didn't seem to think at all, I just wanted to pay them back for all the misery! I thought if they think I am so wicked, then I'll be wicked, but I see now I was foolish! I can have no excuse, except that I was so miserable, I didn't truly care what any of them thought of me!"

"And Libby?" he asked, making his voice harsh lest he betray how he longed to hold her in his arms and sooth her distress. "You couldn't see how a supposed pregnancy of yours might affect my wife?"

She met his hostile eyes fearfully, biting at her lips again. "Not, not at first," she said very quietly. "I truly didn't think of—of all the implications, and then— and then I—I told myself that— that had she—she been kinder to me, not so wrapped up in her own misery, she'd have known the truth!"

"Kinder to you?" he repeated incredulously. "To all intents, you tried to steal her husband and you allowed her to believe you carried his child, yet you accuse her of not being kind!"

"No, no, she was kind, that was the awful thing!" she said, swallowing a sob. "In spite of everything, she tried her best to be kind to me! She wouldn't allow any of them to say anything to me. I would that she'd told me she hated me to my face. It was worse, ten times worse, don't you see, to have her forgiving me!"

"No, I don't see," he replied harshly. "I can well believe she tried to help you, and in return you tormented her—tried to make her believe I'd been unfaithful to her, that you carried my baby. You have blackened my reputation past belief, and driven my wife into an early grave."

She tried to speak, to defend herself from the accusation, but the sight of his implacable face was too much for her. She laid her head on the table and wept copiously. He sat opposite her and watched as if carved of stone, aware that if he gave way and followed his heart by comforting her, he would be lost.

Finally, after some minutes, when the only sounds in the room were her sobs, she showed signs of recovery.

"Then my life is over," she said brokenly, wiping away her tears with the back of her hand. "For plainly, you believe me as wicked as all the gossips in Chawcester say."

"Gossips in Chawcester! What have they to do with this?" he demanded, irritable at her melodramatic ways.

She looked up, her eyes and nose running. "You were in a fever, Hal, we went in fear of your life, so you'll not recollect how it was."

"I was told," he replied curtly. "Once I recovered, Justin took great satisfaction in relaying the gossip in unnecessary detail."

She shrugged her shoulders, her face pinched with misery and wiped her brimming eyes again. "You'll know then how I am already vilified as a murderer," she said starkly.

"Vilified as—what nonsense you talk!" he snapped angrily. "How can it be so? You made your deposition to Dogberry, I saw it for myself."

"Dogberry?" she repeated. "No, I did not—"

"There, if you were better-educated, you'd know I

was speaking of that bungling oaf the constable, what was his name? The town constable, and his witless prig of a master, the bailiff!" he exclaimed.

"Master Keeble and Will Sambourne the constable?" she asked blankly.

"Aye, that brainless pair!" he cried in exasperation. "You told them everything that occurred, I know you did. I read it in the days before I left for France. It tallied remarkably well with my account. Why, even Keeble agreed you'd been courageous to recount all that had gone on."

"Did he?" she replied frowning. "I didn't feel very brave, nor was he very polite to me, but by then, the gossip was at its height, and gossip seldom bothers with the truth, does it?" she tried a valiant smile as he looked amazed. "Recollect, I was not born one of them, and like most small towns, the people were remarkably— parochial, I suppose. They don't even like the folk from Chipping Barbury, never mind Adamsholme. I wasn't one of their own, you see, and they soon remembered my father had been a dissenter, and how I'd spurned several young men of the town. It didn't take them long to decide I'd got above myself, and that I was the sort of wicked hussy who regularly used her beauty as a lure.

Then, having hooked a suitor, blew hot and cold on him until he was driven mad and gave me the chance to kill him with my own hands."

"Giles Durward murdered four of their citizens," said Hal aghast. "By Heaven, I know the mind of the average townsman, but surely, at the very least, they should have been grateful for you saving them the cost of the trial!"

"Oh yes, but that was hardly a matter for public congratulation, or so Mistress Latham said! She merely repeated the gossip—for my own good, of course—telling me how it was common knowledge my wickedness had driven Durwood mad. That I'd used a madman to capture and ruin a well-respected Justice of the Peace."

"I rather think you are being oversensitive," he replied harshly. "That wasn't common gossip at all. My character did not emerge with anything like that much sympathy. Durward may have been proved the man who terrorised their town with a sequence of murders, but I was most certainly the villain who seduced the innocent ward of one of their leading townsmen, whilst sitting in judgement of them all. None of us left that town with a shred of character, or any credit."

"Aye, 'tis so," she agreed, tears falling again. "And you

hold me to blame for it!"

"Don't you think you deserve some blame for it?" he replied.

"Some, perhaps, but not all," she cried, sniffing.

He sighed heavily and produced a handkerchief and handed it to her, saying: "No, not all, but I cannot deny at this moment in time I am very angry with you, Sophie! Maybe you weren't to blame for the fiasco in Chawcester, but since? How could you behave so very badly since then, Sophie?"

She blew her nose and wiped her swollen eyes. "I don't know, Hal," she whispered. "Lest it be that I was so very unhappy that I didn't care. Haven't you ever felt that miserable, Hal, so miserable that you know, even as you are doing a thing, it is wrong—but you just don't care?"

Unbidden, it came into his mind exactly how he'd felt when, as a young boy, very much Sophie's age, he'd fallen under the spell of his stepmother Jacqueline. He had known her to be his father's wife, but that hadn't stopped him wanting her, neither had he cared enough to think of his father's feelings had he discovered the true state of affairs.

"Well, yes," he admitted reluctantly, the harsh lines

of his face softening. "Yes, I can't deny having been that wicked, that unhappy, but by Heaven, I paid dearly for my sins in remorse since."

"Do you imagine I don't?" she cried, a spark of anger coming back into her voice. "Even if I'd been allowed to forget my sins by your family, do you not think I'd be tormented by my own conscience?"

"I am relieved to hear you still have one," he replied austerely, recollecting it was not his part to sympathise with her.

She wiped her eyes again, and looked at him fully. "Tell me, what you would have me do?" she beseeched. "I swear to you, if I thought it would serve a purpose, I'd go barefoot in my shift with ashes in my hair to show my penitence! But whom would that benefit?"

The mental image awoke a well of longing in him, as he remembered her barefoot in her shift when he'd rescued her from Giles Durward the previous summer. He recollected how she'd clung to him in her terror, and how soft she'd felt and how sweet she'd smelt as he'd held her close the remainder of that night. He shrugged his shoulders, his face taut, unable to speak for the wild desire that possessed him.

"I tried my very hardest," she was continuing, more

quietly now. "When I realised what was happening. When I fully understood that Libby was ill, and that it was my wickedness which had caused it. I wanted to go to her, to confess everything and to explain how I'd never meant to injure her, and to beg her to forgive me, but they wouldn't let me. They told me, Justin told me, I'd killed her, and if he had his way, he'd see me hanged for it like a common strumpet! None of them listened or let me explain."

She was silent for a space and still he sat, saying nothing, so she went on. "I thought and thought what to do, and then I realised, I couldn't hope for them to understand, but I saw that Harry was afraid and confused, and I knew I could so something for him, I looked after him." She paused, and this time she didn't weep, but the melancholy look on her young face was enough to make him want to.

"I made it my business to give him as much love and kindness as I possibly could," she said, her voice aching with regret. "Having, in my wickedness, lost to him both his mother and father, I tried, in my poor way, to give as much love as I could. I knew I could never hope to replace her, but at least I could be there—all day and night, too, if need be. I was able to play with him, to talk to him, to cuddle him, to listen to his hopes and fears. To tell him stories when he couldn't sleep, to kiss him when he fell down, and sit by him each night, holding his hand until he'd gone to sleep."

Hal blinked away water from his eyes. "It sounds as if you've been too tender with him," he said, his voice coming gruff. "That will not fit him for the world! He is a motherless child. Few of us have ever known the kiss of love, yet we have survived."

"Have we, Hal?" she asked, looking up at him, her lovely eyes red-rimmed and wet with tears again. "I, like you, grew up a motherless child, with few to show me affection. Don't you think that is partly why we find it so hard to admit our love?"

He looked away from her, knowing if he gave way now, there would be no going back. He wouldn't commit himself to her, and thus condemn them both. "You are wandering from the point," he snapped, fear that he might succumb making him irritable. "The point is that you made my family—inadvertently, mayhap, at first—but you made my family believe I'd sired a child upon you. You, who are little more than a child yourself, who had been left into my care! Don't you comprehend the depth of the wrong you have done me?

The damage you have done, to my personal reputation, even if we put aside the more unprovable accusation of my wife's death?"

She bowed her head. "I am not trying to put any of this aside," she said, her voice aching with misery. "I am fully aware of how my vanity and folly led to this disaster. That I must live the rest of my life in the knowledge that my wickedness caused another to give up her will to live. All I do say, Hal, is that if you'd been here, none of this would have happened."

"Oh, so I must regulate my life now, according to what wicked whim you might chose to take into your head, must I?" he cried angrily. "I must be constantly by to save you from the efforts of your vanity and folly!"

"Is that not what guardians are there for?" she asked humbly, her tears stilled now. "Are they not chosen as older, wiser people to guide those left in their care?"

He turned on her, incensed. "I neither sought, nor gave consent to the charge laid on me."

"No more did I," she returned.

"And I left you in Justin's care. He was named with me," he added.

"And, in effect, left me in a worse case, for Justin hates me," she replied steadily. "Knowing this, you abandoned me to fend for myself."

"Oh, 'tis plain then, all this is my fault," he cried. "I see you and my family are correct. All the wrongs must be laid at my door. Each mishap or mistake has my name upon it!"

"Your family seemed to feel so," she observed dispassionately. "I don't recall one of them doubting for one moment that the child was yours."

He stared at her, his face bitter. "Thank you, I had noticed that."

"Although doubtless, had you been here, you could have scotched such suggestions before they had time to take root in everyone's mind," she continued relentlessly.

"I had important business in France!" he snapped dismissively.

"What?" she asked.

"What I did in France is none of your concern," he cried angrily, turning on her again. "Suffice it to say, I needed to go there!"

"I merely wondered what could be so very important that your wife could die and your children be left in distress," she returned innocently.

"I do not need to explain myself to you!" he exploded, getting to his feet and pacing the room. "At the time, I needed to go to France. With the benefit of hindsight, perhaps, I should have delayed my departure a few weeks, but I was not to know all this would happen."

"No," she agreed simply, "but it has. What shall you do?"

"I do not know," he replied over his shoulder. "I need time to consider. When did you last see Justin?"

"Michaelmas," she replied. "He comes on quarter days to pay my allowance, it would seem."

"Was he not at Libby's funeral?" he asked.

"I believe so, Mary said I'd better not go! I stayed with the little ones and tried my best to comfort Harry."

He nodded. "Very well, I'll consult with him as to what is to be done. In the meantime, continue to make yourself useful to my sister and begin to study the books that will be left out for you."

"I finished my schooling at fifteen!" she snapped.

"You may have completed one phase of it," he returned. "You will now embark on a further course of study. It should serve to keep you out of mischief, and hopefully broaden your outlook beyond the narrow confines of a tradesman's world."

She stared at him in disbelief. "I do not want to go back to school," she cried. "I am nineteen years old."

"And as such, at a marriageable age," he replied. "Unless you intend to marry your innkeeper, you'll need to improve your knowledge of the world."

"I do not want to be married off," she cried, indignant at the jibe. "You promised me a year free of suitors."

"Free of suitors, but not of work," he replied. "If you wish to marry well, and I assume you do, you'll do as I bid you."

"I don't know that I wish to marry at all," she replied, amazed that he could still be thinking of it. That it should be a matter for discussion, when it was plain to her they should be wed after a decent interval.

"Well, fortunately, I don't need to consult you yet," he replied. "In the meantime, you'll do as you are bid. This interview is now over. Oblige me by going at once and getting on with your tasks at hand."

She stood up, looking a little bewildered. "Hal," she said, and there was a note of desperation in her voice. "Hal, don't you love me at all?"

He had returned his attention to his letter, and his hand faltered at these words, splattering the words, but he kept his voice steady as he said: "Don't be so foolish! Shut the door on the way out."

⚜

Chapter Five

Ambrose looked uncomfortable as Hal entered the office of Justin Danvers. "I'm afraid Justin has someone with him, Hal," he said with would be ease. "I, I don't know how long he may be."

"No matter," replied Hal curtly. "I'll wait."

Ambrose indicated a chair. "Bess—Mistress Danvers—is gone to visit an acquaintance, I do believe," he said, taking a chair behind a desk and picking up a roll of parchment.

"So her maid informed me," said Hal. "Odd, when she has been so lately delivered of her child."

"She left her bed last week," said Ambrose frowning. "She invariably says she is well."

"And?" asked Hal.

"Her looks belie it."

"Is the child healthy?" asked Hal abruptly.

"Indeed," said Ambrose. "Yes, very strong and healthy, contrary to Jane's fears. She thought all the misery Bess has had to endure could well have an adverse effect on the child, especially when he came early, but in fact, quite the reverse seems to have occurred."

"That is something to be thankful for, at all events," said Hal austerely.

A burst of laughter from the inner room made Hal raise his brows slightly and brought a faint colour to Ambrose's cheek.

"Mistress Sitwell," he said uneasily. "A widow—a merry widow."

"So it would appear," returned Hal.

"She—she has numerous interests," continued Ambrose, who plainly felt the need to explain. "She is in constant need of advice and guidance."

Hal inclined his head politely and tried not to allow himself to become irritated. After all, he had no appointment. Justin didn't deliberately keep him waiting.

Another burst of laughter followed, and then footsteps, and the inner door opened.

"One moment, Helen, I'll—oh! Sir Henry, was I expecting you?" Justin Danvers halted in the doorway, the laughter dying from his grey eyes, the smile from his lips.

"No," Hal got to his feet. "No, I called to consult you."

"You should have sent for me," he replied sharply. "I'd not put you to the trouble of coming to my humble abode."

"It's no trouble," returned Hal, glancing to the fashionably-dressed woman who'd followed him from the inner office. "I thought to combine my consultation with a visit to my sister."

"I regret my wife is from home," began Justin, but his companion interrupted saying: "Is it Sir Henry Westwood? Good Heavens sir, you bear precious little resemblance to your father."

"No, ma'am," he agreed with a bow.

"Mistress Sitwell, Sir Henry," said Justin woodenly.

"Ma'am, I am honoured to make your acquaintance," Hal bowed again without enthusiasm and kissed the hand she held out.

"Delighted, Sir Henry, I knew your father well," she cried, her painted mouth curved into a smile that held little warmth, calling attention to her rouged cheeks and the heart-shaped patch on her chin. "Manys the time we shared a bottle of wine together at Whitehall just after the King returned," she added. "I mind well how proud he was of you! It was 'my Hal shall do this' and 'my Hal has done that' until one grew quite out of charity with you!"

"I beg pardon, ma'am, for the tedium of it," he replied with the suggestion of gritted teeth.

"Aye, well, to see you, in the flesh, so to speak, makes me appreciate how I never truly believed one half of what he said!" she cried gaily. "But see how I am paid out, you are at least twice as handsome as I imagined. How is it, Justin, you never told me your brother-in-law was such a pretty man?"

"Likely, Mistress Sitwell, I thought it of little moment," he replied sourly.

She chuckled at this. "Aye, likely you did, my dear, but I mustn't detain you any longer if Sir Henry is awaiting you. When shall those documents be ready for me to sign?"

"Ambrose shall begin work on them at once," he replied. "They should be ready by this evening."

"Then, I shall merely expect you, along with them, later to dine," she replied, coming to where Ambrose held out her cloak for her. "Sir Henry, you'll be welcome to join us if you are not otherwise engaged."

"I regret ma'am, I am," he replied swiftly.

"Another time, then," she said with a smile. "Justin, I shall expect you at five sharp."

"Indeed, ma'am, I'll be there," he replied, ushering her to the door. "Ambrose, escort Sir Henry into my chamber, if you please, whilst I see Mistress Sitwell to her coach."

"Is Mistress Sitwell a frequent visitor?" asked Hal, as he followed Ambrose into the book-lined chamber beyond. "She appeared to be on uncommon terms with everyone."

"She has only recently come to live in Adamsholme, I believe," said Ambrose reluctantly. "I think she arrived in the summer with her husband as a result of the plague in London. Mr Sitwell subsequently died of an apoplexy, leaving Mistress Sitwell with precious few acquaintances of her own age."

"Mr Sitwell being considerably her elder, one supposes," remarked Hal grimly, becoming well aware of the lady's status.

"As you say," agreed Ambrose diffidently.

"I assume my sister doesn't make up one of the dinner party?" Hal continued.

"As to that I—I couldn't—indeed she has until lately, of course..."

"Yes, yes, don't trouble yourself, I can see the horns of your dilemma," interrupted Hal, as Ambrose floundered in a morass of half-excuses. "I don't forget he is your employer."

Ambrose threw him a grateful look. "Can I fetch you a cup of wine, Hal?"

"Thank you, I'd sooner it came from your hand," he agreed ironically.

"Justin has recently lost his sister, Hal," said Ambrose with the return of his unease.

"And I my wife," he agreed, handing his hat and cloak to him and sitting down.

"Indeed," he agreed hastily. "You must find everything very strange."

Hal accepted the cup with a sigh. "Very strange," he echoed. "And yet horribly familiar."

"Jane is well?" asked Ambrose wistfully.

"But that she doesn't see enough of you, and my gloom weighs upon her spirit," he replied with a faint smile. "I cannot tell you how grateful I am to her for her constant attention to my wants. I fear I am not a good companion for her." He looked up, seeing the longing in the other's eyes. "When shall you and Jane share a house?"

"We have no clear idea," he admitted. "I've very little other than my wage, and have no home to offer her."

"Libby, surely, suggested you lived at Westwood with us?" he asked, settling comfortably before the fire.

"Yes, indeed, but it seemed rather a liberty with—" He broke off as Justin's step was heard. "Ah, here is Justin now," he added. "I must return to my work. My love to Jane please, Hal, when you return."

Hal nodded, his face stark again as Justin entered. "I'll gladly be the bearer of a letter," he said.

"I imagine he is too busy to waste his time writing love letters," said Justin, closing the door upon him. "I see you have a cup of wine, good! In what way can I serve you?"

"There are various matters we must discuss," said Hal. "I need to know the terms of Libby's will, and to pay up my account with you. I must owe you a considerable sum, I understand you've been put to some inconvenience on my behalf during my absence."

"Considerable," he replied, going to a glazed cupboard and removing a large box.

"Then, perhaps, you could oblige me by making up the account that I may settle it," returned Hal.

Justin turned to face him. "It isn't a quarter day, am I

to understand that you'll be seeking a new man of law to deal with your affairs in future?"

Hal met his eyes, forcing himself to acknowledge how the past six months had laid its hand on his brother-in-law, too. He looked thinner, tired and older, his lank, mousy hair showing signs of grey. "No," he said evenly. "I was meaning for it to be paid by the quarter day. I don't think, whatever our personal differences, I could find a better man of law."

"It is something that you acknowledge that, I suppose," said Justin ungraciously. He took a bundle of papers and laid them on his desk. "You'll not be surprised to learn your wife left everything she owned to you."

"To me?" Hal looked astounded. "I am surprised. Very surprised," he said. "I was under the impression she intended to leave this business to you."

"Whatever her intentions, the fact remains, as you have returned from France alive, you inherit everything," he sighed heavily. "I tried to get her to put it in trust for her children, but the foolish woman adored you to the last, so like as not, her sons will be cheated as she has been."

"Her children are my children, I shall not cheat them," replied Hal sharply.

"Not until you've married your strumpet and she ensures they are cut out by her brats," snapped Justin.

"I do think it essential, if we are to continue in our business relationship, that civility is adhered to," said Hal evenly. "I cannot fail to be unaware of your opinion of my character, it is not necessary to labour the point with snide remarks and ill-founded suppositions."

"Yes, this is very much your way, is it not?" sneered Justin. "To cloak everything in an air of elegant courtesy! To pretend to be so good and virtuous whilst still pursuing your selfish course!"

"You imagine, perhaps, your blunt rudeness is in some way preferable?" replied Hal coldly.

"It has the merit of honesty," Justin snapped.

"It has the merit of ill-manners," Hal returned.

Justin laid the papers before him. "These are yours, sign for them, if you please. There is also this sealed envelope, a letter, written, if not in blood, with the last of her strength, telling of her undying love and unalterable faith in you."

Hal took up the pen and signed as directed, placing the papers carefully within the pouch he carried.

"You do not read it."

"No," replied Hal curtly. " I'll do so at my leisure."

Justin snorted. "It was her dearest wish you read it, she expended much-needed strength in leaving it, and you'll read it at your leisure?"

Hal glanced away. "Yes, Justin, when it is convenient to me to be alone some little while. Now, if you'll excuse me, we come to one final matter. That of our joint ward, Sophie Redcroft."

"I have nothing to say with regard to that evil hussy," he snapped. "She is responsible for all our troubles. Do you realise she is the cause of Libby's death? Well, her and you between you. But she hounded my sister into her grave!"

"Mistress Redcroft is responsible for nothing," he replied firmly. "She cannot be held to blame for others' beliefs."

"She can be held to blame for being your whore!" Justin cried. "You can be held responsible for breaking my sister's heart."

"Indeed I can," he agreed evenly. "But, as Mistress Redcroft has not, and never shall be, my mistress, your accusations with regard to her are unfounded."

"I take leave to doubt that!" cried Justin.

"What proof do you have of this calmany?" asked Hal, keeping a tight rein on his temper. "As a man of

law, talking to a Justice of the Peace, we both understand well the importance of proof!"

Justin glared at him. "I don't need proof, I know."

"But I have told you, and on more than one occasion,
that you are mistaken," returned Hal, seeing clearly that
Justin had nothing but his distress to go on.

"God damn it, Hal, she's carrying your child!" exploded Justin wrathfully, unable any longer to keep
calm.

"Indeed, she is not," said Hal, in the same reasonable
tones which contrasted so strongly with Justin's. "She
could not be, for she is, to my knowledge, a maid."

"A maid!" cried Justin, "A maid, when even your own
sister said she was so far gone with child it showed. What
else do you think took away Libby's will to live?"

"I do not know, to my shame," he replied. "And I am
aware how remiss I am in that respect, but, to come
back to facts—and it is facts we are dealing with, not
female fancies, not gossip, not rumour, but hard facts.
Sophie has never been my mistress and, so she informs
me, was not ravished by Giles Durward. No more is she
with child. I therefore conclude she is still a maid."

"And you'll take her word for it," Justin cried, furious
at this simple logic.

"Why should I not?" he countered. "I have not known her to lie before."

"So she's not with child!" Justin snapped, irritated that he couldn't seek refuge in this belief, couldn't assuage his grief, but could only feed on his hatred of Sophie. "Does she deny trying to make us believe she was?"

"No, she doesn't deny it," replied Hal. "She admits it freely and says you deserved it for thinking the worst of her."

"Libby deserved that torment, did she?" he demanded, anger leaping back into his voice.

"No, Sophie says she truly regrets that she caused Libby distress—"

"Words are cheap," Justin interrupted rudely, glad to be able to brush aside this response. "I see, she still has you in her sway, at all events! So, the conniving little schemer has succeeded so far in her plans! She lays a trap for you, and you fall neatly in it. No doubt, she fell on your neck with tears and kisses and stirred your sympathy, not to mention lust! She's already disposed of your wife, do you want to wager on how long before she's your bride?"

"I agree to whatever odds you care to name," Hal

replied. "I am not about to enter the married state again."

"You may think you are not," retorted Justin. "But you will, just the same! You'll wake up one morning to find her in your bed, and you'll have no choice!"

Hal frowned, for this was so unlike Justin, this angry belief in the worst of a character. "I am aware you don't hold Sophie in high esteem," he observed. "But do you truly believe her capable of such scheming?"

"I believe her capable of anything," Justin snapped coldly.

"My family were right, you have changed, and I am sorry for it. Especially, as they claim, it is my fault you no longer hold the high ideals you once did. That you no longer are the tolerant and just man you were," said Hal uncomfortably.

"I have no time for your family," he returned sourly. "Though I fail to see why my becoming more clear-sighted should be anything to do with you! Until my eyes were opened, I was dazzled, just like Libby was, by your glamour. Now I'm no longer an idealistic fool, I see you for what you are: a pretty sham! Libby thought you a pattern card of every virtue and would have no dispute, thinking your character as handsome as your face, but now 'tis plain you are nought but a hollow man, with no heart or soul! Don't you be sorry for me, I pity you!"

"On that note, then, of mutual despair, I judge it right to part," said Hal, getting to his feet hastily, feeling his patience was being tried too far. "I gather from your conversation you have no care for the charge left you by Edmund Benton."

"No," he replied coldly. "None. Do with her what you will! I know she'll end up where she wants, I know that will be as your wife. Her sort always wins in the end."

"I thank you for the care you have given my affairs in my absence," Hal said formally. "Pray do send in your account promptly. I don't care to have outstanding debts. With regard to my sister and my nephews, I do trust you'll not make difficulties for her family."

"You may visit you sister as much as I do mine!" he returned sharply.

"You are naturally free to visit Libby's grave when, and how, you chose," replied Hal at once. "If you'll be so good as to bring Bess with you, we can kill two birds with one stone."

"How very apt a simile you use," sneered Justin.

"When will Bess return?" asked Hal patiently.

"I do not know," he returned. "Not before nightfall, I dare say."

Hal frowned. "She is well enough to be so long from her home when she has been so recently recovered from child birth?"

"She hasn't gone anywhere near as far as Chawcester," said Justin icily. "And will return to find her husband here. I have no fears for her."

Hal sighed. "Hindsight is a most useful medium," he agreed. "Please give her my love and I'll bid you good-day."

"What use would she have for such a trumpery commodity?" he replied. "Good-day."

"Pray give it to her anyway," replied Hal and left the chamber swiftly.

Ambrose met his eyes sympathetically. "Not good, eh?"

"As you say," agreed Hal, casting him a considering look. "Are you finished with the Inns of Court in London, Ambrose?"

"Yes," he replied. "And ate my dinners. I am a qualified man of law."

"Then why are you employed as a clerk? Where is the

fellow Justin used to have, Nick Robinson?"

"He's at the Temple," said Ambrose. "Justin says there is enough work for at least two men of law."

"So I thought," Hal replied. "Ambrose, ride out to Westwood this evening, will you, I have things I want to discuss with you, and Jane needs your company."

"I would that I could, Hal," he replied quietly. "But I have a great deal to do here, I doubt me I'll be finished before midnight."

"Who do you imagine owns the business, Ambrose?" Hal asked, as Ambrose helped him on with his cloak.

"Justin doesn't? No, it was Libby's, wasn't it?" he said, a sudden gleam entering his eyes. "Do you tell me you, now—"

"Exactly," replied Hal. "We dine at five, Ambrose, I'll tell Jane to expect you. And you may as well remain overnight. I'll probably have further instructions for you to bring back to Justin on the morrow."

Chapter Six

Hal watched his sister as she turned to smile up at Ambrose, whose visit had made her much happier. The news that he'd be joining them had been enough to bring a sparkle to her eyes and a smile to her lips. It did him good to see it and strengthened him in his resolve. Jane was a good sister to him, she'd stood by him these last few days without a word of criticism or complaint. Neither had hers been an easy life, she deserved some happiness.

He was about to speak to Ambrose when the door opened and Sophie entered. Hal cursed under his breath, for he still couldn't stop his heart from leaping at the sight of her. He was angry with himself. He wanted desperately to play the part expected of him, the part his own temperament demanded, that of a grieving widower. Yet every time he saw her or heard her voice raised in the distance, a well of happiness sprang anew in his heart, and he could not but wonder why it was that Sophie should affect him so. He'd loved Libby, he told himself so a dozen times a day, but it had been a thing of duty, she was his wife, a good and dutiful wife, an excellent mother, who had from the first days of their marriage identified herself with his interests. She'd made no demands on him, had seldom held an opinion that hadn't initially been his, and had in every way, conducted herself in a most exemplary fashion.

Yet although he'd often been glad to see her at the end of a long journey, although she had the facility to sooth him and smooth away many minor irritations he could never recall feeling remotely like he did at the sight of Sophie. He'd never felt the smallest desire to crush Libby in his arms and rain kisses on her face. He'd often seem Libby weep, especially at the death of her babies, yet although he'd joined her in that grief, he'd never felt as he did when Sophie wept, that his own heart must surely break, and that he must move heaven and earth to restore her to happiness. The fact that he could do nothing, that he found himself in such a position that he must stand dumbly by only added to his own misery.

"Sir Henry, will you come to little Harry, if you please," Sophie said, approaching the chair where Hal was affecting to be interested in a two week old news-sheet.

"Harry?" he replied. "What is amiss, is he ill?"

"No, indeed no, sir." She returned quickly. "No, nothing like that—he is in good health, I assure you. It is more his spirits." She glanced uneasily to Jane. "I don't know if Mistress Carver has mentioned it but…"

"No, I have not," said Jane quietly. "I beg pardon, Sophie, I know you wanted me to, but it went from my head!"

"You have been more pleasantly amused than rec-ollecting messages for me." Hal agreed with a smile. "Well, ma'am, what is it my sister has forgot?"

"Harry seems to have got it into his head you were go-ing to Adamsholme, to collect his mother, from where she'd been staying with Bess and Justin," said Sophie baldly.

"I think it was the only way his baby mind could make sense of it, Hal," explained Jane, as he looked appalled. "He asked Mary where his mother had gone when he arrived back here, and she replied she'd gone to Heaven."

"So Harry now thinks Heaven is a village the other side of Adamsholme, and he is concerned you've returned without her," continued Sophie. "He keeps thinking of things to account for it, but I am sure, sir, if you would but explain to him, that would be an end of it."

Hal suppressed a groan. The very last thing he wanted to do, but then it was probably the last thing Harry would want to hear, too.

"Poor Harry," said Jane in ready sympathy. "Shall I go and try to explain?"

"No, good heavens no," he said quickly. "You stay here with Ambrose. It's little enough opportunity you get to be in his company. Besides if Harry really is so muddled—" Hal sighed heavily and left the chamber closely followed by Sophie.

"Poor Hal," said Ambrose. "He looks exhausted."

"He was saying earlier how this is the first journey he'd ever returned from in six years, when Libby had not been there waiting. I think it is only just fully sinking in how much he is going to miss her."

Ambrose nodded. "Did he tell you Libby had left everything she owned to him?"

"No, he did not mention it. Why?"

"Well, it means in effect he owns the business, not

Justin. He, Hal, is my employer, not Justin."

"Why, you are right!" she cried. "Libby's father cut Justin out and left it to Libby. Justin has just managed it for her, I'd forgotten that! But surely, Libby always intended to leave it to Justin. Did she not do so?"

"No, for did they not quarrel so bitterly back in the summer, that Justin never set foot at Westwood again? Not until that last week, when Libby was so ill?"

"Indeed," she replied staring. "Good heavens, no wonder he is so bitter! So, Hal is the one who employs you? That is better news at any rate for us."

"Is it?" he asked doubtfully. "I sometimes don't think that Hal greatly cares for me! He has a way of looking at me, which reminds me of your Aunt Margery!"

"Hal isn't a great one for showing his feelings," she replied laughing. "He likes you well enough."

"I am relieved," replied Ambrose. "Tell me, does he care for Sophie at all? Or is it just infatuation on her part?"

"I would that I knew," she said in a meditative tone. "I'm inclined to think he is unsure of his own feelings. He is certainly keeping her at a great distance, is he not?"

"I feel for him," he said nodding. "Whatever his feelings, he is in a most unenviable position." He glanced to her adding; "Unlike me. Is he likely to be long, do you think?"

"Some time, yes," she agreed. "I can't see that explanation being quick or simple."

"Good." He changed his seat to come and sit beside her on the window seat. "Another's trial is one man's pleasure. At least we can be sure of being undisturbed for a while."

Hal sat waiting, holding his son's hand tightly as his eyelids grew heavier and heavier. In the soft light of the candle the child's beauty was unreal; his skin looking like it was carved from ivory, his dark curls clustered about his head like black grapes, his pink moist lips, now breathing regularly. He kept his eyes rigorously on the child's face, watching the glistening track of a tear, determined not to look up to see Sophia on the other side of him. At Harry's insistence she was cuddled up with him, so that his dark head rested against her encircling arm and his other hand held her thumb loosely. That the child feared to loose his loved ones was plain, and no wonder, sighed Hal, feeling his own eyelids droop.

Hal awoke with a start sometime later, to find the candles guttering and Harry cuddled into Sophie's sleeping embrace. The unearthly beauty of the picture they presented quite took his breath away. Harry's small dark head nestled against Sophia's thick gold curls, which had tumbled free of restrain and spilled across her shoulders. Like Harry she slept with childish abandon, her cheeks rosy from sleep, her plump lips parted over regular breathing, her dark eyelashes fringing her cheeks. He watched the rise and fall of her corseted breasts with a great surge of longing. Her bare shoulder was but an inch or two from the tips of his fingers, and before he knew what he was doing, he had caressed it.

Her eyes flew open immediately, and even through the mists of sleep, she could read enough in his face, to tell her all she had wanted to know. Hal indifferent to her—never. She smiled at him in a conspirital fashion.

"He sleeps," she said with simple satisfaction.

"Yes, and so have we," he hissed. "The hour is late. You'd best go to your bed."

Her smile deepened and she stretched her body carefully with the enjoyment of a cat. "I am remarkably comfortable here," she murmured. "I don't recall sleeping so soundly in months. It must be the comfort of knowing you were watching over us! Like a sentinel knight."

"Much use I'd be keeping guard," he replied severely. "I, too, slept."

"Yes, I know, I watched you at first," she whispered. "You sleep exactly like little Harry. It was strange to see you both together. He is very like you."

"Yes, so everyone says," he agreed. "Come, he sleeps, you should be gone lest he wakes."

She laughed a little. "Go where?" she asked. "This is my chamber; I carried him here last night, when he was so afraid."

"Your chamber!" he cried in horror. "Why did you not say so? I should never have come here! Why is it you sleep here, and not in a guest chamber?"

"I moved here to be closer to the children when their nurse took sick last month," she replied. "It was when Libby, Lady Westwood, was so ill, and all the servants were needed to nurse her. They wouldn't let me near her, lest I poison her I suppose, but I could be and was, of real help with Harry."

"I beg pardon for my family's doubts and slurs upon your character, but given the circumstances, and your reckless behaviour, they can hardly be blamed for it," he replied stiffly.

"I wasn't complaining," she replied, smiling a little. "Merely explaining."

"Yes, well, I thank you again for all the trouble you've taken—" he began.

"It was no trouble," she interrupted. "I love them and enjoy looking after them. I told you, I felt so guilty at all the trouble I'd brought to them, that I felt the least I could do was to give them my time and affections, and in doing so I came to love them."

"I see," he replied gravely. "Then I am doubly grateful, but this is no time to discuss it. I must go, lest I be discovered here."

"None are likely to do so," she soothed. "I am left very much to myself and at least you are not avoiding me."

He glanced to her uncertainly in the half light. "I wasn't aware I was avoiding you," he said, as he eased himself gently from Harry's clinging hand.

"I was," she replied smiling. "I am not a fool, Hal."

"No," he agreed tiptoeing across the room, "No indeed. Goodnight, Sophie."

He paused before opening the door, listening for footsteps, and so thought himself particularly cursed that Jane should hasten toward him.

"Hal, I was looking for you," she said. "I thought perhaps you'd gone to bed. Do you recollect you sent for Ambrose?"

"Yes, I am very sorry," he replied, finding to his annoyance he was blushing. "I sat holding Harry's hand because he was so very upset, and fell asleep also."

"Poor Hal," she said sympathically. "You must be so tired. Shall I tell Ambrose to wait until the morning?"

"No, no indeed I'll gladly talk to him now if I may." He held out his hand to her. "Dear Jane, you bear with me admirably."

She smiled faintly as she took it, for her heart was wrung by the anxiety in his face. "Do not so constantly berate yourself, Hal," she murmured. "Be more gentle with yourself."

He frowned as he followed her down the fine oak staircase wondering at her words. He'd been on the verge of beginning a complicated explanation, but he was aware suddenly that it would be futile. The damage to both his and Sophie's reputation was done. No words could repair it. He recollected with a wry grimace also what Justin had thrown at him earlier. He'd been proved right in part, but Hal still couldn't think that it had been done by design. To his mind Sophie wasn't that sort of female. As he hesitated, he began to feel once again a measure of panic, as he had last summer. It was the effect being with Sophie had on him, he suppressed, that he should feel as if he were in a constant state of bewilderment and confusion. Such emotions were so alien to him, that he responded by being constantly on guard, feeling that he might inadvertently commit an unforgivable folly.

He entered the parlour so deep in his thoughts, that he came to stand at the table with Ambrose, not speaking a word. Jane waited, as still Hal stood looking blankly before him, she finally asked.

"Hal—is aught amiss?"

"Amiss?" he glanced to her and then, realising where he was, cried; "Oh, no—no, I beg pardon Ambrose! My wits have gone a begging."

"You were certainly miles away," he agreed pleasantly. "And weary, I believe. I can easily come back another time, Hal, if you'd sooner seek your bed."

"No—no," he said hastily. "I—I don't sleep well. Just —just give me a moment if you will."

"Have you a problem, Hal?" asked Jane, her heart wrung to see the fretting anxiety in his eyes.

He glanced to her and smiled. "Not one I can discuss

freely." He said wryly. "I have little enough credit with my kin these days."

"Don't be silly, Hal," she replied reaching across to squeeze his arm. "You know I'd be happy to help in anyway I can! Is it Sophie?"

He nodded. "Yes, its Sophie." he agreed.

"Is she a trouble to you?" she asked in surprise. "I thought she was quite well behaved now. In fact she has been, well, since we realised how very ill Libby was."

He nodded. "Yes—no, no in truth I can't say it's anything Sophia's done," he said slowly. "I can see she's trying her best to make amends, and her care of Harry is remarkable. No, it's more—"

"More that you fear for your own feelings?" suggested Ambrose gently.

Hal looked taken aback at this, then he shrugged. "Oh, what's the use, I—I love her," he said, and dark colour filled his cheeks as Ambrose looked amazed.

"Have you only just discovered that, Hal?" Jane asked laughing a little.

"No," he said humbly. "But I've been suffering the torments of hell trying to deny it! I know it's obscene with Libby so lately dead, and I did love her, too, but it was nothing like this. I feel I shall go mad if I don't tell someone."

"Wouldn't it be better to tell Sophie?" suggested Ambrose suddenly relaxing, for in his confusion Hal was so much more human and approachable.

"No, on no account," Hal replied, coming to sit with him at the gate-legged table. "Don't you see? That wouldn't be enough for Sophie. She'd be thinking of marriage. I need time and peace to think everything through. I just thought if I told you, you'd be able to help me. To stop me from falling further into this web of deceit. I seem to get more firmly trapped as I try to escape."

"I—we are honoured by your confidence," said Ambrose as Jane smiled, and came to join them. "But do you want to escape? Personally I was glad to hurl myself from a great height into love."

Hal smiled as Jane took the hand Ambrose extended. "Yes, I can see that, and it does my heart good! And yes, half—no, near all of me longs to join you. To throw myself headlong into love, and say the devil take the hindmost. But in my position, with Libby so lately dead, every feeling would revolt."

"True," agreed Jane. "It would be a great scandal and source of gossip. You are right, Hal, you need time, and we'll do our best to help you."

"Will you?" he asked quickly. "I know I should be strong enough to manage on my own, but I would so like some help."

"We would be delighted to help you in anyway we can," Ambrose assured him.

Hal nodded his thanks and sat thinking a moment, before saying, "In reviewing matters since my return from Adamsholme, I've decided, Ambrose, there is no reason you cannot be a junior partner in the business at Adamsholme. I know I own the business, and although Libby was always content to let Justin run it, I don't see why he should have it all his own way in the future. Thus, Ambrose, with your position improved, you can afford to keep a wife in a fit fashion."

"Hal, what can we say?" cried Jane, as Ambrose looked astounded. "Oh, Hal, you are so good, so kind."

"No more of that!" Hal replied quickly as Ambrose hastily added his thanks joyfully.

"It is no more than you deserve. You are a good sister and I love you dearly. I believe Libby owned several properties in Adamsholme," continued Hal. "I can't say that I know of any that are vacant, and in truth, I would prefer your company here. I feel as if the house is so empty as it is. So, I'd like you both to make your home here. Indeed, is not the west wing standing almost un-used, since its restoration? You must take that, and do with it as you wish, so you have your own household and begin married life in a proper fashion."

"Oh, Hal! How kind you are," she cried coming im-pulsively to kiss him. "Do you truly mean it?"

"Indeed I do, as long as Ambrose doesn't mind hav-ing to travel to Adamsholme as often as he will."

"No, not at all," Ambrose replied. "Although Bess will feel more cut off, I imagine, if I desert her, at this point."

"Yes, I am concerned about Bess," agreed Hal, "but with Justin so unreasonable at the moment, I don't know what to do."

"I'm sure as his grief abates a little, he'll become more like his old self," soothed Jane. "However, Hal, here is an-other problem. Aunt Margery wrote this morning from Hetta and Will's home, where she is spending a few days, to say she and Aunt Kate will be with us on Wednesday."

"Aunt Margery?" Hal replied, his voice flat, for this was an encounter he'd been dreading since landing at Dover. "Does she say if she'll be making a long stay with us?"

Jane smiled in a troubled way. "That I cannot say.

You'll know, of course, she decided at one point she could no longer reside in a house which held Sophie? She departed to assist poor Tom Kingscott with all his troubles. But now, reading between the lines, she is torn. Libby's illness and death were a great shock to both aunts, Hal."

"Not only to our aunts, surely." he protested, looking unutterably weary.

"No, indeed," she agreed swiftly, "but they are older, less resilient perhaps? Aunt Margery feels you need her more than Tom Kingscott, you see, but having declared she'll not return whilst Sophie is part of your household?"

"She'll expect me to send Sophie away," he concluded dully.

"No, I don't think she expects that. After all, it is your duty as Sophie's guardian. And then there is the rumour that Tom Kingscott has plans to remarry himself."

"Yes, Mary told me that," replied Hal thoughtfully. "I wish him joy of the project. Surely he is old enough to know his own mind."

"With his son dying like that last year, and the baby, his heir, not overly strong, it does make sense," said Jane. "Not to mention, his daughter-in-law, young

Tom's widow, planning to remarry a neighbour herself." Jane shrugged. "Aunt Margery says Tom plainly feels the need to secure another heir."

Hal blinked at this amazing history of Aunt Margery's step-son. "What does Aunt Margery say of all this?" he asked.

"I have no doubt she'll tell you in great detail when she arrives," replied Jane ruefully. "My guess is she is uncertain as to her best course. On the one hand she is not convinced Tom can be trusted to bring his marriage to a satisfactory conclusion without her help. Nor is she certain in her mind Alice, young Tom's widow will part with the baby, little Tom, as she has promised to do on her re-marriage. On the other hand, you are a Westwood, as she sees it, in great trouble and plainly need her assistance, if you would but ask for it."

Hal groaned. "I can see it all too clearly! What does Aunt Kate say?"

"Not a vast deal," replied Jane smiling. "Mostly that you are a good boy and will do your duty as you always do."

"I see between them I shall be sent back to the nursery with little Harry." he said with a grimace. "Did I say I hated the house so empty and quiet? This unaccustomed peace is about to be shattered."

"Aunt Margery is always an antidote to melancholy, I find." said Jane. "Sooner or later one is forced to laugh at her."

Chapter Seven

The arrival of his aunts was at the back of Hal's mind the next morning when he and Ambrose sat discussing plans, so that the noise of a carriage on the driveway didn't take his attention, but the wail of a baby did.

"That can't be Aunt Margery or Aunt Kate," he remarked, looking surprised.

"No." Ambrose, who was sitting at a table in the window, glanced out. "It's the coach from the Adam and Eve," he said, referring to the inn at Adamsholme.

"Is it?" Hal got to his feet and walked to stand beside him. "Has Justin come seeking you, do you think?" Then, as he caught a glimpse of a maidservant: "Isn't that my sister's nursemaid?"

"Aye, 'tis so," Ambrose agreed. "It's Betty! What does she here?"

Hal crossed swiftly to the door. "I imagine she

accompanied her mistress," he said, his voice echoing his disquiet, as he hurried into the hall. There, he found Jane helping her tearful sister Bess into the parlour, and instructing Harry's nursemaid to go to the assistance of Betty.

"Take Philip and the baby up to the nursery, if you will, Alys," she said. "I'm sure Mistress Sophie will be pleased to help! Come Bess, be calm, please be calm, you'll only distress your boys!"

"What's amiss?" demanded Hal tersely.

"Oh Hal!" Jane turned to him with relief, and Bess, with a sob, ran into his arms. She leant her head on his shoulder, as he stroked her long, dishevelled hair soothingly. "I don't know, something is plainly wrong, but it's not little Philip, or the baby."

"'Tis the Master!" said Betty, who was handing the baby over to Alys. "Been taken up as a murderer, he has."

"Justin?" cried Hal incredulously, as Bess gave a moan of despair. "Justin, taken up for murder!"

"Aye," said the girl with relish. "This morning, he and the missus were ashouting at each other, so's they could be heard all over the house. 'Twere on account of him not coming in until dawn. Then, Mistress Bess, she says to me, 'pack up all my and the boy's things, we're going to Westwood, for remain here I will not'. Then, just as the coach from the Adam and Eve comes, so too does the sheriff's man to take Mr Justin, for the murder of that there Mistress Helen Sitwell! Aye! Her that's no better than she ought to be!"

"Yes, right, thank you, er, Betty!" said Hal, as Ambrose supplied the name. "You go along with Alys and see the children disposed of comfortably. I'll send for you presently. Come Bess," he helped her from her cloak and escorted her into the parlour, where Jane pressed a glass of wine into her hand. "Yes, yes, I know you don't like it, but it might help you to stop weeping."

"Oh, Hal," Bess gasped, after she'd sipped a mouthful of the wine and coughed and choked over it. "Pray, don't make me drink any more."

"One more sip," he commanded, "and keep it there in case you start to weep again. Now come, this is serious, I need a round tale with no fuss. Tell me exactly what has happened."

"Justin didn't come in last night," she said, her voice just above a whisper. "He left word with Betty he'd be working late and taking supper with one of his clients." She cast her brother and sister a tearstained look. "Ambrose will tell you, Justin takes supper at least twice a week with Mistress Sitwell, thought whether 'tis a legal consultation, I take leave to doubt!"

"I met her yesterday afternoon," said Hal. "She was certainly consulting him legally then, and I heard her issue the supper invitation, indeed, she extended it to me, it wasn't an invitation to be lightly denied."

"Yet, you did," she retorted, irked that he sought to justify her husband's neglect.

"I do not need her business," he replied coolly. "So continue—Justin didn't return home last night. You know this? You waited up for him?"

"No!" she said, taken aback. "At midnight I grew weary of waiting, I went to bed, but I slept ill, he wasn't there at one of the clock, nor two…"

"And after that, you slept?" asked Hal swiftly.

"Yes, I slept until dawn, when I heard him coming in. I was angry, and demanded to know where he'd been, and he replied that it was no concern of mine." Her voice trembled over this, and she had recourse to the glass of wine, sipping it distastefully as she mopped at her overflowing eyes. Jane, who sat beside her on the settle, patted her back in a soothing manner. "I knew where he'd been, of course, with that woman!" Bess declared, her gentle face alight with a rare fury. "So I told him I'd tolerate no more of it! He, he replied that I'd do as I was bid, that I was his wife, and that he'd stood enough Westwood tantrums for to last him a life-time!"

Hal raised his brows at this, but nodded for her to continue.

"I, I told him that if he thought he'd seen you in a temper, he'd seen nothing of it yet! That I'd not stand idly by and tolerate his churlish behaviour! Unless he promised to behave in a manner befitting my husband and a gentleman, I must decline to remain under the same roof! Neither would I allow any children to re-main in so contaminated an atmosphere!"

Hal grinned briefly. "Yes, you did lose your temper, sweetheart, didn't you," he agreed, as Ambrose looked dismayed and Jane chuckled. "You sounded exactly like our father."

"He seemed to be at my elbow supplying the words, Hal," she said. "Normally, I am tongue-tied and can-not think what to say, and Justin is so very calm and reasoned in his arguments, but today, such a fury pos-sessed me, that I hardly knew what I said. I only knew I wasn't going to listen to his lies for a moment longer!

So I sent Andrew for the coach and told Betty to pack my bags!"

"And Justin stood by and allowed this?" asked Hal, bemused.

"No, he began quoting law at me, but I told him I cared nothing for his words. He could do his worst, but if he laid a finger on me, or my children to stop us, I'd scream and scream until I fetched all the neighbours. Then I'd tell them how so upright and respectable a citizen conducted himself."

Hal came to sit by his sister, a wry smile hovering on his lips. "Masterly, my dear. Of course, it wouldn't hold water in a court of law, but what cared you for that?"

"Nothing, for I have right on my side," she replied swiftly. "A court of law can find what it may, but it can't condemn me or my children to live with a whoremonger."

"If he is your husband, I believe it can," murmured Hal gently. "Otherwise, half the wives in the land would be estranged from their spouses."

"I care nothing for your precious law!" she snapped, rounding on him. "I am speaking of morals here, Hal!"

"Which has little to do with the law," he agreed. "So, was Justin silenced?"

"No, he flew into a greater fury still, and declared I'd take his children over his dead body! That I could do my worst, and accuse him as I wished, but as I had no proof to support my wild accusations, he was fully within his rights to prevent my and the children leaving, employing force if necessary."

"Dear heavens," Hal made a face. "This sounds as if it's going to be a mess!"

"He threatened to lock me up," she declared, her wan looks fleeing in the warmth of remembered indignation. "That, if I didn't cease this tumult, he'd see my children were kept from me! Into all this fuss, Sergeant Parry walked with a warrant for Justin's arrest."

"A warrant for his arrest!" repeated Hal, as her hot tears spilled over again. "It doesn't bear thinking on. I mean, a warrant? Isaac Hughes must feel very sure of himself to have issued a warrant, and not to have come himself to find out."

Bess blinked back her tears. "It seems that trollop Helen Sitwell was found this morning by her wench, and she and the manservant sent for Sheriff Hughes, claiming that Justin left just before dawn." Her mouth went awry as she struggled with tears. "They say he has been a constant visitor these past six weeks, often spending the night there as her lover!"

Jane hugged her compassionately as her voice became suspended in tears.

"Yes, yes, it probably does look bad," agreed Hal. "But this is Justin we are talking of! Laying aside your quarrel, Bess, and that he may have made this woman his mistress, none of which matters desperately, this is Justin! He cannot have killed her."

Bess nodded through her tears. "I know," she whispered. "But Prescott, her manservant, says he heard them quarrelling violently last night, and that he'd beaten her before!" This last was a wail of despair.

"Justin? I do not believe it!" snapped Hal in exasperation.

"He has changed, Hal," said Ambrose in an aside, as Jane tried to sooth her sister and coax her to sip more wine.

"No man changes that much," declared Hal. "Bess, Bess! No, be calm, I beg you. It is essential that you are calm. Have no doubt we'll all assist you to the utmost of our ability, but you must be calm."

"Excuse me, Sir Henry," Sophie appeared in the doorway, unsure of how welcome she'd be. "I, I thought perhaps Mistress Danvers might care for a tisane to calm her." She indicated the posset dish she held. "'Tis most efficacious, I do believe, your wife taught me the recipe."

Bess, who had looked up in dismay at the sound of Sophie's voice, almost began to shake her head, but Jane got up at once and came to take it. "Oh, what a good idea, Sophie, and how kind of you to take the trouble. Have the boys settled in?"

"They seem to be. Philip is happily trying to play with Harry and his soldiers, and Alys and Betty are nursing the babies. I felt rather in the way of their chatter, so I went to brew the tisane." She glanced uncertainly to where Bess was sipping it.

"Well, either come in, or go back to the children, Sophie," said Hal sharply. "Don't stand hovering in the doorway.

Sophie blushed at his tone. "Will I be in the way here? Perhaps Mistress Danvers would rather the matter kept private between family."

"With her husband arrested for murder, she can hardly hope to keep anything private," said Hal. "Bess, do you object to Sophie joining us?"

Bess glanced up to meet his eyes, her answer plain, for she and Libby had been the closest of friends, but she forced her lips into a patently reluctant negative.

"There," said Hal ironically. "You have Bess's permission to enter my parlour and sit and listen."

"Thank you," Sophie took a seat by the window. "But in truth, I'd rather your sister said she hated and despised me to my face."

"I don't hate and despise you!" cried Bess, turning around to face her. "But you must remember, Libby was my dearest friend, I loved her like a sister! I cannot forget that, nor stop resenting you."

The colour flared in Sophie's cheeks, but she said steadily: "Thank you for your honesty. I, too, came to love Libby, she was so good and kind to me. I hope you'll believe me when I say how sorry I am to have added to her unhappiness, and how much I regret my folly."

"Yes, this is all very well," interrupted Hal. "But we are concerned with Justin, Bess! You just said Mistress Sitwell's man accused him of quarrelling with her violently, and of previously beating her, now this doesn't ring true."

"He had threatened to beat me several times these past months," remarked Sophie. "He said it would give him the utmost pleasure."

Hal frowned and looked annoyed. "He has a personal

grudge against you, Sophie, he held you to blame for all our present problems. The point is, he didn't beat you, did he?"

"No, Libby refused to allow him," she agreed. "But he looked quite murderous when he said it."

"I don't think we'll let Hughes speak to Sophie," remarked Ambrose, with a look of dismay.

"Quite," said Hal. "Bess, never mind what Sophie says. That's a different matter entirely," he commanded, as Bess looked appalled. "This is much more to the point, this man Prescott and her wench, they say Justin was Mistress Sitwell's lover. So, tell me, has Justin ever beaten or attacked you violently?"

"Justin?" Bess replied blankly. "Justin? Violent? No! You know him, Hal, yes he can get angry, furiously angry, but then can't we all? Justin might flay you alive with his tongue, but use physical force? No, never!"

"Well, yes," agreed Sophie. "He certainly liked to use his tongue to make one feel small and foolish. But he also frightened me on several occasions. He shook me once and left bruises on my arm."

"I'm surprised he didn't throttle you, Sophie," said Jane. "The way you two used to quarrel when you first came to Westwood." Then, realising what she'd said, she, too, looked appalled. "I didn't mean to say that. It's just that Justin has plainly been very irked by his various problems lately, that 'tis no wonder his temper's short."

"That is two of them Hughes mustn't talk to," said Ambrose, looking concerned.

"How did Mistress Sitwell die?" asked Hal. "Did Parry say?"

"He said she'd been smothered in her bed," said Bess, who was very pale. "That's why they assumed Justin was the murderer, I suppose."

"But is there any proof?" asked Ambrose. "Or is it just the word of two servants against Justin?"

"I don't know," Bess replied. "But it seems that the man, Prescott, claims that whore left everything to Justin."

"Justin inherits?" said Hal, a surprised inflexion in his voice. "Why?"

"She had no other relations," said Ambrose reluctantly.

"You know this?" Hal turned to him, not bothering to conceal his dismay.

"That's what they were discussing yesterday," he said. "I'd prepared the will as she wished. Justin presumably went over it with her and I amended it, so that he could take it with him to supper to be signed."

"Perhaps there wasn't time," suggested Hal hopefully. "Perhaps that's what they quarrelled over."

"That's what the manservant Prescott said," cried Bess. "That she changed her mind, and Justin forced her to sign it, and then murdered her."

Hal got decisively to his feet. "'Tis plain we must find out more. Ambrose, we'll go to Adamsholme, and talk to Isaac Hughes and Justin himself!"

"They've taken him to Maucester, Hal," said Bess dismally. "To the castle prison."

Hal stared. "I don't understand this," he exclaimed. "Since we helped him solve Johanna Danvers' murder, Hughes has been much more helpful. He seems remarkably hot at hand in this affair."

"It is almost as if someone wanted Justin to be found guilty," agreed Ambrose.

Hal frowned. "Who has he upset lately, do you know?"

"More, who hasn't he upset?" murmured Ambrose.

Hal nodded his understanding. "Time to make a move then. Jane, have a care of your sister. Naturally, you'll remain here, Bess, until everything is resolved. Now, do not trouble yourselves, Ambrose and I will do everything that's necessary!" ⚜

Chapter Eight

"You are not immured in the darkest dungeon, then," remarked Hal, as the turnkey slammed the door, leaving them in the small chamber above the gatehouse.

"No. This is the chamber Hughes held your father in, as I remember it," replied Justin. "It has almost a family atmosphere."

"Speaking of family, yours is at Westwood, safe and well," Hal said, removing his hat.

"Yes, your sister announced her intention of leaving me shortly before Hughes's man arrived to arrest me," Justin snapped, as Ambrose put some books and papers on the table.

"One can appreciate her reasons," said Hal temperately.

"Can one?" Justin flared. "It seems to me you Westwoods have it all your own way. You betray your wife, my sister, with our ward, and then you proceed to desert her. Your sister decides I've taken a mistress, and she deserts me!"

"And is my sister correct? Was Helen Sitwell your mistress?" asked Hal sharply.

"Is Sophie Redcroft yours?" he retorted, equally sharply.

"I am not imprisoned and accused of murder," sighed Hal.

"No, but you should be. You killed my sister!"

Hal walked to the door. "If you come to your senses before they hang you and require help, send for me," he said over his shoulder.

"Hal!" cried Ambrose. "You can't abandon him."

"Yes, he can," snarled Justin. "Take note, it's the Westwood way! They promise you the earth, and then go back on their word."

"You lie!" cried Hal wrathfully. "No Westwood ever went back on their word!"

"No?" sneered Justin. "Did you not promise to love and cherish Libby, forsaking all others, keeping only unto her, so long as you both shall live?"

"Indeed I did," he agreed. "'Tis the words of the marriage service, you were there at mine. I don't know what vows you took, for there were none present at that clandestine ceremony."

"Look, aren't we wandering from the point?" said Ambrose, hoping to establish peace.

"I think not," said Hal at his most haughty. "Surely, the point is that Justin was with Helen Sitwell that night."

"No, I was not," Justin replied sharply. "I left her house at about half-past one in the morning."

"Bess says you came in at dawn, about eight in the morning! What were you doing in the meantime?"

Justin shrugged his shoulders. "Walking."

"Walking! For six hours you were walking?" cried Hal. "On a November night, you chose to take a six hour walk rather than go home to your bed?"

"Yes," said Justin, turning his face away, revealing a long, vivid scar on his cheek, like a scratch.

"Have you told Isaac Hughes this?" asked Ambrose.

"I have sworn a statement, yes," he agreed.

"And I expect he was hard-put not to laugh in your face?" cried Hal. "Come, Justin, every rogue off the street can come up with a better tale than that one. Walking on a winter's night!"

"It is, however, the truth!" replied Justin coldly.

"Then you'll hang," said Hal, with simple conviction.

"Where were you walking to?" asked Ambrose. "One doesn't wander aimlessly in the foul sort of weather it was last night. Was it foggy, perhaps, in Adamsholme, did you lose your way?"

"No, it was a remarkably calm, clear night, with a sharp frost," said Justin.

"So, what was your destination?" asked Hal.

"I decline to say," he replied arrogantly.

"Then you'll hang," repeated Hal.

"For the love of Christ! If you can't think of anything better to say then that, go now!" cried Justin.

"Where were you going that you couldn't summon a coach?" asked Ambrose patiently. "To have walked that far, for in that temperature you couldn't have lingered, it was too cold, you must have gone some distance." Then, as still Justin said nothing, he added: "One could probably walk from Adamsholme to Westwood and back in that sort of time."

"Why on earth would you walk to Westwood at that time of night?" said Hal blankly. "And had you, why return? Why not seek shelter? Why, indeed, come if—"

"Did you go to the church?" asked Ambrose intently,

as Justin clamped his lips together over a retort. "Did you walk to Libby's grave and back?" he added, suddenly inspired.

"I've told you, I am not required to say. I walked," replied Justin stubbornly. "I am innocent of this charge. It is for Hughes to find me guilty."

"Oh, I see!" said Hal, at his most scathing. "This is a test of Hughes's abilities, is it? Oh excellent, so of course, we'll know he's an incompetent bungler when they hang you!"

"Will you stop saying that!" cried Justin angrily.

"Will you wake up to what is happening?" snapped Hal.

"Look!" said Ambrose. "Will you two stop fighting each other! For Heaven's sake, we've enough on our hands proving your innocence, Justin, without having you and Hal squabbling all day long! Can't we just accept you hate each other, and try to behave in more adult manner?"

"I don't hate him," snapped Justin. "Libby and I loved him. He was like a brother to me and he betrayed us both."

"Then you didn't love like a brother," returned Hal quietly, his face pale. "A brother forgives. He understands his brother can be a fool, and forgives. You and Libby thought me a god and you can't forgive my feet of clay."

"Feet of clay!" cried Justin. "You are all clay. There's not one bit of fine metal in you."

"I am what I have always been," Hal said, and he sounded weary. "A man, for better for worse, a man with faults. Libby chose to make me more, and I was vain enough to be flattered by her estimation. If you took her values of me, it is not for me to apologise."

"Damn you, I took my own values of you!" cried Justin. "You were everything I ever wanted to be! Handsome, clever, wealthy, a gentleman, an honourable and respected citizen. Naturally, you were our ideal! Have you any idea of what it's like to not be born a gentleman? To have to work hard to achieve that status, to have it given grudgingly with sneers behind one's back?"

"Or even to lose it?" asked Ambrose suddenly.

"Yes," said Hal honestly. "Never forget, I spent my formative years in France, going from place to place with my father. Often, we were next best things to rogues, certainly we looked what we were—exiles, soldiers of fortune! Don't ever think I can't remember those days, that I've forgotten how lucky I was to take my uncle's eye, to marry Libby and her dowry, and then inherit Westwood! Do you truly imagine I wanted to fall in love with Sophie Redcroft? Did I not do my best to avoid her? Didn't I beg you to leave Chawcester on more than one occasion?"

"Yes," admitted Justin reluctantly.

"Do you imagine I wanted to run away to France? By God, I just said I spent my youth in exile! Don't you think it was a last resort for me to leave my home and family! Don't you think I was praying I'd come back to find her betrothed to a young Adonis! And all I have found is that you conspired to make her so miserable, she's more in love with me than ever!"

"And you?" cried Justin sharply. "Are you more in love with her than ever?"

Hal turned away. "I couldn't understand it, Justin. When you defied your father and married Bess, losing everything," he said quietly. "You see, I'd never been in love. I loved Libby, she was such a dear, sweet and gentle soul, who couldn't? But I was never in love with her—you know the difference. I tried every way to escape it, but the bonds bit deeper with each struggle."

"Libby loved you, heart and soul," cried Justin bitterly.

"I know, and I am grateful for it, and sorry, so very

sorry it wasn't like that for me. I tried to make it appear so, and God willing, if circumstances had been different, she would never have known. But they weren't, and she did, and I'll never forgive myself for it."

"She excused you to the last, do you know that?" cried Justin, his face ravaged with grief . "With her very last breath she said, 'tell Hal I understand and that I love him'."

"No, I didn't know, but I can believe it," Hal whispered. "I would to God I'd been a better man for her."

"I would to God you had, too," snapped Justin, tears crowding his eyes. "Oh God, I would you had, too."

Hal came swiftly, and enfolded him in his arms. "I am sorry, Justin, I am so sorry," he said, hugging him.

Ambrose stood uncomfortably by, as Justin finally wept openly for his sister. He didn't know what to do, but he had a feeling this was for the best. Not one tear had Justin shed, his anger at his sister's death had known no bonds, but his grief had been kept tightly contained. Ambrose slid into the shadows, as the others sat talking quietly, Hal with his arm still about his brother-in-law, and taking up a pen, he began to write quickly.

After some ten minutes Hal glanced round, his face was still pale, but some of the fretting anxiety had gone.

"What are you at in the corner there, Ambrose?" he asked.

"Writing down what we must do," Ambrose replied. "Making lists of people we must seek out and talk to. Justin, on your walk last night, you met none?"

"No," he replied with a sigh. "A dog barked at me at Oakford-by-the-Vale at the big farm there, but I saw none on my way."

"There may have been shepherds on the hill," said Hal. "Harry Riggs at Fordview Farm runs a goodly few sheep on the hill."

"'Tis too early for lambing," said Justin.

"But not for foxes," returned Hal. "They get desperate in winter and will often attack the weaker ewes, 'tis worth trying."

"I walked along the Vale," said Justin. "I wouldn't be visible from the hill."

"These old shepherds have remarkable eyesight and hearing," soothed Hal. "If anything moved in the Vale, they'll know it, for their dogs would have barked, too."

"Now I think of it, another dog did bark in the distance," said Justin dully. "I remember thinking if I wasn't careful, it would wake up the farmer, who'd probably think I was after his hens and take a pot shot at me."

"Why were you stumbling about in the dark, Justin?" asked Hal gently.

Justin sighed and leaned back on his chair in a weary manner. "Helen was becoming too demanding," he said, his voice coming very quietly. "I don't truly know how I got so involved with her, save that nothing has gone right since you went off in June, Hal. I quarrelled with Libby over that wretched girl Sophie, and then with Bess over my quarrel with Libby. It seemed every way I turned, everyone was against me and making excuses for your behaviour. I even had Guy saying he thought you'd taken a courageous step in going to France! Guy, who couldn't see a wider issue if it smacked him in the eye!" he smiled faintly as Ambrose chuckled. "Helen Sitwell was sympathetic, and I needed sympathy from someone. It was only when I was at outs with them that I realised how much my life revolved around the Westwood family, and, by Heaven, I was sick of them! So I spent more and more of my free time with Helen."

"What of Bess in all this?" asked Hal, guessing how his gentle sister must have suffered.

"I don't know, we weren't on such terms as to, to enable me to know her feelings," he replied bitterly.

"Bess, your wife, the woman you loved so much you

threw your fortune away for?" asked Hal incredulously.

"Yes," he snapped. "And that was part of it. After all that sacrifice on my part, she hadn't the loyalty to stay true to me. She sided with the Westwoods."

"Oh, my poor darling," said Hal. "How she must have been torn asunder by this feud."

"She is my wife. She should identify with my interests, not you and your damned family," cried Justin anger coming back into his voice.

"If I know Bess," replied Hal, "she identified, as Libby would have done, with right. Not you, nor I, but right."

Justin looked away. "Yes, well, you would say that," he said, and the resentment was there in his voice again. "Anyway, you'd treated my sister badly, I didn't see why I should have to be so careful of yours."

Hal's eyes darkened. "You punished me through Bess," he said flatly. "That's despicable."

Justin didn't meet his eyes. "Your conduct can hardly be called exemplary," he snapped in reply.

"I hardly think—"

"I know we don't have a great deal more time," interrupted Ambrose. "We need more information, not you two shouting recriminations at each other. You've both behaved extremely badly, but that is in the past. Please, we need to discuss the future."

Both stared indignantly at the other man, then Hal nodded. "Yes, Ambrose, you are right. Come Justin, a straightforward tale, with no excuses or explanations. They can come later, when we've got you out of here."

Justin shrugged. "As I said, I turned to Helen, her company soothed me, but there was a price to pay. It seemed she wanted more than a congenial companion. I probably wasn't a very good companion, now I think of it, forever ranting about one or the other of you. She wanted a man in her bed." He shrugged again. "I, I complied. Truth to tell, I didn't care much. My life was in such ruins. Everything went well enough, until Bess had the baby." He paused to take a breath. "I found out last night she, she was hoping Bess would die. So many women do in childbirth, she said!" His tone expressed his utter horror. "It, it was like the scales falling from my eyes! There was my sweet and gentle Bess, still ill from bearing my child and this—this creature—was calculating on her life expectancy! Hinting—hinting such awful things!" He broke off to cover his eyes for a few seconds. "I was horrified," he said. "And in my horror, I couldn't hide my contempt. She didn't take it well. She flew at me, giving me this."

He turned his head and indicated the livid scratch which ran down his cheek. He sighed heavily. "She reminded me she'd named me as her heir in her will, which she'd signed earlier, and demanded to know if I thought I was getting it for nothing. I replied, as I had done a dozen times before—as you can testify Ambrose—that I cared nothing for it. She was but a few years my senior. It was unlikely I'd inherit, I'd only consented because she was desperate to bind me to her in some way. She kept saying I could have it all now if only Bess were disposed of and I married her. It was like a nightmare in which, whatever way one turns, the same wall confronts one." He shuddered. "In the end, she flew at me again, scratching, kicking, biting like a wild animal. I hit her, just once, across her face, to calm her. She fell back to the bed, I hurriedly dressed and left."

"Did she move again?" demanded Ambrose. "Did you hit her hard enough to knock her unconscious?"

"No!" he replied. "No, she was shouting foul abuse at me as I beat a hasty retreat."

"Did she fall on her back or face?" asked Hal.

"On her side," said Justin, frowning as he recollected. "I hit her with my right hand across her left cheek, and she fell sideways across the bed."

"Did she bang her head, or twist her neck in any way as she fell?" continued Hal.

"Not to my knowledge," he said. "But I was throwing on my clothes and trying to keep control of my temper as she abused me like a tinker."

"And that was the only time you hit her?" asked Ambrose.

"Yes," he said clearly. "But she came after me, throwing her arms about my neck, begging me to remain. Then, as I refused and requested her sharply to release me, her hands went to my neck, and she tried to choke me." He moved his neckcloth to show some red marks on his throat.

"I put my hands up so," he held his hands aloft, "and forced her wrists apart, flinging her from me."

"Did she fall?" asked Ambrose quickly.

He hesitated. "I don't clearly remember. I hurried from the room and down the stairs, straight out of the front door, as quickly as I could. But, I have the feeling she—she may have tripped coming after me. In my mind's eye, I seem to see her stumbling on the hem of her nightgown, but I was too intent on getting away from her before she killed me, or I..."

"Murdered her?" supplied Hal, as he broke off in horror. The silence lengthened. "Did you?" he asked.

"No," Justin replied simply. "The temptation was there, especially when she spoke of disposing of my dear Bess! But no, I just wanted to get away from her."

"And from there you went, where?"

"I stumbled back home," he said. "And then I realised I could not face Bess. I felt such shame, such embarrassment, that I couldn't go in the house to her. I turned away and began to walk. My neck was sore and my cheek was burning, I needed cool air to soothe them. I even walked to the bridge, and looked at the river, wondering if that might not be the answer. For now, I had none to turn to. Bess was estranged from me, Libby dead, I hated you and all Westwoods. I had no friends. I stood there a long time, reasoning that it probably solved all problems. I'd be out of my misery, you could be rid of both Danvers and marry your Sophie, and Bess would be better off without me."

"What stopped you?" asked Ambrose curiously.

"I couldn't convince myself Bess would truly be better off without me," he replied honestly. "Even if she never forgave me, never even spoke to me again, I could be there. I could make sure she and the babies wanted for nothing. That she had no worries to upset her, and no problems to beset her. I knew I'd sinned so greatly I no longer deserved her, but I could still take care of her.

So I walked on and on, out of town, and then I realised my steps were taking me towards Westwood, and I thought, why not? I'll go and talk to Libby, I'd not visited her grave since the funeral. So I walked to the churchyard and sat on the tombstone next to Libby's grave—your uncle Henry's, I think—until I became too damn cold to think anymore. I kept telling myself I'd walk up to the house and awaken someone, but in the end, my courage gave out. Chilled to the bone, I set out back to Adamsholme, thinking of a hot bath and breakfast. I arrived to find Bess in a fury and calling for a coach to leave me, and before I could do anything about it, Hughes's man Parry arrived to arrest me!"

"Yes, Bess told us that part," said Hal thoughtfully.

"Is, is she still as angry?" asked Justin, as they fell silent.

"Bess? Yes," replied Hal bluntly as Ambrose made soothing noises. "I've never seen Bess that furious, not since my father went back on his promise to allow you to marry."

Justin sank his head into his hands, pulling relentlessly at his fine hair. "Then I have ruined everything, and it matters not if they hang me."

"It matters to Bess—aye, and to your children too," said Hal sharply. "The very last thing they need is a convicted felon for a father."

Justin's shoulders shook, and for one dreadful moment, Ambrose thought he was weeping again. Then, Justin looked up to reveal a face lined with anxiety, eyes red-rimmed with sleeplessness, but lips trembling with wry laughter.

"Oh, how true, Hal, and what an embarrassment to Sir Henry Westwood, too," he mocked.

"Not only an embarrassment, a damned shame," Hal said, getting to his feet. "To lose so fine a lawyer and so beloved a brother for the want of a little effort."

"It is so hopeless," said Justin, although he still smiled. "What shall you do?"

"Take your advice," he replied. "For if you didn't kill her, then somebody else did. So if we can't prove you innocent, we must find the guilty one! Come Ambrose, bring your papers, we are off to find out what proof Sheriff Hughes has, and how sure he is of his facts!"

⚜

Chapter Nine

Bess sat in the upstairs chamber given over to the little ones, nursing her baby and watching Sophie cuddle Harry and his cousin as she told them a story. Bess's tears were finally stilled, she noticed with a detached air, but now she wept endlessly inside.

She met Sophie's eyes for a few seconds as her son Philip, suddenly sagged against her, his eyes closing. Sophie smiled and held him closer, and Bess found herself returning the smile. She remembered the words Libby had said back in the autumn, before her illness had truly taken hold. Yes, there was no denying Sophie was a sweet girl, and truly did love children. She could now understand Libby's mixed feelings, how she'd laughed in that wry manner she had and said that she'd love the girl even more, if she hadn't hated her so much. Bess found she was drawn to Sophie more and more, but her love of Libby, and her resentment for the pain she'd caused still held her back. She deliberately shifted the focus of her thoughts to her husband, wondering if Hal had seen him yet, and if he had, what had been achieved. She sighed unhappily as she hugged her baby closer, and wondered how everything could have gone so wrong. She acknowledged she'd been at fault, but should she have denied the truth, and told Justin he was right when she didn't agree? A good wife would have done so, she supposed, but his quarrel with Hal had been bad enough. To compound it by quarrelling with Libby, had seemed to her to be the height of folly, and she'd told him so.

She saw now where her error lay. Having told Justin she didn't agree with him, she should have added that, as his wife, she still supported him, or so Hal said. To her, it didn't make sense, indeed it made her head spin to even think of it, but Hal was clever and so was Justin, so presumably they both understood. She had to confess, she didn't understand that it was quite within her rights to disagree privately with her husband, but totally wrong to say so publicly. To her mind, if that was the case, she might as well keep silent. But, Hal said that was the way to a harmonious marriage, and how Libby had always comported herself. A fact born out by her behaviour back in the summer and autumn. For, although it was plain she hadn't approved of Hal's behaviour in going off to France without telling her and leaving Sophie in her care, never once could she be brought to level one word of criticism at him. Indeed, she had defended him stoutly against all Justin's vilification, and kept her own counsel entirely.

"A coach," said Sophie, with a sigh, as the crunch of gravel and horses' hooves came to their ears. "Aunt Kate and Aunt Margery? I am dreading their return."

"You need not," said Bess, with an equal sigh. "Aunt Kate is kindness itself, and Hal will protect you from Aunt Margery now. Indeed, with this latest scandal, she'll probably forget all about you."

Sophie laid the sleeping little boy in a bed and tried to calm Harry, already at the window, exclaiming in his excitement. "Harry, do come away. Oh! It's not the aunts—it's a stranger—a woman and a baby—and good heavens! Surely that is Phillipe Douay!"

"The French physician who went to France with Hal?" asked Bess, putting her baby into the cradle and coming to stand beside her. "Is it? I don't know, I've never met him."

"No more has Jane," said Sophie. "Should I go down and help her?"

"Yes, yes, do, dear," said Bess absently. "And thank you for soothing the baby to sleep. No, Harry, stay here, let Sophie go on her own, if you please."

Sophie hurried away, pausing at the head of the stairs to marvel again at Phillipe Douay's command of English, and smiled to herself at Jane's flustered protest.

"I am indeed desolated that Sir Henry is from home," the Frenchman was saying, with but the faintest trace of an accent, his hands busily flying about. He was a small, dark, mercurial man with a moustache that seemed to vibrate with suppressed energy. "But I assure you, he is expecting me. I am Phillipe Douay, a friend of his, and we have lately been travelling in France together."

"Indeed sir, I have heard my brother often speak of— Oh Sophie! Thank Heaven you are come."

"Doctor Douay," Sophie curtsied as he crossed the hall to join them.

"Mistress Redcroft, I am delighted to behold you," he replied. "You indeed can vouch for me, I do believe."

"Jane, this is Hal's friend, Doctor Phillipe Douay," said Sophie. "Doctor, may I present Mistress Carver, Hal's sister."

"Ma'am, your servant," he said, bowing very low. "And may I, in turn, introduce another of your brother's wards, Mistress Cordelia Sandys."

"My brother's ward?" said Jane in amazement.

"Yes," he said uneasily, as Sophie looked surprised, and the girl curtsied keeping her eyes averted. "This is a matter best explained by Hal, I do believe. Suffice it to say, Mistress Sandys has resided for the past eighteen years with the nuns at Saint-Sauvy. Where, indeed, her father, a Royalist gentleman, deposited her at that time before returning to England to continue fighting for his King. Mistress Sandys has unequivocally decided against taking the veil, and so Hal promised the Prioress he'd help Mistress Sandys trace any relations she may still have living."

"And the baby?" asked Sophie, as Jane looked bewildered.

"A matter, as I say, best explained by Hal," he replied .

A swift dart of jealousy entered Sophie's breast and stayed there as long as it took her to reckon up times and dates. No, Hal had been gone but five months, the child couldn't possibly be his. Her eyes travelled to the girl, noting her dark eyes, brown hair, and sallow skin. Not a beauty, but there was something there.

"Well, you'd best come in and be welcome," said Jane, at a loss. "Unfortunately, I cannot say when Hal may return. He has been called away to, to deal with a matter in—well, various matters," she glanced wildly to the young woman. "Alas Doctor Douay, I have no French at all, pray convey to Mistress Sandys—"

"Mistress Sandys speaks English, Mistress Eustace," he replied quickly. "Although, but a small child when her father left her with the nuns, she was already fluent in her mother tongue and had the good fortune to be in the care of one of her countrywomen for more than sixteen years, until her recent demise. She is, however, a little overcome at the thought of meeting so many strangers, hers being a very secluded life previously."

Jane face cleared. "Oh, thank heavens! Mistress Sandys, you are most welcome to my brother's home. Come, you must be weary, allow me to show you to a chamber where you may rest and refresh yourself. Is your maid not with you?"

"Unfortunately, the lay sister sent with us to tend the baby and Mistress Sandys' needs, abandoned us on sighting 'Le Manche'," sighed Phillipe Douay. "And Mistress Sandys was good enough to take over looking after the child herself."

"How old is the child?" asked Sophie, bestowing a kindly smile on the nervous girl. "Stay Jane, I'll escort Mistress Sandys to a chamber and summon Alys to attend the child."

"Etienne is but a month short of his first birthday," replied Cordelia quietly, tenderly stroking the head of the sleeping child. She followed Sophie up the staircase.

The newcomer has a sweet husky voice, Sophie noted, and but the slightest trace of a French accent, reminiscent of Doctor Douay himself.

"You surely do speak English well," Jane heard Sophie say. "I would my French were as good."

"Ma'am, I am desolated to have inconvenienced you so," said Phillipe Douay, casting her a sharp look, wondering a little at her calm, matter of fact manner of accepting their arrival.

"No matter, sir, may I press some refreshment upon you?" Jane replied politely, although her thoughts were confused.

"A glass of wine, ma'am, would be a great solace," he said slowly, "before being allowed to seek rest in a chamber? Your brother intimated I might be honoured to reside with him here at Westwood for a short duration."

"Here at Westwood?" said Jane, betrayed into surprised at this. "Oh, I—yes, I see. Then pray excuse me for one moment, sir, whilst I call a servant to bring us some wine."

She hurried away, leaving the Frenchman to smile ruefully and wish for the return of his host to explain matters. That this would always be an awkward introduction, they had both foreseen, but he'd never expected to have to face it alone.

⚜

His host, meanwhile, was sitting waiting for Isaac Hughes with an air of determined patience which amazed Ambrose, who had, on occasions, witnessed Hal's hasty temper.

"I must say, Hal, this is rather ill-mannered, keeping you waiting in this way," said Ambrose, fidgeting about the cramped chamber.

"No, no," soothed Hal. "Hughes was for Parliament, you know, he thinks it's his duty to be boorish to any who served the King."

Ambrose grinned, but said no more as the door opened and the sheriff entered, his arms full of books and papers, some of which began to slip as he stared at

Hal in dawning horror.

"Sir Henry! I hadn't heard you were returned!" he cried, as Ambrose hurried to assist him. "I thought you still in, in—oh, many thanks, sir—in foreign parts," he ended lamely.

"And so, no doubt, felt safe in immuring one of my family in your dungeons," remarked Hal affably.

"No, no, indeed no," he said, somewhat stiffly, and then relaxed, noting the quizzical gleam in Hal's eyes. "It's more that your esteemed brother-in-law hit my sergeant when we asked him to assist us in clearing up this matter."

"That he didn't say!" murmured Hal, glancing to Ambrose.

"Truth to tell, Sir Henry, he was in such a passion, or so the fellow says, I doubt he remembers the incident. Although poor Parry does, of course," he hesitated, his face impassive. "Firstly, pray allow me to express my condolences, Sir Henry, on the sad occasion of your wife's death."

"Thank you," said Hal woodenly.

The man looked uncomfortable, as if not sure how to continue, then he added in more business-like tones: "As for Mr Danvers, it would appear my man had the misfortune to interrupt a misunderstanding between your brother-in-law and his wife, your sister?"

"Yes," agreed Hal, not deaf to the interrogatory note in Hughes's voice. "A slight misunderstanding which will, no doubt, resolve itself as soon as I have secured Justin's freedom."

The sheriff sat down. "He is held on a capital offence, Sir Henry," he said sharply.

"Indeed," agreed Hal, "but not charged, as I understand the matter?"

"No," he replied reluctantly. "Although he will be charged with assault of a public servant."

"But there can be no necessity, surely, in keeping him housed here for so slight a crime," continued Hal firmly. "Mr Danvers is well-known to you as a man of integrity."

"It does make it easier for our investigation," began the sheriff lamely.

"Naturally, one understands that," agreed Hal smoothly. "But Mr Danvers is a man of law, he'll not be interested in flouting it. He'll be happy to report to you on a regular basis and assist you as much as possible in clearing up this matter, as he has done so many times in the past."

"I know his past record is exemplary," agreed the man. "But the evidence suggests—"

"Many things," interrupted Hal. "Come Hughes, I am Justice of the Peace, you can release him into my care with perfect confidence."

The sheriff hesitated. "Are you suggesting house arrest at Westwood?" he asked bluntly.

"No, I was suggesting I stood surety for him," replied Hal frowning. "That he may return to his own affairs."

"I would be more inclined to agree to house arrest," said Hughes tentatively. "The facts suggest very strongly that he is involved, Sir Henry. I should to my mind keep him here, locked up until brought to trial, but to oblige you, and one who has in the past assisted me—"

"Are you so sure of your facts?" demanded Hal, rather appalled at his certainty.

"It would appear on the face of it a simple matter," said the man reluctantly.

"Nothing is ever that simple," replied Hal swiftly.

Hughes shrugged. "I see no need to pursue any other."

Hal got to his feet, anxiety etched on his face. "I'll accept your terms," he said harshly. "Does house arrest mean he cannot even walk in the gardens?"

"Walk, yes, but not ride the estate, or leave the

grounds," said the sheriff. "You'll sign to that effect, Sir Henry?"

"I am more used to giving my hand upon it," he replied, then, as the sheriff hesitated, he said: "Very well, I'll put my name to it if it makes you feel happier."

"No, no, Sir Henry, I beg pardon," he said, hastily recollecting that, in spite of political differences, Hal had always behaved with scrupulous honesty. "Naturally, if you will stand surety for your brother-in-law, that is good enough."

Hal raised his brows. "Then let us have him released at once, if you please," he said. "That he may the sooner turn his mind to finding the villain of this piece."

It was less than an hour later that Hal and Justin were trotting along the road to Westwood, Ambrose having returned to Adamsholme to begin enquiries and attend to matters in Justin's office.

"I think you might try for a little more cheer, Justin," remarked Hal, as Justin replied to yet another of his questions with a sullen monosyllable.

"Do you?" he snapped. "Tell me, what have I to be cheerful about?"

"Well, you are no longer locked up in the county prison," said Hal.

"Only by your good offices," snarled Justin. "He made that very plain, the lickspittle!"

"What does the reason matter," said Hal impatiently. "At least you are free, and can turn your mind to finding the killer of Helen Sitwell."

"I don't even know where to begin!" he said wearily.

"You must do," said Hal sharply. "You were her lover, her closest confidante, and her lawyer. You must know all there is to know about her."

"I know next to nothing," he sighed. "She came here last summer with her husband, a sometime merchant in London, a cordwainer, I do believe, although he must have had other interests, for he was exceedingly wealthy. He came to consult me first, his premises had been destroyed by fire, and they'd left because of the plague. He wanted my advice about disposing of his money. I recommended he bought himself a country estate, which I was assisting him in looking for, when an apoplexy took him off. I was then called upon to help Helen, who had absolutely no idea about money, other then how to spend it! She bought that large house out on the road to Mallen, that rather odd place which wouldn't sell, do you remember?"

"Yes, yes indeed," he replied. "It belonged to the Taplow family, brewers of Adamsholme, all of whom died in the war. A distant cousin inherited it, and was promptly killed in a brawl. Then his wife died in child-birth, and a fever took the other son, meaning that an even more distant relation came into possession, only this one was already on his deathbed and overnight, the place became cursed!"

"Yes, that's the one," agreed Justin. "Well, Helen had never heard of any of these people, to her it was a per-fectly good house."

"Which it was," said Hal.

"Its fate is sealed now," retorted Justin. "Anyway, she bought it lock, stock and barrel, and took possession in a flurry of excitement, determined to create a 'salon'."

"Oh dear," said Hal with foreboding.

"Yes," sighed Justin. "The county ignored her, and the townsfolk laughed at her. She was very lonely."

"Had she no family?" asked Hal. "None to keep her company?"

Justin frowned. "I seem to recollect her mentioning a brother, an older man. But he was a soldier of for-tune—no, a sailor. That's right, he sailed to the West

Indies with Prince Rupert—"

"If he sailed with Rupert, he was a pirate," said Hal dispassionately.

"I gather he didn't come back," continued Justin. "For she said nothing further of him. No more did Nat Sitwell have any family—that came out at his death. She was most anxious that his will couldn't be overturned by his second or third cousin, who's been counting on the inheritance these past five years and was most put out by Helen marrying him."

"She was an adventuress?" said Hal.

"No more than the Castlemaine," replied Justin defensively. "I'll grant she wasn't your tip-top quality, but then she hadn't any advantages. Her family lost everything in the war, and she was forced to live on her wits. I don't know that, in similar circumstances, you or I might not be prepared to sell ourselves for a modicum of security."

"As indeed, I did," said Hal.

Justin stared. "I wouldn't have put it so bluntly."

"But you must have thought it," he said simply. "I married to oblige my uncle, he promised to make me his heir. It gave me security. As I remember it, I prayed devoutly that my future bride would be personable," he sighed, "which she was. Jesus, I recollect the feeling of relief when I first saw her, dear Libby."

"I recollect her look of adoration," said Justin harshly.

"She was everything a man could ever want in a wife," Hal continued, as if he'd not heard. "I doubt we'll ever see her like again."

"Don't!" cried Justin angrily. "Don't play the grieving widower to me! I was with her at the last! You were not! I know you made her last months Hell!"

"May I not grieve over my stupidity, too?" he replied swiftly. "I deny nothing. I was—still am—a knave and a fool, but does that make my love for Libby any less?"

"You abandoned her and went off to France, leaving her heartsick and ill!" he cried wrathfully. "Yet you dare to speak of love!"

"Did you love Bess any less when you were abed with Helen Sitwell?" he countered.

Justin hunched his shoulders and glared at him mutely.

"I know you'll have told yourself you didn't care, that Bess deserved such treatment, that you were fully within your rights, but did you actually love her any less?"

"No," he muttered.

"No," Hal agreed. "I don't think either of us can afford to take the high moral ground, do you? Now, you were talking of Helen Sitwell."

"There is no more," said Justin, as they rode through the gates of Westwood Hall. "I've told you, I know but little of her."

"What did you talk about?" asked Hal. "You can't have spent every moment locked in each other's arms. What did you discuss over dinner?"

"God, I don't know—the weather—the excellence of her cook—the colour of her boudoir—when you were likely to return—the arrangements for Libby's funeral; What does one discuss with one's mistress?"

"I don't know, I've never had one," replied Hal.

"I take leave to doubt that," he sneered.

"I don't claim to be a pattern card of virtue," Hal replied. "But any infidelity I am guilty of has been but a fleeting affair, nothing settled or permanent. I have never had a mistress, as such."

"I don't know that three months is permanent," said Justin, in a mortified tone. "I don't recall what she talked of, merely that she talked, almost incessantly. As I've said, she was lonely, and a great discusser of small things of little importance."

Hal nodded his understanding. "Yes, I see—well I don't doubt you were privy to a vast amount of information, but whether or not you can recollect anything relevant is another matter. Although, you might try to remember if she told you of any past enemies or persons who wished her ill," he sighed, as Justin nodded, looking gloomy as the house came into view. "And if you'll take my advice—which I doubt—you'll seek out Bess immediately, beg her pardon, and try to come to some understanding."

Chapter Ten

Justin climbed the main staircase at Westwood Hall. Supper had been an awkward affair, Hal had disappeared within minutes of their arrival, and had remained closeted with Phillipe Douay until the meal. Bess had been nowhere to be seen, and he'd stood about, feeling very uncomfortable, talking in a disjointed manner to Jane, who was as equally preoccupied until suppertime.

Hal had then emerged in an abstracted mood, Phillipe had been full of nervous hilarity, whilst Jane's bewilderment had only increased, and Sophie was almost as morose as himself. Only Cordelia Sandys had behaved in a rational manner. If speaking only when spoken to, and then in a voice pitched just above a whisper, could be called rational. Of Bess, there had been no sign at all.

The only thing he could be grateful for was that Aunt

Kate and Aunt Margery had been delayed a day by Aunt Margery taking a heavy cold. It seemed to add to his miseries that they would still arrive the following day and be at every meal henceforth. For Margery, the senior of Bess's aunts, never failed but to plant thorn after thorn in his side when they met, and this, surely, would be his lot from now on.

Gloomily, he turned into the chamber where his children slept. Both sons were abed and sleeping soundly. The baby in a crib, and the little one snuggled up with his cousin Harry in a bed. He leaned over the crib, studying the swaddled bundle there. He felt he hardly knew this child of his. He and Bess had quarrelled midway through her pregnancy, and his early arrival, some few weeks ago, had been more a source of irritation to him than joy, especially as he showed a marked resemblance to the Westwood family. His elder son, was plainly a Danvers, and although he had Bess's smile, he had the same fine straight hair. But this child was of a different cast altogether, and to Justin's jaundiced eye, bore a likeness to his namesake, Hal. Not that he called him Henry. Henry Liberty, he had been baptised, and Justin was determined he should be called Liberty in honour Libby, even though she hated that name and always insisted on the softer version.

"Oh!" Bess entered the room, Sophie in her wake. "I wasn't expecting to see you here!"

"I'll go," said Sophie quickly. "Call me should you need my help."

"What the devil does she mean by that?" demanded Justin irritably.

"That it is difficult to manage two little ones, now that Alys is in attendance on Etienne," replied Bess coolly.

"I don't know how you can speak to her. Sophie is responsible for Libby's death," he snapped. "If your nursemaid is busy, send for another, but don't let that hussy near our boys."

"She is not a hussy," said Bess quickly, "but a good and kind girl, just like Libby always insisted. I'll send for Jemima if you are not at the house, but I'll not keep Sophie from my children because you are prejudiced against her," she paused, as he looked angry. "What do you here?"

"I came to see my children," he snapped. "I assume I may do so? Indeed, if a fornicating jade may tend them, I imagine I may look at them."

"If it is your wish," she replied. "Although it has never been so before, I notice. I merely ask that you do not disturb them, it is no easy task to get them to sleep once awakened."

"I shall not disturb them. I am not a complete fool!"

"Are you not?" she returned from the doorway. "I am not arraigned on a murder charge, I wouldn't know. Pray keep your voice down."

"Bess!" he cried, as she made to leave the chamber, and at the suppressed anger and despair in his voice, the baby stirred and whimpered.

"Oh hush!" she cried, hastening back to rock the cradle anxiously.

"I need to talk to you," he said through gritted teeth.

"Then do so, only quietly," she returned coldly, as the baby went back to sleep.

"Not here," he hissed. "Somewhere we can be private."

"Private," she replied, her tone ironical. "Private, with me? This is something new! Alas, I have just explained we are busy because of the extra child. I am therefore required in attendance on him until Jemima is sent for."

"I need to talk to you now," he snapped. "May I not come to your chamber? Can you not set Sophie to watch them for a while? Has Hal not a dozen servants who might tend them over night? Surely, it is not necessary for you to do so."

"Sophie is with little Francis, who depends heavily upon her since Libby's death," she replied coolly. "I can perhaps spare you half an hour, if she'll be so good as to listen out for the children's cries. I take it you have removed your objection to a person accused of fornication attending them?"

"No," he replied, "but I have no choice."

"Neither do they, especially as they are too young to appreciate the difference between an unfounded accusation of fornication and a widespread acceptance of adultery. I find it difficult myself."

Justin set his mouth grimly as she left the room. She'd changed, become harder. His darling Bess of the early days of their marriage would never have spoken so. Her wits had sharpened, and with it, her tongue, as a result of the misery he'd inflicted on them both. He stood dumbly in the doorway, as she and Sophie Redcroft returned. Sophie, who had cast him one timid, frightened glance, assured Bess she'd not leave them unless little Francis woke, and settled down to rock the cradle, humming a gentle tune.

Bess led the way to her chamber, but hesitated outside

the door. "I came here to escape you," she said bluntly. "I do hope you'll respect my desire for privacy, and leave when I ask you to do so."

"I am your husband, by God!" he snapped. "You have no right to leave me! By law I can compel you to allow me entry into your bed."

"Do not be quoting law at me," she replied. "I am discussing moral issues here, and asking for your word as a gentleman that you will not force your attentions on me."

He stared at her for a few seconds, wondering of he could push her into the chamber and compel her to listen to him and forgive him, but caution made him nod grimly.

"I have your word?" she said. "I need and require your verbal assent. See how well you have trained me, indeed, if it is not forthcoming immediately, I may require a written contract."

"You have my word as a gentleman, for what its worth."

She opened the door and entered. "Is that traduced also?"

"It can hardly be enhanced by being accused of murder," he replied, as she crossed to take a position by a window on a cushioned seat.

He selected a chest at the foot of the bed and glanced about him. "You have changed for the better," he remarked bitterly. "This is far more elegantly-appointed than your own chamber. 'Tis no wonder you wished to return to your former home."

"When I lived here, I was housed in a tiny garret," she replied. "Aunt Margery said children should know their place. Libby keeps—kept—a better house, and Hal treats me like a welcome guest. That is the biggest change, to find my company was wanted, not despised."

"I don't despise your company!" he cried, as if in pain. "Can't you see, I am too ashamed to seek it?"

She surveyed him coldly. "Forgive me, no, I was not aware that was the reason I sat alone, evening after evening."

"Oh, God, Bess, how are we come to this?" he cried. "I love you, I have always loved you, can you not forgive me?"

"You love me?" she repeated blankly. "You have a strange mode of showing it, taking a mistress and spending all your time with her."

"I only did so because I was so miserable," he muttered. "Because you were siding with Hal, and I was so alone!"

"I did not side with Hal," she replied sharply. "I disapproved of Hal's behaviour every bit as much as I do yours. You and I disagreed over your quarrel with Libby."

"Yes, but don't you see, with both you and Libby against me, I had nobody!" he cried. He looked so like his little son, who, earlier in the day had thrown a tantrum, that it made her smile. "Oh, you think me amusing, do you?" he added, stung by this.

"No, I think you very foolish," she replied with dangerous candour. "You reminded me of little Philip in a fury because Harry wouldn't share his wooden horse with him. It was the same look of baffled fury."

"I am not a child," he snapped, incensed by the comparison.

"You behave very like one," she observed. "You have done, ever since you quarrelled with Hal. Rather as if you've been in a sulk with everyone," she paused, as he glared at her miserably. "I see you and he are at least talking now, is he forgiven?"

"Yes, no, I don't know!" he replied irritably. "You know Hal, he talks and talks and eventually he ends up half-convincing you he's innocent."

"When you'd much rather believe him guilty," she added.

Again, he glared at her, seeing with a sense of disbelief how she had matured over these few weeks into a woman. The girl he'd married, the shy, timid creature had disappeared and in her place stood a sensible, calm woman who no longer viewed him with naked adoration, but seemed somehow to rank him with his sons. He felt bereft, and yet unconsciously soothed for her attitude of amused tolerance was akin to Libby's, which he had missed so intolerably.

"Not that exactly," he admitted in calmer tones, "but it helped to have a focus for my anger."

"But surely you have one now," she replied. Then, as he looked an enquiry, she added: "you have been wrongfully accused of murder, and presumably a good friend of yours has been killed by an unknown person."

"Helen wasn't a good friend," he said with difficulty. "She, she was just somewhere to go, a stick to beat all Westwoods with!"

"Poor woman, what an epitaph!" said Bess in a wistful tone, trying not to be pleased that he plainly cared little for the woman.

"She was a pleasant enough companion," he said quickly, as if in defence. "Only, she did talk so. But then, she was lonely, poor soul, and so was I."

Bess frowned, her heart touched by this as she recollected his grief for his sister. "I am sorry that I drove you from me. That you thought me so uncaring that you had to seek comfort from another woman," she said slowly.

He hesitated, this was much more the way of things previously, Bess admitting a fault which had caused him sorrow or anger. He could, of course, push all the blame onto her and her brother, but his innate honesty was nagging at him. "You didn't drive me from you," he said roughly. "I snatched at the excuse. I behaved in an abominable manner, just as Libby said! Oh Bess, Bess, please say you'll forgive me."

"I forgive you," she replied, but her voice and face were remote.

He got up and came to sit beside her. "Do you truly forgive me?" he asked, taking her hand, which was lying slackly in her lap, for she did not look as if she did.

"Yes," she replied, turning to meet his eyes, her own calm.

"But you don't love me anymore," he said dully. "I've killed your affection and respect for me. I can see it in your face."

She looked away. How could she tell him she no longer saw him as a god? Neither he nor Hal were now the Colossus-like figures of her girlhood. Both had proved only too human, part of her longed-for a return of that blissful trust, but her more sane side told her that was past, they had all come through a time of testing, they must go on.

"Of course I still love you," she said with a sigh. "But I am still angry, and, and jealous of this woman."

"You have no need to be jealous," he said, clasping her hand urgently. "I had no love for her."

"But she was your mistress," she cried shocked. "You shared most intimate moments with her. How could you not care for her?"

"Yes," he looked shamefaced, "but it meant nothing. Bess, believe me, it meant nothing."

Again, she stared at him. "It meant nothing? Does that mean our love is equally worthless?" she asked. "Could all my love be cast aside in a moment, if another woman entered your sphere? Just as Hal did Libby's? Does the love a man has for a woman mean so very little that it can be over in the twinkling of an eye?"

"No, no!" he cried quickly. "I mean, I tried to convince myself I cared little for you, that you had betrayed me by your loyalty to your family, that I had a right to take a mistress if I wanted, that I really did care for Helen. But, it was all lies, every bit of it, and some lust initially, although that soon faded." He paused again as she looked away, plainly unconvinced. "Bess, I know I can't redeem myself with a few words, that it will take weeks, months to convince you of my unfailing love, that I must prove by my actions what I say is true. But I may only have a few weeks, I need your love and support now."

"Do you truly think they have a good case against you?" she asked quickly, fear entering her voice.

"Helen and I had quarrelled," he said with difficulty. "She—oh Bess, she'd been expecting you to die in childbirth." His clasp on her hand increased, almost making her cry out in pain. "I was so shocked, stunned! I had no idea what she'd been planning! It was like a nightmare. Then she began hinting, and I knew I had to get away from her, quickly."

"What was she hinting?" she asked, rather amazed at these disclosures.

"That women often die after childbirth, that they are worn down by the experience and none are surprised if they succumb to illness and death," he said in a horrified whisper, and she could see he was, indeed, still truly shocked by the woman's plotting.

"Dear God!" exclaimed Bess. "What did she mean? Were you to poison me or smother me?"

"I didn't wait to find out. I wasn't sure if she was mad or I was. I just got away as fast as I could," he said with a shudder, unconsciously confirming what had been proposed.

Bess sat silent, digesting this astonishing news. Trying to assimilate all that had occurred.

"Why did you not come home?" she asked after a few moments.

"I did, I stood in the street outside and realised what I'd done. I realised I wasn't worthy to be your husband anymore, that I'd been such a wicked fool that I didn't deserve you or the children. I felt unclean, sullied, I couldn't contaminate you or the boys by my presence, so I walked away."

"Oh Justin, if only you'd come in, all this would never have happened," she said, with tears in her eyes.

He nodded. "But I didn't come in, Bess, and now Helen is dead, and there are witnesses to say I was the last person with her and they heard us quarrelling. Add to that that she'd made a will in my favour…"

"Why?" she demanded quickly, suspiciously.

"Because she had no other kin," he replied. "Because she knew I was bitter over my father's will, because she knew I resented having to be grateful to the Westwoods for my daily bread."

"Do you truly hate us so much?" she asked, tears falling now.

"You are not a Westwood, Bess," he replied. "And no, I don't, I just tried to tell myself I did, because I was so angry over Libby."

She nodded now, then hesitated before saying: "You've got to rid yourself of that anger, Justin. I know it's difficult, I know how you loved Libby, but the resentment you feel towards Hal is injuring you too, and that's the last thing Libby would have wanted. She loved you and she loved Hal, to think you were quarrelling over her death would have distressed her greatly."

"Yes, I know," he agreed. "And meeting and talking with Hal has helped a little. I suppose I feel a little less like throttling him now, but he's always so damn plausible in his explanations!"

"That's because they are mostly the truth," she replied. "You know Hal, he always tells the truth, however unpalatable."

"You know he loves this—this girl," he said quietly.

"He has not told me so, but I can see she still worships him," replied Bess bleakly, thinking of the looks Sophie cast Hal, and how she had once worshipped Justin like that.

"'Tis there in his face when he talks of her," he said bitterly. "He told me that until he met Sophie, he'd never been able to understand how I'd been prepared to throw up my inheritance. But once he'd fallen in love with her, it all became clear." He waited as Bess said nothing, only sighing a little, then added: "He said he wished he'd loved Libby like that, but he hadn't and he was sorry for it and any pain she suffered on his account! Why couldn't he have loved her like that, Bess? She was so good and she adored him."

"I told you he was painfully honest," she said. "I don't know why."

"Yes, I know, but admitting a fault doesn't automatically mean one must forgive," he objected. "It doesn't stop the pain."

"No, indeed," she agreed. "But all he asks for is understanding. He knows you'll not forgive him, but give him time, Justin, give him time."

"I probably don't have time," he replied bitterly.

"Hal will not let you hang," she whispered. "He told me so this morning, I have faith in him."

"Yes," he laughed rather hysterically. "He'll not have his sister connected to a convicted felon, he told me too!"

"Does the reason matter, if the end is the same?" she asked with a sigh. "Do you know that his reason is total self-interest? I would think he'd feel more that he owed it to Libby to save her little brother."

"Probably," he agreed in a depressed voice. He glanced sidelong to her. "Am I forgiven, Bess?"

She turned to look at him. "Forgiven?" There was a pause as he read the answer in her face, then she added: "I tell you this, Justin, I'll swear to put it all behind me, to forget about it from this moment forth, if you'll do the same with Hal, and as for forgiveness, I'll forgive you when you can forgive Hal."

He stared at her, his eyes dark. "What do you mean by putting it all behind you?" he asked.

"Just that," she replied. "I'll make a conscious effort not to remember these last weeks. I'll try to go on as if they'd never happened. I'll even accept you back as my husband, if it is your wish."

"You know that is my wish," he said, his voice sounding gruff with emotion. "But will you be able to do it?"

"I've said I'll try," she replied with another sigh. "I can say no more than that."

"Then I'll try also," he replied, taking her hand and leaning forward to bestow a light kiss on her cheek. "God grant us success."

"Amen," she replied, holding herself very still in an effort not to shrug him away.

"And I am allowed back?" he glanced about the handsome chamber. "You know I am kept here under house arrest? I'd like to—to think I may seek comfort in your arms."

"I hope to be able to give that at least," she replied reluctantly.

Chapter Eleven

The table in front of Hal was covered in ledgers and papers. He looked up from these in surprise as Sophie entered the Jericho parlour without knocking.

"Yes?" he asked, at his most coldly daunting.

"Who is she?" demanded Sophie breathlessly. "Who is this Cordelia Sandys?"

"What do you mean?" he replied frowning. "Indeed, how dare you burst into my parlour and demand to know who she is? She is Cordelia Sandys."

"Who is she to you?" cried Sophie, advancing on the table he sat writing at. It had taken all her courage to come here. She was shaking with suppressed emotion. She knew he'd be furious, but she couldn't stand not knowing anymore. "Why have you brought her here? Is she your mistress? Is she a trollop you picked up in France and have now brought home to replace your wife?"

Hal stared blankly at her. That his sisters or his aunt might fall into some such vulgar error at first, he'd been prepared for, but not this from Sophie. He recognised its roots in jealousy, but even as he understood, and part sympathised, he was shocked by it.

"Replace my wife," he repeated, his voice falling like drops of ice. "How dare you suggest such a thing? I think you must have taken leave of your senses, to come here in this manner and make insulting suggestions to me! It must be plain to the meanest intelligence that Cordelia Sandys has but recently left the cloister. How dare you suggest she is my mistress?"

"Tell me she is not then!" she demanded hysterically. This was all wrong. She knew it, she knew she'd not get the answers she wanted talking to him this way, but he'd made it impossible for her to talk to him in the usual run of things and she had to know.

"Sophie, get control of yourself," he replied sharply. "And answer me one question: have you ever been my mistress?"

"You know I have not," she cried, tears filling her eyes at his coldness.

"Then how should this girl be? For I barely know her, or she me. If you, who are more than willing, are not my mistress, then how could she be?"

She fell back a few paces at the studied insolence of his words. "M-more than willing…" she gasped.

"What, are you not then?" he rejoined sardonically. "Do you tell me if I had asked, I'd had done so in vain?"

She held his eyes, knowing his words to be true, but intolerably hurt that he held her so light as to say them. That her own behaviour had been at fault, she was well aware, but still couldn't believe that he would rank the love they had as something so tawdry and despicable.

"Is that truly how you see me?" she whispered, appalled. "As a trollop, a slut to be summoned at the lift of a finger?"

He reddened slightly, for he knew this unjust, but irritated by her behaviour, shrugged his shoulders. "Is that not the danger every hoyden exposes herself to?"

Tears slid down her cheeks. "I love you," she whispered. "With all my heart and soul. You know that, and that I'd deny you nothing."

"Yes, I know that," he replied coldly.

"Hal!" she whispered desperately. "Have you no pity?"

He turned from her, determined not to betray himself.

"No, none," he replied in the same tone. "Not for you, not for me, not for anyone! Now go, and if you want to try to redeem yourself, observe Cordelia Sandys. That is how a well-bred young woman conducts herself."

"She is like a puppet! A doll, with no will of her own. The nuns have taken all that from her!" she cried indignantly, stung that he should compare them unfavourably.

"You are wrong," he replied. "She has merely learnt obedience. She has a will of iron, which is just well-held in check, for Cordelia doesn't feel the need to impose it upon others twenty times a day."

"And you admire her?" she cried aghast, as she understood his criticism.

"I admire her behaviour, her courage and her good humour," he replied tartly.

"Am I an ill-tempered coward also, then?" she asked pathetically.

"I said I admired Cordelia's good humour, possibly because I find my own lacking, along with my store of patience. I believe I bade you leave me, you must have duties attendant on you," he returned dismissively.

"I don't seem to know you anymore, you are so changed," she said piteously, not moving but standing numbly before him.

"You never knew me," he replied sharply. "And what man wouldn't be changed by the death of his wife?"

"But you loved me, you said you did!" she wept stormily. "Libby can have been nothing to you."

He glared at her, angered that she should remind him of this. "If, for a few short weeks, I succumbed to a mad infatuation, why do you assume a wife, beloved for five years meant nothing? I loved Libby, I still do love her and I grieve that I ever caused her a moment's pain."

"A mad infatuation?" she repeated. "Is that what you felt for me?"

"What else but that could it have been?" he replied woodenly, not answering the question.

"You lie!" she cried hotly. "You love me, I've seen it in your face."

"You delude yourself, and I've told you to go!" he snapped, knowing the longer this discussion continued, the more likely he was to come to grief.

"Do you think I don't know why you won't be alone with me? Why you avoid my company? Why you constantly hector and lecture me?" she cried, angry tears splashing on the table between them. "But you won't succeed! You can say what you want, use me as ill as you choose, but I'll never stop loving you, and I'll never let you forget me."

He picked up his pen. "If these displays of overemotional tantrums continue, I shall consign you entirely to my Aunt Margery's care. She has had extensive experience in the tuition of young females of uncertain character. She will prevail."

She drew a long, shuddering breath. "Say what you choose, I know better. Pretend to distain all emotion, that you feel nothing, but I remember your arms about me. I remember your lips on mine. You are not a man of ice, but a man of fire, and fire can never be contained long."

"I said, go!" he cried, banging his fist on the table, sorely tried as he, too, remembered the occasion and the feel of her in his arms.

"Aha, not so cool now!" she jibed. "Have a care, lest emotion get the upper hand and you become human again!"

"Sophie, don't try me too far!" he cried, stung into a direct appeal.

"Try you? No, wake you! Shatter this icy indifference you pretend to!" she retorted jubilantly, seeing the mask slip.

"Get out!" he snapped, grasping a firm hold on his temper as he saw what she was at.

"Make me," she retorted pertly.

Caution fled before the desire to be rid of her. He leapt furiously to his feet, and before he'd known it, had fallen into her trap as he grasped her arms, shaking her angrily. She laughed up in his face, triumphant that she'd achieved physical contact with him, and could now control him.

"Why, what would demure Cordelia think of this!" she taunted. "Well, do you beat me?" her eyes sparkled with amusement and excitement that she'd loosed the man of passion within him.

He let go of her abruptly, his senses all ajangle at the touch of her, his head reeling at her closeness, at her beauty. The desire to crush her into his arms ousted all his good intentions.

"What, no beating?" she sighed. "Not even a kiss?" Then, as he made to turn away, she hurriedly caught his arm, and standing on tiptoe, kissed him fully on his lips.

A great surge of longing swept over him, it would take no effort at all to give way, and such a vast effort to withstand her. But he forced himself to it, remaining passive, so that she stepped back from him, stricken by his lack of response, aware suddenly of the enormity of her action by the expression in his eyes.

"Oh, I, I beg pardon," she gasped, her hand coming to cover her mouth in horror.

"You do well to do so," he snapped, glad to vent his passion in anger. "Get gone from this place and don't dare return here again! In future, my instructions will be relayed to you via my aunt."

"No, Hal, please, I beg of you!" she cried in dismay to see her plans in ruins. She clasped her hands before her, as if in prayer. "I will be good, I swear, I'll not trouble you again, but please, don't shut me out of your life altogether."

"You give me no choice. I can no longer tolerate this style of behaviour. You bring us both into disrepute," he muttered.

"I won't, I won't, I promise. Please Hal, I beg you, let me show you how I can model Cordelia's behaviour!"

He glanced doubtfully to her, only too aware that his Aunt Margery had already declined in a long and tedious letter which had awaited him, to moderate his ward's conduct, suggesting that the only solution to control her unruly spirit was a speedy marriage, with a strong-minded man.

"Very well, I'll allow you one more chance, but I warn you, Sophie, if I am forced to endure one more occasion like this, you'll be sent from this house with my aunt until a marriage can be arranged for you."

"I want no marriage, Hal," she cried desperately. "You promised me no marriage until I had finished mourning Uncle Edmund."

"Mourning?" he cried bitterly. "What would you know of mourning? You may have tricked me into giving my word, but should this behaviour continue, I'll have no compunction in breaking it, and wedding you to the highest bidder to be rid of you."

She stared at him bleakly, two large tears welling in her eyes at this. "Do you truly love me so little you could do such a thing?" she whispered.

His heart smote him at the thought of her with Adam Blackwell, and he was forced to back down. "Sophie," he cried as if in pain. "Can't you see I need peace? I cannot endure this any longer! You drive me to this excess, goad me into harsh words! I beg you to let me be!"

She moved closer, her tears stilled by his anguish, clasping his arm. "Hal, I beg pardon," she said quietly. "You do right to reproach me. I am wicked and selfish to goad you so, when you have such troubles. I have only the excuse that, since I met you, I have been so alone and afraid, that I clung to you. Please forgive me, I give you my word, I'll behave in such an exemplary manner in future, even your Aunt Margery will be impressed."

He laughed at that, looking down into her beautiful, honest eyes, and was lost. "Oh Sophie, Sophie!" he murmured. "Why do I punish us both? You are right, you know I love you, but I cannot honestly say so, not for a very long time."

"I can wait, Hal," she replied breathlessly, wonder coming into her face. "I don't care how long, if I know you love me, I can wait forever."

He shook his head. "It wouldn't be right to tie you so," he said gently. "You are young, and ripe for marriage, I would not have all this glorious beauty wasted waiting for me."

"It won't be wasted," she whispered, frightened if she moved or spoke too loud this precious moment would be shattered. "If you see it, if you admire my glory, then that is enough, I need no other."

He drew her closer to him, almost in wonder. "You don't know me, Sophie," he said, and there was an ache of despair in his voice. "You only see the surface, or you'd not be so certain of your love."

She slid into his arms, her head going naturally to his chest, and a sigh of joy escaping her. "I am certain of that, if nothing else, and that this is where I belong." She raised her face for his kiss, and this time it came sweetly, sealing a pact that would never be broken.

"Hal, Hal, sacre bleu! Hal, what are you at? Are you indeed insane?" cried Phillipe Douay, who had opened the door, took in the scene at a glance, and hastily shut it again, himself on the inside. "I beg pardon, Hal, Mistress Redcroft, but your aunt is come, Hal! At least, both your aunts, but your sister Jane bade me tell you Aunt Margery is in some sort of anxiety and requires your attendance upon her at once!"

Hal looked at Sophie, his smile a caress. "So, the trouble begins immediately. Remember, you have given me your word on your behaviour."

"And you have given me yours on my future," she replied.

He nodded. "Very well, it is agreed and sealed with a kiss. We shall not get the opportunity to be alone again for a long time, I fear."

"Oh, we'll contrive something," she murmured.

"Hal," said Philippe uneasily. "Your respected sister indicated time was of the essence!"

"Yes, yes, I'm coming, Philippe," he replied, lingering for one last kiss. "Stay here until Philippe returns, he'll let you know if the coast is clear." With these words, he hurried away.

Chapter Twelve

"Well, Sir Henry, what have you to say for yourself?" Aunt Margery, a stoutish, imposing woman, was seated in an upright chair in the larger parlour, and by the look of her jaw, wasn't going to move until she had answers.

"That I am very pleased to see both you and Aunt Kate, ma'am. I also hope your headcold is improving, Aunt Margery," he replied, pausing to kiss that lady's faded cheek, before bowing elegantly over the elder woman's outstretched hand.

"I haven't got any such malady! Don't try to play off your airs on me!" snapped Aunt Margery. "I am not Kate, here, to be cozened by your pretty manners! Just because you've spent six months in France, don't think we are impressed by you!"

"I wouldn't dream of falling into such vulgar error, ma'am," he replied politely.

"Hmm." She looked him over. Her heart wrung to see him so pale and thin. "You've lost weight," she announced. "No doubt so you can fit into that ridiculous garment! A—what do you call it? A coat? What was wrong with a doublet, may I ask? It was good enough for my husband, for your Uncle Henry, even for that fool of your own father! Men have worn doublets since time immemorial, but it's not good enough now! No, anything English and honest must be cast aside in favour of French kickshaws."

"Fashion is a fanciful, fleeting jade, ma'am," he replied. "No doubt she'll be off down a different byway in no time at all, and men will return to doublets and trunk hose."

"How are you, Hal?" asked Aunt Kate, pressing his hand as he brought her a glass of sack. Her sweet, gentle face echoing her concern. "Margery is right, you have lost weight and look dreadfully tired."

"If he will go gallivanting the length of France, he must expect to be tired," announced Aunt Margery. "Consorting with foreigners and the like, 'tis no wonder you are exhausted."

"'Tis difficult to do anything but in another country," he agreed, "English people being thin on the ground."

"But you managed to bring one back with you, or at least that odd French apothecary did, at your behest, or so he claims, though I take leave to doubt it. Well, sir, what do you mean by it? Answer me that. What do you mean by bringing that young female here?"

"What do I mean by it? Why, I mean nothing," he replied. "I intend to find her family for her, and I am hoping you'll be able to assist me."

"I? Assist you!" she exclaimed. "I perceive you have indeed run mad! Why should Kate or I assist you to blacken dear Libby's name on the road to perdition?"

"I'll help all I can, Hal," said Kate gently, seeing him wince at the sound of Libby's name.

"Thank you, ma'am," he replied, turning to her. "How like you to be so trusting! Libby always said you were the closest thing to a mother we had."

Tears filled her eyes. "Oh, Hal, what a beautiful tribute! Being childless myself, I must confess, I have looked upon you children as my own."

"Even if you are too young to have been our real mother," he said, with his charming smile. "The case is this, Aunt Kate, in searching for Jacqueline's grave…"

"Jacqueline's grave?" interrupted Aunt Margery, who was by no means pleased to be shut out of the conversation in the manner she had. She'd recollected that Hal could be lectured, his manners would keep him still and listening, but his resentment meant loss of communication. Often at the end, he would merely bow, apologise, and depart. Not what she wanted at all.

"Yes, ma'am," he replied. "Contrary to our information, Jacqueline did not die with my father in Auch, but in a nunnery at Saint-Sauvy, a tiny little place with a few sisters on the way, I imagine, to Lyon."

"Why?" demanded Margery.

"That I cannot say, ma'am," he replied with a sigh. "True, Auch was hit by plague and most of the population took it, approximately half surviving, but frankly, there does seem to have been some element of foul play."

"Hal!" cried Aunt Kate. "You cannot be saying your father was killed."

"No, ma'am," he replied. "But I am saying he was abandoned by one he'd cause to trust, and left to die in pain."

"I told him he'd live to rue the day he married a Frenchwoman," cried Margery.

"And that thought must have been a great comfort to him, as he lay dying friendless in an inn," replied Hal, with more bitterness than was his wont.

Margery had grace to blush. "Why, Hal, I am as sorry as can be he died like that," she stammered. "I would that we'd known that we could have gone to him!"

"Indeed, ma'am, as we all do," he returned.

"So you set off in search of Jacqueline when you found she had not died?" asked Aunt Kate diplomatically.

"Yes, it was possible she'd perished later and been thrown into a common grave, but the innkeeper and his wife were adamant that she'd gone, hired a carriage and set off for Lyon, they'd said, claiming it was at her husband's insistence."

"Well that is possible, Hal," said Kate reflectively. "Your father, for all his faults, was a brave man, he may have sent her off as a means of protecting her and her child."

"Indeed, ma'am," he agreed, casting her a warm smile. "My thoughts entirely. What man wouldn't endeavour to send his wife out of danger? And what wife would go?"

"You said you found her grave, Hal, so you mustn't judge her too harshly," said Kate gently.

"Indeed," he agreed again. "As I say, the innkeeper's wife mentioned she was taking the road towards Lyon, and I recollected Jacqueline had actually come from somewhere not far away. So, I followed her trail as far as a small village I remembered her once mentioning, and it being late and cold and wet, halted there for the night. I heard the abbey bells the next morning and remembered that my father had told me once she'd been raised by nuns. It seemed worth a visit."

"Raised by nuns?" gasped Margery. "You mean Papists?"

"Yes," he replied briefly, then, as his Aunt looked horrified, he added: "I don't see that it signifies, ma'am. Jacqueline abandoned her religion as easily as she did her husband. It is my contention she held no strong belief."

"Does that make it any better?" cried Margery in dismay.

"I don't know, ma'am," he sighed. "Jacqueline was a complete puzzle to me at the best of times. I have drawn few conclusions, I have only what I tell you. I crossed the fields to make a visit to the abbey, asking if they had an Englishwoman or child taking refuge with them. They replied by introducing Cordelia Sandys. And she realised I was looking for Jacqueline's child, her English being better than my French."

"But you speak French beautifully, Hal," protested Aunt Kate.

"Not according to these French nuns," he said with a smile. "They insisted my accent was dreadful."

"But Jacqueline had been there?" demanded Aunt Margery. "You are certain this child is indeed Jacqueline's? Might there not be some mistake?"

"No. Jacqueline arrived there on Christmas day last year, she'd been abandoned by her carriage driver on the road because he thought she had the plague. By the time she had walked to the abbey, her confinement was well-advanced. She told the nuns very little but that her husband had died of the plague. They nursed her, in spite of their fear that she also had plague, and delivered her of her child. She died the following day, being much weakened, they said, by the return of her fever. The girl Cordelia has helped look after the baby since, and the nuns, of course, have worshipped him."

"But who is the girl? Why have you brought her here? Is she to be the child's nursemaid? Don't you realise she could be the daughter of any soldier of fortune?" cried Aunt Margery. "I grant you those nuns of yours have taught her well, but she could be anybody!"

"She is, in fact, the daughter of Basil Sandys of Bickmarsh Hall in Lincolnshire," he replied. "Now, doesn't Tom Kingscott have some relations in Lincolnshire?"

"I believe he does," agreed his senior aunt reflectively, insensibly cheered to hear this evidence of landed family. "Is it not the Jeavons of Bominster who have estates there? Indeed, I am sure Tom's widow Alice's sister's son has married a Jeavon. Sir Christopher, I do believe, his elder daughter. They would certainly know of—what was the name again?"

"Sandys, Basil Sandys, of Bickmarsh Hall, although I doubt me he'll still own the hall. An impecunious Royalist is how the Abbess styled him. She took the child only as a favour because his wife had been some distant connection. He promised to return for her in a few weeks, his fortune restored, and left to perish at the Battle of Worcester."

"A common enough tale, Hal," sighed Aunt Kate.

"Mmn," he agreed. "Although, one hopes most such abandoned children had relations who sought them out in the intervening years."

"Surely, 'tis strange none did so," mused Kate. "Poor little mite."

"Lincolnshire was very strong for Parliament," remarked Hal. "Indeed, the East Anglian Association was

Cromwell's home ground, perhaps some family conflict led to a rift."

"Indeed," said Aunt Margery. "I'll write to Tom Kingscott immediately and get him to enquire of his wife's kin. We should soon discover something of her history. In fact, this Cordelia may unwittingly know more. I'll question the girl myself."

"But gently, ma'am," Hal replied. "She has lived quite retired from life, remember."

"But will have been taught obedience," said Aunt Margery. "Unlike some, do you know…!" she began darkly.

"Before you launch into a recital of Sophie's wrongdoing, Aunt, may I point out that as you have declined to assist me with her education, something well within your rights, I must decline to discuss her with you," he smiled limpidly. "I'm sure that is only fair. Let us instead talk of the matter of Justin Danvers."

"What is there to discuss?" cried Aunt Margery, going for a softer prey. "I told Bess blood will out, but she wouldn't heed me! A pompous, boorish young man with ideas above his station, I always said so."

"Poor Bess, she must be so worried," sighed Aunt Kate. "Jane was telling me there is a good case against him. How can this be, Hal?"

"Well, there is no dispute he had made this woman his mistress," he replied. "And that he did, indeed, quarrel with her on the night in question."

"There, you see, no gentleman of breeding would subject his poor wife to such disgrace!" declared Aunt Margery.

"Are you suggesting that a gentleman would remain silent and suffer the consequences of the law?" demanded Hal, in patent disbelief.

"Most certainly, in my day!" she replied grandly.

"Then I thank God your day is over, ma'am, and men are no longer required to make such fools of themselves. I wouldn't give a groat for the sort of wife that would expect such a sacrifice!"

"It is patently obvious you didn't give a groat for your poor wife at all," she snapped, angry by having taken such a foolish stand.

"You'll forgive me, Aunt, if I refuse to discuss my wife with you!" he replied, his voice cold. "I'd not like to offer you a discourtesy, which I fear would be the result if we proceed with this conversation."

"Tell me more about poor Justin, Hal," said Aunt Kate in some haste, as Margery turned a dull red and appeared at a loss for words. "Jane said he was initially detained, but that you obtained his release."

"I am standing surety for his behaviour," he agreed. "He is, in effect, under house arrest here."

"Oh, the shame of it!" moaned Aunt Margery. "To bring such a scandal down upon our name!"

"Oh, surely not, Aunt," replied Hal. "To my mind, it can't compare with my father being accused of killing my brother, his uncle, or Mary being accused of poisoning Sir Edward, nor Jane's husband running amok last year as he did, leaving bodies littering the stairs! Indeed, I was beginning to think life was a little tame, but here, sure enough, is another riddle."

"Can you solve this one, Hal?" asked Aunt Kate anxiously.

"I must, ma'am," he replied. "The happiness of Bess and her children depends upon it. Besides which, I owe it to Libby."

"Yes, of course!" she agreed. "I might have known you'd say that. Libby would have expected us all to assist her brother, just as she never failed us. And I, for one, won't fail her or Justin."

"Well, I hope you aren't suggesting I would, Kate," said Margery indignantly. "I'm sure I'm happy to do all

I can to assist Libby's brother."

"Then, ma'am, you must regulate your tongue and your looks," said Hal bluntly. "If, for no reason than to make Bess's life easier. She needs to be able to find the ability to laugh again."

"Laugh! Surely you jest?" cried Aunt Margery. "I cannot believe Bess took him back!"

"Surely, 'twas her Christian duty to forgive him," said Aunt Kate. "Bess would never do other."

"And her inclination, for she loves him," said Hal gently.

"Loves a man who betrayed her!" cried Aunt Margery.

"Yes, Aunt, a good woman, a truly good woman, like Aunt Kate or Libby or Bess, forgive heart and soul, and keep on loving regardless. I doubt we men deserve them, but by heaven, we are thankful for them!"

"I am sure you must be, Hal," said Aunt Kate sympathetically, seeing again how bleak he looked. "The thought of Libby will always be a comfort to you."

"It was a comfort to me to see Hetta so very well when we called in on her yesterday. You know, Hal, she is in a delicate state."

"I did not know that, aunt," he replied. "What excellent news. When does she expect to be confined?"

"Within the next week or so, Hal," replied Kate. "Margery and I shall go to be with her."

"Are you not going to tell Hal your news too, Kate?" said Margery, sniffing.

Aunt Kate blushed. "I was going to pick my moment, Margery," she replied. "Hal has much to trouble him at this time."

"Then he'll be all the happier for some good news! I don't know why you're getting so red-faced and figety. Good heavens, you look like a bashful maid, rather than a middle-aged woman!"

"Pray, ma'am, don't speak if you don't care to," said Hal quickly. "Good news will keep."

"No, Margery is right, Hal. It's just that I'd not like anyone to think I'm injuring dear Henry's memory."

"Oh, good heavens!" exclaimed Margery. "Henry has been dead these past five years, Kate. Your Aunt Kate is to be married again, Hal! There, now, it's out, Kate, you can relax and receive your congratulations."

"Married!" cried Hal, in amazement. "You are to be married, Aunt Kate?"

"Yes," she replied, tears filling her eyes. "You think me too old, don't you, Hal? I can see it in your face."

Hal, who had, indeed, been thinking just that, made a swift recover. "No, I don't, ma'am," he said quickly, to spare her pain. As he spoke the words, he realised it was true. "I think you are a perfect age to be a bride, and I wish you great joy. May I know the name of your prospective husband?"

"Sir Richard Harwich," said Aunt Margery, with evident satisfaction. "He is a connection of the Kingscotts, you know. His wife died last summer, and he came on a visit to his brother's home, and we all met up at Tom's house. I could see at once he was very taken with Kate, so I gave him every encouragement, for Kate has no idea of these things."

Hal glanced to his blushing younger aunt. "You are happy in this, ma'am," he asked softly. "You haven't agreed to anything from pressure? You don't feel you need to be gone from this house because of the scandal? Or because you are no longer needed? For you are, ma'am, now, more than ever."

"Oh, Hal, no!" she cried, lifting her tear-filled eyes to his. "I mean, if you can't spare me, naturally, I'll have to tell him no, but," she smiled, and it was like the sun coming out from behind a cloud, "Richard is the first man I've met since Henry died that I can feel I can trust."

"Tell him no? After all my efforts? You'll do no such thing," cried Margery, incensed, "he has fifteen hundred acres, and only the one son! He is an ideal match. Who knows, you are not so very old that another child is out of the question. Either way, you will have a comfortable home and lots of influence."

"He is a good man, Hal," Kate continued, disregarding this, "a gentle, kind man, I'm sure you and he will deal very well together."

"I'll be happy to make his acquaintance, ma'am," Hal replied, and continued, "I hope you'll let me give you away at your wedding."

"Oh, Hal!" she cried, with a smile. "He is still in mourning, and I have not yet completely made up my mind."

"Well, of course you have, Kate," said Margery sharply. "You can't think of turning him down after all the encouragement you gave him! Anyway, he tells me he has an uncle widowed last winter, I might just consider him myself!"

Both turned to look at her in such amazement, that Margery turned red again. "It was a jest!" she cried. "I was trying to make you both laugh! You said we had to be more cheerful, Hal." ❧

Chapter Thirteen

Hal awoke next morning feeling a lot clearer in his mind about things. He found being in his own home meant he was forced to come to terms with Libby's death. He was still shocked when he thought of it, and he realised he'd grieve for her for many months. But, he knew he had to go on.

He'd successfully introduced Etienne, or, as Hal thought of him, Stephen, into his house, and the anxiety of how to do that without a lot of explanations and recriminations had, he realised, been playing on his mind. Aunt Margery was attending to the matter of Cordelia Sandys. Another burden lifted, he'd reached an understanding with Sophie, who was making him feel so happy that he felt guilty, and he was glad to have Philippe's company once again. He had but to tackle this business of Justin to get everything, if not running smoothly, at least all going in the same direction.

As he shaved and dressed himself, he read over Ambrose's notes and had no hesitation, once he'd eaten breakfast, in calling a council of war of interested parties.

"I don't think there is any great merit in pursuing enquiries here," said Hal. "I mean, I know we must talk to the servants, and I must ask questions of the farmers on the hill, but the answer to this puzzle must lie in this woman's past."

"Her past?" said Bess blankly.

"Yes, if Justin did not kill her, and we are all agreed on that, I think, then somebody else did. Now, I think we can rule out a common thief breaking in to steal money, and then abandoning it. So, that being the case, there must be a reason for her murder, and that reason, not being obvious here, where she has lived for less than six months, may come to light in London, where she lived previously. What do you think, Justin?"

"Possibly," he conceded gloomily.

"I propose that Ambrose goes to wherever she lived in London, do you know where, Justin?" said Hal.

"Yes," Justin replied. "It was in Langley Court, off Covent Garden."

"And asks questions of neighbours, friends, the fellow who bought her husband's business, people in the street, in inns and alehouses, at the theatre, even. Are you willing to do so, Ambrose? I would go myself, but I am obliged to keep Justin within my sight, and he may not leave Westwood."

"Who will run my business whilst Ambrose is gone?" protested Justin, irked at it being made clear he was a prisoner.

"Justin, what business do you think you will have knocking on your door?" asked Hal bluntly. "Adamsholme is a small market town, they all know you were taken up for murder. No new clients will be calling and precious few old ones. Any that do can be directed here to seek your advice."

"So I am to be ruined now, am I?" Justin snapped. "Prevented from plying my craft."

"No, if any, I shall be ruined, as I own the business and you, like Ambrose, are in my employ," returned Hal coldly.

There was a shocked silence at this, for Hal had always been so careful of his brother-in-law's feelings previously.

"I beg pardon!" Justin replied. "No doubt you'll amend any wage accordingly for the time I lose."

"Justin!" said Bess uneasily.

"I have not said so," said Hal evenly. "Ambrose, your answer, if you will."

"I shall be happy to go to London," he replied at once.

"I am sorry, Jane," said Hal, as a look passed between them. "But the quicker he leaves, the sooner he will be back."

"Indeed," she agreed simply. "And it is most necessary that he go."

"Justin will instruct you further," said Hal, running his eye down the list he had before him, "as to where you should best use your questions. I shall, in the meantime, take myself to Adamsholme to talk to these servants of Mistress Sitwell. Is there anything of them, Justin, you can tell me to give me some aid?"

"I doubt they'll help much," said Justin, shrugging. "Prescott is a middle-aged man, a local fellow Sitwell hired when he came here. I arranged the matter for him. He had good references, which I took up, for a position of manservant in Herefordshire to a gentleman of some wealth. In my opinion, he'd been cheating Helen on a regular basis since Sitwell died, and I'd told her so, but she'd done little about it as far as I was aware."

"And the girl?" asked Hal. "The maidservant, what is her name?"

"Hannah Smith," he replied. "A young chit of a wench, too impudent by half. I'd have sent her off within a sen'night if she'd been in my employ. Idle, sharptongued with an inability to know her place, made her most unsuitable for the position she filled."

"'Tis plain why they both spoke out against you," remarked Hal. "Did she have good references?"

"I did not recommend her, she came with Helen from London. She was her maid there, it seemed."

"Ah, excellent news!" cried Hal. "She'll already have background information. I'll certainly seek her out as well."

"I doubt you'll get anything from her," said Justin.

Hal smiled. "Shall we wager on it? You know I can usually charm a pretty face into confiding in me."

Justin snorted, "Well, if you will waste your time."

"And you can occupy yours, Justin, by writing a full account for me of what you did the night Helen Sitwell died, in exact detail, with times and movements, with nothing left out. And when you've done that, perhaps it would be as well to try charming the pretty face that is your wife's."

Bess blushed at this suggestion and Justin looked affronted, but Hal got to his feet, glad to be doing something, to be escaping for a while from the mourning atmosphere of the house.

They dispersed about their various tasks, Justin to wrestle with pen, paper and his memory, Bess to attend to her children, Jane to assist Ambrose in his packing. Hal followed them upstairs to collect his hat and gloves, and then remembered he'd faithfully promised Harry to always tell him where he was going in future, and when he'd be back. He hastened to the nursery quarters to do so, paused to reassure Bess, and hurried back. He stopped in surprise at the sight of Sophie struggling with sheets and the feather bed in her chamber, as seen through the open door.

"Sophie!" he said, tapping and entering. "What are you doing?"

She paused, looking hot and harassed, her curls all tumbled about her brow. "Changing the linen on my bed," she replied blankly.

He was taken aback. "It is not fit you should do so," he protested. "We must have servants to do that."

She frowned. "Well, you are short-handed. It would seem that Kate and Dorcas have both got the quinsies,

Wat the stable lad has a head cold, and cook says she feels none too well."

Not deaf to the note of impending disaster in this catalogue, he came to the far side of the bed to help her straighten the recalcitrant sheet. "There still must be someone more fit than you, this is impossible. What of your maid? Can she not do this?"

She laughed abruptly. "What indeed? I don't have a maid!"

He stared. "You don't have a girl to tend your needs?" he said in disbelief.

"Justin said it wasn't necessary, that Libby's girl would serve," she replied awkwardly, biting her lip. "Only, only Maggie never would be very obliging. Indeed she was so..." She sighed. "In the end, I found it easier to tend to my own wants."

"I cannot believe this! You tell me you've never had a girl to look after you," he cried, tugging at the bolster she was endeavouring to replace. "Let go, stop, I'll find a wench and send her to you at once."

"No," she replied, smiling a little at his quick anger, which was a balm to her injured feelings, for she'd felt it had all been very much part of the way his family had punished her, giving her no servant of her own, to help, or even confide in. "'Tis of little matter after all," she tried to pull the pillow back.

"'Tis of great matter to me!" he cried angrily, tugging in return so that the pillow swung back toward him. "I am ashamed of my people, of how ill you have been treated."

She laughed a little, unhappy laugh. "Oh, let it be. It matters not, I tell you," and she tried to twitch the pillow away.

He saw her intent and pulled harder, so that she was thrown off balance, tumbling onto the bed with a cry of dismay and so comical a look as to make him chuckle, his anger suddenly dispersing. Indignantly, she snatched at the pillow, pulling him over on top of her, laughing in delight to see the gloom disappear from his face and the man she knew from the summer return with his smile.

"Sophie!" he cried in astonishment. "You wretch, how dare you?"

"How dare I? 'Tis you who pulled!" she giggled as, with the pillow between them, he hovered over her, his face close.

"Sophie," he murmured, his lips brushing hers. "I swear you are a witch. God, how I do love you."

Justin, on his way to seek Bess, still talking over his shoulder to Jane, paused at the sound of Hal's voice to stare in disbelief at the sight of his recently widowed brother-in-law rolling on the bed, giggling with his ward. Words failed him, but some sound escaped him, for Hal glanced up to meet his glare of incredulity. Then Justin was gone, hastening away with footsteps that echoed his fury.

"Oh God!" groaned Hal in dismay. "What have I done? Oh, Sophie, Sophie, you'll be the death of me!"

"Why?" she asked innocently, for she'd seen none of this. "What have I done?"

"Nothing," he sighed, sitting up and catching up his hat, which had been abandoned in the proceedings. "Nothing, just been your usual adorable self, it's what I've done!"

"You've laughed," she replied, sitting up also and pushing her dishevelled hair from her face as she leant forward to catch his hand. "For a few moments you forgot your worries and became lighthearted, like the young man I remember, rather than the dotard you've become!"

"Minx!" he replied ruefully, flicking her cheek lightly with his gloves. "I must go, I've things to do. Oblige me by leaving this and keeping well from Justin's path! You might undertake some study, as I've asked of you repeatedly."

She made a face at him. "I can't leave this, it looks disgustingly suggestive, I'll tidy it and then, if it's so important, I'll go and read your fusty books."

He paused before her mirror, putting on his hat. "I'd hate an ignorant wife," he murmured. "Beauty isn't everything, one wants to be able to hold a rational conversation, too."

She eyed him narrowly. "A rational conversation," she repeated. "About what?"

He kept his face straight with difficulty as she rose so easily to his bait. "Oh, I don't know," he said airily. "The political situation, Greek classics, the plays of Shakespeare and Webster, that sort of thing."

She stared at him, her mouth dropped open. "The plays of Webster?"

"And William Shakespeare," he supplied. "Anyway, I mustn't delay. I've to ride into Adamsholme to talk to Helen Sitwell's servants. Be so good as to tell Jane I'll be returned for supper."

With a raised hand, he went on his way, hastily leaving the house, judging it best to leave Justin to cool a little before attempting to explain. Not that he truly could explain in a satisfactory manner. It had happened, that was all, perhaps he shouldn't have gone in to ask, but then she shouldn't have been left without a maid for so long. He sighed and vowed he'd think on it no more, promptly doing so for the remainder of his ride to Adamsholme. Although, it wasn't Justin's reaction to the kiss he dwelt on most.

Justin meanwhile, having raged at Bess and failed to raise more than an abstracted suggestion that he must have been mistaken, and that she couldn't think such wicked things of either, took himself back downstairs to write his report, his fury still simmering, and there, by the greatest mischance, Sophie found him later when she came looking for a book of Shakespeare.

"What do you want?" he snapped, his anger bubbling back up at the sight of her.

"A…a book," she stammered, not truly aware of what had transpired, only knowing that he hated her and found her at fault on every occasion.

"A book? What, do they have books for the likes of your trade?" he cried cruelly. "What's it called? A whore's charter?"

She stared at him in astonishment. "No, I want

Shakespeare's plays," she replied numbly, not quite able to comprehend the vitriol of his attack.

"Aye, he tells of strumpets and jades, he'll serve you well enough!" he cried, getting to his feet and going to the bookcase. "Here, take it, and may you rot in hell, you evil little hussy!" He threw it blindly at her.

She picked up the book from where it landed, splayed out and crushed at her feet. "Oh, please don't!" she cried. "Hal treasures his books!"

"Hal treasures his books!" he repeated contemptuously. "Aye, I would I could say the same for his women! You do realise, don't you, that you are just one in a long line of heartless drabs he's had and forgotten!"

"Why do you say so to me?" she asked, puzzled. "What have I done that—"

"What have you done?" he cried, in a voice of suppressed fury. "You've killed my sister, isn't that enough?"

Tears filled her eyes as she belatedly recollected Hal's instructions to keep well away from Justin. "I never meant to harm her," she whispered.

"Harm?" he ranted. "Harm? What would you know of the harm you inflicted, you worthless trollop?"

"You have no right to speak so to me!" she protested,

amazed at this unprovoked attack, for he'd avoided her ever since he'd arrived.

"Have I not?" he spat. "You forget I am your joint guardian. I can tell you of your errors. I can beat you if I will!"

She backed from him, recollecting Helen Sitwell's fate, and that he'd threatened her before. "Hal loves me," she whispered. "He'll protect me from you!"

"Hal loves you!" he gave a shout of bitter laughter. "Hal loves none but Hal! You imagine you are precious to him, do you?"

"I know I am, he's said so," she faltered.

"You silly, vain, ignorant little fool," he raged. "Hal Westwood is a philanderer, a whoremonger, he tells the same to all his women! Aye, even his poor, love-blinded wife. Don't you realise he promised to love and protect each in turn, that you are just one of many? What do you think took him to France, but the seeking out of another such as yourself to bring back with him? You should have asked his wife, or his father's wife. Oh aye, look shocked, she was his whore, too. That's what took him the length of France to find his bastard! Why do you think he was brought back so carefully, and is now in the nursery with his other children?"

She looked stunned. "I—I don't believe it!" she cried, tears falling down her cheeks, for suddenly, it all made sense.

"Don't you?" he sneered. "You ask his brothers and sisters, you ask his aunts, they'll all tell you the same story. Hal Westwood is a byword for all that is wrong with the world today. He looks perfect, but he's rotten. Rotten to the core!" His voice cracked on this and he turned away, his rage suddenly spent, as Bess, called by the sound of raised voice, entered.

"What is wrong? Oh, Justin! What have you done to Sophie now?" she cried, seeing how the girl sobbed.

"I've done nothing, but tell her the truth," he replied unpleasantly. "It's more what Hal has done! But don't take my word for it, Sophie, ask his sister, she'll not lie. Tell her, Bess, tell her whose child that is up there in the nursery! Tell her why Etienne will look like Hal, rather than Ned! Go on, explain away that little mystery for her and let her see what kind of man she thinks is perfect."

"Justin!" Bess cried in dismay. "Why do you do this? What good can it do either Sophie, or Hal?"

"What good?" he replied jubilantly, as the look of faint hope on Sophie's face was replaced by dull despair. "I'll tell you what good, it will give them both some of the sort of hell that my poor Libby endured. I'll kill that mindless adoration she has of him.It's my duty as her guardian to make her see clearly that Hal Westwood's not a perfect gentleman. I'll not have her living in a land of illusion like Libby. I'll force her eyes open, she'll see him for what he is, a worthless sham! And in that, they'll both be punished for what they did to my poor Libby!"

"You wicked fool!" cried Bess, incensed, as with a wail of despair, Sophie ran from the room. "Are you so intent on revenge you forget all else? What of our agreement yesterday? What of our marriage? Is that, too, to be smashed in this insane desire to destroy Hal? I've said I'll make a conscious effort to forget you disavowed our marriage and took a mistress, but you are wallowing in your desire to be revenged on Hal, who hasn't even broken his vows!"

"Not broken his vows? I've told you, I've just seen him rolling on a bed with that trollop!" he shouted. "His wife is not cold in her grave, and he's romping in a bed with his slut!"

"I was never cold in a grave when you took Helen Sitwell to her bed! Now she's dead and you wait until my brother rides off to assist in clearing you of a murder charge to drag up all this against him. Have you no sense of gratitude?"

"Gratitude?" he sneered. "I vow I am sick unto death of ever having to be grateful to you Westwoods!"

"Then I suggest you cut loose from us!" she cried, in a rage herself now. "If we are so insufferable, have nothing more to do with us! Go back to prison and fend for yourself!"

"I might well do so!" he shouted.

"Do it, but tell me nothing more about it!" she shrieked.

"What is this terrible commotion?" Aunt Margery stood in the door, outraged virtue personified. "Elizabeth, I am not aware of what is going forward in this room any more than I want to hear, but this noise will cease henceforth! This sort of commotion does not occur in a gentleman's house, however much it may be in vogue amongst the tradesmen of the town. Oblige me by going at once to some other place some distance from here, where there are no servants to hear you, if you must continue this conversation, and taking this person with you."

"I am her husband, madam!" Justin snapped.

"I am aware she bears that misfortune, but I see no need to discuss it," she replied majestically, and turned away, shutting the door on any reply.

Chapter Fourteen

There was a silence in Mistress Sitwell's parlour as all those present sat waiting for the man's reply. Hal had heard many men give evidence in the last few years since he'd been a Justice of the Peace, and he thought he could tell these days when someone was lying. To his mind, this man had done little else.

"So, Prescott," he said, as the man came to the end of another long, rambling excuse as to why he couldn't perform the tasks expected of him. "You are willing to remain here and look after the house until such time as some other arrangements can be made, I take it?"

"What will happen to the house, Sir Henry?" asked the cook, a respectable middle-aged woman from a well-known local family, as the manservant assented reluctantly.

"As to that, Mistress Sawsby, things are left very

awkwardly, I cannot say," he replied pleasantly. "By the terms of your mistress's will, everything, barring small legacies for Hannah Smith and Prescott, was left to Mr Danvers. Indeed, I believe you and John Goode, the groom, witnessed the will only a few hours before her death."

"That is so," said Prescott. "That is why I sent straight for the sheriff as soon as I saw Madam next morning! 'You mark my words,' I said to Hannah, I did, 'you mark my words that there lawyer will be behind all this!'"

"Yes, that lawyer, as you call him, is my brother-in-law," said Hal coldly.

"Indeed, I know he is, Sir Henry," he replied. "Don't everybody in Adamsholme know it? But I've seen you at the Petty Sessions, Sir Henry, you're not a man to wink at the truth. He were here all night, the same as he has been two, three times a week these past six months. He were her lover, right enough, for all that they tried to keep it quiet. I'm a light sleeper, I am, and I used to hear him leave most mornings at dawn, and that night it weren't no different!"

"Yet, I do believe, it was!" said Hal sharply. "For didn't they quarrel? Do you tell me they quarrelled constantly?"

"No, that they didn't," said the maid, Hannah Smith, pertly. "A mild-mannered man, Mr Danvers, too mild, to my way of thinking, to make a good lover. But you'd know more about that than me, Sir Henry!"

Hal cast her a reproving look. "You can vouch for the fact they didn't quarrel?" he said sharply.

"Not until that night," she replied, glad to have gained his attention. "He came, same as usual, at five o'clock. Mistress Sawsby served dinner, which took a good three hours. They removed to the parlour when John Goode and Mrs Sawsby were summoned to witness the will. Then, that being done, Mr Danvers put the papers away in his wallet he always carried. My mistress called for some brandy wine to celebrate, and we left them discussing the bottle."

"I fetched a bottle of the late master's finest cognac from the cellar, sir," said the manservant, nodding.

"Your mistress habitually drank brandy wine?" asked Hal quickly.

"No, no, indeed not, sir," she said hastily.

"And did Mr Danvers drink this also?" he continued.

"He drank his glass, sir," she said doubtfully. "Then they retired, as was their custom, to—to Madam's boudoir."

"Taking the wine with them?" asked Hal, trying not to feel as if he were prying, keeping his eyes on his notes, for the girl's scrutiny was, he found, trying.

"I believe so, sir," she said, casting him a look from beneath her lashes. "Usually, I never disturbed my mistress until after dawn the next morning on those occasions, but that night, at about half past ten, or eleven o'clock, a quarrel broke out. Suddenly, there was shouting and screaming, most terrible screaming, and I ran to her chamber, but didn't dare go in. I heard Mr Danvers say, in a voice like I'd never heard before, that he could kill her for that. Then there was sobbing and screaming again, and what sounded like a thwack."

"I'd joined her by this point, Sir Henry," said Prescott. "And I heard the sound of blows. So I opened the door a crack, in time to see Mr Danvers throw my mistress aside and come rushing for the door, looking fit to kill—"

"We hastily hid," interrupted the maid. "For we were afraid of him, he looked like a man possessed, his face all bloody. He pushed past us and clattered down the stairs, my mistress coming after him in her nightgown, her hair all down her back, weeping as if her life were over, begging him to come back. She caught his sleeve, but he shook her off and she overbalanced, falling down the stairs a little way after him. He paid her no heed, but set off through the door and up the lane as if all the hounds in Hell were after him."

"Your mistress was harmed?" asked Hal quickly.

"She turned her ankle, sir, and had a bruised face, but she were that distressed, anyway, that we helped her back to bed and gave her a few drops of laudanum she kept for emergencies," said the manservant. "Thinking, combined with the brandy, she'd sleep until morning. Then, wearied out, we both retired to our beds."

"About an hour later, it were close on midnight, sir, I heard her moving about in her chamber, then she went down to the door and let Mr Danvers back in. I assumed he'd walked off his ill-temper and returned to be reconciled. They went back up to her chamber, and I heard them talking and laughing together for the next hour or more."

"But when Hannah went to call her mistress next morning, she'd been smothered, sir, by her own pillow," said the manservant, shaking his head. "And him leaving at dawn, same as ever."

"But you heard no continuation of the quarrel?" said Hal, frowning, determined to be clear on this point.

"No, as I say, they were reconciled, laughing and talking, they were, just like old friends with no bad blood between them," she repeated.

"And how did you know it was Mr Danvers that Mistress Sitwell let back in?" he asked. "Did you see him?"

"No, sir, but who else could it be at that time of night?" she replied blankly.

"I don't know, you tell me," he replied. "What other visitors did she have? I doubt any escaped scrutiny."

She bridled a little at that. "Well, I don't know, to be sure!" she said, casting the butler a doubtful look. "I don't recall any called on her but Mr Danvers."

"What, none from the old days in London?" he asked. "You were with her in Langley Court in London, weren't you?"

"Only for a few weeks, sir," she said, and he knew at once he'd not get another word from her, for her mouth closed tight like a clam.

"None, then?" he asked, as if it didn't matter. "Oh well, I'll just have to try some other links. In the meantime, you shall stay here, Prescott, you are provided for in her legacy, as are you, Hannah. But Mistress Sawsby, you should think of seeking another employer, indeed, you all should."

Mistress Sawsby's face took on a look of resignation. "Yes, sir," she said. "'Tis Chawcester Mop next Friday."

"So it is," he agreed. "However, Hannah, if you are willing, I could offer you employment in my household. I have recently acquired the wardship of two young women and neither has a maid. I think you might be suitable possibly for both, or maybe, for just one. 'Tis a matter which needs discussing, naturally you'll want to think on it, too, so if you do wish to take up the position, present yourself to Westwood Hall at any time over the next day or so, or if you can come to a decision at once, meet me at The Adam and Eve in one hour. I have business to attend to, but should be ready to leave Adamsholme at that time. In the meantime, I thank you all for your assistance and I'll bid you good day."

"Well, he's a cool one," said the cook presently, when Hal had been seen on his way by Prescott. "Will you go to his place, Hannah?"

"I might do worse," she replied. "I doubt the legacy will last me long."

"I think he'd be a hard master to work for," said the woman. "Hard, but fair, provided you didn't try no tricks on him."

"He surely is a pretty man," she countered wistfully,

not truly listening.

"Handsome is as handsome does," said the cook, shaking her head over the folly of modern youth.

"That's a phrase usually employed by the downright plain," retorted the maid. "I reckon I could get close to him if I put my mind to it."

"They do say he do hold his head up high," said the cook sagely. "And that for all that, he's a wicked one for the women. You take care, Hannah, those that play with fire get burnt."

"Pooh!" replied the girl. "Most just don't know how to play."

Sophie, meanwhile, had returned to her chamber to sob into her pillow. So recently, she'd been laughing, had been kissed with this same pillow between them, and now her dreams were shattered about her. She dimly remembered Eunice Latham talking with Mistress Palmer of her disapproval of Hal Westwood. How she'd implied he was not the best husband to Libby. How their heads had gone together over a whispered conversation which, as she'd not known either of the people, had meant little to her. She remembered, too, the scandal of her own rescue from Giles Durward's hands, how all Chawcester had buzzed about her and the Justice being together all night in a remote farmhouse with naught but a dead body for company. How the worst had been assumed by almost everyone, it seemed. How easily, without a protest, even his closest family accepted he had been the father of her cushion, only Libby maintaining faith in him.

It must be as Justin said, they must all know what he was like and, unable to change him, had become used to his behaviour, but to Sophie, it was a terrible shock.

Had she been a little fool, believing in fairy tales, in castles in the air and happy ever after, or was it that people saw things differently? To her, the love she and Hal had was wonderful, magical, and set apart from everyday things, almost as if when they were together, they inhabited a secret land of their own, where none could reach or intrude, where they were safe from the outside world as long as they believed in each other.

Now Justin had come trampling through the gossamer of their castle in Spain like a marauder, destroying all he touched, and she had never felt so bereft in all her life. Without Hal and her own secret place, she had nothing, and the world became a howling wilderness without aim or purpose.

Dimly, she perceived this was Justin's intention, his idea to make life a hell for them both as punishment, but even as she declared to herself she'd not let him win, she knew he spoke the truth. Hal had had other women, he wasn't the faithful type. She knew that to her cost, for hadn't he betrayed Libby with her, if not in deed, then most certainly in his heart, which was by far the greater sin.

The thought that all their secrets, all their intimacy, everything they shared, he had shared previously with another, possibly shared even now with Cordelia Sandys, was bitter gall to her. True, he'd told her she was special, that what he felt for her had overwhelmed him, but she was aware of her own ignorance, probably every libertine talked like that to every conquest.

In a frenzy of grief and despair, she paced the room. This not knowing was worse than anything. If it was so and he was false, at least she knew where she stood. If he didn't love her, or saw her as only one of many…but here her reasoning gave out. She washed her face carefully and tidied her hair. She'd seek out Cordelia, she'd be able to discover something from her.

She found Cordelia, as she knew she would, with her books and some globes in the Jericho parlour, which Sophie had imagined was purely Hal's, but it now seemed, Cordelia had the license to use at will. Since her arrival, Cordelia had been most diligent in applying herself to her studies. Indeed, after her interview with Aunt Margery, she'd seemed intent on hiding away, only appearing at meal times.

Chapter Fifteen

Cordelia smiled doubtfully as Sophie looked about the door, aware, as she had been from the very first, of the other girl's animosity.

"Busy reading again?" observed Sophie, eyeing her covertly and wondering how it was, although she'd shed her habit, the order of sanctity still seemed to hang about her. She wasn't a beauty as such. Brown of hair and eye, with a sallow complexion, she couldn't hope to compete with Sophie's golden curls and pink and white porcelain perfection, yet there was something in her self-contained air, some inner peace in her tentative smile, which appealed to almost everyone immediately. Make her, within the few hours she'd been there, accepted by the family. Most certainly, Hal had already commended her quiet manners and quick intelligence, and Aunt Kate's ready sympathy had been stirred by her plight, whilst Jane and Bess had both been impressed by her readiness to adapt to each situation. Even Aunt Margery, who had initially been inclined to view her Papist loyalties with the sort of horror reserved for horns and cloven feet, had been quite won over by her air of good breeding. So that she'd quickly been instituted as a pet, whilst Margery pursued the girl's ancestry with a determined tenacity through the labyrinth of her numerous acquaintances.

"Yes," replied Cordelia politely. All her replies were the same, well-mannered, short, and without any elaboration.

"Aren't you fatigued by all these books?" asked Sophie impatiently. She needed to get her to talk, she decided, she'd never do that unless she parted her from a book. "Wouldn't you care to take some air? We could walk in the garden, or better still, ride. Do you ride?"

She smiled again. "I used to go on the back of the old donkey occasionally when we took the laundry to the washerwoman," she replied. "But I don't think that was truly riding."

"I could teach you," said Sophie, thinking how she'd like to escape the confines of the house.

"How very kind of you to offer," replied the girl with

the same polite air.

"'Tis a necessary accomplishment for any gentle-woman," said Sophie.

Cordelia smiled again. "More so than this?" she asked, indicating the books and globes on the table.

Sophie sighed. "I don't see the need to know where all these countries are," she observed. "I don't intend to visit any of them."

"No more did I," said Cordelia. "But I've already been to France, and Sir Henry and Doctor Douay have also been to the Low Countries and the Rhineland."

"My guardian fought in Scotland and Ireland in the war," retorted Sophie, "but he said foreign travel never did him any good."

Cordelia smiled again and returned her eyes to her book. "Well, we are commanded to study the globes at all events."

Sophie sniffed. Hal had, indeed, instructed her to study, but this information she was seeking was by far more important to her. "I don't see why," she muttered rebelliously. "Just because Hal has taken it into his head to say we must. It is just so that he doesn't have to bother with us."

Cordelia cast her a reproving look. "Sir Henry has

been so very good to me that I am greatly obliged to him," the girl said pleasantly. "There is nothing I would not do for him. If he wanted me to study Greek and Hebrew, I would not say nay."

"Well I would! And do!" snapped Sophie impatiently.

"'Tis as well, then, you weren't at the convent, or you'd have spent best part of your life on your knees in the chapel," observed Cordelia.

Sophie shuddered. "That must have been dreadful."

"Dreadful?" The girl smiled. "No, indeed, I knew no other life, and the sisters were all very good and kind to me. Exceptionally good and kind, when I remember how they fed and housed me for sixteen years."

"Did your father never return for you?" asked Sophie anxiously. "Were you just abandoned?"

"Yes, but not of malice," sighed the girl. "He was killed, you see, at the Battle of Worcester."

"My father died many years ago," said Sophie. "And my mother, like yours, at my birth. Hal says we motherless children have difficulty in loving."

"Does he? I had not observed so," she replied quietly. "When did your father die? Did you know him?"

"Oh, yes," Sophie smiled fleetingly. "I was quite eight

years old. He was a preacher, you know. My guardian, Uncle Edmund, that is, my guardian before Hal, he said he was never quite right in his head after my mother died. She was a distant cousin of his and my father left me with Uncle Edmund and his sister Hannah since my childhood, when he went off preaching. It was something he learned in the army, I do believe."

"He was a Puritan, then?" asked Cordelia, rather shocked.

"I don't know that he belonged to any particular sect," she sighed, "but he certainly wasn't for the Catholic Church."

"And you?" asked the girl anxiously.

"I have been brought up in the religion of the country. Uncle Edmund said we common folk had to sway with the breeze. He used to worship at the Abbey until it was closed, then he listened to various preachers, then we went back to the Abbey once it was opened again."

"I have been brought up a Catholic, as my father wished," said Cordelia. "The nuns wished me to take the veil, but the Abbess knew I had no vocation."

"Nor any dowry," murmured Sophie.

"Yes," agreed Cordelia. "I was occasionally reproached for that, but Sir Henry made them a handsome present for mine and Etienne's visit, so they were happy to let us go."

"Were you not afraid?" asked Sophie. "To be let into the charge of a stranger?"

Cordelia considered the question. "I know he'd come seeking a baby, and I guessed it was Etienne, from something his mother had said—"

"You knew the child's mother?" cried Sophie. "Who was she? What was she like?"

"Lady Westwood? Sir Henry's stepmother?" replied Cordelia. "She was very beautiful."

"Lady Westwood, Hal's stepmother, you mean Jacqueline?" cried Sophie quickly, as she recollected Justin's words.

"Yes, I do believe she was called Jacqueline by the Abbess," agreed Cordelia. "She was either a child of the Abbey, as I was, or perhaps a distant relation of the Abbess. I cannot say which, but she was received as one known to them. She was dying, of course, but even so, it was more an act of obligation than charity. As if they felt they owed her something to take in one who, it appeared, had the plague, and care for her and her child."

"Did she have the plague?" asked Sophie in awe.

"Sir Henry's father died of it in Auch, they say."

"The infirmiran said not," sighed Cordelia, "but as she died anyway, 'tis difficult to tell. Certainly, none of us took it from her, and Etienne survived."

"How old is he?" asked Sophie curiously.

"Oh, did you not know? He was born there on St Stephen's day, hence Etienne. She was in the last stage of labour when she arrived and gave birth at dawn the following morning. Sister Marie Claire was for calling him Noel, but Mamére would not have it. He was born on the feast of Stephen, and therefore Stephen he must be."

"Will Hal call him Stephen?" asked Sophie. "He seldom speaks of him."

Cordelia shook her head. "I do not know. I was with him when Sir Henry came to find him. He stood and looked into the crib for quite some while, his face grim, so that the Abbess grew concerned. 'Is this not the child you were expecting, Sir Henry?' she asked."

"And what did he reply?" asked Sophie, in some trepidation.

"That he greatly feared it was," said Cordelia simply.

"Feared?" echoed Sophie in dismay.

"Yes," said Cordelia. "So then the Abbess asked if he

was not the child of his father, and Sir Henry replied that the child was indeed the child of his father, and turned away abruptly, in spite of Etienne laughing up at him and holding out his arms to him. But then I am told men have difficulty expressing their affections to children, so perhaps he is like that and cannot easily come to a child's level."

Sophie, her mind full of how Hal had cradled Harry in his arms and told him rhyme after rhyme when he first arrived, realised that he hadn't indeed visited the children quite so often since Philippe Douay's return, and quickly sought and found excuse for it. "Sir Henry is but recently widowed," she said defensively. "His grief for his wife holds him aloof from the children, it would seem."

"He didn't know his wife was dead at that time," said Cordelia, nodding her understanding. "He came on several occasions after that to talk with the Abbess and indeed, I had been summoned, and we were discussing my removal to England to seek my relations there, when Doctor Douay came seeking him with the news of his wife's illness."

"He was shocked?" asked Sophie, feeling she shouldn't ask, but desperate to know.

"Stunned," said Cordelia. "He sat silent and still for so long that Doctor Douay shook him, thinking him gone into a trance. 'Hal, Hal!' he said, 'Did you not hear me?' 'Yes,' he replied, 'I heard you. I heard your step on the stair, your voice in the hall, I knew you brought my punishment.'"

"Punishment?" repeated Sophie slowly.

"Mamére chided him at that, saying it wasn't for him to say, and to hurry home to his wife, all would be well. But he knew, he said, that she would be dead. 'The innocent must always suffer for the guilty,' he said, and got up and left, there and then. Doctor Douay concluded the negotiations for mine and Etienne's departure the following day."

Sophie looked bewildered by all this. "So that's why he was gone for so long, most surely, to find his stepmother's grave."

"Yes, and the child. Doctor Douay told me that Sir Henry joined him in France at the end of June and assisted him to clear up a little personal matter for a few weeks."

"Philippe Douay had been accused of murder as a young man, just as he finished his apprenticeship to an apothecary," said Sophie, not really concentrating on what she was saying, but trying to correlate all she'd heard to make sense of this gossip. Was Jacqueline, his father's wife, truly the mother of his bastard child? Was Hal capable of such culmany? 'You don't know me,' he'd said, is this what he'd meant? Her head felt as if it must burst with unanswered questions as she listened to Cordelia with an air of great calmness. "Uncle Edmund knew something of the story, that's why he left France and came to England and studied as a physician, it is his dual knowledge which makes him so good a doctor."

Cordelia nodded. "I see, well, he said his father had always supported him, sending him money when he was studying, and it seemed back in the summer, he was dying, so Philippe wanted to go to see him, and in talking to Sir Henry of it, he became convinced Doctor Douay had been wrongly accused."

"When Hal was injured last summer, Philippe Douay attended him every day and as he got better, they spent hours talking together," agreed Sophie, her thoughts going back to that time and recollecting with a sense of shock how the gossip had escalated about them both in a manner she'd found surprising.

"Indeed, I expect they did, for they are fast friends, it

would seem, and Doctor Douay is very proud to own himself such."

"So, after he'd helped Philippe Douay, he then went on to find his father, Sir Francis's grave?" asked Sophie.

"So Doctor Douay said. He left Doctor Douay in attendance on his dying father and went in search of his own father's last resting place."

"And he found him?" asked Sophie, frowning.

"It would appear. Although, there was a question of some doubt, it seemed, to Sir Henry, but I am repeating hearsay. What he didn't find, as he plainly expected to, was the grave of his father's wife and baby."

"Yes, I gather from what has been said, that they'd received news back in the early spring that both had died of the plague in Auch, in France."

"As indeed Sir Francis did, only the report of his wife dying was erroneous. However, it seems the whole town was stricken by a fever and more than half of the inhabitants perished. So I suppose one cannot expect the authorities to be entirely accurate on all counts."

"But how did Hal trace his stepmother to your Abbey?" asked Sophie.

"That I do not know, merely that he arrived one day at the gate asking if we had an English child left with us. Which was why my name was mentioned. Once Sir Henry knew I'd been abandoned, too, he insisted, as I didn't want to take the veil, in restoring me to my home and, if possible, kin."

"Do you think he'll find any?" asked Sophie curiously.

"I think if he could find a tiny baby boy by travelling the length of France, any kin I have will soon be tracked down."

"You admire him?" asked Sophie bluntly.

"So good a gentleman, who could not?" she replied. "I am greatly obliged to him for his kindness, and am his to command."

Sophie's eyes narrowed. The girl seemed an entire innocent, but she wasn't sure. "What do you mean?" she asked bluntly.

Cordelia looked up again, her eyes blank. "Why, that I am so very grateful to Sir Henry for rescuing me from a difficult situation, that there is nothing I would not do."

Sophie digested this statement in silence, feeling somehow she was making little progress. This girl was rather like a plaster saint enclosed behind glass, there was no getting at her. "Sir Henry makes it his practice to rescue pretty young women!" she announced provocatively.

Cordelia smiled in a faintly puzzled way. "He must have been in error when he helped me, then," she remarked modestly.

"But you are quite pretty," said Sophie, subjecting her to an appraising look. "And you are exactly the right age." Then, as the other smiled in her aloof manner and shook her head, Sophie added quickly: "What if Sir Hen…Hal asked you to do something, something truly wicked?"

Cordelia frowned, still puzzled. "He would not," she observed simply. "He is a gentleman."

"That's not what Justin Danvers says!" cried Sophie, allowing her anxiety to override her judgement. "He says Sir Henry has many women, and that Stephen is his bastard!"

Cordelia drew back from her, looking amazed. "I know nothing of Sir Henry's affairs," she said. "Nor would I presume to judge them. Mr Danvers, you say? Is that not the gentleman who stands accused of murder? The man Sir Henry is putting forward all his best efforts to see him fairly brought to trial? The husband of his poor, ill-treated sister? I do not think I'd refine too much on what that gentleman claims. I daresay anxiety has turned his mind."

"You are not Sir Henry's mistress, then, as Justin Danvers claims?" said Sophie, unable to think of any other way of phrasing the question.

Cordelia's amazement deepened to astonishment, and a deep blush spread from her modest neckline to her cheek. "Mistress Redcroft!" she protested. "How could you ask such an indelicate question? How can you so impugn Sir Henry's reputation?"

"Oh, I've already ruined that, didn't you know?" she cried, blushing in turn at the other's scandalised reaction. "I made them all believe, including his wife, that I carried his child."

Shock showed on the girl's face, and for the first time she was shaken out of her calm complacency. "Not deliberately?" she said, horrified.

"Not at first!" replied Sophie defiantly. "But then, when I saw they all thought the worst, I thought I'd give them something to whisper about!"

"One can comprehend your temptation, and your pain, and I am sorry for it," she said with compassion. "But one must always weigh every action. Did you not realise how it would harm Sir Henry?"

"No," she replied honestly. "I only knew I loved him more than anything else on earth." A wistful look replaced Cordelia's smile. "That is understandable, Sir Henry is an impressive figure."

"No he is not!" cried Sophie impatiently. "He's irritable and peremptory, rude and demanding!"

"Poor man! He has much to irk him," agreed Cordelia with a sigh. "Yet, so good, so kind!"

"He's not good and kind, you make him sound remote, he's, he's a darling!" declared Sophie, tears spilling over and running down her cheeks as she realised the truth that, come what may, she still loved him.

"I am not on such terms of acquaintance with him as you are," said Cordelia. "I have only met him recently, and not been in his company more than half a dozen times."

"I knew I loved him within an hour of meeting him," said Sophie.

"Was he not then a married man?" asked the girl, shocked again.

"Yes," sighed Sophie, "but I did not intend for it to happen, it just did."

"I always find it best not to allow such things to occur," remarked Cordelia thoughtfully.

Sophie cast her a scornful look. "Not allow them to occur?" she repeated. "You speak as if you can control fate. You are no longer in a nunnery, you know. There is no protection in the outside world."

"So I observe," she replied, adding, as if compelled: "What made you think I was Sir Henry's miss—I had a close association with Sir Henry?"

"Justin Danvers told me so," repeated Sophie.

"Mr Danvers," she said. "How strange that he should so injure my name and Sir Henry's. He can hardly know me, and surely he must owe Sir Henry much, yet I suppose it is possible with the worry he has. I gather he is at odds with his wife, too, that such may—"

"His sister was Hal's wife," explained Sophie. "He has taken it into his head that Hal was a faithless husband and accuses every female Hal comes into contact with."

"Oh," her face cleared. "Oh, now I understand, poor man, I shall pray for his grief."

"Pray for him—" began Sophie, incensed by this, but stopped, as the door opened to admit Aunt Kate.

Chapter Sixteen

"Sophie," Aunt Kate said evenly. "I never expected to find you here at your books. No matter, it is you I seek. A Master Adam Blackwell has come calling and begs you will receive him."

"Adam?" cried Sophie, diverted. "Oh how wonderful! He has come at last, like he promised."

Aunt Kate smiled a little at this welcome reaction. "I'll send him here to you, shall I? I'm sure Cordelia won't mind playing chaperone for a short while." She retraced her steps to the door and called to the visitor, smiling benignly as he entered and bowed punctiliously over Sophie's hand.

"Adam, you've changed!" Sophie cried in surprise, for gone was his lackadaisical manner and ill-kempt appearance, and in his place stood an elegant gentleman.

"Have I, Mistress Redcroft?" he replied politely. "If it

meets with your approval, I am satisfied."

She laughed. "Oh, do call me Sophie like you used to in the old days! Cordelia, pray meet a friend of mine from Chawcester, Mr Adam Blackwell. Adam, Cordelia Sandys."

Adam bowed again to the young woman, who left her books to curtsey, her dark eyes widening in wonder and a faint flush staining her cheek.

"Cordelia is Sir Henry's ward too, Mr Blackwell," Aunt Kate was explaining.

"And Adam is the innkeeper in Chawcester—" began Sophie.

"Not any more, I'm not, Mistress Sophie," he replied, declining a mug of ale from Aunt Kate, who left the three alone. "No, I sold out to my stepmother and her new husband."

"Mistress Blackwell has remarried?" cried Sophie in amazement, suddenly realizing how much she missed him and glad to put aside her anxieties with regard to Hal. "Oh, Adam, tell me everything that has been happening in Chawcester. It is a perfect age since I was last there. Oh, how I have missed everyone!"

Adam smiled. "I'll gladly tell you everything, Mistress Sophie," he replied. "As long as I don't bore you and the young lady."

"If Cordelia is bored, she'll go back to her books, and as long as you talk about dear Chawcester, I'll never be bored. Mistress Palmer writes, but never any gossip, so I know, for example, you have a new mayor, that Cannon Helithwaite has had inflammation of the lungs, and that there is serious rot in one of the Abbey doors. But not how poor Sally Rose does with her children, nor whether dear Uncle Edmund is missed, and how you've been. Do, do tell me everything, Adam!"

He laughed and took the seat she indicated. "Sally Rose is doing very well. How else could it have been, with you setting her up in business as a dressmaker and getting Kat Snow to help her, whilst her mother looks after the babies. My stepmother says she's never seen Sally look so well, and that for fit and fashion-sense, you'll not find finer than Sally Rose this side of Oxford."

"Oh, I am so glad it has gone well," exclaimed Sophie. "I did have a scrap of a torn note from Sally at Michaelmas, saying that she couldn't take on any more ladies, and that all the children were well. But I was afraid I'd not been able to lend her enough money, for Mr Danvers wouldn't advance me any of my capital. So,

I had to use my allowance, and that was barely enough to keep them all going, what with the cost of materials and food, and the like."

"How did you manage without an allowance?" asked Adam, frowning. "Was it not difficult?"

"Yes, very," she replied frankly. "Especially coming here, where none know me. The servants all thought me very parsimonious. I couldn't give them any presents or payment, and me, reputedly an heiress! So, of course, my laundry was left until last, and I had terrible trouble with my hair." She made a comical face, but her lips trembled, too, as she recollected that time. "Although, in the light of everything else that was going on, it didn't greatly matter."

"I heard about Lady Westwood," he replied, looking serious. "'Tis said the scandal and gossip killed her."

"No," sighed Sophie. "I did that."

"You, Sophie!" he exclaimed. "I can't believe that."

"'Tis what many say, however," she replied. "I behaved very badly, Adam. You see, I was so miserably unhappy, that nothing seemed to matter."

"You've been having a grim time of it," he said, nodding. "But never mind, the worst must be over now?"

"Yes, oh yes," she replied quickly, although tears

glinted on the end of her long lashes. "But tell me more about your stepmother. Has Mistress Blackwell truly remarried? Why, this will be her third husband!"

"Yes," he agreed, smiling. "But this one is truly for the best. She told me she married her first husband to get a decent home, her second to keep it, and her third to enjoy it. That's why she bought me out, she said I reminded her too much of my father, and that made her feel guilty, so would I please take myself off and do something useful!"

Sophie laughed heartily. "Oh, I can imagine her saying it, too. Dear Mistress Blackwell. I must send her a wedding present."

"She'd like that," he replied. "She is forever saying how she misses the sight of your sweet face." He sighed. "It was your leaving that made her consider James Wooley's offer."

"James Wooley? No!" exclaimed Sophie. "She's never married James Wooley! Why, he must be—"

"Half her age? Yes," he agreed with a grin.

"Surely," said Sophie with a gasp. "Doesn't he—"

"Drink? Oh, aye, he did, but that was before he took fright from Sam Rose's end. He's been sober ever since we found Sam drowned in the barrel of ale."

"Good heavens," she exclaimed again. "Who'd have thought it?"

"Aye, those few weeks last summer have changed Chawcester forever," he said reflectively. "It isn't the same place anymore."

"Well, I suppose with so many being killed," she said, her face suddenly white as she recollected the incidents.

"Precisely," he agreed. "Which is what decided me to leave, too."

"You've left Chawcester?" she said, surprised. "I'd have thought you'd have bought land locally."

"No, my stepmother said there was no sense in that," he said simply. "She said it only kept the window open, living so close to Elmley Park. But I had to make a fresh start, and, in truth, once I came to know Guy Armstrong and his wife, I realized she was right. Guy was just the same as me, in exactly the same position, but that he managed to get out of it and get rich enough to buy Elmley Park. To dream of buying it back when he is doing so well is foolish." He smiled faintly. "Guy suggests I get it back by an alliance. He says I am to find me a bride and get a daughter to wed his son, that way, all the old wounds will be healed."

Sophie laughed. "He told me that was the answer to your problem when I was staying with him recently," she admitted. "But tell me more about your land. Where is it? What is it, a farm?"

Adam looked disappointed, for she had sidestepped the obvious question, and he guessed that Guy's robust suggestion that she be his bride, thus helping them all out, had been put to her, too. "It's at Birch Cross," he replied evenly. "On the east side of Tadham Wood. The Old Manor house and the farm there. It's in pretty run-down state, but with hard work, I can bring the land round, I'm sure. The house, of course, is pretty old—"

"Yes, very old. I recollect Ned Westwood exclaiming over the wanton waste of such a lovely old place when that young man finally ruined himself. What was his name?"

"Francis Findlesham," he said. "His father lost the property fighting for the King, Frank gets it back, and is said to have promptly gambled it away in a game of Hazard."

"Dear me, how dreadful," she said. "His father must be turning in his grave."

"Aye, and Frank took to the road, so they say, to escape his creditors."

"Took to the road!" she cried. "You mean he's a foot-pad?"

"A highwayman, so they say," he said, smiling a little as Cordelia's head came up from a book in surprise. She met his twinkling eyes and smiled in return, a faint blush spreading up her cheeks.

"Oh, Cordelia, has that caught your attention at last?" Sophie teased. "I was beginning to think you made of stone to hear such amazing events without turning a hair."

Cordelia came to join them in response to Sophie's outstretched hand, as if drawn by an invisible thread. "I'm sorry," she said quietly, "but I have no knowledge of these people, you see, so I cannot enter into your feelings."

"But you've no knowledge of any people except your nuns," returned Sophie, keeping a grasp on her hand. "I know you've always been forced to sit on the edge of life, but if you don't plunge in, Cordelia, you'll never get any closer."

She nodded in agreement. "What you say is true, Sophie, but everything seems to happen at such a furious rate, and I am frightened of drowning."

"I am sure your new friends, Mistress Sandys, will

be at hand to keep you afloat," said Adam, his glance admiring.

"Of course we will," said Sophie. "I promise you, it will get better very soon, and I'll be there to help you if you get into any difficulties."

"Thank you," she said, squeezing her hand in reply. "You are very kind, but then I think I knew that. Will you tell me more about—Sally Rose, was it?"

"Oh, she was but the poor, unfortunate wife of the baker of Chawcester. He was a drunken fool, and he fell foul of that dreadful man, Durward. I'll tell you the whole sorry tale sometime, but we won't bore Adam with it now."

"'Tis not a boring tale, Mistress Sophie," he protested. "But one that truly illustrates your goodness of heart—"

"Tell me, Adam," Sophie interrupted quickly. "Have you taken possession of your house? What is it called?"

"The Old Manor Farm," he replied. "I was wondering, Mistress Sophie, if you'd ride across one day and take a look at it. I'd be greatly honoured if you would."

"Well, yes, I will do so, if I may, Adam, although I will have to beg permission first. It can't be many miles from here, can it? For Ned Westwood wanted to buy it when it came up for sale, but Sir Henry, still being abroad, meant he couldn't raise the money in time."

"For which, I am most thankful," said Adam. "I didn't need another competing for it. It took every penny I had to purchase it. I'll have to wait some years before I can begin improving it. The house is respectable, if not very modern, and not at all elegant like this," he added, suddenly downcast, as if comparing the two.

"Westwood is incredibly fine," said Sophie, with sympathy. "When I first came here, I felt as if I should be wearing my bettermost dress and company manners every day."

"And don't you?" he asked, for it seemed to him she dressed differently and was more assured in her manners.

"Well, I supposed I don't wear my old puce gown now, unless I am doing my laundry," she admitted reflectively.

"Doing your laundry?" he laughed. "With a house full of servants?"

"Great houses don't work quite like that," she said. "It's much more like a town than you'd think, only with everyone living under the same roof. And, like Chawcester, our mayor hasn't been here, so lots of petty fighting broke out, however, now Sir Henry has returned, I am sure everything will right itself."

As she said the words, a wave of misery spread over her at the recollection of Justin's jibes. True, he may have been lying, as he certainly was about Cordelia. But she had the dreadful feeling he wasn't, that everything else was true, and that she was a fool to put her trust in Hal Westwood.

"And I shall certainly ask leave of Sir Henry that I might visit you as soon as he returns," she continued, her voice sounding desperate, even to her own ears. Yes, that might shake Hal up a bit, make him think Adam a rival for her affections. But, then, on the other hand, Hal might be glad to be done with her, then might begin to seduce Cordelia. "And I'll ask that Cordelia come with me," she added defiantly. "So that Mistress Kingscott cannot accuse me of impropriety."

"I should like that," said Cordelia, "but recollect, Sophie, I do not ride well."

"Nay, Mistress Sophie," Adam firmly interrupted her assurance to Cordelia that to try was the best way to learn. "Don't be in such a great hurry. If Mistress Sandys will honour my home with a visit, I'll come and escort you both. And she can ride pillion with me, that way, she'll be entirely safe."

Cordelia turned very pink at the thought of such close contact with this giant of a man. But, the arrival of Aunt Kate closed the matter, for she brought an invitation for Adam to sup with them. Adam needed no second bidding, and they barely had time to sit down before Hal joined them, fresh from his trip into Adamsholme.

Chapter Seventeen

Everyone was already seated and grace had been said before Hal had time to take stock and look about the table. Something was definitely amiss, he decided at once. Sophie had refused to meet his eyes since his return from town. She was indeed chattering to that fool Adam Blackwell with a determination which made his head ache, whilst he sat by with a singularly foolish smile on his face and Cordelia Sandys watched all with an aloof air.

"I've brought the wench of Mistress Sitwell back with me, Aunt Kate," he said, raising his voice slightly. "It would appear Sophie was never given a maidservant, and now there is Cordelia too, so I've hired her to wait on them both."

"Very well, Hal," said Aunt Kate. "I don't know why Sophie was never allocated a maid, I know Justin was…"

she stopped, recollecting that Justin was at the table.

"Justin said she'd only spend all her time plotting and gossiping with the girl," supplied Aunt Margery. "Which she most probably will. You'll have to learn, Sophia, how to comport yourself with servants, it doesn't do to get over-familiar, or they soon take advantage of one."

"Yet, too great a height doesn't make for loyalty, ma'am," said Hal, flashing Sophie a smile and feeling a little hurt and bewildered as she quickly looked away.

"It wasn't so much that I feared she'd spend her day gossiping, more that I knew she'd use her to cause Libby trouble," remarked Justin. "Libby already had one enemy in her midst to harm her, she didn't need another! In the event, Sophie didn't need assistance, she never will, she'll always get what she wants. You heed my words, all of you sitting here! Sophia Redcroft will marry Hal regardless of your feelings and my protests, regardless of his doubts and shame, she'll marry him and ruin him!"

"What is this maidservant's name, Hal?" asked Aunt Kate into the deadly silence this outburst engendered.

"Hannah Smith, ma'am," he replied, thankful for the question to relieve his chagrin and embarrassment.

"I hope she may be suitable. She appeared a little pert, but I think—"

"That's right, ignore my bad manners!" cried Justin. "Pretend I don't exist!"

"If only one could," sighed Aunt Margery.

"I tell you this," he snarled, rounding on her. "You Westwoods think you are so safe, so—"

"Justin!" Bess dropped the name like a pebble into the boiling pool of his wrath, and although it sank, the wrath subsided, too.

He scraped back his chair. "I beg pardon, my presence is plainly not required, I'll remove myself from Westwood sight."

Bess sighed as she, too, got up from the table. "Pray excuse me, and Justin," she added as the door slammed behind him. "The wound is yet fresh, and there is much here to irk him."

"Elizabeth is a saint," declared Aunt Margery. "I knew she'd rue the day she took that underbred lawyer to husband, but she bears it all with such patience and good humour!"

"I thought it was agreed amongst us, ma'am," said Hal, addressing her. "That we'd refrain from speaking of the many problems that lie between us? It is painful for many of us at this table, but the effort must be made."

"The trouble with that excellent idea, Hal, is that it leaves so few avenues for discussion. One cannot speak of murder, nor disloyalty. Or foolish love affairs, of France, of your father, of a hundred like topics! All roads seem to lead to Rome, as they say," she retorted.

"One may speak of the love of God," suggested Cordelia. "That can never go amiss."

Aunt Margery drew back her chin to show her deep offence. "I do believe, young lady, I'd be termed a god-fearing woman, but you must understand that one cannot be forever dragging His name into everyday things! 'Keep religion away from the table once grace is over,' my father used to say, or we'll all ruin our digestion."

"Indeed, ma'am," replied Hal. "But religion was not a settled question in the time of my respected grand-father. Today it is different, and if Cordelia wishes to speak of her beliefs, I don't think it will harm any of us to hear it."

"It may well harm her chances of a good marriage, if she combines sermons with dinners," retorted Aunt Margery.

"Must one's only thought be of a good marriage?" cried Sophie impatiently. "Perhaps Cordelia doesn't want a good marriage."

"It is every female's duty to make a good match," replied Aunt Margery. "What else were women put on this earth for, but to provide heirs for their husbands and solace for their hours of ease?"

Hal hid a smile at Sophie's look of abject horror and hastily interrupted. "How right you are, Aunt, so the Bible teaches us, and if any man is lucky enough to get an intelligent helpmeet as well, praise be. Philippe, tell me, how goes your search for a house?"

"Well, Hal, at least I hope so," he replied. "For it is my intention to buy the house at Adamsholme on the way to Mallen as soon as it is decided for certain who owns it."

"But Doctor Douay, it is said to be an unlucky house," protested Jane.

"That is so, Mistress Eustace, so I am hopeful at getting it at a good price. Mr Danvers has said he never wishes to set eyes on it again, should it ever be in his power to dispose of it. So I am contented to wait, as long as I don't incommode you, Hal."

"Not at all," replied Hal politely. "We are happy to entertain you at our table, Philippe, for as long as it takes for the matter to be settled. Is that not so, Aunts?"

Whilst Aunt Kate, who would soon be won over by Philippe's Gallic charm, readily assented, Aunt Margery only did so grudgingly when she felt Hal's eye upon her.

As she explained to Kate as they sat in the parlour when supper was over: "I do feel this house seems to be degenerating into something resembling a bear-garden. Sister, do you not agree? I am sure Henry would have been horrified."

"I don't know that horrified is exactly the word—" began Kate uneasily.

"I do!" said Margery. "Why, we are expected to sup betwixt physicians, innkeepers and lawyers, the sort of people who, in Henry's day, would have eaten with the servants. And to be confronted by chits of girls, one an acknowledged Papist, the other next best thing to a witch, if I am any judge of the matter."

"Oh, Margery, do not even say so!" cried Kate. "You know how talk like that gets about. I beg you, do not call Sophie a witch!"

"How else do you explain Hal's behaviour?" Aunt Margery demanded.

"Hal, who has always been so exemplary in the manner in which he behaves himself. Hal, who is Justice of the Peace, to tolerate at his table the minx, who is responsible for his wife's death. To sit by silently as Justin berated him as he did. He'll do it, you know, if we don't take care. Hal is so besotted with her, he'll marry her, just as Justin says, and his good name will be ruined."

"Oh, I don't think it will, Margery," soothed Kate, "if they wait until Hal is out of mourning. He does so love her, doesn't he? One can see it in his face as he looks at her, the tenderness, the adoration."

"The foolishness that will be his damnation," she corrected. "You don't imagine that hussy will wait, do you? No, she'll be in his bed to be sure of him, if she isn't already! Justin caught them rolling in her bed kissing this morning! Most unsuitable for Hal to be caught in such a manner! A man in his position. It doesn't bear thinking of."

"Did Tom Kingscott never kiss you in the morning, Margery?" demanded Kate daringly. "For, I have to tell you, your brother Henry often kissed me at unsuitable times and unsuitable places before and after we were married."

"Thomas always knew the respect due to a lady of quality," Margery declared, getting rather red in the face.

"I am sure he did," she agreed dryly. "But that wasn't

what I asked."

"Well, to—to be sure," she blustered. "When we were younger—but that is neither here nor there, we were married. Our actions were sanctioned by the arms of the Church and the Law."

"Oh, Margery, what a hypocrite you sound, I am talking of simple love-play, such as all men and maids indulge in. There's no harm in it unless we think harm in it."

"So you think Hal's reputation will not be harmed by an early marriage to that saucy jade and a six month's child to keep the bastard boy company?" she asked tartly.

Kate sobered. "I think the less said of Stephen, the better," she replied seriously. "He must be brought up as a son of Francis Westwood. As for Sophie, I will talk to her and watch her actions. She is a good girl at heart, I have no fear of her wantonly spoiling Hal's reputation."

"*Wantonly* being a very apt word," said Margery, as a clincher.

"However, I think we should reconsider your decision not to assist in the girl's education. By refusing to do so, you are pushing Hal and Sophie together. Hal will find Sophie much easier to resist if he has little to do with her. I think I'll have a chat with Hal. He is a good boy, he will understand our fears. Indeed, I have no doubt he shares them."

"I have no doubt, too," Margery agreed. "The question is, will he remember them when that hussy slides into his bed?"

"I thought she seemed to be showing some interest in Adam Blackwell," she said, hoping to give Margery's thoughts another direction.

"Pooh! A sprat to catch a mackerel," Margery said contemptuously. "Not that either fool could see it."

"I don't think I did either, Margery," remarked Kate.

"She was using the innkeeper to show Hal he is not the only fish in the sea," sighed Margery. "And Hal, like a fool, took the bait. What do they see in her, I wonder? Even that dandified French doctor can't keep his eyes from her."

"She's very lovely," sighed Kate.

"That one's a minx, and make no mistake about it. She might have the face of an angel, and golden curls, but she's one of the devil's own," she paused, obviously thinking things over.

"However, I dare say you are right, Kate. I was wrong to refuse to assist Hal. Every effort must be made to part them. Yes, you talk to him, tell him we'll take care of both his wards, 'tis fitting we do so."

❧

The minx with the face of an angel ran into Hal in the stable yard shortly after she'd seen Adam Blackwell on his way with the promise to visit his farm the following morning.

"Sophie," said Hal, glancing about, relieved to see the yard deserted as a freezing fog started to settle around them. "Sophie, what is amiss?"

"Amiss?" she repeated, with a sinking in the pit of her stomach. She didn't know what to say to him. Part of her longed to hear him deny it all, more of her dreaded its confirmation. "Why, nothing is amiss, but that it is very cold out here."

"You are shivering," he observed. "Here, take my cloak."

"No, no, keep it. I am going to the house to seek my bed," she replied awkwardly, her only desire to run away and hide.

"May I not delay you for a moment," he asked, barring her way with the cloak outstretched in his arms. "You'll not be missed for ten minutes, and I'll guarantee to keep you warm."

Her heart lurched with desire to be in his arms, but

misery seeped into her soul like the fog in her hair. "No," she said baldly, still not meeting his eyes. "I must go."

"What is it?" he asked, frowning. "What has happened? This morning, I held you in my arms, kissed you, knew utter bliss, this evening, you'll not even look at me! Do you fear me? Do you think I'll lose control and ravish you like Giles Durward? I swear to you Sophie, you can—"

"No!" tears filled her eyes and clogged her throat. How many times had he used these words to seduce others? They fell from his lips with such ease and promised such heaven. "No, no, I don't fear you, but I beg you, let me pass," she cried.

"Do you fear yourself, then?" he asked, smiling. "You need not. I know you to be a passionate lover, but I am also your guardian. I swear, I'll not let my ward disgrace herself."

"No!" she cried again. She was horrified that he could see into her soul, that he understood her struggle with her own base instincts. "No, let me pass."

Something in the manner in which she spoke drove the loving amusement from his face. "Sophie," he said sharply. "What is it?"

"Nothing, I tell you, let me by!" She tried to push

past him, but only succeeded in ending up in his embrace.

"What is it, sweetheart?" he murmured, his face close to her cheek. "Only tell me what has happened. I beg you not to torment me in this manner. You must know how I long to hold you and to feel your lips on mine again."

"Don't! Don't!" The cry came with such anguish as she broke free from him, that he was left feeling foolish.

"Don't what?" he cried, anger coming into his voice. "For the love of heaven, Sophie, don't blow hot and cold on me. What have I done? This morning, you had no doubts, but were happy to be in my arms. What has changed?"

"I have!" she cried. She slipped his cloak from her shoulders as if it lay across them like a brand "I see how despicable my behaviour has been."

He stood staring at her, his eyes narrowed, as she held out his cloak to him, trembling all the while. "No, this is not right," he said slowly. "You are keeping something from me. What?"

Then, as the obvious answer dawned on him, he said: "No, you haven't changed. Justin!"

As her eyes widened, he leapt upon it. "Justin's taken his revenge, has he? Come, tell me, what did he say? What further could he do to blacken my name?"

Her tears fell in earnest now. "He told me about the baby, Hal. Etienne is your son," she whispered. "He said I am just one of many, that you've had countless women. That you'll never marry me, but seduce me and I'll just be one of a long line of discarded mistresses, unloved and unwanted."

"And you believed him?" Hal's eyes were dark with anger and disbelief.

"Why not?" she asked helplessly. "You betrayed your wife's love with me. Even your aunts think Etienne is your son. None seem surprised by your dreadful behaviour!"

"Item: I did not betray my wife with you," he said, his voice as cold as an Arctic wind. "You are, to my knowledge, a maid yet. Item: none seem surprised by my dreadful behaviour because, unlike you, they have faith in me, and know it isn't so. Item: I was drunk and seduced into the begetting of Etienne, to my eternal shame."

"So it's true," she said, numbly. "You betrayed your own father, too."

"Without knowledge or consent, yes," he said, through clenched teeth.

"Does that make it any better?" she cried, backing from him in horror.

"Do you mean, would I rather be known as a drunk-ard, than the lover of my father's wife? Yes," he replied curtly.

She shook her head. "I can't believe it. I thought you so good and pure—"

"Don't! Don't begin on that track," he snapped. "You thought me what you wanted to think me, but you knew that I was tempted by you, how could I be pure and yet hold you in my arms and tell you I loved you?"

"You couldn't, you never were, I see that now," she cried distraughtly. "And as for your claim not to have betrayed your wife—it's a lie! You betrayed her every time you looked at me and wanted me! Each time you touched my hand and desired me!"

"I know it and do penance for that betrayal daily," he agreed starkly.

"I never knew you!" she cried brokenly.

"So I told you days ago." The words were wrenched from him. "You just didn't want to believe me."

"I made you my knight in shining armour, my ideal

man. Everything I did, I did for you, because I wor-shipped you."

"And now you know better," he said bitterly. "It's taken you a long time, Sophie, but you've finally grown up. Welcome to this tawdry experience we call adult-hood. When you've recovered some of your dreams, let me know."

"I never want to see you again," she stormed, as her castle fell at her feet in ruins. "I hate you! I hate you! I'll marry Adam Blackwell tomorrow!"

"Good," he replied bitterly. "I wish you joy of him. Tell him to arrange a suitable time for us to draw up your marriage contract."

"Hal," she wailed. "Hal!"

"Sophie, if you're not going put that cloak on, then give it back to me, that I may. And take yourself off to bed, you sound frenzied."

"Frenzied!" she cried, gathering the dark material into a ball and throwing it at him. "Frenzied! I'd sooner be that than a man of stone like you!"

"I am what you've made me," he said, picking up his cloak from the damply-glistening cobbles. "What man can look upon Medusa and not be turned to stone?"

"How dare you?" she cried, as he swept the damp

cloak about him.

"Go to bed, Sophia," he commanded over his shoulder, as he crossed the stable yard and was swallowed up by the fog.

Chapter Eighteen

Hannah blinked in dismay as the door was flung back and her new mistress entered, sobbing tempestuously, to throw herself in complete abandonment across the bed.

Tentatively, she got to her feet, forgetting the chest of linen she'd been tidying and crossed to shut out the curiosity of the world. She hesitated as to whether she should also depart, doubtful of her reception should she stay, yet curious herself as to what could cause such grief, and a little sorry for the other's misery.

Uncertain just how to tackle the situation, she returned to her task, only glancing occasionally to the occupant of the bed, and going to gently tap her shoulder and offer her a cup of water when her paroxysms showed signs of abating.

"Begging your pardon, Mistress Sophie, but I'm Hannah, your new maid," she said. "Sir Henry told me I was to wait upon you. I don't mean to intrude," she added, as tears welled in Sophie's eyes again. "If you want me to leave, I'll go, or if you have a task for me, I'll gladly perform it."

Sophie shook her head, despair filling her soul. She'd known it from the start, she'd known it was too good to be true. She had been living in a fool's paradise all these months, imagining Hal as true as Libby claimed, when it was plain to everybody, but a born fool like herself, that he was nothing but a heartless philanderer. He admitted to it without question.

"Has something occurred to distress you?" said the maid, her sympathy stirred by the other's grief.

"Mr Danvers," she whispered. She couldn't tell the girl the truth, she couldn't bring herself to discuss it with her. "Justin Danvers, he said such dreadful things."

"Oh, him!" said the maid, with a wealth of meaning in her voice. "He has an evil tongue, don't he? I can't tell you the times he left my old mistress weeping."

Sophie turned her head to stare at her dully. "Oh, you are that girl, the maid of that woman," she said, realizing for the first time who she was.

"Helen Sitwell, yes," the girl agreed. "God rest her

soul, poor thing."

"Poor thing?" said Sophie. "Bess says she was a monster who wanted Justin to kill her so that he could be free to marry."

"Well, he would say that, wouldn't he?" snapped the maid. "I know he were the last one to see my mistress, and I found her dead next morning."

"That's horrid," said Sophie, with a shudder. "I found my guardian—the old guardian—dead too. He'd been murdered as well—poisoned. I can still see him now, if I don't take care, in my mind's eye."

Hannah nodded. "Yes, as soon as I close my eyes, I see her face, all blue!" She reached out her hand to grasp Sophie's fingers. "Don't weep no more. He ain't worth it, and he'll surely hang."

"Oh, I'm not weeping over him," cried Sophie. "Indeed, but for poor Bess. I'd say hang him, and good riddance! No, it was what he said that made me weep."

"What was that then? As I say, I know he has a wicked tongue on him at times."

"It was the content, rather than the words themselves," she sighed, wiping her eyes. "He was repeating some gossip about Sir Henry—"

"Now, he's a different kettle of fish, ain't he?" sighed

the maid, with a dreamy air. "My, but he's a handsome gentleman. Now, if my mistress had fallen for him, I could have understood it. I'd not refuse him myself, if he were to ask, like—" she broke off at the sight of Sophie's face. "Oh, begging your pardon, mistress, I don't know what I'm at, to let my tongue run away with me so."

"No, it doesn't matter," said Sophie helplessly. "You see, that is exactly what all women say. They throw themselves at him, just as I've done. And who can blame him if he takes them up on it? Certainly not I. For, if only he'd offered, I'd have accepted."

"Oh, dear, dear me, you have got it bad for the knave," she said as Sophie fell to weeping again. "Never you mind, lass, never you mind."

"But don't you see? I thought him so perfect!" said Sophie distraughtly. "I thought him as good as he looks. I thought it was his love of me which made him overcome his scruples, but now I find this show of reluctance is part of his practiced seduction, that I am but one of a long line of foolish females he's had and forgotten."

Hannah looked impressed. "A rake, is he?" she asked, admiration in her tone. "I can't say but I do like a scamp myself. Is he high up in his notions, or none too fussy?"

"He doesn't seem to care one bit," sobbed Sophie. "Any woman will do, his father's wife, a novice straight from a nunnery, or his own ward, all are grist to his mill."

"Happen they are," said the maid happily. "But grieving over him won't do you no good, will it? So, you drink this and dry your pretty eyes. Why, just look at you. You'll be spoiling that lovely complexion next, making it all blotchy."

"If he doesn't love me, what can it matter," cried Sophie, but she took the cup of water anyway.

"Now, now, now, we don't want that, do we?" the maid chided her gently. "That's no way to go about things. You've got to teach him a lesson. Nothing makes gentlemen happier than to think they've got the whip hand, and that you are desperate for their smiles. You've got to show him you care nothing for him, that you'll not share his attentions, that if he wishes to engage your affections, he'll have to be true to you and you alone."

"No, you don't understand," said Sophie wearily. "That could never be. The child, it is his! And Cordelia too, although she denies it—my life is over!"

"No, no, why you're too pretty for that," soothed the maid. "I tell you, you've got to show him what's what.

What you need is another gentleman to make him jealous."

"Another? Do you mean Adam Blackwell?"

"I don't know, is he young and handsome?"

"Like a Greek god," replied Sophie.

"Then take him instead anyway," said Hannah bluntly.

"No, I don't love him. Adam's a good man, and I am fond of him, but I love Hal."

"Then you use this here Adam to make Sir Henry so jealous that he'll dance to your tune," said the maid.

"Oh, I couldn't do that, it would be so wickedly unkind to Adam," cried Sophie, her innate honesty shocked.

"Why, my pretty, you've got two choices. Either you make one of them unhappy, or you're unhappy yourself. Which is it to be?"

Sophie stared. "That seems so very harsh," she whispered.

"'Tis a war, my pretty," she said, smoothing back Sophie's curls. "If you're not to be on the losing side, you've got to win."

Sophie stared at the girl, fascinated by her logic. "Do you truly see it so?" she asked.

"It has always been so, my dear, between men and

maids," she said comfortably. "A maid has but one thing they want, and she has no choice but to sell it to the one she wants."

"But Hal is my guardian," she said. "And he has the final say in who I marry, anyway."

"Oh no, you've got that, mistress, you've always got that. If need be, in public at the wedding," she replied wisely.

"Oh, Hannah, what would you do?" she sighed.

"I don't know either gentleman. I've met Sir Henry, and I can see why you're taken with him. But," she paused, then said, "if I were you, mistress, I'd not let myself be hurried, that's what I'd do."

Sophie looked thoughtful. "Why yes, I was promised until next June. That's when my old guardian will have been dead a year. Hal gave me his word on it, and I can hold him to it, can't I?"

"If you keep your head," said the maid, smiling.

"Oh, Hannah, thank you. You are exactly what I need. Someone to help me think," said Sophie, clasping her hand. Then, as the maid looked away, tears in her eyes, Sophie asked: "Oh, what have I said? Did I hurt you in some way?"

"No mistress," the maid shook her head, sprinkling

tears. "'Tis just that I were close to Helen—Mistress Sitwell."

"Close enough to call her by name?" said Sophie in surprise.

"We came from the same place, you know. The back streets of the City. We played together in the kennel as children. Only Helen were a beauty, like yourself. She knew we had one chance to get out, and she took it. She went as a doxy in one of the gaming houses just off Covent Garden."

"A doxy?" asked Sophie incredulously. "You mean, a woman of the night?"

"Of the night, of the day, it didn't much matter when. She sold herself to get out of that gutter," replied the maid. "First like that, then later, when she'd helped him amass a fortune fleecing young ne're-do-wells, to Nat Sitwell. 'Twas then she came to get me. I was to be her maid, and we'd both be safe in his house," she sighed and suddenly seemed much older than her years. "My choice was stark. I could either go as her maid, or stay and produce a string of brats for any of those fellows who lived on their wits in Seven Dials. I went with Helen."

"Good heavens!" said Sophie in amazement. "I wonder you don't want to slap me, to hear me weeping over which gentleman to take to husband."

Hannah laughed. "Oh, each choice is difficult enough at the time," she replied. "Why shouldn't you weep over yours, if you want to? I could see the chance of bettering myself, only it didn't work out for poor Helen, or me. But at least her last months were happy."

"She was happy with Justin Danvers?" asked Sophie doubtfully.

"At first she were, yes," she replied. "He was pleasant enough, and you know what men are like when you've something they want. All over her, he was. Calling to see how she went on, bringing her posies and pretty things. She only had to say she had a wanting for something for him to get it for her. Oh, she was that in love. She'd never been able to choose before, you see. In the brothel, she had to take any that picked her, and then old man Sitwell had offered marriage. Not that he troubled her too much, she said. But to have a young lover pay court to her—"

"But he was married! Married to Bess!" cried Sophie, shocked.

"His wife was sickly, everyone said so. And that she had two brats in two years. She wasn't expected to survive the last. Helen were heartbroken when she were safely delivered."

"Did Justin promise her marriage?" Sophie was horrified.

"No, he were too clever. He's not a lawyer for nothing. Helen said he'd just clam up when his wife was mentioned. He'd never say a word about her, it was all about how he hated her brother, Sir Henry. It were more that Helen was convinced it would all work out for her. That his wife would die, they could be married, and she'd live happily ever after." She shrugged her shoulders. "That's our problem, we women. We all want to believe in fairy stories."

Sophie laughed bitterly. "Yes, I suppose we do."

"Not that she were that simple, Helen," she continued, thoughtful. "For I remember she said she had a second string to her bow, if Justin Danvers didn't come though with his promises."

Sophie, busy with her own thoughts, merely nodded. "Yes, I can see that's best, if one is to be rational."

"I don't know who he was, of course," she added. "Shall I put out a fresh gown for you tomorrow, Mistress Sophie?"

"Yes, yes, if you please, Hannah," she replied. "And of

course, you are quite right. I shall tell Sir Henry I'm not even thinking of marrying until next summer."

"And in the meantime, let this here Adam court you. That should make Sir Henry sit up and take notice," said the maid. "This blue gown, mistress?"

"No, Hannah, the grey, we are still in mourning for Sir Henry's wife."

"Of course," the girl nodded. "Mr Danvers were furious over that, weren't he? She were his sister, they do say."

"Yes," Sophie sighed. "And I killed her."

"You?" It was the maid's turn to look shocked.

"That's why he hates me, because I drove Libby to her death."

"Of course, I see now, you are his ward, too. The one he holds responsible for everything. The one Sir Henry is so desperately in love with."

"Is he? I don't know. I don't think so. I think I'm just one of many."

"According to Mr Danvers, he were mad for you. Didn't he go off to France rather than stay near you? Good heavens! I begin to see it now. I never realised you were that ward of Sir Henry's. But what are you afraid of? He'll never give you up. Helen said he worshipped you, he'd do anything to make you his. She were that jealous of you. She so wanted Justin to love her like that."

Sophie crossed to brush her hair. "I don't know. I am getting so weary of it all. I don't know who to believe, or what to do for the best."

"Take your time," said the maid, coming to help her undress. "And have a second string, like Helen said. This Adam will do."

Sophie laughed unsteadily. "Who was her second string?" she asked.

"That, I don't know," said the maid. "She were that close about him. But he visited occasionally, I'm sure. And she were a might afraid of him. Are you afraid of Adam Blackwell?"

"Adam Blackwell? No, indeed," Sophie laughed, this time almost lightheartedly. "No, I'd never be afraid of dear Adam. He's like a dear soft bear."

"And Sir Henry, are you afraid of him?" she asked.

"Perhaps not of him, so much as not being loved by him," she said after a moment's thought.

"Dear me, you got it bad and no mistake," said the girl. "I guess it's not going to matter what he does, you'll love him."

❧

Chapter Nineteen

A thick fog lay over the house and grounds next morning, shrouding them in a gloom that was almost tangible. Philippe Douay, who found November the most trying month of the English calendar, hunched over his breakfast in stoic silence, shuddering from time to time as a draught assailed him. Only Hal's step made him look up, a frown in his eyes, as Hal entered, a cough racking at his chest. "You are ill, Hal," he cried at once, his professional instincts stirred.

"I appear to have developed a cough overnight," Hal agreed, with less than his usual good humour. "Thomas, fetch some fresh ale—no, stay! Now I think of it, I brought some coffee back from France with me last week. Tell cook to brew it, I am sure it would be more to Doctor Douay's taste, too."

"Them little brown beans, Sir Henry?" asked the

manservant, wrinkling his nose. "We tried them, nothing happened! We put boiling water on them, just like you said, and they just sat there, doing nothing. So, cook threw them out."

"Threw them out?" cried Hal incredulously. "Do you know what they cost? I told cook to grind them to a fine powder! She cannot have thrown them all out."

The servant shrugged. "She said she weren't putting heathen beans under her pestle. She said we'd never know what might befall us if we started with that nonsense, that she'd seen things go on here as would make the old master turn in his grave, and that she weren't having no truck with the likes of they."

"Hal, be still," said Philippe, as Hal turned on the man in anger. "I'll go to the kitchen and see if I can brew us a decent cup of coffee. You eat some breakfast."

Still raging inwardly, Hal cut himself a slice of bread, and one of beef. He was about to raise the first piece to his mouth, when the door burst open, and Thomas and the cook, both quarrelling fiercely, entered the room. "I'll have my say, and you'll not stop me, Thomas Jenkins!" she cried, her rubicund face redder than ever. "See here, Master Hal, 'tis time you were told what's what! I

won't, and never will, have these damn Frenchies running tame in my kitchen. This used to be a respectable
house, this did. One as a body could be proud to hold
their head up in and say they were part of! But just lately, 'tis plain disgusting the way things are going, what
with foreigners and Papists in every corner, slips of girls
giving orders where they got no right just because they
share your bed, and murderers being entertained like
royalty! It makes a body wonder what the war were all
about, it surely do!"

Hal's eyes blazed at her audacity. "Indeed it does,"
he agreed icily, "when a man can be abused at his own
table by a paid servant! You speak of my uncle, did you
ever dare address him so?"

"Well, no," she agreed, taken aback by the sudden
fury in his face. "But he were a proper, high-up gentleman, he never so much as set foot in his kitchens in all
his…"

"And I am not?" Hal demanded, cutting short her
diatribe.

"Well, no, Sir Henry, I'm sure I didn't mean—" she
said hastily, amending her tone and dropping a belated
curtsey. "But you can't deny, Sir Henry, this house is
like a fair, with tumblers and foreigners and low com-

pany, coming and going at all hours!"

"My guests are my guests," he said, with cold emphasis. "It is not for you to question their quality. If they sit at my table, you may assume they are my equal. Or, you can seek employment elsewhere. Good cooks come ten to the farthing."

"I wouldn't be too sure of that, Sir Henry," she cried, offended she should be held so lightly.

"I am certain of it, and that I can easily find one to brew coffee, tea, or even chocolate, if I so desire it," he snapped. "Either get back to your kitchen and eat humble pie, that Doctor Douay may teach you to make coffee, or go pack your bags."

"Well, I ain't never been spoke to like that before," she cried, quivering with indignation. "I'll speak to Mistress Kingscott, you see if I don't, she won't care for me to be sent off so lightly."

"Speak to whom you choose," he replied. "But remember who pays your wages. Now shut the door on your way out, there's a damn draught."

"I brewed you this whilst I was in the kitchen, Hal," said Philippe, some minutes later. "It should soothe that cough of yours. Who is that red-faced termagent in the kitchen?"

"She is, or rather probably was, the cook. I've just turned her off."

"She'll not be greatly missed," he remarked, sitting down opposite his friend, and subjecting his face to a steady scrutiny.

Hal bore it for some moments and then protested. "For God's sake, Philippe, I seem to hear you cry the coffin-maker!"

Philippe shrugged. "You are heading that way if you don't have care," he said.

"Because I have a cough?" laughed Hal, coughing again.

"No, it's deeper than that. Why were you out so long last night, Hal?"

Hal's face straightened. "How is this?" he asked sharply. "Are you keeping a check on my movements?"

"No," he replied calmly. "But I was up late reading last night, I fell asleep over the book, your coming in at two o'clock in the morning awoke me from my slumbers. Now, if you'd been out to share the bed of your mistress, all well and good. But, if you had, as I suspect, been walking in the fog, which, it seems, it is a peculiarly English pastime which could easily be the death of you, as well as Justin Danvers."

"It is difficult not to walk in the fog in England in November," remarked Hal.

"I have lived here ten years, Hal, longer than you, in fact," he replied. "I am not a fool, where were you for hours?"

"I needed to think, to talk to Libby," he replied.

"You can talk to Libby where you will, Hal," he said patiently. "She doesn't require your attendance at her graveside in the middle of a winter's night." Then, as Hal shrugged and sipped at the concoction before him, he added: "Drink it down, it probably tastes foul. Hal, you cannot believe that Libby would require you to remain a widower forever, surely? I know my acquaintance with her was slight, but she struck me as being a woman of superior sense, and above all, she loved you. It would be your happiness, your comfort, that would be what she wanted." Hal shrugged, bracing himself to swallow the bitter brew. "Hal, this is merely a fidget of the mind, brought on by Justin Danvers and his wild accusations. Take no heed of him, the fool's mind is turned by worry."

Hal sighed. "In essence, he says what others think," he replied quietly.

"Yes, he does, but they'll not think it for long," protested Philippe. "You know each scandal only lasts until the next. Once you and Sophie are married…"

"That will never be," interrupted Hal bitterly.

"Yes, you feel like that now, fresh from your grief, but you can't deny you love Sophie, Hal," he continued patiently.

"I'll not deny it," he agreed. "But I'll merely add, that Sophie tells me she won't marry me."

"Sophie? Sophia Redcroft won't marry you?" he repeated. "My dear fellow, our problem is making her wait until you can do so respectably."

"No, she won't marry one as despicable as I, indeed, she has informed me she'll marry Adam Blackwell tomorrow," he said wretchedly, as a fit of coughing shook him.

"To which you replied?" Philippe asked intently, seeing plainly there had been a quarrel.

"That I wished him joy, and that he should visit me to draw up the marriage contract today," Hal replied with a shrug.

"I was wrong. You are English after all!" exclaimed Philippe. "Only an Englishman could make such a mess of a wooing."

Hal looked bewildered. "Why? What do you mean?"

"Hal, you should have taken her in your arms and demanded that she put all thoughts of Blackwell from her head. That you'd be married as soon as you were able, but until that time, you considered her contracted to you. And finally, that if she dared to look at another man, she'd live to rue the day."

"No, no, Philippe, you don't understand," Hal said, shaking his head miserably. "Justin told her about Etienne. That he is my son. She was horrified that I betrayed my own father."

Philippe sat back in his seat, drawing his breath through his teeth with a little hiss. "He makes it very difficult to save him, this Justin Danvers," he pronounced.

"It was my fault!" said Hal hopelessly. "He caught me kissing Sophie yesterday. It obviously enraged him."

"And?" said Philippe.

"It can't be very gratifying to see a sister so quickly replaced," Hal said wryly. "I feel disgusted with myself, how can I blame him?"

"You want to do what is right, Hal," sighed Philippe. "You tried your hardest to do what was right, you even went away when the situation became so difficult. Yet, then you were blamed further for Libby's death. It seems to me you cannot win."

"I drew the same conclusion last night," he agreed bitterly, as he coughed again.

"This is why I see you so grim today."

Hal shrugged again, as a pot of coffee arrived with Thomas and Aunt Margery. "Sir Henry, what is this cook tells me? Is it true you have turned her off? I cannot believe it! She has been with us these past eighteen years! And you know I go to be with Hetta at any moment."

"It's high time we tried someone new, then," said Hal, refusing to be drawn into an argument. "And that needn't have any effect on your visit to Hetta. Is she well?"

"No, Will is in some anxiety about her. I thought I might visit almost immediately," said Margery, sidetracked, and then, realising she was losing her place in the discussion, cried: "Someone new? Are you mad? Another cook? By suppertime, I suppose?"

"If possible," he agreed mildly.

"Do you imagine good cooks grow on trees?" she cried, aghast.

"I thought they were taught," he said reflectively. "Where's that wench from Adamsholme?"

"Hannah Smith? She's in attendance on one of your wards. Now there's one who is trouble, or my name isn't Margery Kingscott." She eyed the dishes of dark, steaming liquid that was placed before each man. "Whatever is that awful-smelling stuff, Hal? Never say you are going to drink it!"

"It's coffee, ma'am," he replied. "And widely drunk all over London these days."

"I can well believe it, they'll do anything in that godforsaken place!" she snapped. "Your uncle never drank anything but good, honest English ale in all his life, neither did my husband."

"You're wrong, ma'am," he replied simply. "I recollect once accompanying my uncle to a coffee-house in London. Would you be so good as to ask Hannah Smith to come here, Thomas?"

"What am I to do about cook?" demanded Aunt Margery. "I think if you were to apologise, Sir Henry, she might reconsider."

"I, apologise?" He laughed, and began to cough, saying breathlessly: "I think not, Aunt."

"I can explain you are far from well, indeed, you look quite ill, Hal. Have you thought of consulting a physician?"

"I am in the middle of doing so, ma'am," he replied. "Doctor Douay recommends coffee and a new cook. Ah, Hannah, that was quick."

"Sir Henry," she replied, casting him a look from beneath her lashes.

"I hope you've settled in, and will suit Mistress Redcroft and Mistress Sandys. In the meantime, has the cook Jennet Sawsby found employment yet?"

"I do believe she had an offer, Sir Henry, but not accepted it, not being too taken with the conditions, so to speak."

Hal nodded, with a satisfied air. "Thomas, saddle your horse and take yourself to the other side of Adamsholme. At the house of Mistress Sitwell, you'll find a cook called Mistress Sawsby, ask her if she'd like the position of cook here at Westwood Hall."

"Yes, Sir Henry, at once, Sir Henry," he replied, mindful that there was also a manservant without employment. "I see Adam Blackwell is just riding up the drive, Sir Henry."

"Adam Blackwell again!" said Hal, looking disgusted. "What can he want?"

"I rather thought he was to escort Sophia and Mistress Sandys to his new home," said Philippe.

"To his new home?" cried Aunt Margery, scandalized. "I have never heard the like of it. Two young, unmarried females, to go off like that to a man's house? I will not allow it! Hal, as their guardian, you must forbid it."

"I don't see the necessity," said Hal wearily. "Cordelia will chaperone Sophie, and it is Sophie that everyone is so anxious to get married off, isn't it?"

"Yes, yes indeed, but to a man like that? An innkeeper!" she cried in disgust.

"He gave up innkeeping some months ago, ma'am, and bought a property. As a son of a Royalist gentleman, I'd have thought you'd approve of him."

"He certainly is a fine figure of a man," she agreed, viewing him through the window, relieved to hear he no longer ran an inn. "How many acres has he purchased? Of course, the Blackwells used to own Elmley Park, did they not? As I remember it, they were a connection on the Distaff side, to the Twinnings of Boscote."

Hal nodded, trying to keep the dislike from his face, as Thomas ushered the young man in. "Mr Blackwell, were we expecting you?" he asked, with a marked degree of hauteur.

"Yes," Adam replied, reddening. "That is to say, Sophie is. And the other young lady, Mistress Sandys.

They are riding out to the Old Manor, to see my new home."

"The Old Manor? You mean, the Findlesham's property?" said Margery, nodding her approval. "Of course, it can't compare with Elmley Park, but if one is forced to begin again, a splendid old place like the Old Manor is charming."

"I will expect both my wards to be returned in good time," said Hal coldly.

"Adam, are you come?" cried Sophie, coming into the room with an air of over-emphasized liveliness. Her overnight meditations had brought her little counsel. She only knew that she loved Hal quite desperately, that he'd broken her heart, and that she was determined none should know it. "Here is such fun: Cordelia is shy of going with you!"

"How is Mistress Sandys to be conveyed?" asked Philippe. "She is not proficient on horseback."

"I know, I am going to teach her," said Sophie. She suddenly caught sight of Hal's pale face, as a fit of coughing over took him, and realized, with a jolt of dismay, how very dear he was to her. "But for today, Cordelia is going to ride pillion behind Adam."

"I assume you have begged leave of Mistress Westwood?" said Hal.

"Indeed, but she said we must seek permission from you," Sophie replied, anxiety filling her face. "Are you ill, sir?" she asked gently.

Hal shook his head. He was still bitterly angry and disappointed with her. "And?" he asked, inflexibly.

"May Cordelia and I go with Adam to see his new home at the Old Manor?" she asked obediently, although she watched him anxiously, realizing how ill he was.

"You may," he replied austerely. "However, I have just been telling Mr Blackwell that I expect you returned in good time, and remain together at all times, do I make myself clear?"

"Indeed, sir," she agreed, sensing that these precautions had their root in jealousy. "Adam, do you come?" She began to turn away, and then turned back to Hal. She longed to walk away and let him suffer, but the sight of him had frightened her. "Sir," she said. "Shall I brew you a tisane for the headache before I go? I am convinced you have one."

"Thank you, but Philippe has already done so," he replied coldly, looking away from her, determined not to allow her pretty ways to cloud his judgement.

She hesitated still. "You will stay indoors close to the fire today, sir? I think he should, don't you, Doctor Douay? He looks very ill."

"Good heavens, girl, Sir Henry has a dozen people to attend him, should he feel the need," said Aunt Margery in a scolding tone, which showed to the initiated just how anxious she had become. "He is a man full-grown, he can decide for himself what is best for him."

"No, ma'am, he cannot," Sophie replied swiftly, glad to contradict the imposing lady, aware that it was her wish to make Sophie sound foolish. "For it can only be some neglect that has allowed him to become this ill. Doctor Douay, surely Sir Henry should be abed?"

"Mistress Sophie, pray depart upon your errand and leave Sir Henry's health in my hands," Philippe replied bluntly. "See, Mistress Sandys awaits you. Be gone, and do not linger too long, lest the fog come down again."

Again, Sophie looked doubtful, but Hal didn't raise his eyes from the contemplation of his breakfast, and aware that Cordelia's nerves were on edge, she hurried from the parlour, followed by Adam Blackwell in a much-chastened frame of mind and was soon riding along the lane as the fog lifted a little.

She'd not give Hal another thought, she'd vowed last

night, as she'd finally, her tears spent, lain dry-eyed in the dark. She'd put him from her mind completely. He was not worth dwelling on. A libertine and a rake, she'd nearly fallen into his trap. But, even having decided upon this comforting resolution, she felt little happier. Indeed, great waves of desolation had swept over her repeatedly, until finally, worn down by her emotions, she'd slept.

Now, this morning, when confronted with him looking in far from good health, all that love she'd been trying to suppress had just sprung up again, in a whirl of joint anxiety and tenderness. Did it truly matter what he was? She loved him, and to contemplate life without him was unthinkable. How could she even consider marriage to another when her heart jolted, even at the sight of him? She'd been a wicked fool even to think of it, and now, here was poor Adam, filled with such happiness because she'd agreed to see his home. He was a good, kind soul, and didn't deserve to suffer for her foolishness. She must cast a damper over his high spirits. Let him see that, although she would ever want to be his good friend, she could never be more while her heart was not free.

⚜

Ambrose, who had ridden hard the previous day, winced as he walked along the road that afternoon. He was paying for his fast journey, but his desire to be back at Westwood with Jane had driven him. Ahead was a linen draper's, and there, so he was informed, he'd find a friend of Helen Sitwell. He paused outside the shop and peered into the interior. It was dark and hung about by various items of apparel, rather like a cave bestrewn with cobwebs.

"Be you wanting some help, m'lord?" asked a young woman, limping from behind a vast press.

"Oh, yes please!" Ambrose, started at her sudden appearance, which was all the more surprising, as her face underneath the linen cap she wore, in the old manner, was badly scarred. He was about to launch into his investigation but suddenly it occurred to him he might to better if he purchased something initially. "I, I want a, a—" To his horror, he couldn't think of a decent item of feminine apparel he could ask for. "I, I want something for my wife," he said hastily.

A smile flickered across her mouth, showing for an instant how great the tragedy had been to her face. "A pair of gloves, m'lord?"

"Gloves!" Relief flooded across him. "Yes, gloves, they

will do very well indeed, thank you."

"Kid gloves, sir, or velvet?" she asked knowledgeably.

"Er," again, Ambrose hesitated. Hal had indicated he should be made a partner in his law firm and had spoken at some length of an increased remuneration. But exactly when this should be forthcoming, he had no idea. Nor did he think he could claim gloves as a legitimate expense as Hal had bade him. His food and lodgings, of course, and bribes, but gloves? He wasn't sure. "Velvet," he replied firmly.

She crossed unhurriedly to a chest and removed a box, placing it on the surface and laying out various lengths and colours for his inspection. "Has the lady small hands, sir?" she asked.

"Yes, very small," he said, thankful for so easy a question.

She pulled on a ruby red glove, exhibiting it for him with loving care. "This is the small size, sir," she said.

He nodded, thinking he liked the fit but had never seen Jane wear anything in red. She appeared to prefer blue or green. "Have you something like in another colour?" he asked. She sighed and began to go through the box again. "Actually, I was looking for Mistress Nancy Gollen, too," he said uncertainly.

"Oh, and who wants her?" asked the woman sharply.

"Well, I do. I'm Ambrose Carver, a man of law, and I might be able to tell her something to her advantage if she can provide me with certain information."

"Greeny-blue gloves, sir?" she suggested, laying a pair in front of him.

"I like the colour," he replied. "You don't know her, then?"

"I may do," she replied. "But I'm not so sure she should be so free with her information. How do I know you don't mean her harm?"

Ambrose sighed and picked up both pairs of gloves. "I don't, but how can I reassure you?" he said, frowning. "I suppose I could fetch Mr Bennett, of Lincoln's Inn, where I studied. Although, he is but another man."

"Do you want the gloves, or no?" she asked.

"Er, how much are they?" he asked doubtfully.

"Two and eleven pence hapenny, a pair," she replied.

"Really?" he replied. "Then, I'll take them both."

"What information do you want?" she commanded, carrying the gloves across the room to the press. "Shall I wrap these in silvered paper?"

"Please," he agreed. "That is something I must dis-cuss with Mistress Gollen."

"You are," she replied briefly.

"You are Nancy Gollen?" he asked in amazement.

"Yes," she replied.

"But I thought, that is to say, I was given…"

"You thought I was a whore," she replied roughly. "And expected me to be pretty. Yes, well, happen I was, for I fell fowl of Jack Strickland.

"Jack Strickland?" said Ambrose blankly.

"He were my bully-boy, my man." She threw him a look of impatience. "Mercy upon us, here's a green 'un if ever I met one. Doesn't know the price of gloves and has never been with a whore."

"Are the two compatible?" he asked.

She laughed. "Nay then, you've no harm in you, I dare swear. Jack Strickland did this to me because he thought I'd 'peached on him."

"Oh, I see," Ambrose nodded. "Yes, I begin to understand. The information I require regards a Mistress Helen Sitwell."

"Nell?" cried the woman. "Nell Sitwell! Glory be, I thought she'd retired to the country with Nat."

"Indeed, only her husband died recently."

"Husband? That's a good one," laughed the woman. "I can assure you, Mistress Gollen, I have seen her husband's will. He left everything to her," said Ambrose earnestly.

"Lucky bitch," she replied tartly. "Maybe she weren't so daft after all."

"Unfortunately, mistress, her good luck didn't hold, she was murdered last week."

"Murdered?" cried Nancy, her face suddenly pale. "Nell, murdered!"

"I fear so," he said gravely. "And my master accused of it."

"Whose your master?" she asked from narrowed lids.

"Justin Danvers."

"I ain't never heard of him, though wait a bit—ain't he the fellow who used to clerk for Mr Johnson over at old man Steene's a year or so back?"

"Indeed, ma'am, I do believe he did," he replied. "Do you know him?"

"Oh him," she grunted. "Nat Sitwell used to use... Well, what do you want to know?"

"Anything I can about Nathaniel Sitwell and his wife Helen. Their friends and acquaintances, associates and the like. I have been told you were Helen's closest friend."

"I was one of her friends, but not the closest. That

were Hannah Smith, and she disappeared these past six months."

"Hannah Smith? Why, she was her maid, or so she claims," exclaimed Ambrose.

"Do she? Yes, well, happen she were glad to see the back of Jack Strickland, too," she muttered. "Fled to the country, hey? I wonder if he followed?"

"Who is this Strickland fellow?" asked Ambrose.

She glanced up at him. "Look," she said, "this is too risky by half. How much are you offering?"

"I am ordered to offer five pounds for information," he replied promptly.

"It ain't worth it," she said at once. "Not for me skin, it ain't. Look, you can see what he did to me when he thought I'd 'peached. I'm not risking my skin for less than twenty pounds."

"Twenty pounds! That's a vast deal of money!"

"Aye," she replied, her voice hard. "And you're asking for a vast deal of risk."

Ambrose considered as she hastily packaged his parcel. "I don't have that much money at my disposal," he said frankly. "But I could give you, perhaps, as much as ten pounds, and if your information is good, you could come with me to see Sir Henry Westwood and collect the remainder of the money."

"Who's this Sir Henry Westwood?" she demanded suspiciously.

"He's the brother-in-law of Justin Danvers. He and I are trying to clear Justin's name."

"That's five shillings and eleven pence, sir," she replied, placing the parcel before him.

Ambrose drew out his purse and counted a crown and a shilling on the edge of the press. Then, he counted out more coins. "There, that's more than ten pounds."

She eyed the money, licking her lips. "Aye, well, happen I could do with a visit to the country to get some fresh air," she muttered. "But I can't leave this shop just like that, can I?"

"What time do you finish?" he asked.

"Four o'clock," she replied. "As soon as it starts to get dark, Mr Tabit, the mean old skinflint, takes over from me to save himself using candles."

Ambrose nodded. "There's a coach for Oxford at six. Meet me at Charing Cross, I'll procure you a ticket and you can tell your tale to Sir Henry."

"Six at the Golden Keys?" she asked.

"Yes, don't be late."

⚜

Chapter Twenty

"Hal?" Aunt Kate glanced about the door of the Jericho parlour to see him sitting at the table, which, as usual, was covered in documents, his head supported on his hand, his whole body suggesting ineffable weariness. "Hal, Margery says you are ill, can I get you anything? Oh, Doctor Douay, I beg pardon, I didn't see you there! Doubtless, you have made a tisane for Hal."

"Indeed, ma'am," he replied gravely from his seat, concealed by a screen.

Kate's anxious gaze went to Hal's face again as she noticed the dark smudges under his eyes and the lines etched about his mouth. She'd come to love him like the son she and Henry never had, and her heart went out to him in his trouble.

"Was there something else, ma'am?" he asked politely, as she didn't go.

"Well, I did wish to talk to you, Hal, but another time will do."

"I'll leave you and take a walk," announced Philippe, getting to his feet. "See, I become English, I go to walk in the fog!"

"Pray, don't go out on my account, Doctor Douay, not in this intolerable weather," cried Kate, as he went to the door. "I can come another time."

"No need, ma'am," he said. "I need to stretch my legs anyway."

"Don't worry, Aunt. I gather you've been sent to lecture me by Aunt Margery," observed Hal with a faint grin. "That alone accounts for your reluctance to see me."

"As if I have the right to lecture you, Hal!" she said, coming to mend the fire and picking up a cushion, which she plumped up and fitted behind his back. "There, is that a little more comfortable?"

He laughed abruptly. "Yes, thank you, Aunt. How did you know my back and shoulders ached?"

"From the way you are sitting. You are very like your uncle Henry, you know…"

He smiled and caught her hand as she smoothed back his hair, kissing the palm. "Thank you, ma'am," he said, his voice a little husky. "You are too good, too kind. You don't know how much I miss a woman's touch."

"That's the hardest part of bereavement," she agreed. "The feeling of isolation. The lack of a simple caress, the knowledge that you are no longer special to someone." She paused and added: "Although that doesn't apply to you. Sophie thinks you are very special, and doubtless you could have as many of her caresses as you cared to ask for."

"Doubtless," he agreed, his eyes wary. "Is this the burden of this lecture?"

"Margery and I are concerned," she agreed, taking a seat opposite. "Obviously, we know it is no real business of ours, but we both love you, Hal, and you are getting into deep waters with Sophie."

"Am I?" he replied wistfully. "I thought I was managing quite well."

"My dear," she laughed. "You are plainly head over heels in love with her."

"A man cannot always control his heart, ma'am, even if he can rule his head," he agreed.

"Yes," she said vaguely. "'Tis neither your head nor your heart we are concerned with, Hal."

He smiled a little. "I see, 'tis my loins which are causing you both such disquiet, perhaps?"

"Well," she blushed hotly. "I don't imagine you get much assistance from Sophie in that department," she stammered. "Her beauty is provocative, anyway, and I doubt me she is overburdened with moral scruples."

"And then there is the matter of Etienne," he suggested.

"I know you are older and wiser, now, Hal," she agreed. "But you can't deny you are susceptible to a pretty face."

"Or even a desirable body?" he suggested tartly. "One is, one hopes, a gentleman, and acquaintance with my stepmother proved a valuable lesson. After all, Aunt, I am in a position of trust. Sophie is my ward."

"Yes, Hal, I have no doubt you are mindful of the fact, but Sophie won't give it a thought, and if I am any judge of the matter, a born temptress."

He smiled thinly. "I manage, ma'am," he replied starkly.

"Managing is putting too great a strain on you, that much is plain. Margery and I want to help. Margery agrees she was too hasty in refusing to teach Sophie how to conduct herself. We see your need, Hal, and we are not the like to ignore it. Leave the conduct of your wards in our hands. Margery will find Cordelia's kin, indeed, she dispatched a letter to Tom Kingscott as soon as she heard, and she'll bring Sophie's unruly temper under control."

"You are very kind, ma'am, but I cannot put such a burden on you both," he replied. "Aunt Margery was right. I am a man full-grown, if I make a mistake, it is for me to rectify."

"You must not refine too much upon Margery's words, Hal, you know her bark is infinitely worse than her bite. I can assure you neither ward will be a burden to us," she replied quickly.

"I'm sure Sophie will be to Aunt Margery, and she and Sophie do not agree. Giving her over to Margery's care will be the death of one of them."

Kate laughed. "You underestimate Margery, I do believe, Hal, she has just the tiniest admiration for Sophie, in that she won't allow herself to be tamed. I do believe that, in time, they'll come to have a certain respect for each other."

"Perhaps, but what of the casualties along the way, ma'am? For, make no mistake, this will be a war of attrition."

Again, she chuckled. "Indeed it will, won't it, Hal. So

you stand aside, and let them fight it out."

"And you? After all, you are leaving us quite soon to be married," he asked, feeling a distinct longing to allow his aunts to take over his responsibilities to his wards, but still quite anxious as to the consequences.

"Not for some months," she replied quickly. "And then only if I am certain. I am not sure I've not been over-persuaded. But enough of that, you need not fret for me, Hal. You see, I've had long practice in standing aside," she confided. "Margery has her methods, I have my own."

"Mmn," he agreed. "Margery's being the frontal attack with full cannon and cavalry, yours being the undermining of the walls with kindness and common sense." He hesitated as she smiled, and then added with some difficulty: "You, you will take care of Sophie for me, ma'am?"

"You know I will, I can see how you love her, indeed I am fond of her myself! Sophie has many splendid qualities, she just needs to learn to moderate her unruly temper!"

"She does, doesn't she," he agreed, looking gratified. Then, the cloud descended to his face again as the recollected their meeting last evening.

"Why, what is it, Hal?" she asked in surprise.

"Oh, I was remembering. Justin told her of Etienne, the child, and—and my affair with Jacqueline. Sophie was shocked and digusted! I think you need have no fear for me now. She says she'll not marry me anyway."

"Had you asked her?" said Kate, amazed that things had advanced so far.

"No," he replied, "but I hadn't denied that I loved her. We—we had a sort of understanding, I suppose."

Kate digested this, and realised that if he didn't marry this impetuous young woman, he'd be heartbroken. So much for Margery's plans. Hastily, she began to rethink her ideas. "Don't fret, Hal," she said gently, clasping his hand. "Sophie may well appear shocked and dismayed, but to me, it looks as if she is as much in love as you are, my dear! She may say all manner of foolish things, but she loves you."

"Cannot love be tried too far?" he asked. "Have I not sickened her by my lecherous behaviour?"

"True love endureth, Hal," she replied, tears filling her eyes as she recollected her own husband. "It matters not what one of you does in folly. The trust and affection of years weighs heavily against such flotsam."

"I am sorry, Aunt," he returned the pressure of her

hand. "I'd forgotten about Will Cuthbert."

"Yes," she said simply. "Poor Will, if only your uncle had acknowledged him properly, perhaps all that was good and fine in his character might not have turned to evil."

"Yes," said Hal doubtfully.

"Will was like Henry, too, Hal, before you arrived to be Henry's heir and jealousy soured Will's character. None of us know what we are capable of until we are tried by the loss of that most dear to us."

"Indeed," he agreed. "I beg pardon, Aunt, and I heed what you are saying. Etienne, Stephen, I don't know why the French name persists so. Stephen will be brought up in truth as to his birth."

"Not an easy task, Hal," she said with a sigh. "You have no doubts as to who is his father?"

"Few," he replied bitterly.

"It's not as if you can console him with the idea that his mother was a good person," she said thoughtfully.

"No," agreed Hal. "Perhaps misguided would be a better way to explain it. I don't know. We'll have to hope he shows few of Jacqueline's traits."

"Indeed," she agreed with a shudder. "Did you—" she hesitated, unsure how to phrase the question. "Did you explain everything to Sophie?" she asked delicately.

"Did I tell her I was drunk? Yes," he replied shortly.

"Oh Hal, like that?" she cried. "You didn't tell her how Jacqueline tricked you, seduced you?"

"It was hardly an edifying story, ma'am," he replied austerely. "Nor one I can hope to relay to my ward with any degree of credit."

"Your ward, no," she agreed, "but your love, yes."

"I am sorry, I have difficulty in separating the two," returned Hal.

"Yes, that is the main problem," she agreed, getting to her feet. "But don't fret any more. You concentrate on getting Justin off this murder charge. I'll worry about Sophie."

He smiled up at her. "I'd be vastly obliged, ma'am," he said.

The day seemed unending to Hal, listening as he was, constantly for her return, as the afternoon wore on into early evening. Several times, he lifted his head from the account book he was studying, convinced he'd caught the sound of her voice raised in laughter, only to find he'd imagined it. How much worse would it be, when she would come no more? When she departed for her husband's house for good, and he never set eyes on her lovely face again.

"You are melancholy, Hal?" Philippe, who had returned shortly after Aunt Kate's departure, and has been
sitting, apparently with his head in a book most of the
day, but in truth, he was using it as a shield while he
kept an eye on his friend.

Hal smiled. "A little," he admitted. "This weather can
be a trial, I find, and my affairs are in something of a
muddle. I see I am paid out for these past weeks of idle-
ness."

"Yes, the fog is returning again," Philippe rose and
went to the window. "But the young people, they have
not yet returned. Yet you impressed upon Blackwell not
to delay."

"I expect he is in too great a state of bliss to notice the
ugly weather," said Hal grimly.

"Bliss?" mused Philippe. "You think Sophia Redcroft
giving one undivided attention would be bliss?"

Hal kept his head down. "I don't think. I know it,"
he murmured.

"If you truly love her, Hal, you know what to do."

"Yes," he replied starkly.

Philippe sighed and continued to look out of the
window as Hal embarked on a further column of fig-

ures. "Justin Danvers is walking in the garden again," he remarked. "No wonder Englishmen are such dour creatures. I vow I felt very English in my misery earlier. Have you and he quarrelled again, Hal?"

"No," he replied, losing his place with a sigh and realising that with a headache, it really was beyond him. "No, I am avoiding his company, if I speak to him, I might be tempted to cheat the hangman."

"You think he will hang, Hal?" he asked in surprise.

"Unless Ambrose can return with some information of real use, I fear he might yet," he replied. "I can discover nothing locally that helps in any way."

"When are you expecting him?" asked Philippe, as Justin turned back toward the house.

"Not for a day or so," replied Hal. "Although the longer he is gone, the more chance there is of him having found something, I suppose."

"I observe a rider turning in the gateway now," said Philippe. "Is it the young people? No, 'tis merely one horse. It cannot be your sister's husband, it is much too soon."

"Who is it, then?" said Hal, shutting his book. "Let us pray he brings us something we can use in Justin's defence."

"Sir Henry!" Justin opened the door, still clad in his

outdoor garments. "A lone rider is come."

"Yes, we saw from the window," said Hal coolly. "Yet it cannot be Ambrose."

"No, 'tis not his build, nor horse, 'tis a stranger," he replied.

"A stranger," Hal came out into the hall in surprise, going to the door to look curiously at the rider approaching.

"Do not go out in that cold air, Hal!" called Philippe.

Justin cast Hal a bleak look. "'Tis not Ambrose," he repeated.

"No," agreed Hal, as Thomas ran out of the porch to take the horse's head.

"Sir Henry Westwood?" asked the man, as he dismounted.

"Inside, sir," said Thomas.

The man cast a quick look about him, rather impressed by the elegant façade, which, if not entirely symmetrical, was very pleasing to the eye, with its lead-paned windows flanking the porch, suggesting warmth and comfort on a cold, damp evening. He trod up the step and into the porch. "Sir Henry Westwood?" he repeated.

"I am Hal Westwood," said Hal, stepping forward.

"I'm pleased to meet you. I am John Hollingshead,

usually called Jack," he smiled briefly. "I've come in response to an enquiry from kin of mine. It seems your aunt, Mistress Kingscott, who is a distant cousin of ours, is seeking any relations of Cordelia Sandys."

"You are her kin?" asked Hal.

"Only a second cousin, I'm afraid," he replied easily. "But kin, of sorts, yes."

"This is excellent news," said Hal. "Do come in and get warm. Have you had a long journey?"

"I set out from Lincolnshire last Tuesday," he replied, taking off his hat and gloves, and following Hal into the Jericho parlour. "But I've been staying with my mother's family in Oxford. It was my great-aunt who received your aunt's letter."

"This is my good friend Philippe Douay," said Hal, as the physician got to his feet. "Come, warm yourself at the fire, I'll get a servant to bring some broth."

"Stay, Hal, I'll do it. 'Tis time I prepared your physic anyway," said Philippe, heading to the door and almost tripping over Justin. "Oh, Mr Danvers, I beg pardon."

"Justin, this is Mr John Hollingshead, he is Cordelia Sandys's cousin. Mr Hollingshead, my brother-in-law, Justin Danvers."

"Call me Jack, please," he said pleasantly. "Yes, I was

just explaining to Sir Henry, I am a distant cousin of Basil Sandys of Bickmarsh Hall, who was killed at the Battle of Worcester. Is this the right connection?"

"As far as we know," agreed Hal.

"As far as we knew, Cousin Basil had no issue," continued the young man, flinging back his cloak as the warmth of the fire penetrated the numbing cold. "He left England in the Autumn of 1646, after the King was captured," he hesitated to explain. "We are of his father's sister's family, and for Parliament, so we had little contact with him, especially after he left England. He wrote occasionally to my mother, usually asking for money, which angered my father, so she seldom mentioned him. Certainly, we had no idea he'd married again."

"He had been married previously," asked Hal, as Thomas came in bringing a bowl of broth and wine for them.

"Thank you, this is most welcome. The weather is turning very nasty out there," said Jack, surrendering his outer clothes to the servant. "Yes, Basil was married previously to a cousin of my father," he continued. "But unfortunately, she had died in childbirth the previous year, and the older child took a fever shortly after, so that he was left with no family."

"Please, eat your broth, the story has been long waiting, it can wait a few moments more," said Hal, handing a glass of wine to Justin.

"Thank you, you're most kind." The young man took a seat at the table and took up his spoon to make short work of the food, thus giving Hal an opportunity to observe him. If he were seeking any likeness to Cordelia, he couldn't find it. For, they were totally unalike, save in colouring, and perhaps a rather sallow cast of countenance. For, where Cordelia was slight and compact, this fellow was tallish and gangling, although not ill-looking in a nondescript sort of way. He was, Hal surmised, in his early twenties. A little older than Ned. "Will you continue with your story?" asked Hal as the stranger put aside his bowl and accepted the wine Hal offered.

"Thank you, yes. Basil left for France, we assume, and was one of the court at Saint Germain in attendance on Queen Henrietta-Maria. The next we heard of him was that he came back to his home in the August of 1650, to see to matters on his estate, which was in a terrible way. Most of it had been sequestered, so my father said, and sold off to pay fines. Basil had bought some of the land which marched with ours, but all that was left was the ruined house and a few acres. Basil went there to collect together a few of his people, and left for Worcester. They brought him back the following week, and he was buried in the churchyard at Bickmarsh," he paused, taking a deep breath.

"As the only surviving child of Jocelyn Sandys, my grandmother inherited Bickmarsh in the terrible condition it was in, and my father, believing as he did Basil died childless, restored it for me on her death."

"Ah," said Hal as Philippe entered with another of his vile brews.

"Ah, indeed," agreed the young man wryly. "You are certain, are you, that this young woman is Basil Sandys's daughter?"

"I am, and I have a letter written by him to prove it," said Hal, accepting the cup reluctantly. "It would appear that he married the daughter of another penniless exile who died the summer of 1646, leaving her alone. They lived, as you suggest, on the fringes of Queen Henrietta-Maria's court, but the death of the lady in childbirth and the need to find the baby a place of safety, sent Sir Basil to a nunnery in the heart of the country. He deposited the child there because his wife had lived with the nuns in her youth, and it was at this place I found your cousin Cordelia when I was looking for my father's lost child."

Jack Hollingshead sighed. "Does that prove he was legally married to her mother?" he asked rudely.

"No, but the records of the Church of the Blessed Virgin in a small village near Calais do," said Philippe Douay. He nodded at Hal. "How right you were to send me to check them, Hal, and to get that letter from the priest to confirm the date of marriage."

The stranger pulled a face. "Forgive me, but this is the most unwelcome news. For the past eighteen years, ever since I could sit my pony, my father and I have tended the estate. Until his death, slowly, bit by bit, we put it all back together again, buying back the land as it became available. Now to find it isn't mine at all. That Basil had a daughter, and neglected to let us know."

"One can appreciate your chagrin," said Philippe.

"I'm obliged to you," he retorted. "And this leads me to my next question: is my cousin Cordelia married?"

"She left the nunnery a few weeks ago," said Hal. "Where has been the time?"

"Excellent," Jack Hollingshead sighed with relief this time. "Then, as my mother suggests, that is the answer. Luckily, I am unmarried, too."

"Now, wait a moment," said Hal. "This is a girl fresh from a nunnery. I agreed to take her into my guardianship when it became clear she had no vocation as a nun. But I'll not forget my promise to the Reverand Mother, or my obligation to Cordelia herself."

"We are, of course, vastly obliged to you for your rescue of our cousin," the young man agreed. "But now that her kin have been discovered, there can be no occasion to trouble you further. My mother will assume guardianship of her during her minority."

"I'm sorry, but I signed legal papers," said Hal firmly. "Cordelia stays my ward until such time as she comes of age, or is given in marriage, to a bridegroom I am certain she'll be completely happy with."

"But of course," he agreed amicably. "I assure you, we've no intention of treading on any toes. If you wish to retain the guardianship of my cousin, you must indeed do so. My mother merely sought to relieve you of a burden which had no claim upon you." He smiled, but the humour didn't reach his eyes. "After all, Sir Henry, we have no knowledge of your character, as you have no knowledge of ours. You must understand our concern that one of our family is in the wardship of a complete stranger. Naturally, I am relieved to find that she is the ward of a man with integrity. But, you must agree, it could have been otherwise."

Hal nodded slowly. "Indeed, and you must also agree, sir, that I could not allow her to be married off to suit your convenience."

"Indeed Sir Henry, I have no intention of anything other than the hope that we might be found to suit one another. May I, perhaps, meet my cousin?"

"You could, had they returned from their visit," murmured Hal, glancing anxiously to the fast-darkening sky. "They arrived while I was brewing that for you, Hal," said Philippe. "Along with the new cook. All are alive and well, if not damp. I sent them to change their shoes."

"Then you'll meet Cordelia over supper, Mr Hollingshead. I'll call my servant to escort you to a chamber in the west wing. You will, of course, stay long enough with us to make the acquaintance of your cousin."

❧

Chapter Twenty One

Cordelia, meanwhile, had hurriedly changed her shoes and her damp gown, rigorously keeping her mind on the events confided to her by Philippe Douay. A cousin of marriageable age coming seeking her. It was suddenly all too much. She needed Sophie to put things into perspective for her.

From never having met a man other than the ancient gardener, she had, in quick succession, met Hal, for whom she'd immediately developed a youthful admiration. Philippe Douay, who amused her and helped her so with the oddness of her native people. And now, Adam Blackwell. Adam, although he wasn't grand like Hal, and therefore less awe-inspiring, or amusing and witty like the Frenchman, was somehow much more interesting. Indeed, she could frequently have slapped Sophie today for her patent lack of interest in the things Adam had been showing them. It was so plain he'd been on tenterhooks, wanting Sophie's approval of everything, and so obviously proud of what he'd achieved. He only required her interest to transport him into the realms of delight. Yet Sophie accepted everything as normal and his worship as her due.

"Sophie, may I come in?" Cordelia was surprised to see she'd not even changed her shoes, but sat blankly before the bright fire, still warming her hands. "Are you ill, Sophie?" she asked anxiously. "Have you not changed from your boots?"

"Mmn? Oh no, I'd better do it or I'll incur Philippe Douay's displeasure," she agreed, bending down to ease off the little kid-leather boots which had earlier wrung Cordelia's heart with her first stab of envy. There was, she realised, a world of difference between normal life and the cloisters. Within the nunnery, all had worn similar clothing in essence, but out in the read world, she'd been shocked to find how much she admired Sophie's more fashionable clothing. How she longed to be able to turn her rather plain wardrobe the nuns had hastily put together for her from cast-off garments into the modish apparel Sophie habitually wore.

"Shall I find you a drier gown?" suggested Cordelia,

not without the desire to look through her closet.

"Oh, would you be an angel?" said Sophie, unlacing her bodice and allowing her thick riding kirtle to fall in folds to the floorboards. "I'm sorry I'm so late, I've been in something of a daze, but you'll want to talk of this cousin! Of course, you'll have known nothing of him."

"No, nothing," agreed Cordelia, feeling suddenly very flat as she realised, far from wanting to talk of her visitor, she wanted to discuss their visit to Adam Blackwell's.

"It's almost too romantic," murmured Sophie, as she poured water from an ewer over her hands and began to wash her face. "No sooner does he hear of your existence, than he crossed half of England to meet you."

"I thought Doctor Douay said he'd come to see if I had a claim on his estate," she replied rebelliously. "That doesn't seem to me to be romantic, far from it."

"Oh, Philippe Douay is a Frenchman," cried Sophie scornfully. "You know how odd they are about marriage and property. Yes, that one if you please," she added as Cordelia held out a gown.

Cordelia shook her head. "I don't know, are they? I thought everyone considered property when they married."

"Well, yes they do, or at least their families do," conceded Sophie. "But the French are rather cold-blooded about it, or so they say. That's why Hal was so ready to marry his first wife. He'd been reared in France, you see, as you were, and saw nothing amiss in marrying the daughter of a wealthy lawyer to gain her considerable dowry." She stepped into the gown and readily accepted the other girl's help with the lacing of it.

"But surely, if Adam Blackwell marries you, he'll gain control of your money, won't he?" asked Cordelia, frowning.

"Well, yes," she agreed. "But, Adam could hardly be said to be marrying me for my money, why it must be plain to a blind man, he adores me."

"Yes, yes, that is indeed plain," agreed Cordelia in a flat voice, as Sophie ruthlessly brushed her mane of bright curls. "Are you ready? Shall we go down?"

Margery glanced with approval to Hal. Their latest guest was taking great pains to engage his newly discovered cousin's attention. All seemed set in motion for a satisfying conclusion to what had been, after all, virtually an insoluble problem, and Hal could thank her for rescuing him from the results of his improvident folly. For once in these past unhappy, disturbed months, she felt that possibly life could be settling back into some semblance of the old order so beloved by her. Here, before her eyes, was a modest young female being properly courted by a kinsman, approved by his own family, attended by kinsfolk, and well-chaperoned.

Aye, and it would do that minx Sophia good to be forced to play chaperone and second fiddle for a change, she thought, with a further swell of satisfaction. Sophia needed to be shown she wasn't the only fish in the sea, and that for all her beauty, tarnished goods weren't likely to make a good match. It wasn't that she disliked Sophia, as Kate claimed, in fact, in some ways she had a gnawing respect for her independent spirit. But, in spite of that, and the seeds of a fiercely repressed admiration that Sophia would not allow herself to be dominated, Margery knew in her heart she was trouble. Some girls were, and of all she'd ever seen in her life, Sophia Redcroft was potentially the most troublesome.

It was a grave source of concern to Margery that Hal seemed powerless to resist the hussy. She'd seen him and noted his struggles. Hal was intrinsically a good man, she had no doubt of that. As upright as his uncle and namesake, with none of his father's deviousness of character nor slippery principles, Hal was nonetheless a man for all that, with all the frailties it implied. Henry, her brother, hadn't been above blame, he too had had his peccadillos, and much trouble had that led to for them all. Best then, to nip this affair in the bud, before Hal, too, got burnt and they were all plunged into some disgrace or another.

Somehow, she had to get Sophia out of the house and swiftly, before Hal committed them all to the sort of scandal Sophia was sure to trail in her wake. It needed some thought and careful planning.

In the meantime, there was no doubt this Jack Hollingshead was a very well-behaved gentleman. She'd suffered a moment of doubt, for when he'd first clapped his eyes on Sophie, he'd assumed that glazed expression most men did. But she was pleased to see he'd soon recollected what his errand was, and had henceforth devoted his attentions to Cordelia entirely. He had recounted his few memories of her father, talking in great detail of the house that was her home, and all the improvements he'd made to it. He had also assured her of the warm welcome his mother would extend to her on the occasion of her visit.

"A great pity," he was saying. "That you never had the occasion to meet our grandmother. She died but last year aged six and eighty years. She was very much the grand-dame! She'd been at the court of good Queen Bess and, I am sure, modelled herself all her life on that enigmatic lady! By heaven, I can't number the times she'd make us all shake in our shoes, just by her glance! Indeed, your guardian, Sir Henry's excellent Aunt puts me much in mind of her, and I owe that lady a debt of gratitude for being the means of introducing me to so lovely a kinswoman."

"Even if that introduction will rob you of your property?" asked Sophie bluntly, who was bored by his long-winded speeches, and had doubts as to his sincerity.

His smile did not reach his eyes. "No doubt, Mistress Redcroft, if I said I count it well-lost to view such beauty, you'd accuse me of fustian," he replied.

"I'd think you a fool!" she retorted as Cordelia hid a smile and Hal, who'd been eavesdropping, turned a laugh into an unconvincing cough that did indeed soon turn to a bout of coughing.

"No, no keep away from me, Philippe," he gasped, as soon as he could get his breath. "I've had enough of your foul potions for today!"

"But it is efficacious, Hal," he protested. "Since taking the mixture before supper, you'd hardly coughed and you look much improved.

"True," he agreed. "But no more now, I beg of you."

"Later, before you retire, then," said Philippe, his face still anxious.

Hal nodded, his eyes going again to Sophie's averted face, a feeling of depression creeping into his soul. This was how his head told him it should be. Her indifference to him, her lack of interest, was exactly how it should be between a guardian and his ward. But how it broke his heart. The grim despair he'd felt at the news of Libby's death, and which had somehow held off once he'd caught sight of Sophie's beloved face, had him back in its grip. He sat on, listening to the pompous young man, feeling twice his age, and could only be glad when supper was finally over and they dispersed. He soon sought his bed.

❖

However, not everyone was ready for bed. Kate found Sophie, still wide awake. "Sophia, may I come in? You are not too weary for a talk?" asked Aunt Kate, tapping on the half-opened door. "Oh, you are Hannah. Are you settling in well?"

"Thank you, Mistress Westwood, yes," said Hannah promptly, as she picked up Sophie's damp boots and muddy kirtle. "I've just been to see young Master Henry and Master Francis in the nursery."

"And rocked the baby whilst I told them a story," smiled Sophie. "I think Hannah, you'd sooner be a nursery maid than a ladies' maid."

The servant girl smiled faintly. "I'm not one to be choosy, Mistress Sophie," she replied evasively.

"How is cook settling in?" asked Kate anxiously. "That supper she served was certainly excellent. Even Doctor Douay commented upon it."

"Well, she said it were difficult," said Hannah. "Not knowing where everything went, and with some of the servants off sick, but I gave her a hand for a while."

"Yes, do take care, Hannah, you don't take the quinsies too," sighed Kate. "It has gone through almost all the maids like wildfire."

The girl nodded and curtsied, departing with the muddy clothes.

"So, ma'am," said Sophie, taking up a brush to tidy her long hair. "How can I help you?"

Kate smiled at the picture Sophie presented in her

long nightgown, with her golden curls rippling under her brush. She looked much younger than her nineteen years. "Here, let me do that for you," she said, coming to take the brush. "My, what beautiful hair you have, 'tis like spun gold."

Sophie smiled back at her in the mirror and surrendered the brush a shade reluctantly. "I've not had my hair brushed since Mistress Nichols died. My Uncle Edmund's sister," she explained, as Aunt Kate looked blank. "She used to lecture me, too," she added.

"I've not come to lecture you, Sophie," protested Aunt Kate, "merely to talk."

"Have you not?" asked the girl sceptically.

Again, Kate met her eyes in the mirror. "You are right to be wary of us, Sophie," she agreed. "We have not treated you well. I see that now. We were all so taken up with the scandal and then Libby's illness, that very little thought was given to you. I am sorry for it, I should have controlled Justin more, it was for me to see to things."

"You were nursing Lady Westwood, ma'am," replied Sophie, softened by her frank confession.

"Yes, but Margery wasn't here, Libby was ill. As the most senior present, I should at least have seen you had a maid and asked after your welfare. I confess, I never gave a thought to any of the horrors you, a young, friendless girl, had endured at the hand of that man, Durward."

Sophie's mouth went awry, but she lifted her chin, biting at her plump underlip. "I did well enough, ma'am."

"Call me Aunt Kate," she replied. "All the children do. No, Sophie, you did not do well enough. Neither did I. That foolishness with…was it a cushion? Indeed, had I been concerned for your welfare, had I even been on terms of civility with you, that nonsense could have been stopped before any damage was done. I failed you, and Hal, but mostly Libby."

"My dear ma'am, Aunt Kate," Sophie turned on her stool in concern. "Do not be so quick to take on all blame. I am no little fool. I was wicked, I know I was wicked. I feel such shame now for the things I did! For the terrible trouble and pain I've brought on both Lady Westwood and Hal." Tears filled her eyes at this confession and Aunt Kate, abandoning the brush, hugged her close whilst Sophie relieved her overcharged emotions in a bout of tears.

"Oh, ma'am, I mean, Aunt Kate," she whispered, as

soon as she could. "I am sorry, I did not mean to weep all over you."

"No matter, my dear," she replied, laughing a little. "Tears are better shed than hidden!"

"'Tis usually Hal I weep all over," she said, and then began to sob anew.

"What is it, Sophie? Why do you weep so?" asked Kate gently.

"I, I do love him so," she whispered. "But, but…"

"But Justin has spoiled your dreams?" asked Kate.

She nodded, tears running down her cheeks.

"What did Justin say?" she asked.

"That Etienne was Hal's son," she whispered. "That he and Jacqueline were lovers, that Hal was a rake and a libertine who used women. That I was but one of many, that Cordelia was his next target, already he had no use for me."

Kate nodded, stroking her tumbled hair from her tearstained face. "In effect, Justin threw all the mad accusations at you that he could," she said reflectively. "He tried to make you hurt as much as he's hurting."

Sophie sniffed. "Yes, I suppose he did," she agreed. "But, but don't you see? It's all true!"

"And you still love him," finished Aunt Kate as

Sophie began to weep again. "Truth often depends upon how it is presented, you know, let's take these wild accusations, shall we? Firstly, the one about Cordelia is so patently untrue as to be laughable. When have you seen Hal even look at Cordelia?"

"He did rescue her from that French convent," she replied.

"Indeed he did, and I am proud of him for doing it. He knew it wouldn't be easy, but thank God he still has a deep compassion for those less fortunate than himself."

"And he admires her, he told me I should model my behaviour on hers," said Sophie rebelliously.

"Well, and don't you admire her, too?" asked Kate. "Isn't she a very brave young woman?"

"Yes," agreed Sophie pettishly. "Oh yes, but everyone likes her so, and thinks her so much nicer than me! Yet, she is a stranger to them as I was. Why should she be accepted as Hal's ward, without a word, when I am rejected?" Then, as the elder woman met her eyes smiling, she said: "Yes, I know, because her behaviour is much more acceptable."

"Indeed," Kate said. "You have but to moderate your behaviour, Sophie, to see a like acceptance, I am sure.

To our second point, that you were but one of many women and that Hal used women ill. This first is a lie. Hal could not by any means be called a rake. Here, I fear, he suffers for his father's reputation. He was, to my knowledge, a good faithful husband to Libby. None had ever heard her level a word of complaint about him, and believe me, child, a wife knows."

"Until I came onto the scene, ma'am," she said soberly.

"Until he met you, yes," she agreed. "But still, his behaviour didn't, until the very last, when he was ill, if you remember, in any way harm his wife. He treated her as he always had done, with utmost courtesy. If looked at from an impartial standpoint when faced with an impossible situation, Hal took the only way out he could at the time. He left you all and went abroad to, as he himself phrased it, 'hopefully rid his head and heart of you.'"

"Whilst I remained at home to make matters worse," she said penitently.

"Then we come to the last crime, and for this, there is no defence, as such. He is sure Etienne is his son. Have you discussed it with him?"

"Not, not in any detail," she replied in a suffocated voice.

"May I tell you of it?" Kate asked gently.

"If, if you please, ma'am," she agreed.

"We must go back to before the end of Cromwell's reign, shortly before he died. Hal was a young man, growing up abroad. He trailed around Europe with his father, not a pleasant man, my dear. Oh, affable enough to your face, but with few sound principles. Henry, my husband, and he had quarrelled most of their lives. Francis was a jealous man, arrogant, given to seeing slights where none were intended. They had quarrelled bitterly at the end of the fighting in '48. Francis refused to pay fines and fled abroad, taking only Hal with him, Catherine joined him later, leaving the children with us, Mary, Bess, Jane and Ned. Henry and I were childless, it was an eternal grief to us, and we were happy to restore them to some semblance of normality, poor things. They had suffered much, living in lodgings most often in the course of the war. Over the next year, we sent Francis money to support himself, and he continuously wrote home complaining it was not enough, and that we were not to allow this or that to happen to the children. Then Francis decided he wanted his family reunited and sent for them all. Then came the blow of the King's trial and execution. It seemed the end to all Royalists.

I'm sorry if I'm boring you with this, my dear, but it is necessary you understand, if possible. We sent money to the exiles, but Henry had fought, he too had fines to pay. Once again, they all lived, anyhow. Francis went as a mercenary for a while, leaving Catherine in poor circumstances. She lost another baby, and then Hetta was born. It was, at this point in '55, I think, that some sense prevailed and Henry went across to France to bring the children back. Margery was back with us by this time, and we thought they had been abroad too long. Hal was fifteen by now, but Francis wouldn't let him come, although he sent all the other children. Henry had, however, been impressed by Hal. He said he was a good-hearted, serious lad. Well-educated, and plainly not happy in the circumstances he found himself. It was then Henry began to formulate a plan for Hal to be his heir. He had realized I wasn't going to have children, and so began to make provision for the future. At first, Francis wasn't agreeable, and he and Henry quarrelled again, but in '58 or thereabouts, he fell in with a disreputable set of people following Catherine's death, and for some reason, ended up in desperate straights, near death himself. Hal took him to an apothecary to tend his wounds, and it was there he and Francis met the man's daughter, Jacqueline.

What went on, we never found out, but Francis and Jacqueline were married early in '59, and shortly after, Francis wrote to say that he was having difficulty with Hal. That the boy had been dazzled by his new wife, and was deeply in love with her and that for everyone's sake, Hal had better come home to us.

Henry was thrilled and preparations were made, then Oliver Cromwell died and all Royalists jumped for joy. Francis, as ever, in the thick of plot and counter-plot, was too busy and so Hal never came until the King himself returned. Later, he accompanied Francis and Jacqueline to London, and then he came to Westwood with Francis. It was then the marriage Henry had all but arranged the year before was once again mooted for the lad.

I liked Hal immediately. There is an honesty in his character that I loved from the start. He was so very like his uncle, and so unalike his father. He professed himself willing to marry whomsoever his uncle chose, provided he could mend their fortunes. Henry, guessing the lad had been bitterly hurt by Jacqueline, thought a speedy wedding the best thing for all concerned. Hal wed Libby later that summer, meeting her a bare few days before the wedding.

Henry, of course, was killed on that very day by his natural son, Will Cuthbert. Henry had kept Will close to him, which was a mistake, for Will grew to think he should become heir. He had finally to admit Will was not a fit man to take care of an estate. This threw him into a murderous fury and the flaw in his character Henry had foreseen resulted in Will murdering his own father.

Hal, with Justin's help, discovered who was to blame, for Francis looked guilty on the face of it, and Will was brought to justice of sorts, but in the meantime, Jacqueline was at her mischief again. Bored by Francis's frequent trips abroad, she came to Westwood and sought to amuse herself with Hal. It is my belief that she had previously seduced the boy, there was no doubt she considered him her property, and Hal believes she tried to injure Libby. Finally, Francis saw sense and removed her to London again, where the family met infrequently over the next few years. As he grew up and settled more in life, Hal's principles became stronger, and when Jacqueline realised she could no longer tempt him, she resorted to underhand methods.

Hal himself was forced by circumstances to confess

fully to us all what had happened next. He had gone to his father's house in Whitehall one stormy night when he was searching for Justin and Bess. He sought shelter and dry clothes, and it was then that he allowed a combination of sheer physical weariness, coupled with disappointment and anxiety, to lead himself into drinking too heavily for his own good. He said he awoke next morning to find Jacqueline in his bed, and although he hastily decamped, the damage was already done. Jacqueline later announced she was pregnant with what she insisted was Hal's child, although Francis told me he thought it was like to be the child of her lover in Whitehall. To save Hal and Libby any more grief, he took Jacqueline immediately abroad, and as you now realise, they both perished in France shortly after."

"So Jacqueline seduced Hal," said Sophie frowning. "Why did he not tell me so?"

"Apparently not only seduced him, but threatened to cry rape if he tried to accuse her," said Kate. "Jacqueline was not a very pleasant person, my dear. As to why he didn't tell you, well, you know how Hal is. He is deeply ashamed of the whole thing. He said it was hardly an edifying tale with which to entertain his ward."

Sophie gave an abrupt chuckle. "Yes, I can hear him

saying it. He can be so stiff at times! Poor Hal, it must have hurt his vanity, too, to be made a fool of."

Kate smiled. "Male vanity is immense, I'll agree, but best, I always find, if not remarked upon."

Sophie exchanged a grin. "Rather as Mistress King-scott always does."

"Exactly as poor Margery always does," she agreed. "With men, my dear, you must have selective vision."

Sophie thought about that. "And speech, too, surely?"

"Ah, now you are becoming wiser," said Kate nodding.

"Yes," Sophie was pensive for a few moments, then she looked up. "What should I do, Aunt Kate, for the best?"

"Oh, Sophie, that is more than I can say," she replied. "For myself, I think you love Hal so, and he loves you so, that you should eventually marry. But don't be in any hurry to go about it."

"That's what Hannah says!" she exclaimed. "To take my time."

"Then she's no fool," said Kate. "Take your time, do as you are bid, attend your studies and keep compa-ny with Cordelia. Allow everyone a little time to settle down and then see how you and Hal both feel." She rose to her feet. "But I've talked too long, Margery would be so cross if she knew I'd kept you from your rest. Remember, child, I am always here if you need me."

Chapter Twenty Two

Thomas sidled up to Hal at supper next evening, saying, in an undertone: "Mr Carver has arrived back from London, sir. He says he's too dirty to join you all at supper, but will you go to him in the Jericho parlour as soon as possible?"

Hal nodded his assent. It had been another difficult day. Sophie and Margery had spent the whole time sniping at each other, in spite of Aunt Kate's best efforts. Hal wasn't sure who he was crossest with. The atmosphere at the table was electric, and hardly conducive to good digestion. Hal caught Philippe's eye and indicated they should leave with a jerk of his head. The physician needed no second bidding to depart the dining parlour.

"Ambrose," Hal entered the room, and espying him drinking a bowl of broth, added: "No, don't get up, finish that before you talk. Philippe and I will get a cup of wine. We've arrived promptly because we were being bored to death in the dining parlour."

"Your respected aunt looked as if she was very happy," remarked Philippe. "She truly believes Mr Hollingshead a virtuous young man."

"He's an intolerable braggart," said Hal.

"You only thought that when he was admiring Sophie," grinned Philippe. "Once Hollingshead remembered his estate was at stake, he forgot her and became really pompous."

"Why, what has occurred?" asked Ambrose, intrigued.

As the physician outlined the latest developments, Hal got them and Justin, who had just arrived, a glass of wine. He handed Justin his glass, matching black look for black look, and then sat down at the table as Ambrose put his finished supper aside and accepted the wine.

"Thank you, although I bring but a poor budget, I fear."

"Nothing?" cried Hal, in dismay.

"Very little," he said, with a sigh. "I very quickly found the place of Nathaniel Sitwell's business, it is but a blackened ruin now. The biggest problem, really, was the plague last summer, when so many died and all the survivors fled. True, some came back when it was safe this autumn, but very few want to talk about it."

"So, you could discover nothing?" asked Justin, in dismay.

Ambrose shook his head guiltily. "Very little of any moment," he said uncomfortably. "True, I discovered Nat Sitwell had used his business as a cover for his illegal dealings, but I have no hope of persuading anyone to testify to that. The only hope was a young woman who works for a linen draper who has some knowledge. In fact, I brought her with me. Oh, not here!" he added as they all looked amazed. "No, I've left her at the inn at Adamsholme. She says she wants more money than I can offer to tell her tale."

"Oh, that sort of harpy!" said Justin. "You fool, you've been taken in. She'll know nothing."

"I think she is to be trusted!" protested Ambrose. "Yes, she's wary, but when you see her, you'll understand why." He shook his head. "I don't know how a man could treat another being so, let alone one of the weaker sex."

"Nat Sitwell injured her?" asked Hal, with a frown.

"No, not Nat Sitwell. It seems this man, Kit something, I think she called him, was connected with Sitwell's illegal dealings.

"What form of illegal dealings was he involved with?" demanded Hal.

"Plucking green pigeons," said Ambrose, with a grimace.

"Robbing young and foolish gentleman of their money, Philippe," said Hal, as the Frenchman looked puzzled.

"I believe I suspected something of this," said Justin, with a little reluctance. "It was when I was working for Steene and Johnson, Hal. That's where I first met Sitwell. I heard various rumours, but then there are always rumours in that part of the world. When he came to me in Adamsholme, he seemed perfectly respectable."

"But you said you thought he'd made the bulk of his money elsewhere," said Hal.

"Yes, I did," Justin agreed. "Truth to tell, I thought him a moneylender."

Ambrose nodded. "Which, in fact, he was. Only the interest was exorbitant, and his methods probably dubious. And..." he continued slowly, "I think he also used a decoy to get them drunk. It was said he was hand in glove with a lady of the night. She used to encourage the gambling and then, having plied them with drink and seen them fleeced, she'd take them, from the goodness of her heart, you understand, along to Uncle Nat's."

"Yes, one sees the pattern," agreed the physician.

"It would appear, although I must emphasize this is all hearsay, none of the people I spoke to would swear to it, and few would ever enter a court of law, it would appear this doxy later married Nat Sitwell."

"Helen!" gasped Justin in disbelief.

"She went by the name of Nell Riggs," said Ambrose. "At least that's the name on the Register of Births, Marriages and Deaths at St Peter at Gate."

Justin looked amazed. "She spoke of being in business with her husband," he stammered. "But I'd, I'd imagined that to be the cordwainer business."

"Largely a sham," said Ambrose. "Largely a sham."

"I find this difficult to believe," said Justin in dismay.

"As well you might," agreed Hal. "It does, however, open up many more areas of inquiry."

"How so, Hal?" asked Philippe.

"Well, if he was in business long enough to make a

fortune, I imagine he ruined a good few young men. He only needs one of those to be intent on revenge to have a reason for his, or his wife's death."

"True," agreed Justin, his eyes brightening a little at this thought.

"That is what had puzzled me all along about this case all along, lack of motive," said Hal. "Now we have motive enough. Justin, I was not here when Nat Sitwell died. Could that have been foul play, do you think?"

Justin stared. "I never considered it," he replied, taken aback. "I mean, he was elderly, fat, a heavy drinker, and a pig of a man. He was bound to make a bad end. He died back in September. I'd seen him two days previously to discuss his intention of buying a property at Ashton Attwell. Then suddenly, Mistress Sitwell sent word to say that her husband had died of an apoplexy and begged me attend her. I went at once and found him sprawled out on the floor of the inn's best parlour with Cookson raising caine about his good name."

"Why?" asked Philippe blankly.

Justin frowned. "Why, well, it being bad for trade, I suppose," he replied, as if it had never occurred to him. "Innkeepers hate sudden deaths, they always claim it ruins trade."

"I take your point, Philippe," said Hal. "You mean, why should the innkeeper worry that an old gluttonous drunkard of a guest had died of apoplexy? How could that have been prevented?"

"I don't know," Justin shrugged, but he looked puzzled as well. "Helen insisted I looked at him, and that the apothecary attended, but it was too late. The constable confirmed him dead, and he was buried the following Thursday. I hired a house for Helen, who couldn't bear to stay on at The Adam and Eve, and she and her servants moved in until the house at Mallen was purchased."

"The apoplexy could have been caused by an attack, I suppose," said Ambrose. "I shouldn't have thought an unhealthy old man like him... How old was he?"

"In his seventieth year, I believe," said Justin.

"A great age," said Philippe. "And so, as Ambrose suggests, an old man, grossly indulgent, it wouldn't have taken much to send him into an apoplexy. Why, even the mere sight of one he feared, or some rough handling, could have been enough."

"However, he's been underground these past two months, and none notice aught amiss at the time, so we can hardly judge," said Justin.

"Quite," agreed Ambrose. "What we must do now is ask for the names of any of the young men he fleeced."

"Ask?" cried Justin. "Ask who? The innkeeper? The neighbors? You've just said there is nobody to ask. As well ask that table."

"According to Nancy Gollen, there is one who'd know, although finding her may be difficult," said Ambrose. "It seems Helen's maid was a friend of the old days. Although, she disappeared six months ago…"

"But she's here!" cried Hal. "I took her on as Sophie's maid, to attend on Cordelia and Sophia both," he amended. "Did you not hear me say so at dinner the other day?"

"He'd already left by then. So the wench is in the house? Should we not call her down and question her?"

"Wait," said Hal, as Ambrose assented. "Wait, let me think. When I interviewed her before, as soon as I asked her about her mistress, she clammed up on me. It might be as well to get Jane to talk to her. Not Bess, she sees Bess as her mistress's enemy, but Jane might get something from her."

"But she might hold the key!" cried Justin. "Must we wait upon her convenience to get these answers?"

"I think it might be advisable," replied Hal. "She was very wary when I put the simplest of questions."

"Not quite so easy to charm, then?" remarked Justin blandly.

"No indeed," agreed Hal. "But if you think you'll have more success, you're welcome to try."

"We shall see how Mistress Carver manages, and if there are no answers forthcoming, I shall try," announced Philippe. "It is amazing what a female will tell a physician."

Hal grinned at him. "So, matters stand thus. The butler still swears you must be the murderer, Justin, although the cook is wavering. She now says you've too honest a face. The maid, Hannah Smith, has said very little, but that she never saw the man who returned. I, with Ambrose, will go to see this wench, Nancy Gollen, to see what we can get out of her tomorrow. Other than that, my agent has spoke to the shepherds on the hill. It seems they are in agreement that something disturbed the dog at Home Farm in Oakford, but what, they couldn't swear to. This is the first piece of corroborative evidence we've had."

"And probably the only," said Justin.

"Think about it again, Justin. Wasn't there the slightest hint that Nat Sitwell's death was anything other than natural?" asked Hal.

"No, there was nothing, it seemed the most natural thing in the world," Justin replied wearily. "It barely raised a ripple of gossip. It was about the time the mayor was held-up, of course, by that highwayman. Black Jack, do they call him? The gossips in Adamsholme were full of tales of him being somebody special. Nat Sitwell's death went almost unnoticed. But then, this highwayman is young and handsome, and free with his money, it seems. Nat Sitwell was old and drunk, and never gave anybody so much as a groat."

"Oh well, we shall have to see what Jane can get from the maid," said Hal. "In the meantime, Justin, have you finished your report? If Ambrose is to defend you, he'll need all the facts at his fingertips. By the by, Ambrose, did you find Nick Robinson, as I asked, and tell him to return to Adamsholme?"

"How is this?" cried Justin. "I sent Nick Robinson to qualify at Lincoln's Inn as a lawyer."

"Yes, I am aware of that," said Hal, "and once this matter is resolved, and we have another clerk to replace him, he may return thence, for all I care. But, in the meantime, we have need for him in Adamsholme."

"I make the decisions with regard to my practice," said Justin.

"You used to make the decisions when you were employed by your sister," replied Hal. "I now own the business. I've decided upon some changes. In future, you should be a senior partner, and Ambrose the junior, with a clerk to replace the work he does."

Justin's jaw dropped, then he shut his mouth, a sneer coming over his face. "I see! This is your revenge, is it?" he muttered.

"Don't we all require revenge?" retorted Hal blandly. "At least I take mine on you, fair and square, not on a young woman given over to your care."

"Young woman? Young trollop, you mean," sneered Justin.

"From your close association with a trollop, you should know Sophie is no such thing. If you have something to say to me, say it. Don't go shouting around the house about it."

Justin turned on him. "That's right, take a tone of moral outrage! Pretend that you, a widower of less than a month, wasn't tumbling your slut on a bed a few days ago."

"Surely the fault is the same, be the wife alive or dead,"

said Hal his face pale. "I don't set myself in the position to make judgements on another just because my pride is hurt. Ambrose, we are for Adamsholme first thing in the morning."

Chapter Twenty Three

In spite of Hal's best endeavours, the morning was considerably advanced by the time he and Ambrose rode into Adamsholme. Running the gauntlet, as he had not only both of his aunts, but Philippe, concerned with his health. However, as the day was bright and mild for the time of year, he overbore them all and they arrived in the town with his spirits unconsciously lifted by the fresh air, the sunshine and the exercise, and his cough plainly benefited from an untroubled night.

They made their way at once to the major inn, The Adam and Eve, only to find the place in turmoil, with the market crowd gathered in the courtyard, staring, and servants running hither and thither whilst, in the background, someone indulged in a bout of noisy hysterics.

"You, Luke Fletcher," cried Hal sharply. "What goes on here, were is Cookson?"

"Master's with the sheriff's man, your honour," replied the groom, recognising local quality.

"The sheriff's man?" repeated Hal, with a sudden sense of foreboding.

"Aye, that there wench you brought here last night, Mr Carver, her that were so ugly and crooked, well someone's finished her off."

"Dead?" said Ambrose, in horror.

"Life smashed out of her," replied the man with relish. "I doubt she's a whole bone in her body! I don't know who she were, but somebody took powerful agin' her to do that!"

"I shouldn't have left her," cried Ambrose. "I had it in my mind that I shouldn't leave her unprotected, but I thought you'd had so many unpleasant shocks land on your doorstep recently, and that this far from London she should have been safe."

"Where is your master and the sheriff's man?" demanded Hal.

"In the tap, your honour," he said apologetically. "The wench being laid out, so to speak, on a table in the dining parlour."

Hal jerked his head at Ambrose and he followed him under the low thatch of the inn. All was calm inside, by contrast with the throng without, and quiet enough but for the persistent wail of the hysterical voice."

With Ambrose on his heels, Hal entered the tap without so much as a knock in time to hear the landlord's protest.

"Well, I'm sure I don't know, Mr Parry," he said in injured tones. "I'm a telling you, that there clerk of Mr Danvers, him as you yourself arrested for murder, he came in here, bold as brass, with this here doxy on his arm, and him married to Sir Henry's own sister, 'tis said..."

"Good morning, Sir Henry," Sergeant Parry made haste to disassociate himself from the innkeeper's gossip. "Mr Carver!"

"Mr Carver!" The innkeeper's eyes bulged slightly and then he made a good recover. "Aye, well, Mr Carver, you'll surely bear out my story! The wench you brought here last night, you paid for her chamber, didn't you?"

"Indeed, I did," he agreed. "And paid well. I trust she was safely housed as I requested?"

"I put her in my second-best chamber, your honour," he said, his eyes travelling to Hal in appeal. "'Twas the best I had, Sir Roger Twychett and his Lady occupying the best, them laying overnight on their way to visit their daughter at Shallsbury Hall, short of Malvern! I thank the good Lord they were up and out of here at an early hour, Sir Roger hoping to get to the Hall before the fog came down again, and so heard nothing of this!"

"At what time was the body discovered?" asked Hal.

"At ten, Sir Henry," he replied. "My good wife said she'd take her up a morsel of breakfast, as Mr Carver would be sure to visit today, indeed, you said as much sir."

"Indeed, I did," agreed Ambrose again. "I knew I'd be returning with Sir Henry. Nancy Gollen was an important witness in Mr Justin Danvers's defence."

"Is that so?" asked the sergeant with interest. "And now she's dead."

"Yes," said Ambrose bitterly. "Before she had time to tell us her information or swear a deposition."

"It ain't my fault, Sir Henry," cried the innkeeper quickly. "I put her in the best room we had."

"How was she killed?" asked Ambrose.

"Battered to death," replied the sergeant, his face pale as he recollected it. "A vicious attack, it must have gone on long after she was dead."

"And my poor Maggie the one to find her," muttered

the innkeeper. "'Tis no wonder she be still in hysterics. 'Twas sight enough to make a man sick at heart and I fought in the war."

"Did none of you hear anything?" asked Hal. "A vicious beating that went on long after the poor wench was killed, that was not silently accomplished, I know!"

"There was a meeting here last night, Sir Henry," said the innkeeper uneasily. "A group of us who were in the Militia in old Noll Cromwell's time. We keep the feast of St Andrew as the day we get together to remember old friends-in-arms, and drink a health to their memory."

"And your friends were, I suppose, numerous," remarked Hal dispassionately.

"Well, a goodly few, your honour," he agreed apologetically. "And then Ned Tanner were a getting wed again this coming Friday to Widow Tranter and there were much making a May-game of him, indeed, Sir Roger mentioned we were a merry company!" he added in a worried undertone.

"Not so merry for Mistress Gollen," said Hal austerely.

"No, no," he agreed guiltily. "God rest her poor soul."

Hal turned to the official. "Mistress Nancy Gollen

was an acquaintance of Mistress Helen Sitwell. She came from the same part of London as both Mistress Sitwell and her husband, and had information pertaining to their deaths, I do believe."

"So Nat Sitwell were murdered!" cried the innkeeper. "I told Maggie he hadn't gone natural-like."

Hal turned to him. "Did you? Yet you did not report it, as I understand the matter."

"No, well, 'taint good for business, Sir Henry. They say you're a fair man, you'd know that I and Mistress Sitwell, she were anxious for it all to be passed off quick-like! He, he were an old man, Sir Henry."

"Indeed, but the law requires that no man go a day, nay not even an hour, before his appointed time," said Hal. "What made you suspicious that his death was not natural?"

"This should have been reported, Jem Cookson!" said Sergeant Parry, suddenly seeming to grasp what was afoot.

"Well, I couldn't rightly say, and that's why I didn't say aught if you must know, Jack Parry!" he added sharply. "I suppose really it were the look on his face, I've never seen a man die in such terror, and that there Mistress Sitwell so anxious to hush it all up. 'His heart was weak,

Cookson!' she said. 'The physician in London warned him of it. That's why we came here, for a quieter life.' Then when I asked what had happened, she said he suddenly gave a cry and clutched at his chest and died."

"'Tis possible," conceded Hal. "I've seen men taken that way."

"Aye, but that don't explain the curtains ripped off their rings, nay, nor all the apples fallen under the tree outside the window of that chamber next morning."

"You think he had a visitor who was shy of being recognised?" asked Hal as the sergeant sat with a puzzled frown on his face.

"Aye, and an unwelcome one," said the landlord.

Hal nodded. "But if there were no marks of violence on the body, that need not necessarily mean murder. He could just have died of fear. He was old and had a weak heart."

"Indeed, Sir Henry," agreed the landlord with gratitude. "That's why I didn't say anything."

"But if he was old and weak and the visitor knew that…" said Ambrose.

"Too many 'ifs', Ambrose," said Hal. "Stick to facts. Item: he was, in fact, elderly. Item: he did, in fact, have a weak heart. Item: there were no marks of violence on the body. Item: the chief witness said he died as he did. Case proved."

"Item: chief witness murdered, now dead. Item: further witness also murdered! Case stinks to high heaven," Ambrose retorted.

"I agree with you," replied Hal. "But our concern is purely with Justin and ensuring his innocence."

However, when he and Ambrose had seen the battered body of the little crippled draper's assistant laid out on the table in the dining parlour, awaiting the arrival of the coffin maker, Hal turned pale with fury. "I stand corrected, Ambrose," he said curtly. "Our first duty is to prove Justin innocent, then we'll find the madman that did this and see that he is hanged."

Later, back at Westwood, Aunt Margery, having listened to the erudite Mr Hollingshead's petition the previous evening, was moved to bestow a modicum of approval upon it, and promptly sent for her nephew's wards to inform them of the treat in store.

"Ah, come in Cordelia, Sophia," she said as both appeared in the still room where she was engaged with a book and pen, checking the various stores and remedies kept there. "I thought you should both assist me this morning in the still room. Later, dear Kate will teach you to make up the receipts. Indeed, I understand you already have some knowledge of herbs, Sophia."

"Yes, Libby, Lady Westwood taught me a little before she was taken ill," replied Sophie rebelliously.

"And I studied with the infirmarian for many months, ma'am," said Cordelia.

"That is excellent news," said Margery. "But today, we shall be concerned with the keeping of herbs and spices. You see here, I have a ledger in which each herb is kept logged and entries to say who has used what. I see you have brewed several tisanes, Sophia, and made careful notes of the ingredients, that is good."

"Mostly they were for Hal, he is subjected to the headache," said Sophie. "Libby taught me how to do it, although I'd learnt it earlier from Mistress Nichols."

"Indeed," agreed Aunt Margery. "And always has been since he arrived here a young man. Well at least when you two young ladies are off his hands, he'll have less cause for concern."

"What do you mean, off his hands?" demanded Sophie sharply.

"Why that in the fullness of time, you shall be wed.

Cordelia, in a very short space of time, if she is agreeable." Then, as both young women stared, she smiled with a patronising air and said: "Surely you realise Mr Hollingshead is most anxious to make you his wife, Cordelia."

"To claim Cordelia's land, you mean," said Sophie.

"Well, and if he is, where is the harm in that?" replied Aunt Margery. "It shows a level-headedness which one requires in a husband. Naturally, after all the work he'd put into it, Mr Hollingshead would not want to abandon the estate. He came, as he very properly expressed himself to me last evening, prepared to find a compromise, and is delighted to find much that he can admire."

"You mean that, provided Cordelia wasn't a crippled half-wit, he's prepared to marry her anyway to retain his investment," said Sophie bluntly.

Aunt Margery folded her lips over a sharp reproof. "Cordelia is a young woman of sense, of that, I am convinced, even by our short acquaintance. I am certain once she knows Mr Hollingshead better, as indeed we all shall, when we accompany him back to Lincolnshire next week. Once she knows him better..."

"Who'll accompany him back?" cried Sophie, interrupting her rudely.

"Once she knows him better, and remember, my dear, there is no compulsion upon you but common sense and your own best interests, Sir Henry insists I make that clear to you."

"Who is to go with him?" demanded Sophie, refusing to be ignored. "I, for one, shall not."

"Indeed?" snapped Aunt Margery. "You have discretion over your time and movements, do you, Sophia? Has not Sir Henry commanded you to my care? I have decided we shall both go with Cordelia to Lincolnshire, I as chaperone, you as a companion of her own age. Surely you'll agree Cordelia will need a companion to support her in the strange situation in which she finds herself. I do not think she would refuse a like service for you, were the situation reversed."

"You don't care for that, you seek to part me from Hal!" she cried, as usual going straight to the heart of the matter.

"Part you from Sir Henry?" Margery repeated. "Young lady, why should I waste my efforts on such a needless exercise? We merely go to Lincolnshire to assist Cordelia, it is natural she should want to see her home and the grave of her father. You shall accompany so that you can extend your experiences a little. I fear your circle has not been as widened as one would have wished for a young person in your position. You have beauty and wealth, if the habit of consorting with tradespeople can be broken by an acquaintance of gentlefolk, I see no reason for you not making a very good marriage."

"I do not wish to make a good marriage! I shall attend to my own affairs," cried Sophie, white-faced at this.

"Indeed, such is the reaction of most young people of your age and disposition, Sophia, which is why so important a decision is left in the hands of wiser heads."

"Hal has promised me…"

"Hal! What has he promised?" interrupted Margery, in a panic.

"He promised me I need not even think of marriage until next June," said Sophie.

"You certainly cannot be married before then," agreed Margery, breathing again. "But there is no harm in preparing for it, and if you shall meet an agreeable gentleman, entering into a contract with him."

"I do not wish to meet any gentlemen," snapped Sophie.

"Your wishes are not of paramount importance," replied Margery in crushing tones. "You will do as you are bid."

"I shant!" cried Sophie defiantly.

"Sophia, I am not impressed by childish tantrums more suited to the inhabitants of a nursery. I have said we shall go to Lincolnshire. It is not a matter for discussion, but a fact."

Sophie stared at her, tears filling her eyes as she realised what was afoot. Had Hal truly consented to this? She had to know. "I shall ask Hal! He won't want me sent away!" she cried and ran quickly from the room.

Chapter Twenty Four

"Hal!" Sophie burst into the parlour where he sat with the other men, discussing what to do next. Her head was too full of Aunt Margery's masterly plan to recollect how she and Hal had last parted, or how she'd behaved towards him in the interim. "Do you know they are plotting to send me away?" she demanded, her flashing, indignant eyes fixing solely on his face to the exclusion of his astonished and affronted companions.

"To a place where you'll be taught better manners, one presumes?" he replied, his tone cutting, as embarrassment at her familiarity before the others mingled with his bruised feelings of the past few days.

"Who plots to send you away?" asked Philippe, his ready sympathy provoked by her suddenly scarlet cheeks and wavering gaze as she saw Hal was not alone.

Looking about her, she encountered Justin's glare of

hatred and Ambrose's look of blank amazement. "The aunts…Hal…Sir Henry's aunts," she mumbled, recalled to a sense of propriety. "Cordelia's cousin, this Jack Hollingshead, is begging leave to take her on a visit to his mother, to see her home. They plot to send me with her. To be rid of me!" Her voice rose again in an impassioned plea, as she realised how powerless she was against these people.

"Cordelia will require a chaperone, surely," said Philippe, as ever, a Frenchman.

"But not such a hoyden as this, if we are to retain any credit with her kin in the east of the country," remarked Hal austerely. "If a chaperone is required, I have no doubt my Aunt Margery will attend."

"Your aunt is quite elderly, Hal, and not in the very best of health," said Philippe, doubt in his voice. "I think this is, perhaps, not noticed by her family."

"Aunt Margery has never had a day's illness in her life. She will tell you herself, she doesn't approve of ill-health," said Hal, forced to smile at this. "Don't you ever let her catch you saying she is elderly, Philippe, she'd think you highly impertinent and probably eat you for her supper."

"She thinks me lower than a toad anyway, Hal. And

you are wrong. This ague she has is not..."

"She's going anyway!" interrupted Sophie rudely, her cheeks crimson and tears smarting her eyes, to hear Hal's opinion of her. "She says it will do me good to widen my circle of acquaintance beyond farmers and merchants, and to see how well-bred people behave themselves."

"I see nothing to dispute in that," Hal observed coldly, fully aware that Justin's scorching contempt was expressed in his eyes, which never left Hal's face.

"But Hal, don't you see what they are at?" she cried, tears sliding down the side of her nose. "They think to introduce me about, so as to marry me off to someone! They seek to part us!"

"There is, to my knowledge, no 'us' to part," Hal replied cruelly. He knew he should reassure her, as his words were like blows inflicted. But the intolerable situation her impetuous behaviour had precipitated them into, and the recollection of the misery he'd endured these past days, had him in its grip. "To my mind, the plan has certain merits, and, I am sure, when discussed in a rational, level-headed way, when you are less agitated, you'll come to understand."

"Rational? Level-headed? You talk like, like one of

your aunts," she cried passionately. "Don't you see? They'll send me away and never allow me to see you again? Don't let this happen, Hal, you know how much I love you and how much you love me!"

Hal shut his eyes momentarily in anguish, and Philippe, seeing this, caught her beseeching hands in his, and tucking one hand under his arm, said: "I think you are in need of some chamomile tisane," he announced, forcing her to walk with him to the door. "Just to calm the nerves a little." Then, he added in an undertone: "When will you learn, ma petite, not to embarrass a man with an hysterical scene in front of others?"

Ambrose exchanged a frowning glance with Hal. "So, what shall we do now? Now Nancy Gollen is dead, we need to talk to this Hannah Smith urgently if we are to have a chance of proving Justin innocent," he said, hoping to continue the interrupted conversation, and so smooth over any unpleasantness from Justin.

"Hannah?" Sophie stopped in her tracks, her tears stilled. "What do you want with my maid?"

"'Tis nothing to concern you, pray, don't let us detain you," said Hal dismissively, anxious she should depart before she compromised him further.

"It is everything to do with me." She pulled herself

free of Philippe's restraint and returned to the room. "I'll not see Hannah bullied."

"We don't want to bully her," said Ambrose quickly. "Merely to ask her some questions about her mistress, Helen Sitwell."

"She wasn't her mistress, she was her friend," said Sophie bluntly. "They grew up together, and when Helen, the prettier one, got established, she sent for Hannah to come live with her. I think they are probably kin, cousins, perhaps."

"You have talked to her, then?" observed Hal, looking astounded that she'd discovered so much.

"Yes," Sophie looked nettled, sensing she would be censured. "She's one of the few people who does speak to me." She glared at them defiantly.

"No, Sir Henry means she talks freely to you," Ambrose interposed swiftly. "Do you think if you were present, she'd answer some of our questions?"

"She might," Sophie replied, "if you don't all look down your noses at her. But mind, I won't have her bullied."

"We shall be as gentle as lambs with her," Philippe assured her. "Will you not call her here, Sophie?"

"No, I'll fetch her myself," she replied.

"Pray, do not discuss with her what we want," said Hal, concerned she might forewarn the girl.

"I'd be at pains to do so, as I don't know myself," Sophie retorted and flounced out.

The men talked in a muted way for some moments, their thoughts plainly not on the subject, until the sound of Sophie's voice was heard. The door opened to reveal Sophie and the maid, Hannah Smith, who looked distinctly apprehensive. Hal got up. "Pray, come in, Hannah." He got up to meet her and get her an upright chair by the fire. "Your mistress will have told you we'd like to talk to you about Helen Sitwell."

"I don't know much," she replied, her voice defensive.

"Hannah, I give you my word you may trust Sir Henry." Sophie came to sit by her on a footstool, clasping the maid's roughened hand in support. "If only you'll trust him, he'll see you come to no harm."

The girl glanced to her, and then to Hal, standing gravely, watching her. She nodded her head slowly.

Hal smiled at her encouragingly and took a seat opposite, noting with relief that the others were keeping very much in the background. "Hannah, thank you very much for trusting us," he said, his smile warm. "Mistress

Redcroft is quite right, you'll come to no harm, you have my word upon it." He paused, gathering his thoughts, whilst Hannah, dazzled by the smile, began to relax. "You'll understand, our interest here is to assist Mr Danvers," he began, a shade tentatively. Then, as she nodded, her gaze going to Justin in the gloom: "You'll know Helen Sitwell enjoyed a liason with Mr Danvers?"

"She were his mistress," she nodded. "I don't know that she enjoyed it, leastways, not at the end."

"What do you mean, Hannah?" he asked, frowning.

"Well, it were all fine at first, she were so happy, for he were a-courting her, so to speak, with soft words and pretty presents and such. She went singing about the house, she'd never had that much joy with Nat Sitwell, you see. What with him being a cross-grained old miser. But after a few weeks, just like a man, once he got what he wanted, he changed his tune."

"I see," said Hal, thinking this boded ill. "In what way did he, forgive me, Justin, but I beg you'll not interrupt! You'll be allowed to question Hannah, with her permission, presently. Tell me, Hannah, how did he, uh, change his tune?"

"There ain't no call for him to forgive you!" said Hannah sharply. "I'm only telling you how it was. And that, the gentleman can't dispute, I'll be bound! 'Twas more that he kept her waiting, and went early. His mind was playing on other things, and he got difficult to please, like all men."

Hal smiled ruefully. "I see you don't rate us highly as a race, Hannah. When did this unfortunate development take place?"

"Along of the end of October, aye, I mind it were the time of Hallowe'en, or thereabouts, that Helen began to look woebegone."

"I see. About the time of his wife's confinement and the birth of his son?" asked Hal sapientially.

Hannah looked blank, as this had never occurred to her. "Aye, I suppose it were," she agreed, her voice echoing a vague disquiet.

"Did not you, and indeed, your mistress, understand that he would be abstracted at such a time? That he might be concerned for the safety of his wife and his baby?"

"No," she replied honestly. "Truth to tell, I never gave a thought to it. And well, Helen, she said…she said his wife were a nasty spoiled brat, sickly-like, who'd be better off in the next world."

This time, Justin wouldn't be silenced. "As God is my witness, Hal, she never had that from me!" he cried in anger.

"No," Hannah, albeit reluctantly, agreed with him. "No, that were one of her whines. That he could never be brought to say a word against his sainted wife," she admitted. "Too good for the likes of him, Helen reckoned. Now you, sir, there weren't nothing he'd not lay at your door! All the evils of Christendom were to be held as your fault. But Mistress Bess, she were sacrosanct."

"Mistress Sitwell told you much of her life?" asked Hal, nodding as if this didn't matter greatly.

"I knew most of it," she replied. "We were little ones together, you see, sir, playing in the kennels of Shoreditch. Her mother was my father's sister, who her father was, heaven alone knows. There were a crowd of us, Helen, Nancy, Kate, Molly, not that there's many of us left now Helen's gone, what with Kate dying of the cough and Molly being drowned in the Thames…"

"I'm afraid Nancy has been murdered," said Hal gently.

"Nance? Nancy Gollen?" cried Hannah, a strident note entering her voice. "Who did for Nancy?"

"That's what we're trying to discover, Hannah," Hal

replied. "Who would have had reason to kill both Nancy Gollen and Helen Sitwell?"

The colour had all drained from the girl's comely face, and she shook her head, part in disbelief, but more in denial. "I don't know, and I don't want to know, so don't you go asking me!" she cried. "I don't care what Helen and Nat Sitwell were up to. It weren't none of my doing, and I never got a penny out of it. Neither did Helen, come to that. We just both got out of that flesh market. But I know Helen knew too much, and I don't want to go the same way as her."

"I can assure you, you won't," he replied in soothing tones. "Are you not here in my house? Here where you are safe, where Mr Carver was bringing Nancy, too. We thought that getting her from London meant she'd be safer, whereas, in fact, she was in more danger." He leaned forward. "Please, Hannah, put your trust in us, we'll protect you, but we do need the truth."

The girl was deathly pale and breathing fast. She stared at Hal for a few pregnant seconds, and then let go a sigh. "I dare say I'll regret it," she muttered, glancing to Sophie doubtfully. "You'll see me all right, won't you, Mistress Sophie?"

"You know I will, Hannah, pray tell Sir Henry all you

know. It's the only way if we are to find out the truth."

The girl nodded again, and stared down at her tight-ly-clasped hands for a few moments. "That night, the night Helen were killed, I don't think it were him…Mr Danvers, who came back!"

"That's what I've said from the beginning!" cried Justin, incensed.

"Shush!" interrupted Hal. "You don't think it was Mr Danvers, Hannah, why not?"

She looked up again, a tight smile on her face. "Well, he weren't the only one to visit Helen," she disclosed.

"Indeed," said Hal swiftly, as Justin exclaimed in anger.

"Oh, don't you get into a pucker, 'twas you she wanted, you she loved," cried the maid pertly. "But 'twas something she said, after you'd gone, and I were fetching the laudanum. Something about you not being the only apple on the tree."

"But do you have any proof of this man's existence?" asked Philippe, who had been listening with barely-concealed impatience.

"No," she said. "But he'd been before. About every month, he came, and if it's who I think it is, then she'd been with him in London, too."

"In London?" said Hal intently.

"Aye, you'll know, I guess, that Helen were a doxy. She started off working for old Mother Underhill, like we all did. She were something more, Helen. Out of rags, and with a decent gown and her hair curled, she could have competed with Castlemaine herself. She moved on to one of those gaming hells in Long Acre. She used to deal cards for young bucks and encourage them to drink the wine. I lost touch with her for nearly a year, or so. Well, it didn't do with her to be seen with my sort. I weren't pretty enough to be going anywhere. But then, one day last summer, when the plague were getting bad, I were walking by Temple Bar, and a coach stopped. It was Helen, she bade me get in, which I did, and she told me what had happened to her. We talked for a bit, and then she asked me if I wanted to go and live in the country to get away from the plague."

"Which, presumably, you did!" cried Justin. "Can you not stick to the point?"

Hal frowned him down. "Let Hannah tell the story in her own way. Go on, Hannah, you thought you'd take advantage of her offer, did you?"

"Aye, well Robin, my man, had taken the shilling. And I were getting older. It were either go as a servant, or take to the Geneva. I never cared for Geneva above half, so I went with her. We left within the hour, and I never went back. That was part of it, you see. Nat Sitwell was in fear of his life."

Justin looked amazed at this. "In fear of his life? He told me he'd sold up!"

"Aye, so he had, what was left of it. But his true trade were as a moneylender. Helen were in league with him. She'd get the young bucks drunk on a mixture of brandy wine and Geneva. And when they lost heavily, the cards were crooked so the house always won, she'd tell them she knew where they could get money to win it back. I don't know how many she ruined that way, a dozen, I dare say. And Nat Sitwell charging his percentages all the time. Why, she'd even visit them in the King's Bench prison."

"Was it one of these young men that was after them?" asked Hal.

"'Tis my guess," she replied. "Certainly Nat Sitwell were desperate to get away. That's why we came to this backward place."

"We don't need guesses, we need facts. Unless we have proof, I'm a dead man!" cried Justin.

"Hush!" repeated Hal. "Who is your guess, Hannah?

Who would be desperate enough to kill three people?"

"There's only one that wicked," she replied, her face pale. "I met him once. In the old days, he weren't above Mother Underhill's. Indeed, he suggested to Helen she went to Long Acre. And bought her the gowns too, I dare say. He were a devil, he were. One of those who enjoyed living dangerously. Aye, 'tis him, I'm sure. For, she said he took to the road to pay his debts. 'Tis Kit Swithland."

"Kit Swithland?" repeated Hal blankly. He glanced to the others. "It means nothing to me." Then, as they, too, shook their heads, he added: "Are you sure of the name?"

"'Twas the name he went by," she replied tartly. "I don't know any more than that. Nat Sitwell ruined him. He were a returned Royalist, so Helen said. A fine gentleman with a taste for women and cards. Between then, Helen and Nat bled him until he was forced to sell everything, even his land, a ramshackle place, by all accounts. He took to the road, as a highwayman."

"It's a common enough tale," said Hal. "I believe my aunt was talking of a similar occurrence only the other day. But this is nothing to the point, at least now, we have a name with which to pursue our investigation.

Thank you, Hannah, for your trust, and be assured, I'll see no harm comes to you."

"Do you think this man visited Helen on the night she died?" asked Justin intently, seeming to Hal, for the first time, to turn his mind from its senseless raving against him, and consider the problem as a lawyer.

"Well, someone did," Hannah replied pertly. "And you say it weren't you."

"No." He shook his head impatiently. "No, go through it with us again, girl. There must be a reason you didn't think it was me."

Hannah flashed him a look of dislike. "I've told you, there was this big row, shouting and screaming alongside of midnight. I were nervous for Helen, I don't know why." She paused, thinking. "I suppose, because she'd been nervous herself," she said reflectively. "Ever since Nat died, she'd been jumpy. Looking out of the window, listening for sounds, I don't know, not at ease."

"As if she was expecting someone," said Justin.

"Yes," she replied slowly. "But not like when she were waiting for you. Then, she were happy and excited. This was different waiting."

"I see," said Justin. "On the night in question, did you see me leave?"

"Aye," she said, her smile faintly mocking. "You went down those stairs like a bat out of hell."

Justin returned her look grimly. "I'd had a shock," he said. "Until that time, I'd not realised how ruthless your mistress could be."

"Until that time, she'd not realised you were prepared to keep her as a mistress, so long as you could keep your wife too," she retorted. "Helen was just a realist, not a romantic fool. What was in it for her? Do you really think she wanted you as a lover for the rest of her life?"

"I really don't think we can achieve much if we descend to trading insults," said Hal. "Please oblige us, Hannah, by going over, in as much detail as possible, what happened."

Hannah sighed. "As I said, there were shouting and screaming and weeping. Then, you pushed Helen aside and ran down the stairs. She stumbled after you, catching her foot in her nightgown." She sighed again. "I ran with Wat Prescott to help her to her feet. She'd banged her head on the banister, and it were bleeding a little, but nothing much. We helped her back to her chamber, because she'd twisted her ankle. And I bathed her head while Wat Prescott put some cordial in brandy wine for her, to soothe her nerves, like." "Did she show any ill-effects from her fall?" asked Hal.

"No, none, apart from being angry once she'd stopped weeping," replied the maid. "I tell you, 'twere naught but a scratch," she repeated. "Eventually, we got her into bed…"

"You say 'eventually'," interrupted Justin. "How long after I'd left?"

She paused, considering the question. "Well, perhaps as much as an hour, by the time she stopped weeping, and then spitting fury," she replied. "I know it was gone one o'clock in the morning when I heard voices again."

"Raised voices?" asked Hal. "Angry voices?"

"No," she replied. "It was as if she was talking to someone a distance away. Outside, I thought. But, when I went to the window, I couldn't see anyone."

"Is that all you heard?" asked Hal, disappointed.

"Yes, until a bit later. Then, I heard laughing."

"What sort of laughing? Was it your mistress?" demanded Justin.

"Yes, it was Helen, and she was laughing. Laughing fit to split her side," she said blankly.

"Are you sure?" asked Hal. "You couldn't be mistaken?

Or was it a man? Perhaps, it was a wicked, evil laugh."

"No," she laughed briefly. "No. Oh, I think there was a man laughing, too. I think I caught the echo of it, but I couldn't swear to it. It was just a happy sound."

"And then?" asked Hal.

"Nothing," she said. "I went to sleep again. I assumed the quarrel was over and they were happy again. I couldn't believe it when I found her dead next morning."

"Yet, you don't think it was Mr Danvers who returned to the house? In spite of assuming it was at first," continued Hal.

"No," she was silent again, thinking. Hal waved Justin down as he went to break in impatiently. "It wasn't his laugh," she said finally, indicating Justin. "I've not heard him laugh more than once or twice. But he laughs like a lawyer. You know, wondering how much it will cost him. The other man laughed from pure joy."

Hal hid a grin. "That's a very good point, Hannah, and one, if I were sitting on the case, I'd give heed to. But we desperately require facts."

"Horse droppings where he left his mount," sighed Ambrose.

"Only if you could prove they came from his horse

and he was riding it, whoever he is," said Justin bitterly.

"Well, we know who he is," said Hal. "He's Kit Swithland. All we have to do is prove he exists."

"That should be simplicity itself," snapped Justin.

Hal sat silent for a while, then he said: "I think we must try to find some trace of this fellow. Tomorrow, Ambrose, and Philippe, if you please, will visit all the inns, taverns and ale-houses within riding distance of Mallen. If he's in the area, he must be staying somewhere."

"But who are we looking for, Hal? He won't go by his name, you can be sure of that," demanded Justin.

"Possibly not," Hal agreed. "But you'll know him, should you see him. He'll be young, devil-may-care, with no fixed purpose. Probably handsome, certainly charming, and with an attractive laugh."

"Mon ami, you should put Sophie and Cordelia on this trail," said Philippe. "They are much more likely to find him than we are."

"Cordelia and Sophie should be safe, out of harm's way, before we begin to search for this fellow," said Hal, glancing to Sophie, who sat silently listening in an abstracted fashion.

"We haven't much time," said Justin impatiently. "The Assizes are the week after next. If we don't find something soon, I will be hanged."

"We will find something," soothed Ambrose. "Already, we can show their case is flawed. Don't fret, Justin, we'll find something."

"I am convinced we will," agreed Hal. "In the meantime, its but half an hour 'til supper. Perhaps, we can run over our plans again. Thank you, Hannah, for your valuable assistance. And you, Sophie, for persuading her to speak."

Thus dismissed, the women went on their way, Hannah to return to her duties, Sophie to take herself to her chamber to consider her position.

❧

Chapter Twenty Five

Hal set down his candle with a sigh of relief, hearing the clock strike midnight. He shrugged off his coat, casting it to a chest, and tugged at his cravat. It had been a long evening. Justin was in the depths of despair, convinced they'd never find this Kit Swithland, and his spirits seemed to have infected everyone. Aunt Margery had given her cold to Aunt Kate, who was unusually silent all evening, and his sisters were plainly as apprehensive as Justin. He'd been finally glad to escape the oppressive atmosphere.

The cravat followed the coat and, as he unbuttoned his waistcoat and top buttons of his shirt, he turned and gave a start of surprise.

"Sophie! What the devil are you doing here?" he exclaimed.

"Oh hush!" she hissed, as Bess's voice called out goodnight to her sister. "I had to see you alone, and they keep preventing me!"

He stared at her. "With good reason!" he spluttered. "With damn good reason! Are you mad, girl, to come here to my chamber at this time of night?"

"It is the only place and time I can be sure of seeing you alone!" she snapped. "All day long, I am kept at my lessons or running errands for Aunt Margery."

He couldn't prevent the faint smile which flickered across his lips as he reflected that few could prevail against his aunt, but Sophie correctly interpreted it and flew into a sulk.

"Oh, it amuses you, does it? That I should be at the beck and call of your aunt? That she should have the power to send me hither and thither like a servant?"

"My aunt wouldn't send a servant hither and thither," he replied. "A servant would be expected to be gainfully employed at all times. My aunt treats you as an equal, you may be easy on that score."

"Easy?" she cried, only further annoyed.

"Hush!" He caught the echo of Justin's voice and came hastily to catch hold of her, placing his hand over the intemperate words spilling from her lips. "Hush! 'Tis Justin!"

She immediately relaxed against him, forming her lips into a kiss against his palm. He felt his pulses begin to race at the nearness of her, and had to remember to hold himself away from her until all danger of discovery was past.

He released her abruptly and crossed the room, making a play of hanging up his coat so as to get away from her. "Say what you want quickly and go," he said sharply. "This is utter folly for you to be here, and so you know!"

She stared resentfully at his broad back as he removed his waistcoat and hung that up too. "Are you not concerned at this plan of your aunt?" she asked piteously.

He considered the question as he came to take a chair by the table, motioning for her to do the same. "Concerned," he replied. "Yes, I suppose I am concerned," he said in meditative tones. "Aunt Margery has been so much of my life since my return that I'd not realised she is a great age. I fully understand that she'd not be prepared to take things easier, but I must find a way to ease her path without offending her."

Sophie stared at him again, unable to comprehend his words for a few seconds, then amazed that he could have any concern other than her. "No!" she protested.

"No, I mean about me!"

He sighed. "Sophia, when will you come down out of the clouds? My aunt is proposing you accompany her and Cordelia on a visit to East Anglia for a few weeks to enable Cordelia to meet such kin as she possesses. Where is the harm in it?"

"She'll find a way of keeping me there," she cried. "I just know she'll not allow me to return!"

"Now you are being wantonly dramatic," he replied patiently. "Not allow you to return! Do you imagine she proposes to sell you to the gypsies or some such foolish thing? It is late November, any visit made would naturally conclude before Christmastide."

"But you've only just returned!" she cried. "I've hardly had an hour with you! Now she wants to take me away for weeks."

"Sophie, I am your guardian," he said with emphasis. "No more than that. Until your marriage, or your majority, you reside in my home as a matter of course, it does not mean we must live in each other's pocket."

"No more than my guardian?" she repeated, forgetting how badly she'd been treating him since Adam's return to the scene. "How can you say that! I love you, you love me!"

"The feelings you have for me and those I might have for you are neither here nor there," he said coolly, blinking to hear this passionate avowal. Did she still love him, or was she blowing hot and cold? It was all too confusing. "We are both bound by the code of mourning, you for your former guardian, me for my wife. You are very young, I'll grant, but do even you fondly imagine I am going to cast aside convention and marry you? Do you have so little concern for my feelings? So little consideration for my estimation in the world? What would you think if you heard of a man who married a maid considerably his junior within weeks of his wife's death?"

"I'd think they must be very much in love," she replied defiantly.

"You'd think, quite rightly, he was a knave, and she little better than a fool or a harlot," he replied roundly. "And the world would agree with you."

"I don't care for what people say!" she cried, tears filling her eyes. "I love you."

"To keep repeating something which should fill you with shame does not make it better," he snapped, now thoroughly confused and, deciding his only safe course was to take refuge in formality. "You have no right to love me now any more than you did when Libby was alive. You insult her now as you did then, and I shall not allow her memory to be further traduced."

She shook her head in bemused disbelief, unable to comprehend that she could not bend him to her will. "Then you cannot love me," she cried desperately.

"My feelings are not a matter for discussion between us, he replied curtly. "I've told you I shall be observing the correct period of mourning for my wife at the very least. I need, therefore, to discuss my emotions with none until after Christmastide next year."

"By which time, your Aunt Margery will have me married," she wept, sinking her head into her hands.

"My aunt has not so much power," he replied. "None can force you into a marriage not of your choosing, Sophie."

She raised her head and looked at him, her eyes beseeching. "Hal, do you not love me, only a few days ago you said you did."

He closed his eyes. "I explained my position, Sophie, on more than one occasion," he said woodenly. "I think I can say that my affections will not alter, but I have no intention of discussing or parading them until after Christmas next year, do I make myself clear?"

"Yes!" she sobbed. "And what am I to do in the meantime?"

"That is for you to decide," he returned. "As your guardian, I've already indicated that I could consider a further course of study necessary, not to say desirable, if you are to become the wife of any man of sense. There are also a hundred valuable lessons to be learned about the running of a house, which is why I've placed you under the tutorage of my aunts. I'm sure once you stop behaving like as spoilt child you will come to understand that most projected suggestions are for your own good, and are aimed at an ultimate objective."

She set her jaw mulishly. "To make me a copy of Libby, you mean!" she snapped.

"To make you a fit helpmeet for any man," he replied sharply.

She turned from him pettishly. "For any man," she repeated. "Why do you not say for you?"

"Because I cannot forsee the future," he replied, weariness creeping into his voice. "You have known me six months, and claimed to have loved me all the while, yet at one time you entertained the notion of Giles Durward as a suitor, another, Adam Blackwell. You are young," he repeated as she protested with some heat. "Such veering affections are natural, which is why the question of marriage for a minor is left to older heads."

"I have never wavered in my love of you," she cried passionately. "I told you within hours of meeting you I knew no other man could compare!"

"Yet you also told me last Wednesday that you would marry Adam Blackwell," he replied coldly, unable to stop himself allowing his resentment to show.

"I was in a rage with you!" she cried, in exasperation.

"And sound little better now," he concluded.

"You wilfully misunderstood me!" she cried, tears filling her eyes again.

"No, you wilfully misunderstood me," he countered, convinced by her passionate declarations that she had no true understanding of her own feelings, and that she must have time to consider her position. "You only want to hear what you want to hear, not what I say!"

"You don't give me any choice but to hear," she retorted.

"But you still don't listen," he said patiently. "I am telling you clearly, Sophia, to behave in the manner which is expected of you, or suffer the consequences."

"What consequences?" she demanded.

He sighed. "There are other means I can employ if you continue in this outrageous manner, intent on disgracing yourself and me. I am not obliged, for instance, to house you in my own home, or to ask my own family to tutor you. It is quite within my rights to pay a third party to do this for me, should you prove too troublesome. In effect, I can send you to an academy for young ladies where it is solely their business to bring rebellious heiresses to heel."

"You would not dare!" she cried, shocked.

"Don't try me too far," he snapped. "Because I have been too soft with you in the past does not mean I shall always remain so."

She stared at him, finally shocked into silence.

"You'd sent me away!" she whispered in despair. "To, to school!"

He kept his face cold and his sympathy under control. "If I consider it necessary," he agreed, relieved to see this was finally having some effect in stopping her more outrageous behaviour.

"I'd sooner die!" she cried passionately.

He sighed. "No doubt you believe so," he remarked. "Although in practice, I think you might care to reconsider."

Her face crumpled and her tears fell again. "What has happened to you?" she wept. "You never used to be like this! You've grown so cold and grim and grown-up!"

This forced a bitter laugh from him. "One of us needs to be, Sophie," he said ruefully, but mostly dismissive, glad to see that she was wavering. "Now trot along to bed, if you please, and do try to remember what I said."

Chapter Twenty Six

Ned cantered along the road from Rushington Manor towards Westwood Hall, the fog had lifted temporarily, and early morning sunlight dappled the forest floor. Ned's thoughts were far away from his actions. He'd imagined himself doing this so much, indeed, had often done it in the last few years in Hal's company. They'd turned the run-down manor into a tidy little property for Ned's inheritance. Now, riding this stretch alone seemed suddenly empty and pointless. He'd always imagined he and Hal would continue to go on as they had before. They'd do things together, consulting each other in everything, helping where possible. Yet here it was, near a week since Hal's return and he'd not come to visit them. No more, had he sent him word of Justin's being held on a charge of murder. He was aware he was to blame, that he'd taken too rigid a stand over that girl, but in heaven's name, he'd been fond of Libby. He'd felt Hal was in the wrong, hadn't someone to take the courage to tell him so?

Of course, he should have known better, Hal accepted the rebuke as just, even agreed he had to make it. Even said, he'd not dream of intruding on them whilst he was still absent from a state of grace. Any more than he'd dream of contaminating dear Cecily with his reprobate presence. The result was that Ned was damned lonely, and somehow, the wonderful achievement of his marriage was a little soured.

To be sure, Cecily was perfectly happy playing house, and he'd been content enough at first to join her. But when it was left to Guy Armstrong to tell him Justin Danvers was to stand trial for murder, and was as like as not to hang, well it was time something was done.

Still smarting from not having been informed by Hal himself, he cantered along at a spanking pace, alternately forming and discarding various methods of reproach for his brother, and trying desperately not to sound plaintive.

It was this matter which so occupied his mind, as to make him quite unconscious of his surroundings, so that somehow, he was confronting the muzzles of a pair of pistols before he knew what was afoot. He stopped dead, his horse slithering a little on the damp leaves of the overhanging trees, and stared at the highwayman in incredulous amazement.

"Come along, look sharp about it," growled the man, waving his pistols. "Get off your beast and hand over your valuables!"

"I'll not," cried Ned indignantly, his hand going for his sword.

A shot whistled past his ear, taking Ned's hat from his head, making him jump in the saddle in astonishment.

"The next will find your heart," snarled the highwayman. "I'm not fussed, 'tis easier to rob a dead man. Now, your valuables and your horse, or I'll dispatch you to Kingdom Come in the twinkling of an eye."

Ned toyed with the idea of rushing him. After all, the highwayman had but the one bullet left, but the accuracy of his other shot gave him pause. He slid reluctantly from the saddle.

"That's my fine fellow," encouraged the highwayman. "No sense in losing your life over a horse and a few trinkets. My, he's a handsome chestnut."

"A wedding present," snapped Ned, incensed to think

how Cecily would be distressed at the loss of her gift.

"What, have I stopped a bridegroom?" he laughed. "Oh joy! This must be my lucky day! Well, my fine friend, you may keep your wedding ring to show you I'm not an inhuman monster. But I'll have your purse, aye, and that pretty pin you wear at your throat. Put them in your saddlebag and I'll be on my way!" He rode forward, pistol cocked at the ready, trained at Ned's heart. "Stand back from the beast," he warned. Then, as with gritted teeth and a face of fury Ned complied, he reached down and caught the bridle over his arm adding, "I trust you've not too far to walk home, and I'm sorry for it, but I can't take chances."

And before Ned could fully comprehend, he felt a searing pain in his shoulder as he crumpled to the trodden leaves.

It wasn't much later when he awoke, but he knew he was in trouble. His head was muzzy and his shoulder felt like a leaden weight. For a few seconds, he couldn't remember anything, then suddenly it all came back to him with startling clarity. He tried to sit up, and found, to his horror, his body wouldn't obey him. With a great effort, he lifted his other hand and brought it across to his shoulder, feeling it wet and sticky and trying to focus on the blood dripping from his fingertips. A slightly incredulous tremor of annoyance ran though him. This couldn't be it, surely? Was he, Ned Westwood, to die alone in a wood like the victim of a damned highwayman? Never! He set his teeth and tried again to raise himself, and succeeded in rolling across to a tree and half-propping himself against it before passing out again.

Sophie, meanwhile, made miserable by the air of censure she felt she met at every turn in the house, settled for open defiance. Let Hal dare to try to send her away to school, she'd make him sorry he even thought of such a thing. She'd make them all sorry. She lost patience with Cordelia's temperate suggestions, and expressed nothing but scorn for Mr Hollingsworth's endless anecdotes. In a desire to be free of everyone and all restraint, she ordered Hal's horse from a newly-hired stable lad, against Aunt Margery's express ban. She set out in the crisp morning air, determined to gallop the fidgets out of her soul and show Hal just how tiresome she could be if she truly set her mind to it.

Fortunately for her neck, Hal's horse had been ridden

a vast distance the previous day, and so it was unnaturally docile. So, far from coming to grief, as she'd half-expected, she convinced herself she was a splendid rider and enjoyed a good canter over the hill. The ride brought the colour back into her pale cheeks, and all the pins out of her hair, so that by the time she dropped down onto the path from Westwood to Adamsholme, her mood was vastly improved, and although she looked a perfect hoyden, she was more at peace with mankind.

It was at this point, as the trees grew thick overhead to form a tunnel even at this late season of the year, that she saw a man sprawled in the road ahead under a tree. All thoughts of her future fled, as she jumped from the horse and hurried up to him, half afraid he was dead.

"Oh sir, are you? Oh, Ned! It is you, Ned Westwood!" she cried in dismay.

Ned opened his eyes with difficulty. He'd been dreaming of Cecily and the light hurt him. He squinted up at the vague female outline and then placed the voice. "Oh, 'tis you," he said in a thread of a voice. "Go away."

"Ned, you are hurt. Dear God, you are hurt!" she cried in horror. "What happened?"

"Highwayman," he replied. "Go away, I say, I don't like you. You killed Libby."

Tears filled her eyes at this, but anger came to her aid. "I don't like you either," she snapped. "But I'll not go away and let you die too. Hal loves you."

"No," he muttered. "Loves you better, not seen him since I told him I'd not meet you."

She paid no heed to this but was considering what was to be done. He was bleeding badly, and although they weren't far from the house, he'd never make it unless she could stop the flow of his blood. "Let me see," she commanded, kneeling at his side.

"Go away, 'tis useless," he replied querulously. "If you've any pity at all, fetch Hal."

She pulled his hand away and ripped open his shirt, looking at horror in the small hole in the pearly flesh of his shoulder. That he could lose so much blood from such a small hole amazed her.

"Where is your handkerchief?" she demanded, her brain racing.

"In my sleeve," he replied. "Couldn't get it."

She plucked it from the sleeve of his useless hand and swiftly fashioned it into a pad, placing it over the wound on his chest and pressing down firmly as she unwound his neck-cloth. "Lift your head, do," she cried impatiently. "I'm trying to save you."

"I wish you'd let me die in peace," he snarled. "What an awful girl you are, troublesome, interfering, always there when you're not wanted…Oh!"

This last came as she, in a temper, pulled his body against her to ease his coat and waistcoat off. "Do stop wasting your breath!" she snapped. "And try to help! You aren't exactly a lightweight, you know."

"Damn you, woman, you are hurting me!" he screamed as the waistcoat finally tore free of his arm and the shirt was ripped to give her a clear area to bind his wound. She saw, with fear, the wound on his back was much larger than she'd thought, and was bleeding copiously. With teeth gritted to stop them chattering, she snatched his neck-cloth and formed another pad for his back. He gave a grunt of anguish and promptly lost consciousness again, which gave her the opportunity to bind her scarf as securely as she could about his arm and neck, holding the pads firmly in place.

She laid him back against the tree, seeing with satisfaction the blood flow cease, and took stock of her progress. He was fearfully pale, but breathing yet. She was smothered in blood and almost as dirty as him, and the mist was coming down again. He had to be got to safety before they fell foul of another footpad.

The problem was, could she lift him onto her horse? She was strong, she knew, but he was a heavy man, and without his help, she doubted she could do it. She set about bringing him back to consciousness.

Ned had never felt so tired, he wanted nothing but to sleep, and the foolish woman kept nagging him to wake up. Reluctantly, he opened an eye. "I told you, go away," he snapped.

"Ned, you must get up," she said. "You can lean on me, but you've got to get to your feet and on my horse!"

"What are you talking about? I don't need to lean on you, or anyone else for that matter, of course I can get up!" he growled deliriously.

"Come on, then," she grabbed his sound arm and pulled, and he, indignant that she should imply weakness, forced his screaming body to push his muscles upward. She received him into her arms, tottering with his weight and stumbled across to her patient horse.

"Oh God, Ned, thank Heavens I've galloped the fidgets out of Hal's horse," she cried, as the animal stayed still as they staggered to it. "Now, one last push, Ned, to get you into the saddle, one last try!" she coaxed. "But don't put any pressure on your arm."

"I'm not a child!" he murmured. "I've been mounting horses since before you were born!" He grasped the pommel and allowed her to guide his foot into the stirrup. "No, no, it's the wrong one, it's a side saddle, I can't ride this."

"You must!" she cried desperately. "We've no other chance!"

He sighed, and from somewhere, gathered the strength to come up behind the saddle, giving her the chance to slide up in front of him and take the reins. She took his useless arm, seeing in dismay how the bandages had slipped, and pulled him hard against her back.

"Hold me, Ned!" she commanded. "Hold me tight, for we must gallop!"

With the last of his strength, he linked his arms about her small waist and thankfully laid his head on her slender shoulder. "Take me home," he muttered. "Take me to Hal."

Chapter Twenty Seven

"Help me! Somebody help me!" yelled Sophie as they came galloping up to the front of Westwood Hall. "Help me! Please!"

Hal, who'd been talking to Philippe Douay, stared at him in surprise, crying: "Sophie!" He hastened to follow the physician from the Jericho parlour, where they'd been discussing Philippe's future.

"Sophia?" Philippe hurried over the threshold, his jaw dropped in dismay.

"Oh! Doctor Douay! Help me, please! He is sorely wounded and has lost much blood. I staunched the wound, but the dressing came adrift as I got him into the saddle."

"Ned!" cried Hal, in horror, as Philippe gently lifted him from behind her. "Dear God! Ned!"

"He is much hurt, Hal!" cried Philippe, his face pale.

"Come quickly, assist me!"

He turned with his limp burden into the house, almost tripping over Hal's man, who'd come running.

"Thomas, take Mistress Redcroft from the saddle," called Hal, as he helped Philippe by taking Ned's legs. "In the parlour, Philippe, put him on the daybed!"

"Never mind me, help them!" cried Sophie, sliding down from the saddle. "They'll need hot water and bandages! Send a groom for my horse!" She ran into the house after them and arrived in the parlour in time to see them lay the young man out on the daybed.

"Oh, he is so pale!" she cried, as Philippe began to unravel the makeshift blood-soaked scarf, calling for water. "I tried to keep the pads in place, but they slipped, so I galloped here as fast as I could, I am so sorry!"

"Was he conscious at all?" asked Philippe, pressing harder on the blood-soaked cloth and feeling for Ned's pulse.

"Yes, oh yes! I came up on him on the Rushington road!" she cried. "He said he'd been shot by a highwayman. He was conscious right up until we entered the park. Then he passed out. I was afraid he'd fall off, so I held onto his arms for dear life and gave Hector his head."

"You did very well, Sophie," agreed the physician as Hal exclaimed in horror. "Hal, I need some cloths to... Oh!"

He broke off as Thomas, followed by a worried-looking Aunt Kate, entered. "What is this Thomas says? Oh dear heavens! 'Tis indeed Ned!"

"The cloths, mistress!" cried Philippe, snatching one from her. "Hal, make this into a pad, yes, so, excellent." He took it, deftly replacing Ned's handkerchief. "Now we can begin to repair things a little! Another soaked in water, if you please, mistress, yes, do get out of the way, Hal, your respected Aunt is much more handy than you! Talk to Sophia, who will shortly be feeling sick as a result of the shocks she has sustained. A little brandy wine would help all round, I feel."

"Thomas, bring some wine!" cried Hal, taking Sophie's arm. "Tell me what happened! Good God, your back is soaked in blood!"

"Yes, I know, I could feel it ebbing into my gown all the way up the drive," she replied. "Oh, Doctor Douay, will he survive? I pray you, don't let him die!"

"I am doing my very best, Sophie," he replied. "Place your hand on that pad, ma'am, and hold it firmly," he instructed Aunt Kate. "Let me look at him. Yes, well, the bullet passed right through him, which is a mercy, for we won't further have to inflame the wound getting it out, but he has lost much blood, Hal, even before Sophie attempted her gallant rescue. But on the credit side, he is young and surrounded by excellent nurses, he may survive."

"He must!" cried Hal. "He is not yet twenty, Philippe, he has barely begun to live, he cannot die!"

"Hush, hush, Hal," Sophie took his arm and led him to a chair. "Don't fret now, Doctor Douay will do his utmost! How lucky that he was here with you and so able to bring immediate assistance! See how your fore-thought may have saved his life!"

"Nay then, Sophie, you will have done that by get-ting him to my care so promptly," said Philippe, tak-ing a fold of paper from his pouch and pouring a little powder from it into a cup, which he then filled with the wine Thomas presented. "This will make him sleep," he announced. "At this moment in time, if we can get him to sleep and keep down his fever, we stand a chance. Take a cup to your master, man."

Hal took a cup and drained it, refilling it for Sophie. "Drink this down," he said firmly. "And then go and get from those gory clothes!"

It was a clear hour later that Sophie returned to the parlour. She'd removed every one of her garments, and with Cordelia's help, had taken a bath, for Ned's blood seemed to be all over her and she felt sticky with it. Her linen was taken to be soaked in cold saltwater and her gown, totally ruined, to be burned. She came down the stairs feeling shivery, despite her bath, and fretted with anxiety.

"Hal," she paused in the doorway, looking across to the fire where both brothers were outlined by the flames. "How is he?" she asked.

"He lives," he replied. "Philippe has gone to concoct a potion for when his fever comes. He is weak, but still clinging to life."

"Has poor Cecily been told?" she asked.

"I've sent Thomas over to Rushington Manor," he replied. "He'll probably bring Cecily at once. Poor Cecily, barely a bride, and her husband at death's door, just like Hetta. Speaking of Hetta, did you know that Aunt Margery and Jane went off this morning? Will had sent word she'd begun with her baby. Dear God, I hope she comes through it safe, I begin to think we Westwoods are unlucky."

"No, no," she soothed. "Lucky, look how Will lived

because of Hetta's devoted nursing when so many others died. Ned was found and brought home when he may have perished out there on the road. And I'm sure Hetta will be safely delivered of a fine baby. No, Westwoods are the fortunate ones!"

"Perhaps we just bring grief to those that love us, then," he said quietly, adding after a few moments: "Sophie, I haven't thanked you for your quick thinking which meant Ned didn't die on the roadway."

"Are thanks necessary between us, Hal?" she replied. "You saved me from Giles Durward, I helped your brother. I'd have tried to help anyone I found injured."

"Later we'll discuss what you were doing alone on the roadway to Rushington Manor," he replied, with a return of his old manner. "But for now, I thank you with all my heart, and tell you I am deeply in your debt."

"Good, I'll remind you of it the next time you start to lecture me," she retorted pertly.

"It can't have been easy for you to have helped him," he remarked as a silence fell between them and he bathed Ned's face in sweet-smelling water.

"No more it was," she agreed. "He abused me roundly and told me to go away. He said he'd sooner die there than accept my help!"

Hal looked horrified, for although she said it lightly, there was a tremor in her voice.

"I meant the sheer man-handling of one who must be much your superior in weight," he said. "Not that you were treated ill by him. I apologise for it, as will he when, if he recovers."

"It doesn't signify," she replied, coming to sit alongside him. "Ned is nothing if not constant. He disliked me from the first meeting, and said so. At least one knows where one stands with Ned."

He laughed a little, his anxiety shown more by this than by any other thing. "True, he is forthright to a fault, but he is also honest. And his honesty will mean that he must apologise."

"He'll hate that," she observed. "I don't doubt he'll do it if you say so, but he'll hate it. I do believe he would rather have died there than accept my help. It is necessary to admire the person who puts one under an obligation."

"Ah," Hal glanced up, a gleam in his eyes as he suddenly understood why she'd altered in her attitude to him. Shaken by Ned's attack, he was moved to speak from his heart. "And now you know the truth about me, you can no longer tolerate being in debt to one so base," he concluded. "That is easily remedied, your obligation to me is over, you've rescued my brother, we are quits."

She looked into the fire. "We can never be quits whilst I love you quite so desperately, Hal," she said in a half-whisper.

He had to stoop to catch the words and looked at her quizzically. "Do you love me truly?" he asked. "This is not a childish whim on your part? You sound as if you really mean it. As if your love is strong enough to endure. To withstand all the things you've heard, all you've found out about me."

She smiled. "Of course. Love edureth. If little Harry is naughty, I am sometimes cross with him, but I still love him," she replied.

"I am not a child," he replied, put out by the simile.

"No," she agreed. "Your faults are not so easily put aside, but I still love you, I'll always love you."

"I do not know that I care to be patronized," he said in a haughty tone. "A wife must have respect for her husband."

"Like poor, blind Libby, making you a hero, come what may?" she replied shrewdly. "No, I don't think I care for that."

"There was nothing amiss with my marriage until I met you," he snapped angrily, wishing he'd never initiated the conversation.

"If there was nothing amiss with your marriage, you would not have even noticed me. Neither would you have a bastard son," she replied candidly.

He was silenced by this logic for a few minutes, then he said painfully: "Libby knew the whole truth about that episode."

"Dear Libby, what a saint she was," remarked Sophie tartly. "Always so ready to forgive."

"Do you dare to sneer at my wife so recently dead by your hand!" he cried, so angry at this jibe as to forget himself.

"By my hand?" she repeated, her face pale. "So, like Justin and Ned, you lay all the blame at my door."

"No, no, that was unforgivable, I beg pardon!" Hastily, he got control of his temper. "But to hear you denigrate Libby…"

"There can be no future for us, Hal, if I must live in the shadow of a saint!" she said bluntly. "I'll never measure up to her perfections, and in no time at all, you'll be comparing me unfavourably. I know I have many faults, just as you do, but I'll not hide from mine any more than yours."

He frowned. "'Tis less than a month since Libby died," he replied. "I loved her, I cannot bear to hear of her being spoken of lightly. She was a good woman, but I acknowledge the truth of your remarks and I'll try not to make her into a plaster saint."

"Thank you," she said, looking away to hide her tears at this honest avowal of his love for his wife.

"What you cannot comprehend, Sophie," he continued. "Is the feeling of guilt that I have. Libby was a good woman, an excellent creature who devoted herself to me from the day of our wedding. I like to think I am an honest man, true, our marriage was a bargain, but I tried to stick to my half always. That I failed miserably is my eternal shame, but until you came into my sphere, I wasn't doing so very badly. You see, once I'd seen you, once I'd met you, then the love I talk of for Libby was like that of a candle flame to the sun. She guessed it. I couldn't conceal it, not from you, my family, nor her, and it is so difficult, with her so lately dead. Respect must be maintained for her memory, for the sake of my own character, if nothing else."

She nodded, accepting the justice of his words. "Where does that leave us?" she asked.

"Nowhere," he replied. "I cannot marry until I am out of mourning. And even then, with so many of my family opposed to us, I must seriously consider, taken all in all, it were much better if you married Adam Blackwell."

"Better for whom?" she asked, numbly, unable to believe he truly meant it. "For me, loving you as I do, to cheat poor Adam? For you, loving me as you say you do, to see me married to another?"

"At least the temptation would be removed!" he cried harshly. "Don't you see how this tears me apart? My brother, he's near death, and I haven't spoken to him since we quarrelled over you! My wife is dead and I didn't see her in her dying moments because I was trying to escape you! I must mourn my wife, my duties, my responsibilities demand it, as does my better self, yet you are constantly at my side, reminding me how much I love you, how much I want you!"

Philippe entered the parlour in time to hear the throbbing passion in these last words. His mobile brows rose. Never tell him Englishmen were cold hearted, but then, Hal had been raised in France. "Hal, Cecily is come and Guy Armstrong, too," he said. "Go to them whilst I see Ned is fit to be viewed. Then I shall give him this potion and sit by him as he sleeps. Tomorrow, if all is well, we'll remove him to a bedchamber."

"I'll sit up with him through the night," said Hal quickly.

"No, you shall not, but you can relieve me in the early hours if you seek your bed after supper," he replied firmly. "Go now, if you please, Hal, and you too, Sophia."

Chapter Twenty Eight

For a few anxious days, Ned's life hung very much in the balance, and all those who loved him went about with worried faces, scarcely daring to breathe. Until one morning, almost a week later, he came out of the fever which had set in, in spite of care, and demanded a mug of ale and some breakfast. His relations were left to congratulate themselves and him on his robust constitution, and the French physician to marvel at the English desire to drink ale at such ungodly hours.

Justin, meanwhile, had become a shadow of his former self with worry. For, although Ambrose had continued diligently, aided in his spare time by Adam Blackwell, to search for Kit Swithland, neither hide nor hair of such a man could be found, nor even any report of him.

It was now but a week to the Assizes, and Isaac Hughes

had made it plain on his increasingly regular visits, that unless some strong evidence was forthcoming immediately to clear Justin of any suspicions, he would have no choice but to bring him before the court as charged.

With this in mind, having seen Ned sitting up in bed attended by Cecily and Philippe, Hal decided he must join in the search. After some consultation with Ambrose, he collected his horse and set off in the direction of Neats Hill.

Hardly had he left his own land, than he caught the sound of a rider behind him, and mindful of Ned's fate, he rode on swiftly. He took the opportunity, as soon as it presented itself, to hide in the undergrowth to see who followed him and with what intent.

The sight of Sophie, happily cantering into his ambush, filled him with anger all the more because he knew he was beholden to her. Waiting until she was almost level, he rode out to confront her.

"Oh, Hal! What a fright you gave me," she cried, clutching her very becoming hat as her horse shied. For a few seconds, she struggled to control the gentle mare, as her hat tumbled to a bush and her hair spilled free. "Why did you jump out at me like that?" she demanded indignantly.

"What if I'd been that damned highwayman?" he snapped, his irritation only fanned by her beauty as he bent to catch up her hat. "You'd be dead by now, or worse! How dare you defy Aunt Margery and ride out yet again?"

"I knew I couldn't come to any harm as I was following you. As for riding out..." she hesitated, shrugging her shoulders.

"You feel that your rescue of Ned entitles you to continue in your intransigence in spite of all I've said," he snapped. "Here, put this back on and pin your hair away. You look like a gypsy!"

As this was entirely the case, she was silenced, but she ignored his latter instruction, merely cramming her hat back on over her curls. "Gypsies are dark," she observed with a baleful look.

"They are also notoriously dishevelled and undignified," he snapped. "Oblige me by returning to the safety of my land where none can at least see the manner in which you choose to comport yourself."

"Shan't," she replied, returning to schoolgirl tactics.

"Sophia, don't try me too far," he warned. "I know I am vastly obliged to you, but I think we agreed, you must cease this tiresome behaviour. Now, be a good girl, turn your horse about and go back to Westwood Hall as I bid you."

"Where I should study at a vast tome, or take up my tapestry, I suppose," she retorted, only further incensed by his patronizing air. "Well, I agreed to nothing, I'm not your good girl, and I shan't do as you bid me! I'm going with you to look for this Kit Swithland. Hannah has told me all about him, I'm as likely to find him as you are."

"No, you're not. Neither shall I take you with me," he cried hotly. "Now go back, or I'll take my crop to you."

She made no reply to this threat, although her eyes narrowed and her mouth set mulishly.

"Did you hear me!" he demanded, a sinking suspicion filling his stomach as he realised she was about to call his bluff.

Her eyes flashed a challenge, and for a second, she stiffened in amazement as he made as if to ride forward, only relaxing slightly as he thought better of it and said weakly: "Sophia, please do be reasonable, you must see I can't take you with me."

"I see nothing of the sort!" she replied tartly.

"It isn't fitting we should be riding about the countryside together," he said desperately. "You should be at home with the other women of the family, you know you should. This behaviour will occasion just the sort of talk we are anxious to avoid!"

"You are anxious to avoid," she said flatly. "No, I shan't go home, I'm going with you."

"It is too dangerous," he cried, his tone almost pleading. "I'm going to taverns, ale-houses, places of ill-repute!"

"Then I shall wait outside with your horse," she replied. "To make sure it's not stolen whilst you pursue your enquiries."

"Sophia, please," he cried, knowing even as he said it, he'd lost.

"I'd have thought time was of the essence," she remarked, glancing ahead. "Do you really have time to linger here, bandying words with me?"

"No, I do not!" he snapped, seeing she would not heed him. "So will you please go home!"

"No, I am going with you," she replied implacably.

There was a short silence and a battle of wills, then he gave way with the little grace he could muster. "You are a damned nuisance!" he cried angrily. "You know I can't beat you on a public highway! You are to keep close to me at all times and to keep a bridle on that tongue of yours, do you hear?"

Again, she made no reply, merely opening her violet eyes wider at him in a mocking manner.

"Don't push me too far, Sophie!" he warned, his eyes flashing. "I might yet forget I was bred a gentleman and treat you like the hoyden you are!"

He brought his horse alongside, still fuming, and they continued on their way in prickly silence.

"How many ale-houses are on Neats Hill?" she asked, after they'd covered a mile in silence and began the gradual ascent of the escarpment.

"Three. One in the village, at the foot, one at the summit, and another in a hamlet half a mile toward Lesser Budding. We'll go beyond and pretend we are on a return journey. The tale is this: your horse got away from you and took you too far, I've come in search of you."

"That will account for your ill-humour," she agreed.

"And your sulky face," he countered.

True to his word, this was the story he told at the rudimentary ale-house near Lesser Budding, where they stopped, ostensibly to procure a cup of water for the faint Sophia, whose wayward mare had proved a little too much for her horsemanship. The ale-wife there was all sympathy but had little information to pass on. Although, she ran her neighbours demented in the next few days, recounting to each in turn how, contrary to report, Sir Henry Westwood was a pleasant, easygoing gentleman, none too high in his notions as to enjoy a gossip with his fellow creatures.

It seemed as if fate would serve them a like turn at the next tavern. But Sophia, descending from her horse in Hal's wake, gave the reins to a vacant-looking stable lad. She walked off in the opposite direction to her companion and the inn, coming to pause at a gate into a field of horses which gave a magnificent view of the valley from which they ascended.

She stood motionless, her eyes on the panorama spread out before her, but her thoughts miles away. What was she to do, she wondered, rather helplessly. Hal seemed to be coming more and more adamant that they shouldn't be married. And whereas, whilst he had been away and on his initial arrival, she'd been confident of changing his mind, now she had doubts. Once again, she witnessed the machinery by which his life was directed, and say what he will, she had the uncanny feeling she'd not prevail against it, at least not without his help.

If only she could get him to agree to a form of betrothal now, she thought, then she could be sure of him. If he would but give his word before witnesses, then she wouldn't mind waiting until he was out of mourning. Well, she would, but she would be able to bear it better.

It was at this point, that her gaze finally fell upon the trio of horses which were in the muddy field, and she realized that one of them bore a passing likeness to Ned's stolen horse.

She frowned over the recollection. She remembered how very tedious Cecily had been in her detailing of each of the finer points of the handsome chestnut. Guy had gone with Cecily to purchase the animal at Gloucester horse fair as a wedding gift for her future husband. Three white socks, Cecily had confided, and a funny little mark, just hidden by the forelock on his handsome head, which looked like a crown. This had convinced Cecily to buy the horse and to call him Prince, it made a fitting gift, she'd said, for a prince among men.

Sophia remembered sniffing at this, to her mind, Ned, already her most outspoken critic, couldn't hold a candle to his elder brother. She grabbed a handful of grass from her side of the fence, and her pulses quick-ened as the animal came in response to her waving at it. There was even something familiar in the animal's gait as it trotted toward her. "Prince, Prince, it is you!" she exclaimed, brushing aside the animal's forelock. "Now, what in heaven's name are you doing here in this field?" Then, as the obvious truth dawned on her, she swung about to run to tell Hal, and she found herself con-fronting a man with a pistol.

"Well, here's an interfering jade," he remarked in a pleasant voice. "My, and a very pretty one, too! Hmm, it would be a definite waste to shoot you, now wouldn't it?"

"Ned's highwayman!" she cried in dismay.

"Was he called Ned?" he replied lightly.

"Yes, and you nearly killed him," she snapped.

"Only nearly?" he said, his brows snapping together.

"Yes, he lives," said a quiet voice behind him. "He'll be able to identify you and bring you to the gallows."

"Hal!" cried Sophie in horror, as the highwayman spun round sharply, and seeing a man with a pistol trained on him, took a step backwards to as to include Hal in his range. "Hal, this is Ned's mare!"

"So I gathered," Hal replied. "And, by my guess, this

is also Kit Swithland. The landlord became most eva-
sive when I mentioned his name."

"At your service." Taking care to keep both covered,
he sketched an ironical bow.

"Then empowered by my position of Justice of the
Peace, I arrest you for the murder of Nathaniel Sitwell,
his wife Helen, and Nancy Gollen. Doubtless there are
others, like my brother, left for dead on the road!"

The man looked intrigued. "Justice?" he said. "Are
you the fellow whose been hunting me these past ten
days? Sir Henry Westwood? Never tell me I shot your
brother."

"My most beloved brother," he replied sharply. "And
I saw what you did to Nancy Gollen."

"I warned Nancy back last summer. I told her not to
'peach on me," he replied. "As for Nat Sitwell and Helen
Riggs, they deserved what they got. I don't know how
many men they've ruined between them, aye, and not
all green ones. A good friend of mine blew his brains
out over that precious pair, I'll not weep for them."

"The law is in place to take care of the likes of Nat
Sitwell and his wife," said Hal, walking slowly forward. "You have no right to take the law into your own
hands."

"Stand still, Sir Henry," the highwayman commanded. "I've not lived on my wits these past three years to
be outmanoeuvred by a country magistrate. You, my
pretty, come here to me, or I'll blow his brains out."
He waved his pistol at Hal and indicated for Sophie to
come closer.

"Stay still, Sophie," commanded Hal. "He cannot kill
both of us!"

"No, but he might kill you, Hal!" she said doubtfully.

"And then you," the highwayman agreed. "Come
here, my pretty!" He inched towards her where she
stood, still by the horses at the gate.

Hal saw his worst nightmare developing. "Sophie!"
he cried, guessing this ruthless fellow would hold her
hostage and use her as he would, once he'd killed him.
He'd already killed many, one or two more would not
matter. "Sophie, get away! God in heaven, you foolish
girl, don't you see the risk?"

"Indeed I do," she cried. "If I move, he'll kill you,
Hal. I love you too much to let him do that!"

"He'll kill me anyway," he cried in exasperation. "Run
Sophie, get free, he can't shoot us both!"

"Oh, I can!" he countered. "Once I've shot you, I can

use my other pistol on her. So stand still, my pretty, and you might live," he added, as he grabbed her arm and pulled her to him to protect himself. "So now, Sir Henry, what will you?"

"Sophie!" Hal cried, part in exasperation, more in fear. "Dear God, Sophie, why must you always be in the wrong place?"

"The place seems good enough to me," said Swithland, getting his arm about her and giving her a squeeze. "I don't think I will shoot you after all, you're much too beautiful. Would you like life on the open road, my dear?"

"Not with you!" she replied, gritting her teeth.

"Well now, you have a choice," he remarked blandly. "I can kill Sir Henry here now, or you can agree to go with me and I'll just stop him following us."

"Leave him for dead as you did Ned, you mean!" she replied, her voice coming high with fear as she struggled to be free of him.

"Stand still now, or I'll kill him anyway," he snapped as Hal inched forward again. "I'm warning you both, I'll shoot if I have to…" His voice rose sharply as Sophie wriggled free and at the same moment, Ned's horse gave him a nudge with its nose so that he stumbled forward, discharging his pistol uselessly into the damp earth. Hal's shot rang out immediately and embedded high up into the highwayman's chest, disabling his pistol arm.

"You've hit me!" he cried in an astounded voice and lurched forward onto his knees. "You've got me!" He pitched to the mud in a heap, rolling onto his side.

"Get his other pistol, Sophie!" cried Hal, as he sprang forward.

"Oh, Hal, have you killed him?" she cried as Hal came to help her pull back the highwayman's enveloping cloak and snatch away his other pistol, as the highwayman tried to raise himself on his arm.

"No, I think not," Hal said. "I want this one to stand trial. Yes, he'll make it. But I'll need to get him back to Westwood." He handed her the pistol he took from the highwayman and stood up. "Stand guard over him, Sophie. Don't let him move a muscle! I'll go and get this rascally landlord to assist!"

"I don't think I can move, Sir Henry. I'd never have guessed you were such a good shot," said Swithland in a weak voice, falling back in the mud with a heartfelt groan. "Damn you and all your family to perdition!"

"Are you in much pain?" asked Sophie doubtfully, as

Hal strode off in the direction of the inn.

"What, are you a ministering angel now?" he mocked, grimacing through his pain. "Help him to shoot me and then tend my wounds?"

"I'd do the same for any man if they were in pain," she said coldly.

"Sit me up, then, do," he gasped. "I'd sooner not meet my Maker flat on my back."

"I doubt very much you'll meet your Maker at all," observed Sophie dispassionately, carefully holding the pistol on him. "And I'm afraid you'll have to suffer as you are until Sir Henry returns. He said you're not to move a muscle."

"And you always do as Sir Henry says, do you?" he muttered through clenched teeth. "Damn him, I'm done for! Who'd have thought him a crack shot!"

"I've heard it said," she replied distantly, shaking like a leaf.

"I've heard it said he told you to kill his wife so you could be wed. Is that true?" he remarked provocatively.

She frowned. "Where heard you that? No, of course it's not true!"

"'Tis the gossip going the rounds. Well, Jack?" This last as the landlord, much crestfallen, and the stable boy accompanied Hal back across the yard, carrying either end of a hurdle. "This is a pretty come out, and you no more idea of who I am than this pretty lady knows how to add poison to a posset!"

"Now, do hold thy tongue Master Frank," said the innkeeper sourly. "Or 'twill be the worst for you."

Hal crossed to take the pistol from Sophie, keeping it trained firmly on the highwayman. "Frank?" cried Sophie, turning to Hal. "I thought you said this was Kit Swithland!"

"That's but one of my many names, my dear," he said, with a laugh that turned into a groan as the innkeeper and the stable lad lifted him onto the hurdle. "I'm also commonly known as Black Jack, and John Loseby."

"'Tis Francis Findlesham, if it please your honour," said the innkeeper, a sob in his voice. "And what old Sir Edward would be saying if he were alive to see this day, I don't know! He must be spinning in his grave to see his only son brought so low!"

"Hold your tongue, Wilks," snapped the highwayman, reaching down and struggling with the cuff of his boot. "Damn me, I've never heard such…" He suddenly whipped out a small pistol from inside his boot and without waiting to take aim, loosed it off at Hal, who had bent to collect the highwayman's spent pistol.

The shot grazed his temple and nicked his ear, taking the hat from Hal's head. The blood began to stream down his cheek into his cravat. He staggered a little and regained his footing in time to hear Sophie's scream.

"Hal!" she screamed as she suddenly swayed and crumpled where she stood. "Hal!"

"Sophie!" Blind fear that she was killed overcame his own injury. "Sophie, my love!"

Chapter Twenty Nine

"Are you absolutely sure, Hal, that you are not much injured?" asked Ned, with all the anxiety of an invalid. It was much later that day, and most of the family were finally gathered in the parlour. "You are certainly covered in blood."

"Most of it is Sophie's," he replied, glancing at his bloodied shirt. "You should see my new coat and waistcoat! They are totally ruined. Aunt Margery will be pleased. Sophie, you owe me a new coat."

Sophie smiled wanly from where she was propped up in a chair, her arm in a sling, sipping one of Philippe's horrid concoctions. "I think I shall soon be bankrupt, Hal, what with all the clothes I have ruined lately!"

"I gather I owe you a gown," Ned remarked to Sophie, awkwardly.

"You also owe Sophie for the return of your horse,"

said Ambrose.

"Not to mention saving your life," Cecily reminded him.

"But everything is settled now, isn't it?" Bess asked anxiously. "This Kit Swithland, or Frank Findlesham, whatever his name is, he is safely in custody? And Sophie will take no lasting harm?"

"No lasting harm, she has been very lucky," said Philippe, shaking his head at her.

"Sheriff Hughes was actually here on our somewhat dramatic arrival, although for high drama, it did not compare to yours, Ned. I thank the Lord, that ale-house keeper, Wilkes, was an honest man, or I guess we'd both be dumped on the road," said Hal, reflectively. "I think Frank Findlesham terrified him too. Leastways, he and the lad with the perpetual sniff tied up our highwayman, whilst I took a look at Sophie's wound, which, as Philippe has said, isn't life-threatening …"

"It may not be life-threatening, but it hurts a lot," interrupted Sophie, as Cordelia took the cup from her and gently smoothed back Sophie's tangled hair. "I was jolted to death in that cart. And I had to travel with Kit Swithland making horrid comments until he finally passed out."

"Frank Findlesham," Hal corrected her. "Anyway, he

made a recover, when we gave him some brandy wine, which Wilkes had the forethought to bring with him on the drive. I wonder where he gets it? I suspect he doesn't pay duty on it, but no more of that now. As I said, Hughes was here when the sorry cavalcade made its way up the avenue, and he had no hesitation in taking Findlesham back to Maucester with him. He is certain in his mind the fellow had killed many, and he admitted to killing Nat and Helen Sitwell in front of Sophie and I, so Justin is finally cleared of all charges."

Aunt Margery, lately returned with the news that Hetta would be a good few more weeks before becoming a mother, shook her head over the degeneration of modern youth. She agreed in an undertone with Aunt Kate how shocking it was that the son of so landed a family should come to such a bitter end.

"Then Sophie is responsible for saving Justin's life, too," said Cecily.

There was an abrupt silence in the room after Cecily's artless remark, with none caring to meet Justin's eye, although Hal grinned and winked at his favourite sister-in-law.

"Yes," said Bess, after a pause in which it became plain Justin wasn't going to speak. "It would appear we are very much beholden to Sophie."

"No, no, you are not," said Sophie, looking dismayed. "None of you like me, so you'll not want to be grateful to me. Just call it a settling of debts. Hal helped me, now I've helped his family."

Again there was a shocked silence, as they recognised the truth of her words, and Hal's smile became a little set, then Ned stirred. "No, that's not good enough," he said flatly. "I may not have liked you, Sophie, but I'm damned glad you saved my life, and Cecily and I thank you from the bottom of our hearts."

"Oh, well said, Ned!" Cecily smiled mistily upon her husband whilst Hal looked gratified.

"I agree it is difficult to be grateful if you dislike someone, but as most of my dislike had its roots in jealousy. I can damn well put that aside and ask you to forgive me, Sophie, if you will, and accept the payment of the finest gown you can find," continued Ned with the air of one determined to get everything off his chest.

"A wedding gown, I should think," said Cecily with a provocative glance in Hal's direction, as Aunt Margery called Ned to order for his strong language.

Sophie, who had endured all the hostility of Hal's family, looked as if this kindness might be her undoing. Weak tears suddenly filled her eyes. "You are t-too kind," she stammered. "I know I've, I know how I injured you all by my behaviour toward Libby…"

"Me most of all," Justin's voice cut across the polite disclaimers. "However, it is plain you'll never injure Hal, so besotted as he is with you." Again, there was an electric pause, then he continued bitterly: "I doubt I'll ever like you, Sophie, or forgive you entirely, but I am grateful for you being such a disobedient, interfering wench, so that the truth came out, and I am sorry you were injured in doing it." Again, he seemed to struggle with words, before adding finally: "A life for a life, they say. You saved mine, and Libby would have said you've paid your debts."

"But she has saved mine, too!" cried Bess. "For without you, Justin, I would have had no life. Sophie has more than paid her debts, we owe her much."

Justin reddened and blinked furiously to rid his eyes of unaccountable water. "Do I truly mean that much to you, Bess?" he asked gruffly.

"You know you do," she replied, clasping his hand.

"Which is more than he deserves," said Aunt Margery. "I vow, you are a saint, Elizabeth. After all the shame and…"

"I agree with you, ma'am," Justin said quickly. "Much,

much more than I deserve. Bess is entirely correct, I owe much to Sophie."

"So do I," said Hal. "She has given me a reason to live."

"Then, as a whole family, we must thank her," said Jane. "And apologise to her for our quite dreadful behaviour." She smiled at the now pink-faced girl. "We are very sorry for the unkindness of the past, Sophie. I think Ned was the most correct when he said we've been jealous of the love Hal has for you, and so made it an excuse to treat you badly. I do hope in time you'll be able to forgive us."

"Well," said Aunt Margery, as everyone felt uncomfortable. "It is to be hoped you've all learned something from this unfortunate episode. If Justin is cleared of murder and we can all hold up our heads again, perhaps this time of trial has not been entirely in vain. As for Sophia, I agree, she has shown a degree of loyalty which is encouraging, but, as I am sure she knows, she has a long way to go before she reaches that state of…"

"No, Aunt, you are wrong," said Hal, as Sophie's eyes flashed. "Sophie needs to learn nothing more, she is, as you rightly say, loyal, generous, kind-hearted and right-thinking. In fact, in my eyes, she is perfection, and I thank God for the day she walked into our lives." ❧ ✺

Last Chapter of the Previous Book
"Dancing with Fire"

Libby stood in the window, much as Hal had done the previous Tuesday, looking down over the busy High Street, but seeing nothing.

"I thought you said he'd promised not to go?" Justin said, trying to keep the incredulity and fury out of his voice.

"No, he didn't promise," she replied, her face strained, and as ever, she was scrupulously honest. "He merely said if I were so distressed over his going, he'd have to think again."

"Aye, but that was when he was too weak to leave," exclaimed Justin, his anger boiling over. "And as a result of his prolonged thinking, he went anyway, without a word to anyone. I'd never have believed it of him!"

"I should never have asked it of him," she returned quietly. "I could see he was hard-pressed by all his problems, and in great distress of mind. I should not have tried to keep him. T'was plain he felt trapped."

"Hard pressed be damned!" he cried angrily, as a single tear slid down her chalk-white cheek, and he felt a measure of guilt that his demands on her husband might had contributed to his flight.

"Anyone would think he was the first man to have fallen for a pretty face he couldn't have! I don't know how many men have endured such a state of things, still do, for all I know. But Hal, he needs must make a song and dance of it, and take himself off abroad in this damned theatrical manner! And to France, of all places!"

"Well, you know, he has not been happy in his mind since the reports came through of his father's death," she began, her tone excusing. "It must be hard to be a long way distant, when one's parent dies."

"And hear of it third hand?" Justin demanded, incensed. "Aye, 'tis damned hard, I recollect the circumstance well!"

"Yes Justin, but you were able to talk to me eventually! You could have come in time perhaps, if only you'd not been so very stubborn! Hal must travel to a foreign land for information, I am sure in my mind that is the main reason for his going. That—and to assist Doctor Douay in his desire to clear his name so that he can return from exile."

"Well, you believe that, if it makes you happier," replied Justin roughly. "But I know better, though surely that is an odd friendship."

"It seems very sudden, does it not?" agreed Libby, her voice unhappy. "I mean, I know Doctor Douay had called every day since Hal was wounded and spent at least an hour talking with him. But to—to go off together like that, without a word to anyone? For Monsieur Douay to abandon all his patients, and just up and leave? It has caused such gossip and speculation!"

"Yes," said Justin, and he folded his lips over further words. He'd not been able to conceal a certain jealously of the foreign doctor, who had so neatly stepped, it seemed, into his shoes, to become Hal's friend and confidante. Once, he and Hal had been close enough to spend hours talking, but his accusations had closed forever the door on that friendship. They'd never sit in comfortable companionship again. He found he missed him, missed him horribly, but, that being the case, how much more miserable must Libby be feeling? "Well, what can't be cured must be endured," he said in calmer tones. "At least we shall be at home tomorrow."

"Yes, I hope never to set foot in Chawcester again," replied Libby.

"That's what Hal kept saying, poor devil! He did try every way to escape the little hussy's clutches," Justin remarked, recollecting his friend's efforts to escape earlier.

"She's not a little hussy, Justin," said Libby, with her innate honesty. "She's a poor, misguided child, who has had much to endure these past few months."

"You do have your own way of seeing things, don't you?" he cried in amused exasperation. "If neither Hal nor Sophie is the villain, who the hell is?"

Her eyes reproached him for his intemperate language. "I thought the depositions Hal and Sophie made were clear. Giles Durward," she replied primly.

"Oh yes, he's the murderer," agreed Justin impatiently. "But there's been wider mischief than that, even, in this affair," his voice echoed his dissatisfaction.

"Indeed," she agreed. "Perhaps Master Benton himself was at fault. If he'd left well enough alone, none of those people may have died."

"Robin Tripp certainly did," said Justin hastily, his feelings still raw from Hal's earlier accusations that his interference had lost four innocent people their lives. "Durward's man confessed to setting the other fire, which caused the smoke. He said he didn't know what Giles intended, but once he was implicated, he had to keep on helping, or Giles had threatened to accuse him! Anyway, Libby, I had this dispute with Hal. We are not fit to judge, we can only seek the truth, and the truth shall set us free."

"I don't always want to know the truth," she replied dully, thinking of the long summer days ahead, without her husband. "I think the truth is overrated. I'd prefer a little common ignorance, personally. I think I'd be happier if I'd never known of all this."

Justin looked appalled. "But that strikes at the foundation of our existence," he cried desperately. "You are saying ignorance is bliss."

"Were Adam and Eve not blissful, in their ignorance in the Garden of Eden?" she returned. "Do you truly think they were happier cast out of the Garden to fend for themselves?"

"Yes, yes!" he cried passionately. "They were like innocent children, they had to grow up, to learn to live their own lives."

She sighed, her thoughts distracted from the philosophical to the purely practical. "As do all children. What shall I tell little Harry?"

"He'll manage," soothed Justin. "And I know Hal, he won't be long gone. He loves England and was too long in exile to remain away for very long. You'll see, he'll be back home in no time."

"And in the meantime, what do we do with Sophie?" she replied.

Enjoy the

First Chapter

of the next book in the series:

"Repenting at Leisure"

which begins on the next page

Chapter One of the next book in the series
"Repenting at Leisure"

July 1666

The sun shone brightly, a faint balmy breeze rustled the leaves of the trees which lined the path, the sky was a clear cloudless blue, the grass a perfect green sward. The birds sang for joy, bees buzzed industriously, God was in his heaven, all was right with the world.

The wedding party which walked the path was equally satisfactory. The bride was bright-eyed and beautiful, the groom young and handsome. The bride's maidens were happy and attentive, the groomsmen sprightly and jocular, and the wedding guests for the most part well-disposed to enjoy themselves at someone else's expense as they followed the newly-wedded couple cross the park to the handsome house on the hill.

"What was that scuffle as we left the church, did you

notice?" asked Justin Danvers as he walked beside his widowed brother-in-law Hal Westwood.

"I did not," he replied. "I was receiving Sir Edgar's congratulations on acquiring so excellent a husband for our ward."

Justin snorted. "It looked like some of the local tenantry, they were certainly armed with clubs and sticks, but the groomsmen saw them off in no uncertain fashion."

Hal glanced ahead to their host. "Sir Edgar is reckoned a warm man. Likely he is hard on his tenants."

"He certainly doesn't appear to be overflowing with the milk of human kindness," agreed Justin, recollecting the older man's stern visage and gimlet eye.

"A companion at arms of the late Oliver Cromwell, I believe," remarked Hal maliciously.

"I doubt he is any the worst for that," snapped Justin swiftly. Then, as Hal only smiled thinly, he glanced to him sidelong and added, with an uncomfortable attempt at sympathy: "This must be difficult for you."

"Difficult?" repeated Hal. "How so?"

"Well, was 'twas but six months ago Sophia Redcroft was declaring undying love for you and vowing she'd marry you."

"I don't recall her ever saying she'd marry me," he replied distantly. "As for swearing undying love, she is but nineteen, emotions are rarely fixed at so early an age."

"Bess was but eighteen when we were wed," remarked Justin evenly.

"Dear Bess," Hal smiled at the thought of his sister. "She may have been eighteen in years, but she was at least thirty in common sense."

Justin grinned his agreement. "Aye, but I was convinced Sophia wouldn't alter," he said.

"Plainly Aunt Margery was correct," said Hal. "She said Sophia merely needed to enlarge her acquaintances to meet and fall in love with another younger man. One much more suitable all round."

"I don't care for the fellow," observed Justin.

Hal shrugged. "You don't care for Sophia either," he said blandly.

"No, but this Gervase Harcourt is somehow, different."

"How so?" repeated Hal.

Justin frowned. "I don't know, I mean, he is in essence quite perfect, don't you think? He has good looks, charming manners, he's educated, affable, cuts a good figure on a horse, talks hunting with Ned, law with you, family with your Aunt Margery, children with Bess, as

I say, quite perfect."

"All two guardians of an heiress could require," agreed Hal.

"Yet something, something doesn't smell right," continued Justin. "Do you know when you pick an apple from a tree, and you look at it and see its rosy and plump, smells crisp, yet somehow you have an uneasy feeling as you bite into it, and sure enough, you find a worm at its heart."

Hal smiled faintly. "You sound jaundiced to me, Justin. You drank too much ale last night."

"There was too much ale last night," he remarked. "Far too much."

Hal glanced up to the house, noting how the bride and groom paused at the threshold. "I think we begin to feel our years," he said. "They were, for the most part, young men, all of Gervase's own age."

"Aye," he agreed. "Too many of them, too!"

"Too much of everything in fact," murmured Hal, and then fell silent as they mounted the steps and the moment he was dreading approached. So it was over, truly over, and all the trouble and turmoil of the past year could be put behind him. All the pain and grief, joy and ecstasy which he had experienced since Sophia Redcroft burst unceremoniously into his life could be categorised, and then shut away forever.

It was strange how one became used to pain, he'd noticed it in sick people of course, how a cripple soon managed to accommodate a damaged leg and walk again, albeit with a shuffling gait. Well, he was like that, he supposed, an emotional cripple. He'd not been lame for long, none had noticed, and he could walk forward again even if it was with an ungainly mental limp.

The dreaded moment over, congratulations and compliments expressed and exclaimed, they joined the groom's parents in a place of honour and the wedding feast proceeded along conventional lines, with much gaiety brought about by copious amounts of wine, so that after a time even Hal's pain dulled a little and he was able to make a speech of such eloquence and erudition as to bring tears to Sophia's eyes and thunderous bursts of approval and gusts of laughter from the other guests.

This over, and the meal brought to a somewhat tedious and wine-sodden conclusion, it seemed to Hal that events began to move out of his control. Before he knew it, the bride and her maidens were withdrawing and the groom and his fellows indulging in overexcited horseplay and yet more drink. Suddenly he felt once again his years as he stood alone and contemplated a rather bleak future.

Justin, seeing his expression, moved to join him, a wine jug in his hand. Wordlessly, he refilled his cup and began a monologue about a recent case which was notable for its circumlocution and the grasping natures of both parties.

His ploy had the desired effect, Hal drank and listened, occasionally nodding as Justin recounted his steps and his protagonists' actions, but although he added the odd comment or two, his attention was but poorly given. Only the surface of his mind was dealing with the actuality of the moment, deep down, he was miles away, back in the haloyan few days of last spring and deeper even than that he was conscious of his heart creaking and bending in pain.

It was much later, as the short summer night was fast becoming dawn that Justin's attention was finally taken by another guest and Hal's mind was free to wonder. He stared into the bottom of his wine as recollections of the evening came to him. The ceremony of putting the bride to bed with its attendant laughter and ribaldry was long past. Neither he nor Justin had been of their riotous number, there were some duties he found it best not to attempt. Instead he'd sought solace in a jug of wine, aided by Justin, and now as he emptied the last of it into his cup; he knew he was stone-cold sober.

He glanced restlessly about him, noting with distaste the feast was fast reaching its natural conclusion. The table was a wreck of broken meats and wine stains with dogs snarling over a bone. Two guests, more energetic than their peers still danced in the centre of the scuffed floor to the strains of a violin player, whilst the rest of the musicians had long lain aside their instruments and were talking and drinking in a corner amongst themselves. In the far corner a goodly crowd of youths were gathered about a game of dice, betting heavily on each fall and over by the old front door, which had been set open wide to let in some cooler night air and a panoply of moths into the over-heated chamber, sat several older and more earnest looking men who were discussing politics with an avid air.

He felt an overwhelming weariness with himself, his companions and the world in general. He drunk off the remainder of his wine, and noting that Justin had been caught up in talk of the dreadful events in London, he got up. Passing two over-tired children squabbling over sweet meats he went out through the open door and into the velvet night.

He paused looking up into the sky, the stars still twinkling, but less brightly, and already dawn's pink glow was predicted in the eastern sky. Resolutely he walked towards that faint light between an avenue of chestnut trees and only when he'd reached the ornamental gates a clear mile from the house did he falter and turn round.

It was over and his heart was breaking. Sophie was another man's wife and he had never felt so alone in his life. He'd read all the poets, heard many men speak of being in love, but never until he'd met Sophie had he fully comprehended how the experience could alter a man. The affection he'd felt for Libby, the love he had for his children, they were nothing beside the blind adoration he had for this girl he'd met just one short year ago.

In the last year since this momentous event had occurred he'd felt as if his life had been turn asunder. He'd lost all sense of direction in his life, and could not find any clear idea of what he wanted for the future of what he should do. He who had prided himself since his return from exile in having purpose and order in his life, had found his plans and dreams in ruins. All he'd known in all that time had been an empty void where his heart was an overwhelming longing to be with Sophie at all times. All he wanted was to see her, to hear her sweet voice, her step, her laughter, to see her lovely smile and to feel the infinite comfort of her presence.

He'd allowed none of this to show of course. As her reluctant guardian and a married, and later bereaved man, how could he have possibly done so and retained but a vestige of honour. He may have stumbled many times, especially in the beginning, but eventually he'd schooled himself to conceal the depths of his love. The result of which had convinced Sophie, already made doubtful by the efforts of his family and his own cold demeanour towards her, she'd sought love elsewhere. His Aunt Margery had been right. How could a widowed father of two children hope to compare with the handsome, dashing heir to a baronacy.

He felt a prickle of tears against his eyelids, and recognised in horror, he wasn't as sober as he'd imagined, but was on the verge of maudling tears. The mere suggestion did much to sober him. He opened the heavy gates and turned his steps towards the church. There was nothing like a brisk walk to clear the head. ❧